CITIES IN FLIGHT

VOLUME 2

JAMES BLISH

BAEN
BOOKS

CITIES IN FLIGHT, VOL. II

A Baen Books Original

Baen Publishing Enterprises
P.O. Box 1403
Riverdale, N.Y. 10471

ISBN: 0-671-72070-8

Cover art by David Mattingly

First Baen printing, July 1991

Distributed by
SIMON & SCHUSTER
1230 Avenue of the Americas
New York, N.Y. 10020

Printed in the United States of America

CONTENTS

Part I:
EARTHMAN, COME HOME   1

Part II:
THE TRIUMPH OF TIME   249

EARTHMAN, COME HOME

To John W. Campbell, Jr.

PROLOGUE

Space flight got its start as a war weapon amid the collapse of the great Western culture of Earth. The invention of Muir's tape-mass engine carried early explorers out as far as Jupiter; and gravity was discovered—though it had been postulated centuries before—by the 2018 Jovian expedition, the last space flight with Muir engines which was completed on behalf of the West before that culture's final extinction. The building, by remote control, of the Bridge on the face of Jupiter itself, easily the most enormous (and in most other respects the most useless) engineering project ever undertaken by man, had made possible direct, close measurements of Jupiter's magnetic field. The measurements provided final confirmation of the Blackett-Dirac equations, which as early as 1948 had proposed a direct relationship between magnetism, gravitation, and the rate of spin of any mass.

Up to that time, nothing had been done with the Blackett-Dirac hypothesis, which remained a toy of pure mathematicians. Then, abruptly, the hypothesis and the mathematicians had their first innings. From the many pages of symbols and the mumbled discussions of the possible fieldstrength of a single electronic pole in rotation, the DillonWagonner gravitron polarity generator—

3

almost immediately dubbed the "spindizzy" in honor of what it did to electron rotation—sprang as if full-born. The overdrive, the meteor screen, and antigravity had all arrived in one compact package labeled "$G = 2(PC/BU)^2$."

Every culture has its characteristic mathematic, in which its toriographers can see its inevitable social form. This expression, couched in the algebra of the Magian culture, pointing toward the matrix mechanics of the new Nomad Era, remained essentially a Western discovery. At first its major significance seemed to lie in the fact that it was rooted in a variation of the value of C, the velocity of light, as a limit. The West used the spindizzy to scatter the nearby stars with colonists during the last fifty years of its existence; but even then, it did not realize the power of the weapon that it held in its faltering hands. Essentially, the West never found out that the spindizzy could lift *anything*, as well as protect it and drive it faster than light.

In the succeeding centuries, the whole concept of space flight was almost forgotten. The new culture on Earth, that narrow planar despotism called by historiographers the Bureaucratic State, did not think that way. Space flight had been a natural, if late, outcome of Western thought patterns, which had always been ambitious for the infinite. The Soviets, however, were opposed so bitterly to the very idea that they would not even allow their fiction writers to mention it. Where the West had soared from the rock of Earth like a sequoia, the Soviets spread like lichens over the planet, tightening their grip, satisfied to be at the bases of the pillars of sunlight the West had sought to ascend.

This was the way the Bureaucratic State had been born and had triumphed, and it was the way it meant to maintain its holdings. There had never been any direct military conquest of the West by the Soviets. Indeed, by 2105, the date usually assigned to the fall of the West, any such battle would have depopulated the Earth almost overnight. Instead, the West helped conquer itself, a long and painful process which many people foresaw but no one was able to halt. In its anxiety to prevent infiltration by the enemy, the West developed thought controls of its own, which grew ever tighter. In the end, the two opposing

cultures could no longer be told apart—and since the
Soviets had had far more practice at running this kind of
monolithic government than had the West, Soviet leadership became a bloodless fact.

The ban on thinking about space flight extended even to
the speculations of physicists. The omnipresent thought
police were instructed in the formulae of ballistics and
other disciplines of astronautics, and could detect such
work—Unearthly Activities, it was called—long before it
might have reached the proving-stand stage.

The thought police, however, could not ban atomic
research because the new state's power rested upon it. It
had been from study of the magnetic moment of the
electron that the Blackett equation had emerged. The new
state had suppressed the spindizzy—it was too good an
escape route—and the thought police had never been told
that the original equation was one of those in the "sensitive area." The Soviets did not dare let even that much be
known about it.

Thus, despite all of the minority groups purged or "re-
educated" by the Bureaucratic State, the pure mathematicians went unsuspected about the destruction of that state,
innocent even in their own minds of revolutionary motives.
The spindizzy was rediscovered, quite inadvertently, in
the nuclear physics laboratories of the Thorium Trust.

The discovery spelled the doom of the flat culture, as
the leveling menace of the nuclear reactor and the Solar
Phoenix had cut down the soaring West. Space flight
returned. For a while, cautiously, the spindizzy was installed only in new spaceships, and there was another
period—comically brief—of interplanetary exploration. The
tottering edifice fought to retain its traditional balance.
But the center of gravity had shifted. The waste inherent
in using the spindizzy only in a ship could not be disguised. There was no longer any reason why a man-carrying
vehicle to cross space needed to be small, cramped, organized fore-and-aft, penurious of weight. Once antigravity
was an engineering reality, it was no longer necessary to
design ships specially for space travel, for neither mass nor
aerodynamic lines meant anything any more. The most
massive and awkward object could be lifted and hurled off

the Earth, and carried almost any distance. Whole cities, if necessary, could be moved.

Many were. The factories went first; they toured Earth, from one valuable mineral lie to another, and then went farther aloft. The exodus began. Nothing could be done to prevent it, for by that time the whole trend was obviously in the best interests of the State. The mobile factories changed Mars into the Pittsburgh of the solar system; the spindizzy had lifted the mining equipment and the refining plants bodily to bring life back to that lichen-scabbed ball of rust. The blank where Pittsburgh itself had been was a valley of slag and ashes. The great plants of the Steel Trust gulped meteors and chewed into the vitals of satellites. The Aluminum Trust, the Germanium Trust, and the Thorium Trust put their plants aloft to mine the planets.

But the Thorium Trust's Plant No. 8 never came back. The revolution against the planar culture began with that simple fact. The first of the Okie cities soared away from the solar system, looking for work among the colonists left stranded by the ebb tide of Western civilization. The new culture began among these nomad cities; and when it was all over, the Bureaucratic State, against its own will, had done what it had long promised to do "when the people were ready"—it had withered away. The Earth that it once had owned, right down to the last grain of sand, was almost deserted. Earth's nomad cities—migratory workers, hobos, Okies—had become her inheritors.

Primarily the spindizzy had made this possible; but it could not have maintained it without heavy contributions from two other social factors. One of these was longevity. The conquest of so-called "natural" death had been virtually complete by the time the technicians on the Jovian Bridge had confirmed the spindizzy principle, and the two went together like hand in spacemitt. Despite the fact that the spindizzy would drive a ship—or a city—at speeds enormously faster than that of light, interstellar flight still consumed finite time. The vastness of the galaxy was sufficient to make long flights consume lifetimes, even at top spindizzy speed.

But when death yielded to the anti-agathic drugs, there was no longer any such thing as a "lifetime" in the old sense.

The other factor was economic: The rise of the metal germanium as the jinn of solid-state physics. Long before flight into deep space became a fact, the metal had assumed a fantastic value on Earth. The opening of the interstellar frontier drove its price down to a manageable level, and gradually it emerged as the basic, stable monetary standard of space trade. Nothing else could have kept the nomads in business.

And so the Bureaucratic State had fallen; but the social structure did not collapse entirely. Earth laws, though much changed, survived, and not entirely to the disadvantage of the Okies. The migrant cities found worlds that refused them landing permits. Others allowed them to land, but exploited them mercilessly. The cities fought back, but they were not efficient fighting machines. Steam shovels, by and large, had been more characteristic of the West than tanks, but in a fight between the two, the outcome was predictable; that situation never changed. It was, of course, a waste to bottle a spindizzy in so small an object as a spaceship, but a war vessel is meant to waste power—the more, the more deadly. The Earth police put the rebel cities down; and then, in self-protection, because the cities were needed, Earth passed laws protecting the cities.

Thus the Earth police held their jurisdiction, but the hegemony of Earth was weak, for the most part. There were many corners of the galaxy which knew Earth only as a legend, a green myth floating unknown thousands of parsecs away in space, known and ineluctable thousands of years away in history. Some of them remembered much more vividly the now-broken tyranny of Vega, and did not know—some of them never had known—even the name of the little planet that had broken that tyranny.

Earth itself became a garden planet, bearing only one city worth noticing, the sleepy capitol of a galaxy. Pittsburgh valley bloomed, and rich honeymooners went there to frolic. Old bureaucrats went to Earth to die.

Nobody else went there at all.

——ACREFF-MONALES: *The Milky Way: Five Cultural Portraits*

CHAPTER ONE: Utopia

As John Amalfi emerged onto the narrow, worn granite ledge with its gritty balustrade, his memory encountered one of those brief boggles over the meaning of a word which had once annoyed him constantly, like a bubble in an otherwise smoothly blown French horn solo. Such moments of confusion were very rare now, but they were still a nuisance.

This time he found himself unable to decide on a name for where he was going at the moment. Was it a belfry, or was it a bridge?

It was, of course, only a matter of simple semantics, depending, as the oldest saying goes, on the point of view. The ledge ran around the belfry of City Hall. The city, however, was a spaceship, much of which was sometimes operated from this spot, and from which Amalfi was accustomed to assess the star-seas that the city sailed. That made it a bridge. But the ship was a city, a city of jails and playgrounds, alleys and alley cats, and there was even one bell still in the belfry, though it no longer had a clapper. The city was still called New York, N.Y., too, but that, the old maps showed, was misleading; the city aloft was only Manhattan, or New York County.

Amalfi's step across the threshold struck the granite

8

without perceptible interruption. The minute dilemma was familiar: he had been through others of its kind often in the years immediately after the city had taken to the skies. It was hard to decide the terms in which one thought about customary things and places after they had become utterly transformed by space flight. The difficulty was that, although the belfry of City Hall still looked much as it had in 1850, it was now the bridge of a spaceship, so that neither term could quite express what the composite had become.

Amalfi looked up. The skies, too, looked about as they must have in 1850 on a very clear night. The spindizzy screen which completely englobed the flying city was itself invisible, but it would pass only elliptically polarized light, so that it blurred the points which were stars seen from space, and took them down in brilliance about three magnitudes to boot. Except for the distant, residual hum of the spindizzies themselves—certainly a much softer noise than the composite traffic roar which had been the city's characteristic tone back in the days before cities could fly—there was no real indication that the city was whirling through the emptiness between stars, a migrant among migrants.

If he chose, Amalfi could remember those days, since he had been mayor of the city—although only for a short time—when the City Fathers had decided that it was time to go aloft. That had been in 3111, decades after every other major city had already left the Earth; Amalfi had been just 117 years old at the time. His first city manager had been a man named deFord, who for a while had shared Amalfi's amused puzzlement about what to call all the familiar things now that they had turned strange—but deFord had been shot by the City Fathers around 3300 for engineering an egregious violation of the city's contract with a planet called Epoch, which had put a black mark on the city's police record which the cops still had not forgotten.

The new city manager was a youngster less than 400 years old named Mark Hazleton, who was already as little loved by the City Fathers as deFord had been and for about the same reasons, but who had been born after the city had gone aloft and hence had no difficulty in finding the appropriate words for things. Amalfi was prepared to believe that he was the last living man on board the flying city who still had occasional bubbles blown into his stream of consciousness by old Earthbound habits of thinking.

In a way, Amalfi's clinging to City Hall as the center of operations for the city betrayed the mayor's ancient ties to Earth. City Hall was the oldest building on board, and so only a few of the other structures could be seen from it. It wasn't tall enough, and there were too many newer buildings around it. Amalfi didn't care. From the belfry—or bridge, if that was what he had to call it now—he never looked in any direction but straight up, his head tilted all the way back on his bull neck. He had no reason to look at the buildings around Battery Park, after all. He had already seen them.

Straight up, however, was a sun, surrounded by starry sable. It was close enough to show a perceptible disc, and becoming slowly larger. While Amalfi watched it, the microphone in his hand began to emit intermittent squawks.

"It looks good enough to me," Amalfi said, lowering his bald head grudgingly a centimeter or two toward the mike. "It's a type G star, or near to it, and Jake in Astronomy says two of the planets are Earthlike. And Records says that both of 'em are inhabited. Where there's people, there's work."

The phone quacked anxiously, each syllable evenly weighted, but without any overall sense of conviction. Amalfi listened impatiently. Then he said, "Politics."

The way he said it made it sound fit only to be scrawled on sidewalks. The phone was silenced; Amalfi hung it on its hook on the railing and thudded back down the archaic stone steps which led from the belfry/bridge.

Hazleton was writing for him in the mayor's office, drumming slim fingers upon the desk top. The current city manager was an excessively tall, slender, disjointed sort of man. Something in the way his limbs were distributed over Amalfi's chair made him also look lazy. If taking devious pains was a sign of laziness, Amalfi was quite willing to call Hazleton the laziest man in the city.

Whether he was lazier than anybody outside the city didn't matter. Nothing that went on outside the city was of real importance any more.

Hazleton said, "Well?"

"Well enough." Amalfi grunted. "It's a nice yellow dwarf star, with all the fixings."

"Sure," Hazleton said with a wry smile. "I don't see why you insist on taking a personal look at every star we go by. There are screens right here in the office, and the City Fathers have all the data. We knew even before we could see this sun what it was like."

"I like a personal look," said Amalfi. "I haven't been mayor here for five hundred years for nothing. I can't really tell about a sun until I see it with my own eyes. Then I know. Images don't mean a thing—no *feel* to 'em."

"Nonsense," Hazleton said, without malice. "And what does your feelership say about this one?"

"It's a good sun; I like it. We'll land."

"All right, suppose I tell you what's going on out there?"

"I know, I know," Amalfi said. His heavy voice took on a finicky, nervous tone, his own exaggerated version of the mechanical speech of the City Fathers. " 'THE POLITICAL SIT-UATION IS *VER*-Y DISTURBING.' It's the food situation that I'm worried about."

"Oh? Is it so bad, then?"

"It's not bad yet. It will be, unless we land. There's been another mutation in the *Chlorella* tanks; must have started when we passed through that radiation field near Sigma Draconis. We're getting a yield of about twenty-two hundred kilograms per acre in terms of fats."

"That's not bad."

"Not bad, but it's dropping steadily, and the rate of decrease is accelerating. If it's not arrested, we won't have any algae crops at all in a year or so. And there's not enough crude-oil reserve to tide us over to the next nearest star. We'd hit there eating each other."

Hazleton shrugged. "That's a big *if*, boss," he said. "We've never had a mutation we couldn't get under control before. And it's very nasty on those two planets."

"So they're having a war. We've been through that kind of situation before. We don't have to take sides. We land on the planet best suited——"

"If it were an ordinary interplanetary squabble, okay. But as it happens, one of those worlds—the third from the sun—is a sort of free-living polyp of the old Hruntan Empire, and the inner one is a survivor of the Hamiltonians. They've been fighting for a century, on and off, without any contact with Earth. Now—the Earth's found them."

"And?" Amalfi said.

"And it's cleaning them both out," Hazleton said grimly. "We've just received an official police warning to get the hell out of here."

Above the city the yellow sun was now very much smaller. The Okie metropolis, skulking out from the two warm warring worlds under one-quarter drive, crept steadily into hiding within the freezing blue-green shadow of one of the ruined giant planets of the system. Tiny moons, a quartet of them, circled in a gelid minuet against the chevrons of ammonia-storms that banded the gas giant.

Amalfi watched the vision screens tensely. This kind of close maneuvering, involving the balancing of the city against a whole series of conflicting gravitational fields, was very delicate, and not the kind of thing to which he was accustomed; the city generally gave gas giants a wide berth. His own preternatural "feel" for the spatial conditions in which he spent his life must here be abetted by every electronic resource at his command.

"Too heavy, Twenty-third Street," he said into the mike. "You've got close to a two-degree bulge on your arc of the screen. Trim it."

"Trim, boss."

Amalfi watched the image of the giant planet and its chill hand-maidens. A needle tipped gently.

"Cut!"

The whole city throbbed once and went silent. The silence was a little frightening: the distant hum of the spindizzies was a part of the expected environment, and when it was damped, one felt a strange shortness of breath, as if the air had gone bad. Amalfi yawned involuntarily, his diaphragm sucking against an illusory shortage of oxygen.

Hazleton yawned, too, but his eyes were glittering. Amalfi knew that the city manager was enjoying himself now; the plan had been his, and so he no longer cared that the city might be in serious danger from here on out. He was taking lazy folks' pains.

Amalfi only hoped that Hazleton was not outsmarting himself and the city at the same time. They had had some narrow squeaks with Hazleton's plans before. There had been, for instance, that episode on Thor V. Of all the planets in the inhabited galaxy on which an Okie might choose to throw his weight around, Thor V was easily the worst. The first Okie city Thor V ever saw had been an outfit which had dropped its city name and taken to calling itself the Interstellar Master Traders. By the time it had left Thor V again, it had earned itself still another appellation: the Mad Dogs. On Thor V, hatred of Okies was downright hereditary, and for good reason. . . .

"Now we'll sit tight for a week," Hazleton said, his spatulate fingers shooting the courser of his slide rule back and forth. "Our food will hold out that long. And that was a very convincing orbit Jake gave us. The cops will be sure we're well on our way out of this system by now—and there aren't enough of them to take care of the two warring planets and to comb space for us at the same time, anyhow."

"You hope."

"It stands to reason, doesn't it?" Hazleton said, his eyes gleaming. "Sooner or later, within a matter of weeks, they'll find out that one of those two planets is stronger than the other, and concentrate their forces on that one. When that happens, we'll hightail for the planet with the weaker police investiture. The cops'll be too busy to prevent our landing there, or to block our laying on supplies once we're grounded."

"That's fine as far as it goes. But it also involves us directly with the weaker planet. The cops won't need any better excuse for dispersing the city."

"Not necessarily," Hazleton insisted. "They can't break us up just for violating a Vacate order. They know that as well as we do. If necessary, we can call for a court ruling and show that the Vacate order was inhumane—and in the meantime, they can't enforce the order while we're under the aegis of an enemy of theirs. Which reminds me—we've got an 'I want off' from a man named Webster, a pile

engineer. He's one of the city's original complement, and
as good as they come; I hate to see him leave."

"If he wants off, he gets it," Amalfi said. "What does he
opt?"

"Next port of call."

"Well, this looks like it. Well——"

The intercom on the flight board emitted a self-deprecatory
burp. Amalfi pressed the stud.

"Mr. Mayor?"

"Yep."

"This is Sergeant Anderson at the Cathedral Parkway
lookout. There's a whopping big ship just come into view
around the bulge of the gas giant. We're trying to contact
her now. A warship."

"Thanks," Amalfi said, shooting a glance at Hazleton.
"Put her through to here when you do make contact." He
dialed the 'visor until he could see the limb of the giant
planet opposite the one into which the city was swinging.
Sure enough, there was a tiny sliver of light there. The
strange ship was still in direct sunlight, but even so, she
must have been a whopper to be visible at all so far away.
The mayor stepped up the magnification, and was rewarded
with a look at a tube about the size of his thumb.

"Not making any attempt to hide," he murmured, "but
then you couldn't very well hide a thing that size. She
must be all of a thousand feet long. Looks like we didn't
fool 'em."

Hazleton leaned forward and studied the innocuous-
looking cylinder intently. "I don't think that's a police
craft," he said. "The police battleships on the cleanup
squad are more or less pear-shaped, and have plenty of
bumps. This boat only has four turrets, and they're faired
into the hull—what the ancients used to call 'streamlin-
ing.' See?"

Amalfi nodded, thrusting out his lower lip speculatively.
"Local stuff, then. Designed for fast atmosphere transit.
Archaic equipment—Muir engines, maybe."

The intercom burped again. "Ready with the visiting
craft, sir," Sergeant Anderson said.

The view of the ship and the blue-green planet was
wiped away, and a pleasant-faced young man looked out at

them from the screen. "How do you do?" he said formally.
The question didn't seem to mean anything, but his tone
indicated that he didn't expect an answer to it anyhow. "I
am speaking to the commanding officer of the . . . the
flying fortress?"

"In effect," Amalfi said. "I'm the mayor here, and this
gentleman is the city manager; we're responsible for different aspects of command. Who are you?"

"Captain Savage of the Federal Navy of Utopia," the
young man said. He did not smile. "May we have permission to approach your fort or city or whatever it is? We'd
like to land a representative."

Amalfi snapped the audio switch and looked at Hazleton.
"What do you think?" he said. The Utopian officer politely
and pointedly did not watch the movements of his lips.

"It should be safe enough. Still, that's a big ship, even if
it is a museum piece. They could as easily send their man
in a life craft."

Amalfi opened the circuit again. "Under the circumstances, we'd just as soon you stayed where you are," he
said. "You'll understand, I'm sure, Captain. However, you
may send a gig if you like; your representative is welcome
here. Or we will exchange hostages——"

Savage's hand moved across the screen as if brushing
the suggestion away. "Quite unnecessary, sir. We heard
the interstellar craft warn you away. Any enemy of theirs
must be a friend of ours. We are hoping that you can shed
some light on what is at best a confused situation."

"That's possible," Amalfi said. "If that is all for now——"

"Yes sir. End of transmission."

"Out."

Hazleton arose. "Suppose I meet this emissary. Your
office?"

"Okay."

The city manager went out, and Amalfi, after a few
moments, followed him, locking up the control tower. The
city was in an orbit and would be stable until the time
came to put it in flight again. On the street, Amalfi flagged
a cab.

It was a fairly long haul from the control tower, which
was on Thirty-fourth Street and The Avenue, down to

Bowling Green, where City Hall was; and Amalfi length-
ened it a bit more by giving the Tin Cabby a route that
would have put folding money into the pocket of a live one
of another forgotten age. He settled back, bit the end off
a hydroponic cigar, and tried to remember what he had
heard about the Hamiltonians. Some sort of a republican
sect, they'd been, back in the very earliest days of space
travel. There'd been a public furor . . . recruiting . . .
government disapproval and then suppression . . . hm-m-m.
It was all very dim, and Amalfi was not at all sure that he
hadn't mixed it up with some other event in Terrestrial
history.

But there *had* been an exodus of some sort. Shiploads of
Hamiltonians going out to colonize, to set up model planets. Come to think of it, one of the nations then current in
the West on Earth had had a sort of Hamiltonianism of its
own, something called a timocracy. It had all died down
after a while, but it had left traces. Nearly every major
political wave after space flight had its vestige somewhere
in the inhabited part of the galaxy.

Utopia must have been colonized very early. The Hruntan Imperials, had *they* arrived first, would have gar-
risoned both habitable planets as a matter of course.

It was a little easier to remember the Hruntan Empire,
since it was of much more recent vintage than the Hamiltonians; but there was less to remember. The outer margins of exploration had spawned gimcrack empires by the
dozen in the days when Earth seemed to be losing her
grip. Alois Hrunta had merely been the most successful of
the would-be emperors of space. His territory had expanded as far as the limits of communication would allow
an absolute autocracy to spread, and then had been destroyed almost before he was assassinated, broken into
duchies by his squabbling sons. Eventually the duchies
fell in their turn to the nominal but irresistible authority of
Earth, leaving, as the Hamiltonians had left, a legacy of a
few remote colonies—worlds where a dead dream was
served with meaningless pomp.

The cab began to settle, and the façade of City Hall
drifted past Amalfi's cab window. The once-golden motto—
MOW YOUR LAWN, LADY?—looked greener than ever in the

light of the giant planet. Amalfi sighed. These political squabbles were dull, and they were guaranteed to make a major project out of the simple matter of earning a square meal.

The first thing that Amalfi noticed upon entering his office was that Hazleton looked uncomfortable. This was practically a millennial event. Nothing had ever disturbed Hazleton before; he was very nearly the perfect citizen of space: resilient, resourceful, and almost impossible to surprise—or bluff. There was nobody else in the office but a girl whom Amalfi did not recognize; probably one of the parliamentary secretaries who handled many of the intramural affairs of the city.

"What's the matter, Mark? Where's the Utopian contact man?"

"There," Hazleton said. He didn't exactly point, but there was no doubt about his meaning. Amalfi felt his eyebrows tobogganing over his broad skull. He turned and studied the girl.

She was quite pretty: black hair, with blue lights in it; gray eyes, very frank, and a little amused; a small body, well made, somewhat on the sturdy side. She was dressed in the most curious garment Amalfi had ever seen—she had a sort of sack over her head, with holes for her arms and neck, and the cloth was pulled in tightly above her waist. Her hips and her legs down to just below her knees were covered by a big tube of black fabric, belted at the top. Her legs were sheathed into token stockings of some sleazily woven, quite transparent stuff. Little flecks of color spotted the sack, and around her neck she had a sort of scarf—no, it wasn't a scarf, it was a ribbon—what *was* it, anyhow? Amalfi wondered if even deFord could have named it.

After a moment the girl began to seem impatient of his inspection, and he turned his head away and continued walking toward his desk. Behind him, her voice said gently, "I didn't mean to cause a sensation, sir. Evidently you didn't expect a woman . . . ?"

Her accent was as archaic as her clothes; it was almost Eliotian. Amalfi sat down and collected his scattered impressions.

"No, we didn't," he said. "However, we have women in

positions of authority here. I suppose we were misled by
Earth custom, which doesn't allow women much hand in
the affairs of the military. You're welcome, anyhow. What
can we do for you?"

"May I sit down? Thank you. First of all, you can tell us
where all these vicious fighting ships come from. Evidently they know you."

"Not personally," Amalfi said. "They know the Okie
cities as a class, that's all. They're the Earth police."

The Utopian girl's piquant face dimmed subtly, as though
she had expected the answer and had been fighting to
believe it would not be given.

"That's what they told us," she said. "We . . . we couldn't
accept it. Why are they attacking us then?"

"It was bound to happen sooner or later," Amalfi said as
gently as possible. "Earth is incorporating the independent planets as a matter of policy. Your enemies the
Hruntans will be taken in, too. I don't suppose we can
explain why very convincingly. We aren't exactly in the
confidence of Earth's government."

"Oh," the girl said. "Then perhaps you will help us?
This immense fortress of yours——"

"I beg your pardon," Hazleton said, smiling ruefully.
"The city is no fortress, I assure you. We are only lightly
armed. However, we may be able to help you in other
ways—frankly, we're anxious to make a deal."

Amalfi looked at him under his eyelids. It was incau-
tious, and unlike Hazleton, to discuss the city's armament
or lack of it with an officer who had just come on board
from a strange battleship.

The girl said, "What do you want? If you can teach us
how those—those police ships fly, and how you keep your
city aloft——"

"You don't have the spindizzy?" Amalfi said. "But you
must have had it once, otherwise you'd never have got
way out here from Earth."

"The secret of interstellar flight has been lost for nearly
a century. We still have the first ship our ancestors flew in
our museum; but the motor is a mystery. It doesn't seem
to *do* anything."

Amalfi found himself thinking: Nearly a century? Is that

supposed to be a *long* time? Or do the Utopians lack the anti-agathic drugs, too? But ascomycin was supposed to have been discovered more than half a century before the Hamiltonian Exodus. Curiouser and curiouser.

Hazleton was smiling again. "We can show you what the spindizzy does," he said. "It is too simple to yield its secret lightly. As for us—we need supplies, raw materials. Oil, most of all. Have you that?"

The girl nodded. "Utopia is very rich in oil, and we haven't needed it in quantity for nearly twenty-five years— ever since we rediscovered molar valence." Amalfi pricked up his ears again. The Utopians lacked the spindizzy and the anti-agathics—but they had something called molar valence. The term told its own story: anyone who could modify molecular bonding beyond the usual adhesion effects would have no need for mechanical lubricants like oil. And if the Utopians thought they had only *re*discovered such a technique, so much the better.

"As for us, we can use anything you can give us," the girl went on. Abruptly she looked very weary in spite of her healthy youth. "All our lives we have been fighting these Hruntan barbarians and waiting for the day when help would arrive from Earth. Now Earth has come—and its hand is against *both* worlds! Things must have changed a great deal."

"The fault doesn't lie in change," Hazleton said quietly, "but in that you people have failed to change. Traveling away from Earth for us is very like traveling in time: different distances from the home planet have different year-dates. Stars remote from Earth, like yours, are historical backwaters. And the situation becomes complicated when the historical periods interpenetrate, as your Hamiltonian era and the Hruntan Empire have interpenetrated. The two cultures freeze each other the moment they come in conflict, and when history catches up with them—well, naturally it's a shock."

"On a more practical subject," Amalfi said, "we'd prefer to pick our own landing area. If we can send technicians to your planet in advance, they'll find a lie for us."

"A lie?"

"A mining site. That's to be permitted, I presume?"

"I don't know," the girl said uncertainly. "We're very short on metals, steel especially. We have to salvage all our scrap—"

"We use almost no iron or steel," Amalfi assured her. "We reclaim what we need, as you do—steel's nearly indestructible, after all. What we're after is germanium and some other rare-earth metals for instruments. You ought to have plenty of those to spare." Amalfi saw no point in adding that germanium was the base of the present universal coinage. What he had said was true as far as it went, and in dealing with these backward planets, there were always five or six facts best suppressed until after the city had left.

"May I use your phone?"

Amalfi moved away from the desk, then had to come back again as the girl dabbed helplessly at the 'visor controls. In a moment she was outlining the conversation to the Utopian captain. Amalfi wondered if the Hruntans understood English; not that he was worried about the present interchange being overheard—the giant planet would block that most effectively, since the Utopians used ordinary radio rather than ultraphones or Dirac communicators—but it was of the utmost importance, if Hazleton's scheme was to be made workable, that the Hruntans should have heard and understood the warning the Earth police had issued to the city. It was a point that would have to be checked as unobtrusively as possible.

It might also be just as well to restrict sharply the technical information the city passed out in this star system. If the Hamiltonians—or the Hruntans—suddenly blossomed out with Bethé blasters, field bombs, and the rest of the modern arsenal (or what had been modern the last time the city had been able to update its files, not quite a century ago), the police would be unhappy. They would also know whom to blame. It was comforting to know that nobody in the city knew how to build a Canceller, at least. Amalfi had a sudden disquieting mental picture of a mob of Hruntan barbarians swarming out of this system in spindizzy-powered ships, hijacking their way back to an anachronistic triumph, snuffing out stars like candle flames as they went.

"It is agreed," the girl said. "Captain Savage suggests that I take your technicians back with me in the gig to save time. And is there also someone who understands the interstellar drive——"

"I'll go along," Hazleton said. "I know spindizzies as well as the next man."

"Nothing doing, Mark. I need you here. We've plenty of grease monkeys for that purpose. We can send them your man Webster; here's his chance to get off the city before we even touch ground." Amalfi spoke rapidly into the vacated 'visor. "There. You'll find the proper people waiting at your gig, young lady. If Captain Savage will phone us exactly one week from today and tell us where on Utopia we're to land, we'll be out of occultation with this gas planet, and will get the message."

There was a long silence after the Utopian girl had left. At last Amalfi said slowly, "Mark, there is no shortage of women in the city."

Hazleton flushed. "I'm sorry, boss. I knew it was impossible directly the words were out of my mouth. Still, I think we may be able to do something for them; the Hruntan Empire was a pretty nauseating sort of state, if I remember correctly."

"That's none of our business," Amalfi said sharply. He disliked having to turn the full force of his authority upon Hazleton; the city manager was for Amalfi the next best thing to that son his position had never permitted him to father—for the laws of all Okie cities include elaborate safeguards against the founding of any possible dynasty. Only Amalfi knew how many times this youngster's elusive, amoral intelligence had brought him close to being deposed and shot by the City Fathers; and a situation like this one was crucial to the survival of the city.

"Look, Mark. We can't afford to have sympathies. We're Okies. What are the Hamiltonians to us? What are they to themselves, for that matter? I was thinking a minute ago of what a disaster it'd be if the Hruntans got a Canceller or some such weapon and blackmailed their way back to a real empire again. But can you see a rebirth of Hamiltonianism any better—in *this* age? Superficially it would be easier to take, I'll admit, than another Hruntan tyranny—but historically, it'd be just as disastrous. These two planets have been fighting each other over two causes that played themselves out half a millennium ago. They aren't either of them *relevant* any more."

Amalfi stopped for a breath, taking the mangled cigar out of his mouth and eyeing it with mild surprise. "I knew that the girl was disturbing your judgment the moment I realized that I'd have to read you the riot act like this. Ordinarily you're the best cultural morphologist I've ever had, and every city manager has to be a good one. If you weren't in a sexual uproar, you'd see that these people are the victims of a pseudomorphosis—dead cultures both of 'em going through the pangs of decay, even though they both do think it's rebirth."

"The cops don't see it that way," Hazleton said abstractedly.

"How could they? They haven't our point of view. I'm not talking to you as a cop. I'm trying to talk like an Okie. What good does it do you to be an Okie if you're going to mix in on some petty border feud? Mark, you might as well be dead—or back on Earth, it's the same thing in the end."

He stopped again. Eloquence was unnatural to him; it embarrassed him a little. He looked sharply at the city manager, and what he saw choked off the springs of his rare volubility. He felt, not for the first time, the essential loneliness that went with perspective.

Hazleton wasn't listening any more.

There was a battle in progress when the city made its run to Utopia. It was rather spectacular. The Hruntan planet, military in organization and spirit down to the smallest detail of daily living, had not waited for the Earth police to englobe it. The Hruntan ships, though they were nearly of the same vintage as those flown by the Utopians, were being fought to the limit, fought by experienced officers who were unencumbered by any sniveling notions about the intrinsic value of human life. There was not much doubt as to the outcome, but for the time being, the police were unhappy.

The battle was not directly visible from the city; the Hruntan planet was nearly forty degrees away from Utopia now. It was the steady widening of the distance between the two planets that had first given Hazleton his idea for a sneak landing. It had also been Hazleton who had dispatched the proxies—guided missiles less than five meters long—which hung invisibly upon the outskirts of the conflict and watched it with avid television eyes.

It was an instructive dogfight. The police craft, collectively, had not engaged in a major battle for decades; and individually, few of the Earthmen had ever been involved in anything more dangerous than a pushover. The Hruntans, vastly inferior in equipment, were rich in experience, and their tactics were masterly. They had forced the engagement in a heavily mined area, which was equivalent to picking a fight in the heart of a furnace—except that the Hruntans, having sown the mines, knew where the fire was hottest. Their losses, of course, were terrific—nearly five to one. But they had the numbers to waste, and it was obvious that officers who did not value their own lives would be unlikely to value those of their crews.

After a while, even Hazleton had to turn the screen off and order O'Brien to recall the proxies. The carnage was frightening, not just per se, but in the mental attitude behind it. Even a hardened killer, after a certain amount of watching men trying to snuff out a fire by leaping into it, might have felt his brains cracking.

The city settled toward Utopia. Outlying police scouts reported the fact—the reports were plainly audible in the city's Communications Room—and those reports would be exhumed later and acted upon. But now, in the midst of the battle, the cops had no time to care about what the city did. When they began to care again, the city hoped to be gone—or invulnerable.

The question of how Utopia had resisted the Hruntan onslaught for nearly a century remained a riddle. It became more of a riddle after the city landed on Utopia. The planet was a death trap of radioactivity. There were no cities; there were seething white-hot pools that would never cool within the lifetime of humanity to show where cities once had stood. One of the continental land masses was not habitable at all. The very air disturbed counters slightly. In the daytime, the radioactivity was just below the dangerous limit; at night, when the drop in temperature released the normal microscopic increase in the radon content—a phenomenon common to the atmospheres of all Earthlike planets—the air was unbreathable.

Utopia had been bombarded with fission bombs and dust canisters at every opposition with the Hruntan planet for the past seventy Utopian years. The favorable oppositions occurred only once every twelve years—otherwise even the underground life of Utopia would have been impossible.

"How have you kept them off?" Amalfi asked. "Those boys are soldiers. If they can put up this much of a battle against the police, they should be able to wipe up the floor with you folks."

Captain Savage, perched uncomfortably in the belfry, blinking at the sun, managed a thin smile. "We know all their tricks. They are very fine strategists—I will grant you that. But in some respects they are unimaginative. Necessarily, I suppose; initiative is not encouraged among them." He stirred uneasily. "Are you going to leave your city out here in plain sight? And at night, too?"

"Yes. I doubt that the Hruntans will attack us; they're busy, and besides, they probably know that the police don't love us, and will be too puzzled to call us an enemy of theirs right off the bat. As for the air—we're maintaining a point naught two per cent spindizzy field. Not enough to be noticeable, but it changes the moment of inertia of our own atmosphere enough to prevent much of your air from getting in."

"I don't think I understand that," Savage said. "But doubtless you know your own resources. I confess, Mayor Amalfi, that your city is a complete mystery to us. What does it do? Why are the police against you? Are you exiled?"

"No," Amalfi said. "And the police aren't against us exactly. We're just rather low in the social scale; we're migratory workers, interstellar hobos, Okies. The police are as obligated to protect us as they are to protect any other citizen—but our mobility makes us possible criminals by their figuring, so we have to be watched."

Savage's summary of his reaction to this was the woeful sentence Amalfi had come to think of as the motto of Utopia. "Things have changed so much," the officer said.

"You should set that to music. I can't say that I understand yet how you've held out so long, either. Haven't you ever been invaded?"

"Frequently," Savage said. His voice was half gloomy and half charged with pride. "But you have seen how we live. At best, we have beaten them off; at worst, we cannot be found. And the Hruntans themselves have made this planet a difficult place to live. Many of their landing parties succumbed to the results of their own bombing."

"Still——"

"Mob psychology," Savage said, "is something of a science with us—as it is with them, but we have developed it in a different direction. Combined with the subsidiary art of camouflage, it is a powerful weapon. By dummy installations, faked weather conditions, false high-radioactivity areas, we have thus far been able to make the Hruntans erect their invasion camps exactly on the spots we have previously chosen for them. It is a form of chess: one persuades, or lures, the enemy into entering an area where one can dispose of him in perfect safety and with a minimum of effort."

He blinked up at the sun, nibbling at his lower lip. After a while he added, "There is another important factor. It is freedom. We have it. The Hruntans do not. They are defending a system which is ascetic in character—that is, it offers few rewards to the individual, even once it has triumphed. We on Utopia are fighting for a system which has personal rewards for us—the rewards of freedom. It makes a difference. The incentive is greater."

"Oh, freedom," Amalfi said. "Yes, that's a great thing, I suppose. Still, it's the old problem. Nobody is ever free. Our city is vaguely republican, it might even be Hamiltonian in one sense. But we aren't free of the requirements of our situation, and never can be. As for efficiency in warfare being increased by freedom—I question that. Your people are not free now. A wartime political economy has to tend toward dictatorship; that's what killed off the West back on Earth. Your people are fighting for steak tomorrow, not steak today. Well—so are the Hruntans. The difference between you exists as a potential, but—a difference which makes no difference is no difference."

"You are subtle," Savage said, standing up. "I think I can see why you would not understand that part of our history. You have no ties, no faith. You will have to excuse us ours. We cannot afford to be logic-choppers."

He went down the stairs, his shoulders thrown back unnaturally. Amalfi watched him go with a rueful grin. The young man was a character; talking with him was like being brought face to face with a person from a historical play. Except, of course, that a character in a play is ordinarily understandable even at his queerest; Savage had the misfortune to be real, not the product of an artificer with an ax to grind.

Amalfi was reminded abruptly of Hazleton. Where was Hazleton, anyhow? He had gone off hours ago with that girl upon some patently trumped-up errand. If he didn't hurry, he'd be trapped underground overnight. Amalfi did not mind working alone, but there were managerial jobs in the city which the mayor simply could not handle efficiently—and besides, Hazleton might be committing the city to something inconvenient. Amalfi went down to his office and called the Communications Room.

Hazleton had not reported in. Grumbling, Amalfi went about the business of organizing the work of the city—the work for which it had gone aloft, but which it found so seldom. It disturbed him that there was no official work contract between the city and Utopia; it was not customary, and if Utopia should turn out, as so many ideals-ridden planets had turned out, to be willing to cheat on an astronomical scale for the sake of its obsession, there would be no recourse under the Earth laws. People with Ends in view were quick to justify all kinds of Means, and the city, which was nothing but Means made concrete and visible, had learned to beware of short cuts.

Hazleton, it appeared, was off somewhere on a short cut. Amalfi could only hope that he—and the city—would survive it.

The Earth police did not wait for Hazleton, either. Amalfi was mildy appalled to see how rapidly the Earth forces reformed and were reinforced. Their logistics had been much improved since the city had last seen them in action. The sky sparkled with ships driving in on the Hruntan planet.

That was bad. Amalfi had expected to have several months at least to build up a food reserve on Utopia before making the run to the Hruntan planet that Hazleton's strategy called for. Evidently, however, the Hruntan world would be completely blockaded by that time.

The mayor sent out an emergency warning at once. The thin resistance which the spindizzy field had offered to Utopia's atmosphere became a solid, hard-driven wall. The spindizzies screamed into the highest level of activity they could maintain without snapping the gravitational thread between the city and Utopia. Around the perimeter of that once-invisible field, a flicker of polarization thickened to translucence. Drive-fields were building, and only a few light rays, most of them those to which the human eye was least sensitive, got through the fields and out again. To Utopian onlookers the city went dark blood-color and became frighteningly indistinct.

Calls began to come in at once. Amalfi ignored them; his flight board, a compressed analog of the banks in the control tower, was alive with alarm signals, and all the speakers were chattering at once.

"Mr. Mayor, we've just made a strike in that old till; it's lousy with oil-bearing shale—"

"Stow what you have and make it tight."

"Amalfi! How can we get any thorium out of——"

"More where we're going. Damp your stock on the double."

"Com Room. Still no word from Mr. Hazleton——"

"Keep trying."

"Calling the flying city! Is there something wrong? Calling the flying——"

Amalfi cut them all off with a brutal swipe at the toggles. "Did you think we'd stay here forever? Stand by!"

The spindizzies screamed. The sparkling of the ships coming to invest the Hruntan planet became brighter by the minute. It would be a near thing.

"Whoop it up there on Forty-second Street! What d'you think you're doing, warming up tea? You've got ninety seconds to get that machine to take-off pitch!"

"Take-off? Mr. Mayor, it'll take at least four minutes——"

"You're kidding me. I can tell. Dead men don't kid. *Move!*"

"*Calling the flying city——*"

The sparks spread over the sky like a Catherine wheel whirling into life. The watery quivering of the single point of light that was the Hruntan planet dimmed among them, shivered, blended into the general glitter. From Astronomy, Jake added his voice to the general complaint.

"*Thirty seconds,*" Amalfi said.

From the speaker which had been broadcasting the puzzled, fearful inquiries of the Utopians, Hazleton's voice said calmly, "Amalfi, are you out of your mind?"

"No," Amalfi said. "It's your plan, Mark. I'm just following through. *Twenty-five seconds.*"

"I'm not pleading for myself. I like it here, I think. I've found something here that the city doesn't have. The city needs it——"

"Do you want off, too?"

"No, hell no," Hazleton said. "I'm not asking for it. But if I had to take it anyhow, I'd take it here——"

A brief constriction made Amalfi's big frame knot up tightly. Nothing emotional—no, nothing to do with Hazleton; probably some spindizzy operator was hurrying things. He staggered to his feet and threw up in the little washstand. Hazleton went on talking, but Amalfi could hardly hear him. The clock grinned and rushed on.

"*Ten seconds,*" Amalfi gasped, a little late.

"Amalfi, listen to me!"

"Mark," Amalfi said, choking, "Mark, I haven't time. You made your choice. I . . . *five seconds* . . . I can't do anything about that. If you like it there, go ahead and stay. I wish you, I wish you everything, Mark, believe me. But I have to think of——"

The clock brought its thin palms together piously.

" . . . the city——"

"Amalfi——"

"*Spin!*"

The city vaulted skyward. The sparks whirled in around it.

CHAPTER TWO: Gort

The flying of the city normally was in Hazleton's hands. In his absence—though it had never happened before—a youngster named Carrel took charge. Amalfi's own hand rarely touched the stick except in spots where even the instruments could not be trusted.

Running the Earth blockade to the Hruntan planet was no easy job, especially for a green pilot like Carrel, but Amalfi did not greatly care. He huddled in his office and watched the screens through a gray mist, wondering if he would ever be warm again. The baseboards of the room were pouring out radiant heat, but it didn't seem to do any good. He felt cold and empty.

"Ahoy the Okie city," the ultraphone barked savagely. "You've had one warning. Pay up and clear out of here, or we'll break you up."

Reluctantly Amalfi tripped the toggle. "We can't," he said uninterestedly.

"What?" the cop said. "Don't give me that. You're in a combat area, and you've already landed on Utopia in defiance of a Vacate order. Pay your fine and beat it, or you'll get hurt."

"Can't," Amalfi said.

"We'll see about that. What's to prevent you?"

"We have a contract with the Hruntans."

There was a long and very dead silence. At last the police vessel said, "You're pretty sharp. All right, proof your contract over on the tape. I suppose you know that we're about to blow the Hruntans to a thin haze."

"Yep."

"All right. Go ahead and land if you've got a contract. The more fools you. Make sure you stay for the full contract period. If you do get off before we reduce the planet, make sure you can pay your fine. If you don't—good riddance, Okie!"

Amalfi managed a ghost of a grin. "Thanks," he said. "We love you, too, flatfoot."

The ultraphone growled and stopped transmitting. There was a world of frustration in that final growl. The Earth police accepted officially the Okie cities' status as hobos— migratory workers—but unofficially and openly the cities were called tramps in the wardrooms of the police cruisers. Opportunities to break up a city did not come very often, and were met with relish; it must have been quite a blow to the cop to find the vanadium-clad, never-varying Contract in his way.

But now there were the Hruntans to cope with. This was the penultimate and most delicate stage of Hazleton's plan—and Hazleton wasn't on deck to administer it. As a matter of fact, if his Utopian friends had heard Amalfi admit to a contract with the Hruntans, he was probably in the hottest water of his career right now. Amalfi tried not to think about it.

The plan originally had not included signing any contracts with either planet; so long as the city was not committed legally, it could refuse jobs, leave them when it pleased, and generally exercise the freedom of the unemployed. But it hadn't worked out that way. The speed with which the police had been reinforced had made it impossible even to approach the Hruntan planet without uncrackable legal protection.

At least the city's stay on Utopia had accomplished some part of its purposes. The oil tanks were a little over half full, and the city's treasury was comfortable, though still not exactly bulging. That left the rare-earth and the power metals still to be attended to; collecting and refining them was unavoidably time-consuming and would take even longer on the Hruntan planet than on Utopia—the Imperial world, farther out from its sun than Utopia, had been given a correspondingly smaller allowance of heavy elements.

But there was no help for it. To stay on Utopia while the Hruntans were being conquered—or "consolidated," as it was officially called on Earth—would have left the city completely at the mercy of the Earth forces. Even at best, it would have been impossible to leave the system without paying the fine for violating the Vacate order, and Amalfi was constitutionally unwilling to part with the money for which the city had labored. Even at the present state of the treasury, it might easily have bankrupted them, for work had been very scarce lately.

The intercom had been modestly calling attention to itself for several minutes. Answered, it said, "Sergeant Anderson, sir. We've got another visitor."

"Yes," Amalfi said. "That would be the Hruntan delegation. Send 'em up."

While he waited, chewing morosely on a dead cigar, he checked the contract briefly. It was standard, requiring payment in germanium "or equivalent"—the give-away clause which had prevented its use on Utopia. It had been signed by ultraphone—the possession of that tight-beam device alone "placed" the Hruntans as to century—and the work the city was to do was left unspecified. Amalfi hoped devoutly that the Hruntans would in turn give themselves away when it came to being specific on that count.

The buzzer sounded once more, and Amalfi pushed the button that released the door. The next instant he was not sure it had been a wise move. The Hruntan delegation bore an unmistakable resemblance to a boarding party. First of all, there were an even dozen soldiers, clad in tight-fitting red leather breeches, gleaming breastplates, and scarlet-plumed casques; the breastplates, too, were emblazoned with a huge scarlet sun. The men snapped to attention in two files of six on each side of the door, bringing to "present arms" weapons which might have been copies of Kammerman's original mesotron rifle.

Between the files, flanked by two lesser lights as gorgeously and unfunctionally clad as macaws, came a giant carved out of gold. His clothing was interwoven with golden threads; his breastplate and helmet were gilded; even his complexion was tanned to a deep golden tone; and he sported a luxuriant golden-blond beard and flowing mustache. He was altogether a most unlikely-looking figure.

He spoke two harsh-sounding words, and boot heels and weapons slammed against the floor. Amalfi winced and stood up.

"We," the golden giant said, "are the Margraf Hazca, Vice Regent of the Duchy of Gort under his Eternal Eminence, Arpad Hrunta, Emperor of Space."

"Oh," Amalfi said, blinking. "My name's Amalfi; I'm the mayor here. Do you sit down?"

The Margraf said he sat down, and did. The soldiers remained stiffly "at ease," and the two subsidiary nobles posed themselves behind the Margraf's chair. Amalfi subsided behind his desk with a muffled sigh of relief.

"I presume you're here to discuss the contract."

"We are. We are told that you have been among the rabble of the second planet."

"An emergency landing only," Amalfi said.

"No doubt," the Margraf said dryly. "We do not concern ourselves with the doings of the Hamiltonians; we will add them to our serfs in due time, after we have driven off these upstarts from decadent Earth. In the meantime, we have use for you; any enemy of Earth must be friends with us."

"That's logical," Amalfi said. "Just what can we do for you? We have quite a variety of equipment here——"

"The matter of payment comes first," said the Margraf. He got up and began pacing slowly up and down with enormous strides, his golden cloak streaming out behind him. "We are not prepared to make any payment in germanium; we need all we have for transistors. The contract speaks of equivalents. What counts as equivalent?"

It was remarkable how the regal manner was snuffed out when it got down to honest haggling. Amalfi said cautiously, "Well, you could allow us to mine for germanium ourselves——"

"Do you think this planet's resources will last forever? Give us the equivalent, not some roundabout scheme for being paid in the metal itself!"

"Equipment, then," Amalfi said, "or skills, at a mutually agreed valuation. For instance, what are you using for lubrication?"

The big count's eyes glittered. "Ah," he said softly. "You have the secret of the friction-fields, then. That we have long sought, but the generators of the rabble melt when we touch them. Does Earth know this process?"

"No."

"You got it from the Hamiltonians? Excellent." The two minor nobles were beginning to grin wickedly. "We need babble no further of 'mutually agreed valuations,' then." He gestured. Amalfi found himself looking down a dozen rifle barrels.

"What's the idea?"

"You are within our defensive envelope," Hazca said with wolfish gusto. "And you are not likely to survive long among the Earthmen, should you by some miracle break free of us. You may call your technicians and tell them to prepare a demonstration of the friction-field generator; also, prepare to land. Graf Nandór here will give you explicit instructions."

He strode toward the door; the soldiers parted deferentially. As Amalfi's hand reached for the button to let him out, the big man whirled. "And you need not attempt to trip any hidden alarms," he growled. "Your city has already been boarded in a dozen places and is under the guns of four cruisers."

"Do you think you can win technical information by force?" Amalfi said.

"Oh yes," said the Margraf, his eyes shining dangerously. "We are—experts."

Carrel, Hazleton's protégé, was a very plausible lecturer and seemed completely at home in the echoing, barbaric gorgeousness of the Margraf's Council Chamber. He had attached his charts to the nearest tapestry and had propped his blackboard on the arms of the great chair in which, Amalfi supposed, the Margraf usually sat; his chalk traced swift symbols on the slate and squeaked deafeningly in the groined vault of the room.

The Margraf himself had left; five minutes of Carrel's talk had been enough to arouse his impatience. The Graf Nandór was still there, wearing the suffering expression of a man delegated to do the dirty work. So were four or five other nobles. Three of these were chattering in the back of the room with muffled sniggers, and a raucous laugh broke in upon Carrel's dissertation every so often. The remaining peacocks, evidently of subordinate ranks, were seated, listening with painful, brow-furrowing concentration, like ham actors overregistering Deep Thought.

"This will be enough to show the analogy between atomic and molecular binding energies," Carrel said smoothly. "The Hamiltonians"—he had seen that the word annoyed the peacocks and used it often—"the Hamiltonians have shown, not only that this binding energy is responsible for the phenomena of cohesion, adhesion, and friction, but also that it is subject to a relationship analogous to valence."

The appearance of concentration of the nobles became so grave as to be outright grotesque. "This phenomenon of molar valence, as the Hamiltonians have aptly named it, is intensified by the friction-fields which they have designed into a condition analogous to ionization. The surface layers of molecules of two contiguous surfaces come into dynamic equilibrium in the field; they change places continuously and rapidly, but without altering the *status quo*, so that a shear-plane is readily established between the roughest surfaces. It is evident that this equilibrium does not in any sense do away with the binding forces in question, and that a certain amount of drag, or friction, still remains—but only about a tenth of the resistance which obtains even with the best systems of gross lubrication."

The nobles nodded together. Amalfi gave over watching them; the Hruntan technicians worried him most. There were an even dozen of them, a number of which the Margraf seemed fond. Four were humble, frightened-looking creatures who seemed to regard Carrel with more than a little awe. They scribbled frantically, fighting to take down every word, even material which was of no conceivable importance, such as Carrel's frequent pats on the back of the Hamiltonians.

All but one of the rest were well-dressed, hard-faced men who treated the nobles with only perfunctory deference, and who took no notes at all. This type was also quite familiar in a barbarian milieu: head scientists, directors, entirely committed to the regime, entirely aware of how crucial they were to its successes, and already infected with the aristocratic virus of letting lesser men dirty their hands with actual messy laboratory experiments. Probably some of them owed their positions as much to a ruthless skill at court intrigue as to any great scientific ability.

But the twelfth man was of a different order altogether. He was tall, spare, and sparse-haired, and his face as he listened to Carrel was alive with excitement. An active brain, this one, doubtless politically unconscious, hardly caring who ruled it as long as it had equipment and a free hand. The man would be tolerated by the regime for his productivity, but would be under constant suspicion. And he was, by Amalfi's judgment, the only man capable of going beyond what Carrel was saying to what Carrel was leaving unsaid.

"Are there any questions?" Carrel said.

There were some, mostly dim-witted, from the technies—how do you build this, and how do you wire that; no one with any initiative would have wanted to be led by the nose in such a fashion. Carrel answered in detail. The hardfaced men left without a word, as did the nobles, who lingered only long enough to save face. The scientist—he was *the* scientist for Amalfi's money—was left alone to launch into an ardent stammering dispute over Carrel's math. He seemed to consider Carrel as an equal as a matter of course, and Carrel was beginning to look uncomfortable by the time Amalfi summoned him to the back of the hall.

The scientist left, pocketing his few notes and pulling thoughtfully at his nose. Carrel watched him go.

"I can't hide the kicker from that boy long, sir," he said. "Believe me, he's got *brains*. Give him about two days and he'll have the whole thing worked out for himself. He won't get any sleep tonight for thinking about it; I know the type."

"So do I," Amalfi said. "I also know barbarian council halls—the arrases have ears. Just pray you weren't overheard, that's all. Come on."

Amalfi was silent until they were safe within the city and in a cab. Then he said, "You have to be careful, Carrel, in dealing with outsiders. You take to it well, but you're inexperienced. *Never* say anything outside the city, even to me, that doesn't fit your part. Now then—I agree with you about that scientist; I was watching him. And now he knows you, so I can't use you against him. Is there someone in your organization who's done undercover work for Mark who hasn't been out of the city since we hit Gort? An experienced hand?"

"Sure, four or five, at least. I can put my finger on any of 'em."

"Good. Find a fairly husky one, a man that could pass for a thug with a minimum of make-up, and send him to Indoctrination for hypnopaedia. In the meantime, you'll have to see that scientist again. Get a picture of him somewhere, a tri-di if they have them here. When you talk to him, answer any questions he asks you."

Carrel looked puzzled. "*Any* questions?"

"Any technical questions, yes. It won't matter what he knows very shortly. Here's another lesson in practical public relations for you, Carrel. When on a strange planet, you have to use its social system to the best advantage possible. On a world like this one, where the struggle for power is plenty raw, assassination must be very common—and nine chances to one there's a regular Assassins' Guild, or, at least, plenty of free-lance killers for hire."

"You're going to—have Doctor Schloss assassinated?"

The shocked expression on Carrel's face made Amalfi abruptly sodden with weariness. Training a new city manager up to the point where his election would be endorsed by the City Fathers was a long and heartbreaking task, for so much of the training had to be absorbed the hard way. He felt too old for such a job now, and much too aware of some failure in his methods, the failure which alone had made the job necessary now.

"Yes," he said. "It's a shame, but it has to be done. In other circumstances we'd take the man into the city—*he* doesn't care who he works for—but the Hruntans would look for him, and find him, too. There has to be an inarguable corpse, and if possible, a local culprit. Your operative, after a suitable course in this Balkanese they speak here, will scout the rivalries among the scientific clique and try to pin the killing on one of those hawk-nosed laboratory chieftains. But the man must be killed—for the survival of the city."

Carrel did not protest, for the final formulation was the be-all and end-all of Okie logic; but it was plain that the waste of intelligence the plot necessitated upset him. Amalfi decided silently to keep Carrel exceptionally busy in the city for a while—at least until the Hruntans had their anti-friction installation well under way.

Now, anyhow, was the time to put another needle into the cops; Hazleton's timetable called for it, and although Amalfi had already been forced to abandon much of Hazleton's strategy—Hazleton's timetable, for instance, had called for a treacherous Utopian landing on Gort, with the full force of the Hamiltonians thrown behind delivering the Hruntan planet into the hands of the Earth police— the notion of bargaining with the cops for the planet still seemed to have merit.

Dismissing Carrel, Amalfi went to his office, where he took the flexible plastic dust cover off a little-used instrument: the Dirac transmitter. It was the only form of communication which the Hruntans—and, of course, the Hamiltonians—did not have; the want of it had cost them an empire, for it operated instantaneously over any distance. Amalfi thrust a cigar absently between his teeth and sent out a call for the captain of police.

The obsolete model had no screen, but the captain's voice conveyed his feelings graphically. "If you're going to rub my nose in the fact that we're obliged to protect you because the Hruntans have violated the contract," he snarled, "you can save your breath. I've half a mind to blow up the planet anyhow. Some one of these years the Okie laws are going to be changed, and then——"

"You wouldn't have blown up the planet in any case,"

Amalfi said tranquilly. "The shock wave would have detonated the local sun and destroyed the whole system, and your superiors would have had your scalp. What I'm trying to do is save you some trouble. If you're interested, make me an offer."

The cop laughed.

"All right," Amalfi said. "Laugh, you jackass. In about ten months you'll be yanked back to patrolling a stratosphere beat on Earth that sees a plane once every two years, and braying about how unjust it all is. As soon as the home office hears that you let the Hruntans and the Hamiltonians join forces, and that the war is going to cost Earth two or three hundred billion Oc dollars and last maybe twenty-five years——"

"You're a bum liar, Okie," the cop said. The bravado behind the pun seemed a little strained, however. "They been fighting each other a century now."

"Times change," Amalfi said. "In any event, the merger will be forcible, because if you don't want the Duchy of Gort, I'm going to offer it to Utopia. The combined arsenal will be impressive—each side has some stuff the other hasn't, and we couldn't prevent either of them from learning a few tricks from us. However——"

"Wait a minute," the cop said cautiously. He was quite aware, Amalfi was more than certain, that this conversation was inevitably being overheard by hundreds and perhaps thousands of Dirac receivers throughout the inhabited galaxy, including those in police headquarters on Earth. That was one of the major characteristics of Dirac transmission—whether you called it a flaw or an advantage depended largely on what use you made of it. "You mean you got the upper hand there already? How do I know you can hold it?"

"You don't risk a thing. Either I deliver the planet to you, or I don't. All I want is for you to rescind the fine against the city, wipe the tape of the earlier Vacate order, and give us a safe-conduct out of this system. If we don't deliver, you don't pay."

"Hm-mm." There was a muttering in the background, as though somebody were talking softly over the cop's shoulder. "How'd you pull it off?"

"That," Amalfi said dryly, "would be telling. If you want to play, proof over the agreement."

"No soap. You violated the Vacate order and you'll have to pay the fine—that's flat."

That was good enough for Amalfi. The cop certainly was not going to promise to wipe his tape of evidence of a tort while he was talking on the Dirac; that he had picked this particular point to stick on indicated general agreement, however.

"Just send me a safe-conduct under seal, then. I'll put the whole thing in the Margraf Hazca's strong room; you get it back when you get the planet."

After a short silence, the cop said, "Well . . . all right." The tape began to whir at Amalfi's elbow. Satisfied, he broke the contact.

If this coup came off on schedule, it would become legendary—the police would be mighty tight-lipped about it, but the Okie cities would spread the tale all over the galaxy.

Somehow, the desertion of Hazleton made the prospect savorless.

Someone was shaking him. He wanted very badly to awaken, but his sleep was as deep as death, and it seemed that no possible struggle could bring him up to the rim of the pit. Shapes and faces whirled about him, and in the blackness he felt the approach of great steel teeth.

"Amalfi! Wake up, man! Amalfi, it's Mark—wake up——"

The steel jaws came together with a terrible snapping report, and the wheeling faces vanished. Bluish light spilled into his eyes.

"Who? What is it?"

"It's me," Hazleton said. Amalfi blinked up at him uncomprehendingly. "Quick, quick. There's only a little time."

Amalfi sat up slowly and looked at the city manager. He was too stunned to know whether he was pleased or not, and the oppression of his nightmare was still with him, a persistent emotion lingering after dreamed events he could no longer remember.

"I'm glad to see you," he said. Oddly, the statement seemed untrue; he could only hope it would become true later. "How'd you get through the police cordon? I'd have said it couldn't be done."

"By force, and fraud, the old combination. I'll explain later."

"You nearly didn't make it," Amalfi said, feeling a sudden influx of energy. "Is it still night here? Yes. The big blowup isn't due much before noon, otherwise I wouldn't have been asleep. After that, you'd have found no city here."

"Before noon? That isn't according to the timetable. But that can wait. Get up, boss, there's work waiting."

The door to Amalfi's room slid aside suddenly, and the Utopian girl stood at the sill, her face pinched with anxiety. Amalfi reached hastily for his jacket.

"Mark, we must hurry. Captain Savage says he won't wait but fifteen minutes more. And he won't—he hates you underneath, I can tell, and he'd love to leave us here with the barbarians!"

"Right away, Dee," Hazleton said, without turning.

The girl disappeared. Amalfi stared at the prodigal city manager. "Wait a minute," he said. "What *is* all this, anyhow? Mark, you haven't sold yourself on some idiotic personal rescue mission?"

"Personal? No." Hazleton grinned. "We're getting the whole city out of here, right on the timetable. I wanted to get word to you that we were following through as planned, but the Utopians have no Diracs, and I didn't want to tip off the cops. Get dressed, that's a good fellow, and I'll explain as we go. These Hamiltonians have been working like demons, installing spindizzies in every available ship. They'd about decided to surrender to the cops—after all, they've more in common with Earth than with the Hruntans—but when I told them what we planned, and showed them how the spindizzy works, it was like giving them all new hearts."

"They believed you as quickly as that?"

Hazleton shrugged. "No, of course not. To be on the safe side, they made up an escape fleet of twenty-five ships—reconverted light cruisers—and sent them out on this mission. They're upstairs now."

"Over the city?"

"Yes. I heard the hijacking of the city—I gather you had the radio on for the benefit of the cops, but it came through pretty clearly on Utopia, too. So I sold them on combining their escape project with a sneak raid to escort the city out. It took some selling, but I convinced them that they'd get out of this system easier if the cops had two things to think about at once. And so here we are, right on the timetable." Hazleton grinned again. "The cops had no notion that there were any Utopian ships anywhere near this planet, and they keep a sloppy watch. They know now, of course, but it'll take them a little while to mass here—and by that time, we'll be gone."

"Mark, you're a romantic ass," Amalfi said. "Twenty-five light cruisers—archaic ones at that, spindizzies or not!"

"There's nothing archaic about Savage's plans," Hazleton said. "He hates my guts for swiping Dee from him, but he knows space combat. This is a survival fleet, for Hamiltonianism, not just people. As soon as we're attacked, all twenty-five of them are going to take off in different directions, putting up a stiff battle and doing their best to turn the affair into a series of individual dogfights. That insures the survival of some of them, of their ideology—and of the city."

"I expected something more from you than a gesture out of a bad stereo," Amalfi said. "Napoleonism! Heedless of danger, young hero leads devoted band into enemy stronghold, snatching beloved sovereign from enraged infidel! Pah! The city's staying where it is. If you want to go off with this suicide squadron, go ahead."

"Amalfi, you don't understand——"

"You underestimate me," Amalfi said harshly. He strode across the room to the balcony, Hazleton at his heels. "Sensible Hamiltonians stayed home, that's a cinch. Giving them the spindizzy was a smart idea—it made them fight longer and kept the cops busy when we needed the time. But these people who are trying to escape toward the edge of the galaxy—they're the incurables, the fanatics. Do you know how they'll wind up? You should, and you would if there wasn't a woman in your head addling your brains with a long-handled spoon. After a few generations on the rim, none of 'em will remember Hamiltonianism.

Making a new planet livable is a job for a carefully prepared, fully manned expedition. These people are the
tatters of a military debacle—and you want us to help set
up the debacle! No thanks."

He threw the door to the balcony open so hard that
Hazleton had to jump to avoid being hit, and went out. It
was a clear night, bitterly cold as always on Gort, and
hundreds of stars glared through the glow the city cast
upon the sky. The Utopian ships, of course, could not be
seen: they were too high, and probably were as well near
to invisible and undetectable, even close up, as Utopian
science could make them.

"I'll have a job explaining this to the Hruntans," he said,
his voice charged with suppressed rage. "The best I'll be
able to do is to claim the Hamiltonians were trying to
destroy us before we could finish giving away the friction-
field plans. And to do that, I'll have to yell to the Hruntans
for help right away."

"You gave the Hruntans——"

"Certainly!" Amalfi said. "It was the only weapon we
had left after we had to sign a contract with them. The
possibility of a Utopian landing in force here vanished the
moment the police beat us to the punch. And here you are
still trying to use the blunted tool!"

"Mark!" the girl's voice drifted out from the room, frantic with anxiety. "Mark! Where are you?"

"Go along," Amalfi said, without turning his head. "After a while they'll have no time to cherish their ritual
beliefs, and you can have a nice frontier home, on the
ox-bone plow level. The city is staying there. By noon
tomorrow, the Utopians who stayed will be put in an
excellent position to bargain with Earth for rights, the
Hruntans will be horn-swoggled, and we'll be on our
way."

The girl, evidently having noticed the open door, came
through it in time to hear the last two sentences. "Mark!"
she cried. "What does he mean? Savage says——"

Hazleton sighed. "Savage is an idiot and so am I. Amalfi's
right; I've been acting like a child. You'd better get aloft
while you have the chance, Dee."

She came forward to the railing and took his arm, looking up at him. Her face was so full of puzzlement and hurt that Amalfi had to look away; that look reminded him of too many things best forgotten—some of them not exactly remote. He heard her say, "Do you—do you want me to go, Mark? You're staying with the city?"

"Yes," Hazleton muttered. "I mean, no. I've made a terrific mess of things, it appears. Maybe I can help now—maybe not. But I've got to stay. You'd be better off with your own people——"

"Mayor Amalfi," the girl said. Amalfi turned unwillingly. "You said when I first met you that there was a place for women in this city. Do you remember?"

"I remember," Amalfi said. "But you wouldn't like our politics, I'm sure. This is not a Hamiltonian state. It's stable, self-sufficient, static—a beachcomber by the seas of history. We're Okies. Not a nice name."

The girl said, "It may not always be so."

"I'm afraid it will. Even the people don't change much, Dee. I suspect that you haven't been told this before, but the great majority of them are well over a century old. I myself am nearly seven hundred. And you would live as long if you joined us."

Dee's face was a study in mixed shock and incredulity, but she said doggedly, "I'll stay."

The sky began to pale slightly. No one spoke. Aloft, the stars were dimming, and there was no sign to show that a tiny fleet of ships was dwindling away into the boundless universe.

Hazleton cleared his throat. "What's for me to do, boss?" he said hoarsely.

"Plenty. I've been making do with Carrel, but though he's willing, he lacks experience. First of all, make us ready to take off at the very first notice. Then cudgel your brains to think up something to tell the Hruntans about this Utopian fleet. You can fancy up my excuse, or think up one of your own—I don't care which. You're better at that kind of thing than I ever was."

"So what's supposed to happen at noon?"

Amalfi grinned. He realized with a subdued shock that he felt good. Getting Hazleton back was like finding a flawed diamond that you'd thought you'd lost—the flaw

was still there and would never go away, but still the
diamond had been the cleanest-cutting tool in the house,
and had had a certain sentimental value.

"It goes like this. Carrel sold the Hruntans on building a
master friction-field generator for the whole planet—said
it would make their machines consume less power, or
some such nonsense. The plans he gave them call for a
generator at least twice as powerful as the Hruntans think
it is, and with nearly all the controls left off. It will run
only one way: full positive. Tomorrow at noon they're
scheduled to give it a trial run.

"In the meantime, there's a Hruntan named Schloss
who probably has the machine tabbed for what it actually
is, and we've set up the old double-knife trick to get him
out of the picture. It's my guess that this should start a big
enough rhubarb among the scientists to keep them from
prying until it's too late. Since this whole deal looked as
though it would work out the same way that the Utopian
landing would have, I also called the cops according to
your timetable and got a safe-conduct. Simple?"

Halfway through the explanation, Hazleton was far enough
back to normal to begin looking amused. When it was
over, he was chuckling.

"That's a honey," he said. "Still, I can see why you
weren't too satisfied with Carrel. Amalfi, you're a prime
bluffer. Telling me to go off with Savage in that dramatic
fashion! Do you know that your fancy plot isn't going to
come off?"

"Why, Mark?" Dee said. "It sounds perfect to me."

"It's clever, but it's full of loose ends. You have to look
at these things like a dramatist; a climax that *almost* comes
off is no climax. We'd better——"

In the bedroom, Amalfi's private phone chimed melodi-
ously, and a neon bulb went on over the balcony doorway.
Amalfi frowned and flicked a switch on the railing.

"Mr. Mayor?" a concealed speaker said nervously. "Sorry
to wake you up, but there's trouble. First of all, at least
twenty ships were over here a while back; we were going
to call you for that, but they went away on their own. But
now we've got a sort of a refugee, a Hruntan who calls
himself Doctor Schloss. He claims the other Hruntans are

all out to get him and he wants to work for us. Shall I send him to Psych or what? It might just be true."

"Of course it's true," Hazleton said. "There's your first loose end, Amalfi."

The affair of Dr. Schloss proved difficult to untangle; Amalfi had not studied his man closely enough. Carrel's agent had done a thorough job of counterfeiting local politics. It was always preferable, when the city needed a man's death, to so arrange matters that the actual killing was done by an outsider, and in this case that had proven absurdly easy to arrange. There were four separate cliques within the scientific hierarchy of Gort, all of them under-cutting each other with fanatical perseverance, like ship-mates trying to do for each other by boring holes in the hull. In addition, the court itself did not trust Dr. Schloss, and took sides sporadically when the throat-cutting became overt.

It had been simple enough to set currents in motion which would sweep Dr. Schloss away, but Schloss had declined to be swept. The moment he became aware of any threat, he had come with disconcerting directness to the city.

"The trouble is," Carrel reported, "that he didn't realize what was flying until it was almost too late. He's a pecu-liarly sane character and would never dream that anybody was 'out to get him' until the knife actually pricked him."

Hazleton nodded. "It's my bet that it was the court itself that finally alarmed him—they wouldn't bother trying to sneak up on him."

"That's correct, sir."

"Which means that we'll have Bathless Hazca and his dandies here looking for him," Amalfi growled. "I don't suppose he bothered to cover his tracks. What are you going to do, Mark? We can't count on their starting the anti-friction fields early enough to get us out of this."

"No," Hazleton agreed. "Carrel, does your man still have contact with the group that was going to punch Schloss's ticket?"

"Sure."

"Have him rub out the top man in that group, then. The time is past for delicate measures."

"What do you propose to gain by that?" Amalfi asked.

"Time. Schloss has disappeared. Hazca may guess that he's come here, but most of the cliques will think he's been killed. This will look like a vengeance killing by some member of Schloss's group—he has no real clique of his own, of course, but there must be several men who thought they stood to gain by keeping him alive. We'll start a vendetta. Confusion is what counts in a fight like this."

"Perhaps so," Amalfi said. "In that case I'd better tackle Graf Nandór right away with a fistful of accusations and complaints. The more confusion, the more delay—and it's less than four hours to noon now. In the meantime, we'll have to hide Schloss as best we can, before he's spotted by one of Hazca's guards here. That invisibility machine in the old West Side subway tunnel seems like the best place . . . do you remember the one? The Lyrans sold it to us, and it just whirled and blinked and buzzed and didn't do a thing."

"That was what my predecessor got shot for," Hazleton said. "Or was it for that fiasco on Epoch? But I know where the machine is, yes. I'll arrange to have the gadget do a little whirling and blinking—Hazca's soldiery is afraid of machinery and would never think of looking inside one that's working, even if they did suspect a fugitive inside it. Which they won't, I'm sure. And . . . gods of all stars, what was *that?*"

The long, terrifying metallic roar died away into a mutter. Amalfi was grinning.

"Thunder," he said. "Planets have a phenomenon called weather, Mark; a nasty habit of theirs. I think we're due for a storm."

Hazleton shuddered. "It makes me want to hide under the bed. Well, let's get to work."

He went out, with Dee trailing. Amalfi, reflecting on the merits of attack as a defensive measure, waved a cab up to the balcony and had himself ferried to the first setback of the midtown RCA building. He would have liked to have landed at the top, where the penthouse was, but the cornices of the building now bristled with pom-

poms and mesotron rifles; Graf Nandór was taking no chances.

The elevator operator was not allowed to take Amalfi beyond the seventieth floor. Swearing, he climbed the last five flights of steps; the blue rage he was working up was not going to be counterfeit by the time he reached the penthouse. At every landing he was inspected with insolent suspicion by lounging groups of soldiers.

There was music in the penthouse, and it reeked of the combination of perfume and unwashed bodies which was the personal trademark of Hruntan nobility. Nandór was sprawled in a chair, surrounded by women, listening to a harpist sing a ballad of unspeakable obscenity in a quavering, emotionless voice. In one jeweled hand he held a heavy goblet half full of fuming Rigellian wine—it must have come from the city's stores, for the Hruntans had had no contact with Rigel for centuries—which he passed back and forth underneath his substantial nose, inhaling the vapors delicately.

He lifted his eyes over the rim of the goblet as Amalfi came in, but did not otherwise bother to acknowledge him. Amalfi felt his blood pressure mounting and his wrists growing cold and numb, and tried to control himself. It was all very well to be properly angry, but he needed some mastery over what he said and did.

"Well?" Nandór said at last.

"Are you aware of the fact that you've just escaped being blown into a rarified gas?" Amalfi demanded.

"Oh, my dear fellow, don't tell me you've just circumvented an assassination attempt on my behalf," Nandór said. His English seemed to have been picked up from a Liverpudlian—only the men of that Okie city spoke through their adenoids in that strange fashion. "Really, that's a bit thick."

"There were twenty-five Hamiltonian ships over the city," Amalfi said grimly. "We beat 'em off, but it was a close shave. Evidently the whole business didn't even wake you or your bosses up. What good are we going to be to you if you can't even protect us?"

Nandór looked alarmed. He pulled a mike from among the pillows and spoke into it for a moment in his own tongue. The answer was inaudible to Amalfi, but after it came, the Hruntan looked less anxious, though his face was still clouded.

"What are you selling me, my man?" he said querulously. "There was no battle. The ships dropped no bombs, did no damage; they have been pursued out as far as the police englobement."

"Does a deaf man recognize an argument?" Amalfi said. "And how do you dazzle a blind man? You people think that all weapons have to go 'bang!' to be deadly. If you'll look at our power boards, you'll see records of a million megawatt drain over one half hour at dawn—and we don't chew up energy at that rate making soup!"

"That's of no moment," the Graf murmured. "Such records can be faked, and there are a good many ways of consuming energy anyhow—or wasting it. Let us suppose instead that these ships who 'attacked' you landed a spy—eh? And that subsequently a Hruntan scientist, a traitor to his emperor, was taken from your city, perhaps in the hope of carrying him back to Utopia?"

His face darkened suddenly. "You interstellar tramps are childishly stupid. Obviously the Hamiltonian rabble hoped to rescue your city and were frightened off by our warriors. Schloss may have gone with them—or he may be hiding in the city somewhere. We will have our answer directly."

He waved at the silent women, who crowded hastily out through the curtained doorway. "Do you care to tell me now where he is?"

"I keep no tabs on Hruntans," Amalfi said evenly. "Sorting garbage is no part of my duties."

Coolly Nandór threw the remainder of his wine in Amalfi's face. The fuming stuff turned his eye sockets into fire. With a roar he stumbled forward, groping for the Hruntan's throat. The man's laughter retreated from him mockingly; then he felt heavy hands dragging his arms behind his back.

"Enough," the Graf said. "Hazca's chief questioner will make some underling babble, if we have to hang them all up by their noses." A blast of thunder interrupted him; outside the penthouse, rain roared along the walls like surf, the first such shower the city had experienced in more than thirty years. Through a haze of pain, Amalfi found that he could see the lights again, although the rest of the world was a red blur. "But I think we'd best shoot this one at once—he talks rather *more* freely than pleases me. Give me your pistol, you there with the lance-corporal's collar."

Something moved across Amalfi's clearing vision, a long shadow with a knot at the end of it—an arm with a pistol. "Any last words?" Nandór said pleasantly. "No? *Tsk.* Well, then——"

A thousand bumblebees took flight in the room. Amalfi felt his whole body jerk upward. Oddly, there was no pain, and he could still see—things continued to take on definition all around him. The clear sight of the dying? . . .

"*Proszáchá!*" Nandór roared. "*Egz prá strasticzek Maria, dó——*"

The thunder cut him off again. Somewhere in the room one of the soldiers was whimpering with fright. To Amalfi's fire-racked sight, everyone and everything seemed to be floating in midair. Nandór sprawled rigidly, half-erect, his body an inch or so off the cushions, his clothing standing away from him. The pistol was still pointed at Amalfi, but Nandór was not holding it; it hung immobile above the carpet, an inch away from his frozen fingers. The carpet itself was not on the floor but above it, a sea of fur, every filament of which bristled straight up. Pictures had sprung away from the walls and were suspended. The cushions had risen from the chair and moved away from each other a little, then stopped, as if caught by a stroboscopic camera in the first stages of an explosion; the chair itself was an inch above the rug. At the far side of the room, a bookshelf had burst, and the cans of microfilm were ranked neatly in front of the case, evenly spaced, supported by nothing but the empty air.

Amalfi took a cautious breath. His jacket, which, like Nandór's, had ballooned away from his chest, creaked a little, but the fabric was elastic enough to stretch. Nandór saw the movement and made a frantic snatch for the pistol. His left forearm was glued to its position above the chair and could not be moved at all. The gun retreated from his free hand, then followed it back obediently as Nandór pulled back for another try.

The second try was an even greater fiasco. Nandór's arm brushed one of the arms of the chair, and then it, too, was held firmly, an inch away from the wood. Amalfi chuckled.

"I would advise you not to move any more than you can help," he said. "If you should bring your head too close to some other object, for instance, you would have to spend the rest of your time looking at the ceiling."

"What . . . have you done?" Nandór said, choking. "When I get free——"

"You can't, not as long as your friends have their friction-field in operation," Amalfi said. "The plans we gave you were accurate enough, except in one respect: your generator can be operated only in reverse. Instead of allowing molecular valence full play, it freezes molecular relationships as they stand, and creates adherence between *all* surfaces. If you had been able to put full power into that generator, you would have stopped molecular movement in place, and frozen all of us to death in a split second—but your power sources are rather puny."

He realized suddenly that his feet were aching violently; the plastic membrances of his shoes were trying to stand away from his flesh and pressing heavily against his skin. His jaw muscles were aching, too; only the fact that the field traveled over surfaces had protected him from having his teeth jammed away from each other, and even at that it was an effort to part his lips to talk against the pressure.

He inhaled slowly. The jacket creaked again. His ribs ground against his sternum. Then, suddenly, the fabric gave way, and the silver belt which had been stitched into it snapped into a tense hoop around his body. His soles hit the straining carpet heavily, and the air puffed out of his shoes.

He swung his arms experimentally, brushing his hands past his thighs. They moved freely. Only the silver belt maintained its implausible position, girdling the keg of his chest like a stave, soaking up the field.

"Good-bye," he said. "Remember not to move. The cops will let you go in a little while."

Nandór was not listening. He was watching with bulging eyes the slow amputation of six of his fingers by the rings he was wearing.

There was now, Amalfi knew, no longer than fifteen minutes before the overdriven friction-field would begin to have more serious effects. Normal molecular cohesion could not be disturbed; homogeneous objects—stones, girders, planks—would remain as they were, but things which were made up of fitted parts would soon begin to yield to the pressure driving them away from each other. After that, structures joined by binders of smaller coherence than the coherence of their parts would begin to give way; older buildings, such as City Hall, would become taller and of greater volume as the ancient bricks pulled away from each other—and would collapse the moment the influence of the friction-field was removed. More modern constructions and machines would last only a little longer. By the time the cops inherited Gort, the planet would be a mass of rubble.

And eventually the human body, assembled of a thousand tubes, tunnels, caverns, and pockets, would strain, and swell, and burst—and only a few city men had the silver belt; there had not been time.

Puffing, Amalfi threw himself down the stairs, dodging among the paralyzed, floating guards. The bumblebee sound was very hard on the nerves. At the seventieth floor he found an unexpected problem; the lights on the elevator board told him that the car had been sealed in the shaft, probably by the action of the safety mechanisms when it had been derailed by the friction-field.

Going down by the stairs was out of the question. Even under normal conditions he could never have traveled seventy flights of stairs, and in the influence of the field, his feet moved as if in thick mud, for the belt could not entirely protect his extremities. Tentatively he touched the wall. The same nauseous sucking sensation enfolded his hand, and he pulled it away.

Gravity . . . the quickest way down . . .

He entered the nearest office, threading his way among the four suspended, moaning figures who belonged there, and kicked the window out. It was impossible to open it against the field, which had sprung it an inch from its lands; only the amazing lateral strength of glass had preserved the pane, but against a cross-sectional blow, it shattered at once. He climbed out.

It was twenty stories down to the next setback. He planted his feet against the metal, and then his hands. As an afterthought, he also laid his forehead against the wall. He began to slide.

The air whispered in his ears, and windows blinked past him. His palms were beginning to feel warm; they were not actually touching the metal, but the reluctant binding energies were exacting a toll. It was the penalty he had to pay for the heightened pull of friction.

As the setback rushed up to him, he flattened his whole body against the side of the building. The impact of the deck was heavy, but it did not seem to break any bones. He staggered to the parapet and climbed over, without allowing a split second for second thoughts. The long, whistling slide began again.

For a moment after he fell against the concrete of the sidewalk, he was ready to get up and throw himself over still another cliff. His hands and his forehead were as seared as if they had been dipped in boiling oil, and inside his teflon shoes his feet seemed to be bubbling like lumps of fat in a rendering vat. On the solid ground, a belated vertigo knotted him helplessly for long, valuable minutes.

The building whose flank he had traversed began to groan.

All along the street, men stood in contorted attitudes. It was like the lowest circle of hell. Amalfi got up, retching, and lurched toward the control tower. The bumblebee sound filled the universe.

"Amalfi! Gods of all stars, what happened to you——"

Someone took Amalfi's arm. Serum from the enormous blister which was his forehead flooded his eyes.

"Mark——"

"Yes, yes. What's the matter—how did you——"

"Get aloft. Get——"

Pain wrenched him into a ringing darkness.

* * *

After a while he felt his head and his hands being laved with something cool. The touch was very delicate and soothing. He swallowed and tried to breathe.

"Easy, John. Easy."

John. No one called him that. A woman's voice. A woman's hands.

"Easy."

He managed a croaking sound, and then a word or two. The hands stroked the coolness across his forehead, gently, monotonously. "Easy, John. It's all right."

"Aloft?"

"Yes."

"Who's . . . that? Mark——"

"No," said the voice. It laughed, surprisingly, a musical sound. "This is Dee, John. Hazleton's girl."

"The Hamiltonian girl." He allowed himself to be silent for a while, savoring the coolness. But there were too many things that needed to be done. "The cops. They should have the planet."

"They have it. They almost had us. They don't keep their bargains very well. They charged us with aiding Utopia; that was treason, they said."

"What happened?"

"Doctor Schloss made the invisibility machine work. Mark says the machine must have been damaged in transit, so the Lyrans didn't cheat you after all. He hid Doctor Schloss in it—that was your idea, wasn't it?—and Schloss got bored and amused himself trying to figure out what the machine was for; nobody had told him. He found out. He made the whole city invisible for nearly half an hour before his patchwork connections burned out."

"Invisible? Not just opaque?" Amalfi tried to think about it. And he had nearly had Schloss killed! "If we can use that——"

"We did. We sailed right through the police ring, and they looked right through us. We're on our way to the next star system."

"Not far enough," Amalfi said, stirring uneasily. "Not if we're charged with technical treason. Cops will detect us, follow us. Tell Mark to head for the Rift."

"What is the Rift, John?"

At the word, the bottom seemed to fall out of things, and Amalfi was again sinking into that same pit in which he had been floundering in dream the night that Hazleton had come back to the city. How do you tell a planetbound colonial girl what the Rift is? How do you teach her, in just a few words, that there is a place in the universe so empty and lightless that even an Okie dreams about it? Let it go.

"The Rift is a hole. It's a place where there aren't any stars. I can't explain it any better. Tell Mark we have to go there, Dee."

There was a long silence. She was frightened, that much was plain. But at last she said, "The Rift. I'll tell him."

"He'll argue. Say it's an order."

"Yes, John. The Rift; it's an order."

And then she was silent. Somehow she had accepted it. Amalfi was surprised; but the steady, uneventful passage of the cool hands was putting him to sleep. Yet there was still something more . . .

"Dee?"

"Yes, John."

"You said—*we're* on our way."

"Yes, John."

"You, too? Even to the Rift?"

The girl made her fingertips trace a smile upon his forehead. "Me, too," she said. "Even to the Rift. The Hamiltonian girl."

"No," Amalfi said. He sighed. "Not any more, Dee. Now you're an Okie."

There was no answer, but the movement of the cool fingers did not hesitate. Under Amalfi the city soared outward, humming like a bee, into the raw night.

CHAPTER THREE: The Rift

Even to the men of the flying city, the Rift was awesome beyond all human experience. Loneliness was natural between the stars, and starmen of all kinds were used to it—the star-density of the average cluster was more than enough to give a veteran Okie claustrophobia. But the enormous empty loneliness of the Rift was unique.

To the best of Amalfi's knowledge, no human being, let alone a city, had ever crossed the Rift before. The City Fathers, who knew everything, agreed. Amalfi was none too sure that it was wise, for once, to be a pioneer.

Ahead and behind, the walls of the Rift shimmered, a haze of stars too far away to resolve into individual points of light. The walls curved gently toward a starry floor, so many parsecs "beneath" the granite keel of the city that it seemed to be hidden in a rising haze of star dust.

"Above" there was nothing; a nothing as final as the slamming of a door. It was the empty ocean of space that washes between galaxies.

The Rift was, in effect, a valley cut in the face of the galaxy. A few stars swam in it, light millennia apart—stars which the tide of human colonization could never have reached. Only on the far side was there likely to be any inhabited planet, and, consequently, work for the city.

On the near side there was still the police. It was not, of course, the same contingent which had consolidated Utopia and the Duchy of Gort; such persistence by a single squadron of cops, over a trail which had spanned nearly three centuries, would have been incredible for so small a series of offenses on the city's part. Nevertheless, there was a violation of a Vacate order still on the books, and a little matter of a trick . . . and the word had been passed. To turn back was out of the question for the city.

Whether or not the police would follow the city even as far as the Rift, Amalfi did not know. It was, however, a good gamble. Crossing a desert of this size would probably be impossible for so small an object as a ship, out of a sheer inability to carry enough supplies; only a city which could grow its own had much chance of surviving such a crossing.

Soberly Amalfi contemplated the oppressive chasm which the screens showed him. The picture came in from a string of proxies, the leader of which was already parsecs out across the gap. And still the far wall was featureless, just beginning to show a faintly granular texture which gave promise of resolution into individual stars at top magnification.

"I hope the food holds out," he muttered. "If we make this one, it'll make the most colossal story any Okie ever had to tell. They'll be calling us the Rifters from one end of the galaxy to the other."

Beside him, Hazleton drummed delicately upon the arm of his chair. "And if we don't," he said, "they'll be calling us the biggest damned fools that ever got off the ground—but we won't be in a position to care. Still, we do seem to be in good shape for it, boss. The oil tanks are almost full, and the *Chlorella* crops are flourishing. Both breeders are running, so there'll be no fuel problem. And I doubt that we'll have any mutation trouble in the crops out here—isn't free-field incidence supposed to vary directly with star-density?"

"Sure," Amalfi said, irritated. "We won't starve if everything goes right." He paused; there had been a stir behind him, and he turned around. Then he smiled.

There was something about Dee Hazleton that relaxed him. She had not yet seen enough actual space cruising to acquire the characteristic deep Okie star burn, nor yet to lose the wonder of being now, by Utopian standards, virtually immortal, and so she seemed still very pink and young and unharried.

Someday, perhaps, the constant strain of wandering from star to star, from crisis to crisis, would tell on her, as it did upon all Okies. She would not lose the wanderlust, but the wanderlust would take its toll.

Or perhaps her resiliency was too great even for that. Amalfi hoped so.

"Go ahead," she said. "I'm only kibitzing."

The word, like a great part of Dee's vocabulary, was a mystery to Amalfi. He grinned and turned back to Hazleton. "If we hadn't been sound enough to risk crossing," he went on, "I'd have let us be captured; we could have paid the fine on the Vacate violation, just barely, and with luck we could have gotten a show-cause injunction against breaking us up slapped on the cops for that 'treason' charge. But just look at that damned canyon, Mark. We've never been as long as fifty years without a planet-fall before, and this crossing is going to take all of the hundred and four the Fathers predicted. The slightest accident, and we'll be beyond help—we'll be out where no ship could reach us."

"There'll be no accident," Hazleton said confidently.

"There's fuel decomposition—we've never had a flash fire before, but there's always a first time. And if that Twenty-third Street spindizzy conks out again, it'll damn near double the time of the crossing——"

He stopped abruptly. Through the corner of his eye, a minute pinprick of brightness poked insistently into his brain. When he looked directly at the screen, it was still there, though somewhat dimmed as its image moved off the fovea centralis of his retina. He pointed.

"Look—is that a cluster? No, it's too small and sharp. If that's a single free-floating star, it's close."

He snatched up a phone. "Give me Astronomy. Hello, Jake. Can you figure me the distance of a star from the source of an ultraphone videocast?"

"Why, yes," the voice on the phone said. "Wait, and I'll pick up your image. Ah—I see what you're after: something at ten o'clock, can't tell what yet. Dinwiddlie pick-

ups on your proxies? Intensity will tell the tale." The
astronomer chuckled like a parrot on the rim of a cracker
barrel. "Now if you'll just tell me how many proxies you
have ahead, and how far they——"

"Five. Full interval."

"Hm-m. A big correction, then." There was a long,
itching silence. Amalfi knew that there would be no hurrying Jake. He was not the city's original astronomer; that
man had fallen victim to a native of a planet called St.
Rita's after he had insisted once too often to said native
that St. Rita's was not the center of the universe. Jake had
been swapped from another city for an atomic-pile engineer and two minor protosynthetics technicians under the
traditional "rule of discretion," and he had turned out to
be interested only in the behavior of the more remote
galaxies. Persuading him to think about the immediate
astronomical situation of the city was usually a hopeless
struggle; he seemed to feel that problems of so local a
nature were nearly beneath notice.

The "rule of discretion" was an Okie tradition which
Amalfi had never before invoked, and never since, for it
seemed to him to smell suspiciously of peonage. It had
evolved, the City Fathers said, from the trading of base-
ball players, a term which meant nothing to Amalfi. The
results of his one violation of his own attitude toward the
rule sometimes seemed to him to smack of divine retribution.

"Amalfi?"

"Yeah."

"About ten parsecs, give or take four-tenths. That's from
the proxies, not from us. I'd say you've found a floater, my
boy."

"Thanks." Amalfi put the phone back and drew a deep
breath. "Just a few years' travel. What a relief."

"You won't find any colonists on a star that isolated,"
Hazleton reminded him.

"I don't care. It's a landing point, possibly a fuel or even
a food source. Most stars have planets; a freak like this
might not, or it might have dozens. Just cross your fingers."

He stared at the tiny sun, his eyes aching from sympa-
thetic strain. A star in the middle of the Rift—almost
certainly a wild star, moving at four hundred or five hun-

dred kilometers per second, but not, as such stars usually
were, a white dwarf; by eye alone, Amalfi estimated it to
be an F star like Canopus. It occurred to him that a people
living on a planet of that star might remember the moment when it burst through the near wall of the Rift and
embarked upon its journey into the emptiness.

"There might be people there," he said. "The Rift was
swept clean of stars once, somehow. Jake claims that this
is an overdramatic way of putting it, that the mean motions of the stars probably opened the gap naturally. But
either way, that sun must be a recent arrival, going at
quite a clip, since it's moving counter to the general
tendency. It could have been colonized while it was still
passing through a populated area. Runaway stars tend to
collect hunted criminals as they go by, Mark."

"Possibly," Hazleton admitted. "Though I'll bet that if
that star ever was among the others, it was way back
before space flight. By the way, that image is coming in
from your lead proxy, out across the valley. Don't you
have any outriggers? I ordered them sent."

"Sure. But I don't use them except for routine. Cruising
the Rift lengthwise would *really* be suicide."

"I know. But where there's one isolated star, there may
be another. Maybe a nearer one."

Amalfi shrugged. "We'll take a look if you like."

He touched the board. On the screen, the far wall of the
Rift was wiped away. Nothing was left but what looked
like a thin haze; down at that end, the Rift turned and
eventually faded out into a rill of emptiness, soaking into
the sands of the stars.

"Nothing on that side. Lots of nothing."

Amalfi moved the switch again.

On the screen, apparently almost within hallooing distance, a city was burning.

It was all over in a few minutes. The city bucked and
toppled in a maelstrom of lightning. Feeble flickers of
resistance spat around its edges—and then it no longer
had any edges. Sections of it broke off and melted like
wraiths. From its ardent center, a few hopeless life craft
shot out into the gap; whatever was causing the destruc-

tion let them go. No conceivable life ship could live long enough to get out of the Rift.

Dee cried out. Amalfi cut in the audio circuit, filling the control room with a howl of static. Far behind the wild blasts of sound, a tiny voice was shouting desperately, "Rebroadcast if anyone hears us. Repeat: We have the fuelless drive. We're destroying our model and evacuating our passenger. Pick him up if you can. We're being blown up by a bindlestiff. Rebroadcast if——"

Then there was nothing left but the skeleton of the city, glowing whitely, evaporating in the blackness. The pale, innocent light of the guide beam for a Bethé blaster played over it, but it was still impossible to see who was wielding the weapon. The Dinwiddie circuits in the proxies were compensating for the glare, so that nothing was coming through to the screen that did not shine with its own light.

The terrible fire died slowly, and the stars brightened. As the last spark flared and went out, a shadow loomed against the distant star wall. Hazleton drew his breath in sharply.

"*Another* city! So some outfits really do go bindlestiff! And we thought we were the first ones out here!"

"Mark," Dee said in a small voice. "Mark, what is a bindlestiff?"

"A tramp," Hazleton said, his eyes still on the screen. "The kind of outfit that gives all Okies a bad name. Most Okies are true hobos, Dee; they work for their living wherever they can find work. The bindlestiff lives by robbery—and murder."

His voice was bitter. Amalfi himself felt a little sick. That one city should destroy another was bad enough; but it was even more of a wrench to realize that the whole scene was virtually ancient history. Ultrawave transmission was somewhat faster than light, but only by about 25 percent; unlike the Dirac transmitter, the ultraphone was by no means an instantaneous communicator. The dark city had destroyed its counterpart years ago and must now be beyond pursuit. It was even beyond identification, for no orders could be sent now to the lead proxy which would result in any action until still more years had passed.

"Some outfits go bindlestiff, all right," he said. "And I

think the number must have been increasing lately. Why that should be, I don't know, but evidently it's happening. We've been losing a lot of legitimate, honest cities lately—— getting no answer to Dirac casts, missing them at rendezvous, and so on. Maybe now we know why."

"I've noticed," Hazleton said. "But I don't see how there could be enough piracy to account for all the losses. For all we know, the Vegan orbital fort may be out here, picking off anybody who's venturesome enough to leave the usual commerce lanes."

"I didn't know the Vegans flew cities," Dee said.

"They don't," Amalfi said abstractedly. He considered describing the legendary fort, then rejected the idea. "But they dominated the galaxy once, before Earth took to space flight. At their peak they owned more planets than Earth does right now, but they were knocked out a hell of a long time ago. . . . I'm still worried about that bindlestiff, Mark. You'd think that some heavy thinker on Earth would have figured out a way to make Diracs compact enough to be mounted in a proxy. They haven't got anything better to do back there."

Hazleton had no difficulty in penetrating to the real core of Amalfi's grumbling. He said, "Maybe we can still smoke 'em out, boss."

"Not a chance. We can't afford a side jaunt."

"Well, I'll send out a general warning on the Dirac," Hazleton said. "It's barely possible that the cops will be able to invest this part of the Rift before the 'stiff gets out of it."

"That'll trap *us* neatly, won't it? Besides, that bindlestiff isn't going to leave the Rift, at least not until it's picked up those life craft."

"Eh? How do you know?"

"Did you hear what the SOS said about a fuelless drive?"

"Sure," Hazleton said uneasily, "but the man who knows how to build it must be dead by now, even if he escaped when his city was blasted."

"We can't be sure of that—and that's the one thing that the 'stiff *has* to make sure of. If the 'stiffs get ahold of that drive, there'll be all hell to pay. After that, 'stiffs won't be a rarity any more. If there isn't widespread piracy in the galaxy now, there will be—if we let the 'stiffs get that no-fuel drive."

"Why?" Dee said.

"I wish you knew more history, Dee. I don't suppose there were ever any pirates on Utopia, but Earth once had plenty of them. They eventually died out, thousands of years ago, when sailing ships were replaced by fueled ships. The fueled ships were faster than sailing vessels— but they couldn't themselves become pirates because they had to touch civilized ports regularly to coal up. They could always get food off some uninhabited island, but for coal they had to visit a real port. The Okie cities are in the same position now; they're fueled ships. But if that bindlestiff can actually get its hands on a no-fuel drive—so he can sail space without having to touch civilized planets for power metals—well, we just can't allow it to happen, that's all. *We've got to get that drive away from them.*"

Hazleton stood up, kneading his hands nervously. "That's perfectly true—and that's why the 'stiff will knock itself out to recapture those lifeships. You're right, Amalfi. Well, there's only one place in the Rift where a lifeship could go, and that's to the wild star. So the 'stiff is probably there, too, by now—or on the way there." He looked thought-fully at the screen, once more glittering only with anony-mous stars. "That changes things. Shall I send out the Dirac warning, or not?"

"Yes, send it out. It's the law. But I think it's up to us to deal with the 'stiff; we're familiar with ways of manipu-lating strange cultures, and we know how Okies think— even 'stiffs. Whereas the cops would just smash things up if they did manage to get here in time."

"Check. Our course as before, then."

"Necessarily."

Still the city manager did not go. "Boss," he said at last, "the outfit is heavily armed. They could muscle in on us with no trouble."

"Mark, I'd call you yellow if I didn't know you were just lazy," Amalfi growled. He stopped suddenly and peered up the length of Hazleton's figure to his sardonic, horselike face. "Or are you leading up to something?"

Hazleton grinned like a small boy caught stealing jam.

"Well, I did have something in mind. I don't like'stiffs, especially killers. Are you willing to entertain a small scheme?"

"Ah," Amalfi said, relaxing. "That's better. Let's hear it."

"It centers on women. Women are the best possible bindlestiff bait."

"I grant you that," Amalfi said. "But what women would you use? Ours? Nix."

"No, no," Hazleton said. "This is predicated on there being an inhabited planet going around that star. Are you still with me?"

"I think," Amalfi said slowly, "that I may even be a meter or so ahead of you."

The wild star, hurling itself through the Rift on a course that would not bring it to the far wall for another ten thousand Earth years, carried with it six planets, of which only one was even remotely Earthlike. That planet shone deep chlorophyll green on the screens long before it had grown enough to assume a recognizable disc shape. The proxies, called in now, arrived one by one, circling the new world like a swarm of five-meter footballs, eyeing it avidly.

It was everywhere the same: savagely tropical, in the throes of a geological period roughly comparable to Earth's Carboniferous Era. Plainly, the only habitable planet would be nothing but a way station; there would be no work for pay there.

Then the proxies began to pick up weak radio signals.

Nothing, of course, could be made of the language; Amalfi turned that problem over to the City Fathers at once. Nevertheless, he continued to listen to the strange gabble while he warped the city into an orbit. The voices sounded ritualistic, somehow.

The City Fathers said:

"THIS LANGUAGE IS A VARIANT OF HUMANOID PATTERN G, BUT THE SITUATION IS AMBIGUOUS. GENERALLY WE WOULD SAY THAT THE RACE WHICH SPEAKS IT IS INDIGENOUS TO THE PLANET,

A RARE OCCURRENCE, BUT BY NO MEANS UN-
HEARD OF. THERE ARE TRACES OF FORMS WHICH
MIGHT BE DEGENERATES OF ENGLISH, HOW-
EVER, AS WELL AS STRONG EVIDENCES OF DIA-
LECT MIXTURES SUGGESTING A TRIBAL SOCIETY.
THIS LATTER FACT IS NOT CONSONANT WITH THE
POSSESSION OF RADIO NOR WITH THE UNDER-
LYING SAMENESS OF THE PATTERN. UNDER THE
CIRCUMSTANCES, WE MUST POSITIVELY FORBID
ANY MACHINATION BY MR. HAZLETON ON THIS
VENTURE."

"I didn't ask them for advice," Amalfi said. "And what
good is a lesson in etymology at this point? Still, Mark,
watch your step——"

" 'Remember Thor Five,' " Hazleton said, mimicking
the mayor's father-bear voice to perfection. "All right. Do
we land?"

For answer, Amalfi grasped the space stick, and the city
began to settle. Nothing that appeared to answer as a
ready-made landing area offered itself, and the mayor had
already decided that nothing would. He sidled the city
downward gently, guiding himself mainly by the increasingly
loud chanting in his earphones.

At four thousand meters there was a brief glitter from
amid the dark green waves of the treetops. The proxies
converged on it slowly, cautious of their prim electronic
lives, and on the screens a turreted roof showed—then
two, four, a dozen. There was a city there—not an Okie,
but a homebody, grown from the earth. Closer views
showed it to be walled, the wall standing just inside a clear
ring where nothing grew; the greenery between the towers was camouflage.

At three thousand, a flight of small ships burst from the
native city like frightened birds, molting feathers of flame.
"Gunners!" Hazleton snapped into his mike. "Posts!"

Amalfi shook his head, and continued to bring his city
closer to the ground. The fire-tailed birds wheeled around
them, weaving a pattern in smoky plumes; yet an Earthman would have thought, not of birds, but of the nuptial
flight of drone bees.

Amalfi, who had not seen an Earthly bird or bee for neatly a millennium now, nevertheless sensed the ceremony in the darting cortege. With fitting solemnity, he brought the city to a stop not far from its jungle counterpart, hovering just above the tops of the giant cycads. Then, instead of clearing a landing area with the usual quick scythe of the mesotron rifles, he polarized the spindizzy screen.

The base and apex of the Okie city grew dim. What happened to the giant ferns and horsetails directly beneath it could not be seen—they were flattened into synthetic fossils in the muck in a split second—but those just beyond the rim of the city were stripped of their fronds and splintered, and farther out, in a vast circle, the whole forest bowed low away from the city to a clap of sunlit thunder.

Unfortunately, the Twenty-third Street spindizzy blew out under the strain at the last minute, and the city dropped the last 150 meters in free fall. It arrived on the surface of the planet rather more cataclysmically than Amalfi had intended. Hazleton hung on to his bucket seat until the control tower had stopped swaying, and then wiped blood from his nose with a judicious handkerchief.

"That," he said, "was one dramatic touch too many. I'd best go have that spindizzy fixed again, just in case. Someday that machine is going to sour for good and all, boss."

Amalfi shut off the controls with a contented gesture. "If that bindlestiff should show now," he said, "they'll have a tough time amassing any prestige *here* for a while. But go ahead, Mark, it'll keep you busy."

The major eased his barrel-shaped bulk into the lift shaft and let himself be slithered through the friction-field to the street. It was certainly a much faster and pleasanter way of traveling than elevators—or skidding down the face of a building using your forehead for a brake shoe. Outside, the face of the control tower shone with hot sunlight, reminding Amalfi that the front of City Hall faced the same way, and that on it the city's motto would be clear even under its incrustation of verdigris. He hoped that the legend could not be read by any of the local folk—it would spoil the effect of the landing.

Suddenly he was aware that the chanting he had been hearing for so long through his earphones was thrilling through the air around him. Here and there the sober workaday faces of the Okie citizens were turning to look down The Avenue, and traces of wonder, mixed with amusement and an unaccountable sadness, were in those faces. Amalfi turned.

A procession of children was coming toward him—children wound in mummylike swatches of cloth down to their hips, the strips alternately red and white. Several free-swinging panels of many-colored fabric, as heavy as silk, swirled about their legs as they moved.

Each step was followed by a low bend, hands outstretched and fluttering, heads rolling from shoulder to shoulder, feet moving in and out, toe-heel-toe, the whole body turning and turning again. Bracelets of objects like dried pods rattled at wrists and bare ankles. Over it all, the voices chanted like water flutes.

Amalfi's first wild reaction was to wonder why the City Fathers had been puzzled about the language. *These were human children.* Nothing about them showed any trace of alienage.

Behind them, tall black-haired men moved in less agile procession, sounding in chorus a single word which boomed through the skirl and pitter of the children's dance at widespaced intervals. The men were human, too: their hands, stretched immovably out before them, palms up, had five fingers, with fingernails on them; their beards had the same topography as human beards; their chests, bared to the sun by a symbolic rent which was torn at the same place in each garment, and marked identically by a symbolic wound rubbed on with red chalk, showed ribs where ribs ought to be, and the telltale tracings of clavicles beneath the skin.

About the women there might have been some doubt. They came at the end of the procession, all together in a huge cage drawn by lizards. They were all naked and sick, and could have been any kind of primate. They made no sound, but only stared out of purulent eyes, as indifferent to the Okie city and its owners as to their captors. Occasionally they scratched, reluctantly, wincing from their own claws.

The children deployed around Amalfi, evidently picking him out as the leader because he was the biggest. He had expected as much; it was but one more confirmation of their humanity. He stood still while they made a circle and sat down, still chanting and swaying and shaking their wrists. The men, too, made a circle, keeping their faces toward Amalfi, their hands outstretched. At last that reeking cage was drawn into the double ring, virtually to Amalfi's feet. Two male attendants unhitched the docile lizards and led them away.

Abruptly the chanting stopped. The tallest and most impressive of the men came forward and bent, making that strange gesture with fluttering hands over the asphalt of The Avenue. Before Amalfi quite realized what was intended, the stranger had straightened, placed some heavy object in his hand, and retreated, calling aloud the single word the men had been intoning before. Men and children responded together in one terrific shout, and then there was silence.

Amalfi was alone with the cage in the middle of the double circle. He looked down at the thing in his hand.

It was an ornate wrought-metal key.

CHAPTER FOUR: He

Miramon shifted nervously in the chair, the great black saw-toothed feather stuck into his topknot bobbing uncertainly. It was a testimonial to his confidence in Amalfi that he sat in it at all, for in the beginning he had squatted, as was customary on his planet. Chairs were the uncomfortable prerogatives of the gods.

"I myself do not believe in the gods," he explained to Amalfi, bobbing the feather. "It would be plain to a technician, you understand, that your city is simply a product of a technology superior to ours, and you yourselves are men such as we are. But on this planet, religion has a terrible force, a very immediate force. It is not expedient to run counter to public sentiment in such matters."

Amalfi nodded. "From what you tell me, I can believe that. Your situation is unique, to the best of our knowledge. What, precisely, happened when your civilization fell?"

Miramon shrugged. "We do not know. It was over eight thousand years ago, and nothing is left but legend. There was a high culture here then—the priests and the scientists agree on that. And the climate was different; it got cold regularly every year, I am told, although how men could survive such a period is difficult to understand.

68

Besides, there were many more stars—the ancient carvings show *thousands* of them, although they fail to agree on the details."

"Naturally. You're not aware that your sun is moving at an abnormally fast relative speed?"

"Moving?" Miramon laughed shortly. "Some of our more mystical scientists are of that opinion—they maintain that if the planets move, so must the sun. It is an imperfect analogy, in my opinion; after all, planets and suns are not otherwise alike as far as we can see. And would we still be in this trough of nothingness if we were moving?"

"Yes, you would—you are. You underestimate the size of the Rift. It's impossible to detect any parallax at this distance, although in a few thousand years you'll begin to suspect it. But while you were actually among the other stars, your ancestors could see the motion very well, by the changing positions of the neighboring suns."

Miramon looked dubious. "I bow to your superior knowledge, of course. But, be that as it may—the legends have it that for some sin of our people, the gods plunged us into this starless desert, and changed our climate to perpetual heat. This is why our priests say that we are in hell, and that to be put back among the cool stars again, we must redeem our sins. We have no heaven as you have defined the term; when we die, we die damned; we must win 'salvation' right here in the mud while we are still alive. The doctrine has its attractive features under the circumstances."

Amalfi meditated. It was reasonably clear, now, what had happened, but he despaired of explaining it to Miramon—hard common sense sometimes has a way of being impenetrable. This planet's axis had a pronounced tilt, and the concomitant amount of liberation. This meant that, like Earth, it had a Draysonian cycle: every so often the top wobbled, and then resumed spinning at a new angle. The result was a disastrous climatic change. Such a thing happened on Earth roughly once every twenty-five thousand years, and the first one in recorded history had given birth to some extraordinarily silly legends and faiths— sillier than those the Hevians now entertained, on the whole.

Still, it was miserably bad luck for the Hevians that a Draysonian overturn had occurred almost at the same time that the planet had begun its journey across the Rift. It had thrown a very high civilization, a culture just entering its ripest phase, forcibly back into the Interdestructional period without the slightest transition.

The planet of He was a strange mixture now. Politically the regression had stopped just before barbarism—a measure of the lofty summits this race had scaled before the catastrophe—and was now in reverse, clawing through the stage of warring city-states. Yet the basics of the scientific techniques of eight thousand years ago had not been forgotten; now they were exfoliating, bearing "new" fruits.

Properly, city-states should fight each other with swords, not with missile weapons, chemical explosives, and supersonics—and flying should be still in the dream stage, a dream of flapping wings at that, not already a jet-propelled fact. Astronomical and geological accident had mixed history up for fair.

"What would have happened to me if I'd unlocked that cage?" Amalfi demanded abruptly.

Miramon looked sick. "Probably you would have been killed—or they would have tried to kill you, anyhow," he said, with considerable reluctance. "That would have been releasing Evil again upon us. The priests say that it was women who brought about the sins of the Great Age. In the bandit cities, to be sure, that savage creed is no longer maintained—which is one reason why we have so many deserters to the bandit cities. You can have no idea of what it is like to do your duty to the race each year as our law requires. Madness!"

He sounded very bitter. "This is why it is hard to make our people see how suicidal the bandit cities are. Everyone on this world is weary of fighting the jungle, sick of trying to rebuild the Great Age with handfuls of mud, sick of maintaining social codes which ignore the presence of the jungle—but most of all, sick of serving in the Temple of the Future. In the bandit cities the women are clean, and do not scratch one."

"The bandit cities don't fight the jungle?" Amalfi asked.

"No. They prey on those who do. They have given up

the religion entirely—the first act of a city which revolts is to slay its priests. Unfortunately, the priesthood is essential; and our beast-women must be borne, since we cannot modify one tenet without casting doubt upon all—or so they tell us. It is only the priesthood which teaches us that it is better to be men than mud-puppies. So we—the technicians—follow the rituals with great strictness, stupid though some of them are, and consider it a matter of no moment that we ourselves do not believe in the gods."

"Sense in that," Amalfi admitted. Miramon, in all conscience, was a shrewd apple. If he was representative of as large a section of Hevian thought as he believed himself to be, much might yet be done on this wild runaway world.

"It amazes me that you knew to accept the key as a trust," Miramon said. "It was precisely the proper move—but how could you have guessed that?"

Amalfi grinned. "That wasn't hard. I know how a man looks when he's dropping a hot potato. Your priest made all the gestures of a man passing on a great gift, but he could hardly wait until he'd got it over with. Incidentally, some of those women are quite presentable now that Dee's bathed 'em and Medical has taken off the under layers. Don't look so alarmed, we won't tell your priests—I gather that we're the foster fathers of He from here on out."

"You are thought to be emissaries from the Great Age," Miramon agreed gravely. "What you *actually* are, you have not said."

"True. Do you have migratory workers here? The phrase comes easily in your language, yet I can't quite see how——"

"Surely, surely. The singers, the soldiers, the fruit-pickers—all go from city to city, selling their services." Then, much faster than Amalfi had expected, the Hevian reached bottom. "Do you . . . do you imply . . . that your resources are *for sale?* For sale to *us?*"

"Exactly, Miramon."

"But how shall we pay you?" Miramon gasped. "All of what we call wealth, all that we have, could not buy a length of the cloth in your sash!"

Amalfi thought about it, wondering principally how much of the real situation Miramon could be expected to understand. It occurred to him that he had persistently underestimated the Hevian so far. It might be profitable to try the full dose—and hope that it wouldn't prove lethal.

"It's this way," Amalfi said. "In the culture we belong to, a certain metal serves for money. You have enormous amounts of it on your planet, but it's very hard to refine, and I'm sure you've never done more than detect it. One of the things we would like is your permission to mine for that metal."

Miramon's pop-eyed skepticism was close to comical. "Permission?" he repeated. "Please, Mayor Amalfi—is your ethical code as foolish as ours? Why do you not mine this metal without permission and be done with it?"

"Our law-enforcement agencies would not allow it. Mining your planet would make us rich—almost unbelievably rich. Our assays show, not only fabulous amounts of germanium on He, but also the presence of certain drugs in your jungle—drugs which are known to be anti-agathics."

"Sir?"

"Sorry. I mean that, used properly, these drugs indefinitely postpone death."

Miramon rose with great dignity.

"You are mocking me," he said. "I will return at a later date, and perhaps we may talk again."

"Sit down, please," Amalfi said contritely. "I had forgotten that aging is not everywhere known to be an anomaly, a decrease in the cell-building efficiency of the body which can be circumvented if you know how. It was conquered a long time ago—before interstellar flight, in fact. But the pharmaceuticals involved have always been in very short supply, shorter and shorter as man spread through the galaxy. Less than a two-thousandth of one per cent of our present population can get the treatment now, and most of the legitimate trade goes to the people who need life-extension the most—in other words, to people who make their living by traveling long distances in space. The result is that an ampul of any anti-agathic, even the least efficient ones, that a spaceman thinks he can spare can be sold for the price the seller asks. Not a one of the anti-agathics has ever been synthesized, so if we could harvest here——"

"That is enough; it is not necessary that I understand

more," Miramon said. He squatted reflectively, evidently having abandoned the chair as an impediment to thought. "All this makes me wonder if you are not from the Great Age after all. Well—this is difficult to think about reasonably. Why would your culture object to your being rich?"

"It wouldn't, as long as we came by it honestly. We'll have to show that we worked for our riches—otherwise we'll be suspected of having peddled cut drugs on the black market, at the expense of the rank-and-file people on board our own city. We'll need a written agreement with you. A permission."

"That is clear," Miramon said. "You will get it, I am sure. I cannot grant it myself. But I can predict what the priests will ask you to do to earn it."

"What, then? This is just what I want to know. Let's have it."

"First of all, you will be asked for the secret of this . . . this cure for death. They will want to use it on themselves, and hide it from the rest of us. Wisdom, perhaps; it would make for more desertions otherwise—but I am sure they will want it."

"They can have it, but I think we'll see to it that the secret leaks out. The City Fathers know the therapy, and you have so rich a supply of the drugs here that there's no reason why you shouldn't all get it." Privately, Amalfi had an additional reason: If He reached the other side of the Rift eventually with enough anti-agathics to extend coverage much among the galaxy's general population, there would be all kinds of economic hell to pay. "What next?"

"You will be asked to wipe out the jungle."

Amalfi sat back, stunned, and mopped his bald head. Wipe out the jungle! Oh, it would be easy enough to lay waste to almost all of it—even to give the Hevians energy weapons to keep those wastes clear—but sooner or later the jungle would come back. The weapons would short out in the eternal moisture; the Hevians would not take proper care of them, would not be able to repair them—how would the brightest Greek have repaired a shattered X-ray tube, even if he had known what steps to take? The technology didn't exist.

No, the jungle would come back. And the cops, in

pursuit of the bindlestiff on the city's own Dirac alarm, would eventually come to He to see whether or not the Okies had fulfilled their contract—and would find the planet as raw as ever. Good-bye to riches. This was jungle climate. There would be jungles here until the next Draysonian catastrophe, and that was that.

"Excuse me," he said, and reached for the control helmet. "Get me the City Fathers," he said into the mouthpiece.

"SPEAK," the spokesman vodeur said after a while.

"How would you go about wiping out a jungle?"

There was a moment's silence. "SODIUM FLUOSILICATE DUSTING WOULD SERVE. IN A WET CLIMATE IT WOULD CREATE FATAL LEAF BLISTER. HARDIER WEEDS COULD BE SPRAYED WITH 2, 4-D. OF COURSE THE JUNGLE WOULD RETURN."

"That's what I meant. Any way to make the job stick?"

"NO, UNLESS THE PLANET EXHIBITS DRAYSONIANISM."

"*What?*"

"NO, UNLESS THE PLANET EXHIBITS DRAYSONIANISM. IN THAT CASE ITS AXIS MIGHT BE REGULARIZED. IT HAS NEVER BEEN TRIED, BUT THEORETICALLY IT IS QUITE SIMPLE; A BILL TO REGULARIZE EARTH'S AXIS WAS DEFEATED BY THREE VOTES IN THE EIGHTY-SECOND COUNCIL, OWING TO THE OPPOSITION OF THE CONSERVATION LOBBY."

"Could the city handle it?"

"NO. THE COST WOULD BE PROHIBITIVE. *MAYOR AMALFI, ARE YOU CONTEMPLATING TIPPING THIS PLANET?* WE FORBID IT! EVERY INDICATION SHOWS——"

Amalfi tore the helmet from his head and flung it across the room. Miramon sprang up in alarm.

"*Hazleton!*"

The city manager shot through the door as if he had been kicked through it on roller skates. "Here, boss—what's the——"

"Get down below and turn off the City Fathers—*fast*, before they catch on and do something! Quick, man——"

Hazleton was already gone. On the other side of the

room, the phones of the helmet squawked dead data in anxious, even syllables.

Then suddenly they went silent.

The City Fathers had been turned off, and Amalfi was ready to move a world.

The fact that the City Fathers could not be consulted—for the first time since the Epoch affair five centuries ago, when the whole city had been without power for a while—made the job more difficult than it needed to be, barring their conservatism. Tipping the planet, the crux of the job, was simple enough in essence; the city's spindizzies could handle it. But the side effects of the medicine might easily prove to be worse than the disease.

The problem was seismological. Rapidly whirling objects have a way of being stubborn about changing their positions in space. If that energy were overcome, it would have to appear somewhere else—the most likely place being multiple earthquakes.

Too, very little could be anticipated about the gravitics of the task. The planet's revolution produced, as usual, a sizable magnetic field. Amalfi did not know how well that field would take to being tipped in the space-lattice which it distorted, nor just what would happen to He when the city's spindizzies polarized the whole gravity field. During "moving day" the planet would be, in effect, without magnetic moment of its own, and since computation was a function of the City Fathers, there was no way of finding out where the energy would reappear, in what form, or at what intensity.

He broached the latter question to Hazleton. "If we were dealing with an ordinary problem, I'd say the energy would show up as velocity," he pointed out. "In which case we'd be in for an involuntary junket. But this is no ordinary case. The mass involved is . . . well, it's planetary, that's all. What do you think, Mark?"

"I don't know what to think," Hazleton admitted. "The equations only give us general solutions, and only quanticised solutions at that—and this whole problem is a classical field problem. When we move the city, we change the magnetic moment of its component electrons; but the city itself is a low-mass body with no spin of its own, and doesn't have a *gross* magnetic moment."

"That's what stuck me. I can't cross over from probability into tensors any more than poor old Einstein could. As far as I know, nobody's ever really faced up to the discontinuity between what the spindizzy does to the electron and what happens to a body of classical mass in a spindizzy field."

"Still—we could control velocity, or even ignore it out here. Suppose the energy reappears as heat, instead? There'd be nothing left of He but a cloud of gas."

Amalfi shook his head. "I think that's a bogey. The gyroscopic resistance may show up as heat, sure, but not the magnetogravitic. I think we'd be safest to assume that it'll appear as velocity, just as in ordinary flight. Use the standard transformation and see what you get."

Hazleton bent over his slide rule, the sweat standing out along his forehead and above his mustache in great heavy droplets. Amalfi could understand the eagerness of the Hevians to get rid of the jungle and its eternal humidity. His own clothing, sparse though it was, had been sopping ever since the city had landed here.

"Well," the city manager said finally, "unless I've made a mistake somewhere, the whole kit and kaboodle, the planet itself, will go shooting away from here at about twice the speed of light. That's not too bad—just about coasting speed for us. We could always loop around and bring the planet back to its orbit."

"Ah, but could we? Remember, we don't control it! The vector appears automatically when we turn on the spindizzies. We don't even know in which direction that arrow is going to point. The planet could throw itself into the sun within the first second as far as we know. We can't predict the direction."

"Yes, we can," Hazleton objected. "Along the axis of spin, of course."

"Cant? And torque?"

"No problem—no, yes, there is. I keep forgetting that we're dealing with a planet instead of electrons." He applied the slipstick again. "No soap. Too many substitutions. Can't be answered in time without the City Fathers

—and torque might hype the end-velocity substantially. But if we can figure a way to control the flight, it won't matter in the end. Of course there'll be perturbations of the other planets when this one goes massless, whether it actually moves or not—but nobody lives on them anyhow."

"All right, Mark, go figure a control system. I'll see what can be done on the geology end——"

The door slid back suddenly, and Amalfi looked back over his shoulder. It was Sergeant Anderson. The perimeter sergeant was usually blasé in the face of all possible wonders, unless they threatened the city. "What's the matter?" Amalfi said, alarmed.

"Mr. Mayor, we've gotten an ultracast from some outfit claiming to be refugees from another Okie city—they claim they hit a bindlestiff and got broken up. They've crash-landed on this planet up north, and they're being mobbed by one of the local bandit towns. They were holding 'em off and yelling for help, and then they stopped transmitting. I thought you ought to know."

Amalfi heaved himself to his feet almost instantly. "Did you get a bearing on that call?" he demanded.

"Yes sir."

"Give me the figures. Come on, Mark. That's our life craft from the city with the no-fuel drive. We need those boys."

Amalfi and Hazleton grabbed a cab to the edge of the city and went the rest of the way to the Hevian town on foot, across the supersonics-cleared strip of bare turf which surrounded the walls. The turf felt rubbery. Amalfi suspected that some rudimentary form of friction-field was keeping the mud in a state of stiff gel. He had visions of foot soldiers sinking suddenly into slowly-folding ooze as the fields were turned off, and quickened his pace.

Inside the gates, the Hevian guards summoned a queer, malodorous vehicle which seemed to be powered by the combustion of hydrocarbons, and the Okies were roared through the streets toward Miramon. Throughout the journey, Amalfi clung to a cloth strap in an access of nervousness. Traveling right *on* a surface at any good speed was a rare experience for him, and the way things zipped past the windows made him jumpy.

"Is this bird out to smash us up?" Hazleton demanded petulantly. "He must be doing all of four hundred kilos an hour."

"I'm glad you feel the same way," Amalfi said, relaxing a little. "Actually, I'll bet he's doing less than two hundred. It's just the way the——"

The driver, who had been holding his car down to a conservative fifty out of deference to the strangers from the Great Age, wrenched the machine around a corner and halted it neatly before Miramon's door. Amalfi got out, his knees wobbly. Hazleton's face was a delicate puce.

"I'm going to figure out a way to make our cabs operate outside the city," he muttered. "Every time we make a new planetfall, we have to ride on ox carts, the backs of bull kangaroos, in hot air balloons, steam-driven air-screws, things that drag you feet first and face down through tunnels, or whatever else the natives think is classy transportation. My stomach won't stand much more."

Amalfi grinned and raised his hand to Miramon, whose expression suggested laughter smothered with great difficulty.

"What brings you here?" the Hevian said. "Come in. I have no chairs, but——"

"No time," Amalfi said. "Listen closely, Miramon, because this is going to be complex to explain, and I'm going to have to give it to you fast. You already know that our city isn't the only one of its type. Well, the fact is that we aren't even the first Okie city to enter the Rift; there were two others ahead of us. One of them, a criminal city that we call a bindlestiff, attacked and destroyed the other; we were too far away to prevent it. Do you follow me?"

"I think so," Miramon said. "This bindlestiff is like our bandit cities——"

"Yes, precisely. And as far as we know, it's still in the Rift, somewhere. Now the city that the 'stiff destroyed had something that we want very badly, and that we *must* have before the 'stiffs get it. We know that the dead city put off some life craft, and that one of those craft has just landed on your world—and has fallen afoul of one of your own bandit cities. We've got to rescue them. They're the sole survivors of the dead city as far as we know, and it's vital for us to question them. We need to know what they know about the thing we want—the no-fuel drive—and what they know about where the bindlestiff is now."

"I see," Miramon said thoughtfully. "Will this—this bindlestiff follow them to He?"

"We think it will. And it's powerful—it packs all the stuff we have and more besides. We have to pick up these survivors first, and work out some way to defend ourselves *and you people* against the 'stiff when it gets here. And above all, we must prevent the 'stiff from getting the secret of that fuelless drive!"

"What would you like me to do?" Miramon said gravely.

"Can you locate the Hevian town that's holding these people prisoner? We have a fix on it, but only a blurred one. If you can, we'll be able to get them out of there ourselves."

Miramon went back into his house—actually, like all the other living quarters in the town, it was a dormitory housing twenty-five men of the same trade or profession— and returned with a map. The map-making conventions of He were anything but self-explanatory, but after a while Hazleton was able to figure out the symbolism involved. "There's your city, and here's ours," he said to Miramon, pointing. "Right? And this peeled-orange thing is a butterfly grid. I've always claimed that it was a lot more faithful to spherical territory than our Geographic projection, boss."

"Easier still to express what you want to remember as a topological relationship," Amalfi said impatiently. "Nobody ever confuses a table of symbols with the territory. Show Miramon where the signals came from."

"Up here, on this wing of the butterfly."

Miramon frowned. "There is only one city there—Fabr-Suithe. A very bad place to approach, even in the military sense. But if you insist on trying, we will help you. Do you know what the end result will be?"

"We'll rescue our friends, I hope. What else?"

"The bandit cities will come out in force to hinder the Great Work. They oppose it; the jungle is their life."

"Then why haven't they impeded us before now?" Hazleton said. "Are they scared?"

"No. They fear nothing—we think they take drugs—but they have seen no way to attack you without huge losses, and their reasons for attacking you have not been sufficiently compelling to make them take the risk up to now. But if *you* attack one of *them*, that will give them reason enough. They learn hatred very quickly."

"I think we can handle them," Hazleton said coldly.

"I am sure you can," Miramon said. "But you should be warned that Fabr-Suithe is the leader of all the bandit cities. If Fabr-Suithe attacks you, so will they all."

Amalfi shrugged. "We'll chance it. We'll have to: We must have those men. Maybe we can make it quick enough to crush resistance before it starts. We can pick our own town up and go calling on Fabr-Suithe; if they don't want to deliver up these Okies——"

"Boss——"

"Eh?"

"How are you going to get us off the ground?"

Amalfi could feel his ears turning red, and swore. "I forgot that Twenty-third Street machine. Miramon, we'll have to have a task force of your own rockets. Hazleton, how are we going to work this? We can't fit anything really powerful into a Hevian rocket plane—a pile would go into one easily enough, but a frictionator or a naval-size mesotron rifle wouldn't, and there'd be no point in taking popguns. Do you suppose we could gas Fabr-Suithe?"

"You couldn't carry enough gas in a Hevian rocket either. Or carry enough men to make a raid in force."

"Excuse me," Miramon said, "but it is not even certain that the priests will authorize the use of our planes against Fabr-Suithe. We had best drive directly over to the temple and ask them for permission."

"Belsen and bebop!" Amalfi said. It was the oldest oath in his repertoire.

Talk, even with electronic aids, was impossible inside the little rocket. The whole machine roared like a gigantic tam-tam to the vibration of the venturis. Morosely Amalfi watched Hazleton connecting the mechanism in the nose of the plane with the power-leads from the pile—no mean balancing feat, considering the way the craft pitched in its passage through the tortured Hevian crosswinds. The pile itself, of course, was simple enough to handle; it consisted only of a tank about the size of a glass brick, filled with a fine white froth: heavy water containing uranium^{235} hexafluoride in solution, damped by bubbles of cadmium vapor. Most of its weight was shielding and the peripheral capillary network of the heat-exchanger.

There had been no difficulty with the priests about the little rocket task force itself; the priests had been delighted at the proposal that the emissaries from the Great Age should teach an apostate Hevian city the error of its ways. Amalfi suspected that the straight-faced Miramon had invented the need for priestly permission just to get the two Okies back into the smelly ground car again and watch their faces during the drive to the temple. Still the discomforts of that ride had been small compared to this one.

The pilot shifted his feet on the treadles, and the deck pitched. A metal trap rushed back under Amalfi's nose, and he found himself looking through misty air at a crazily canted jungle. Something long, thin, and angry flashed over it and was gone. At the same time there was a piercing, inhuman shriek, sharp enough to dwarf for a long instant the song of the rocket.

Then there were more of the same: *ptsouiiirrr! ptsouiiirrr! ptsouiiirrr!* The machine jerked to nearly every one and then shook itself violently, twisting and careening across the jungle top. Amalfi had never felt so helpless before in his life. He did not even know what the noise was; he could only be sure that it was ill-tempered. The coarse *blaam* of high explosive, when it began, was recognizable— the city had often had occasion to blast on jobs—but nothing in his experience went *kerchowkerchowkerchowkerchow*, like a demented vibratory drill, and the invisible thing that screamed its own pep yell as it flew— *eeeeeeeyokKRCHackackarackarackaracka*—seemed wholly impossible.

He was astonished to discover that the hull around him was stippled with small holes, real holes with the slipstream fluting over them. It took him what seemed to be three weeks to realize that the whooping and cheerleading which meant nothing to him was riddling the ship and threatening to kill him at any second.

Someone was shaking him. He lurched to his knees, trying to unfreeze his eyeballs.

"Amalfi! Amalfi!" The voice, although it was breathing on his ear, was parsecs away. "Pick your spot, quick! They'll have us shot down in a——"

Something burst outside and threw Amalfi back to the deck. Doggedly he crawled to the trap and peered down through the now-shattered glass. The bandit Hevian city swooped past, upside down. The mayor felt a sudden wave of motion sickness, and the city was lost in a web of tears. The second time it came by, he managed to see which building in it had the heaviest guard, and pointed, choking.

The rocket threw its tail feathers over the nearest cloud and bored beak-first for the ground. Amalfi hung on to the edge of the suddenly blank trap, his own blood spraying back in a fine mist into his face from his cut fingers.

"*Now!*"

Nobody heard, but Hazleton saw his nod. A blast of pure light blew through the upended cabin, despite the shielding between it and the pile. Even through the top of his head, the violet-white light of that soundless blast nearly blinded Amalfi, and he could feel the irradiation of his shoulders and chest. He would develop no allergies on this planet, anyhow—every molecule of histamine in his blood must have been detoxified in that instant.

The rocket yawed wildly, and then came under control again. The ordnance noises had already quit, cut off at the moment of the flash.

The bandit Hevian city was blind.

The sound of the jets cut off, and Amalfi understood for the first time what an "aching void" might be. The machine fell into a steep glide, the air howling dismally outside it. Another rocket, under the guidance of Carrel, dived down before it, scything a narrow runway in the jungle with portable mesotron rifles—for the bandit towns kept no supersonic no-plant's-land between themselves and the rank vegetation.

The moment the rocket stopped moving, Amalfi and a hand-picked squad of Okies and Hevians were out of it and slogging through the muck. From inside Fabr-Suithe drifted a myriad of screams—human screams now, screams of rage and grief, from men who thought themselves blinded for life. Amalfi did not doubt that many of them were. Certainly anyone who had had the misfortune to be looking at the sky during that instant when the entire output of the pile had been converted to visible light would never see again.

But the laws of chance would have protected most of the renegades, so speed was vital. The mud built up heavy pads under his shoes, and the jungle did not thin out until they hit the town's wall itself.

The gates had been rusted open years ago, and were choked with greenery. The Hevians hacked their way through it with practiced knives and cunning.

Inside, the going was still almost as thick. Fabr-Suithe proper presented a depressing face of proliferating despair. Most of the buildings were completely enshrouded in vines, and many were halfway toward ruins. Iron-hard tendrils had thrust their way between stones, into windows, under cornices, up drains and chimney funnels. Poison-green succulent leaves plastered themselves greedily upon every surface, and in shadowed places there were huge blood-colored fungi which smelled like a man six days dead; the sweetish taint hung heavily in the air. Even the paving blocks had sprouted—inevitably, since, whether by ignorance or laziness, most of the recent ones had been cut from green wood.

The screaming began to die into whimpers. Amalfi did his best to keep himself from inspecting the stricken inhabitants. A man who believes he has just been blinded permanently is not a pretty sight, even when he is wrong. Yet it was impossible not to notice the curious mixture of soiled finery with gleamingly clean nakedness. It was as if two different periods had mixed in the city, as if a gathering of Hruntan nobles had been sprinkled with Noble Savages. Possibly the men who had given in completely to the jungle had also slid back enough to discover the pleasures of bathing. If so, they would shortly discover the pleasures of the mud-wallow, too, and would not look so noble after that.

"Amalfi, here they are——"

The mayor's suppressed sympathy for the blinded men evaporated when he got a look at the imprisoned Okies. They had been systematically mauled to begin with, and after that sundry little attentions had been paid to them which combined the best features of savagery and decadence. One of them, mercifully, had been strangled by his comrades early in the "questioning." Another, a basket case, should have been rescued, for he could still talk rationally, but he pleaded so persistently for death that Amalfi had him shot in a sudden fit of sentimentality. Of the other three men, all could walk and talk, but two were mad. The catatonic was carried out on a stretcher, and the manic was bound, gagged, and led gingerly away.

"How did you do it?" asked the rational man in Russian, the dead universal language of Earth. He was a human skeleton, but he radiated an amazing personal force. He had lost his tongue early in the "questioning," but had already taught himself to talk by the artificial method—the result was weird, but it was intelligible. "The savages were coming down to kill us as soon as they heard your rockets. Then there was a sort of flash, and they all started screaming—a pretty sound, let me tell you."

"I'll bet," Amalfi said. "Do you speak Interlingua? Good, my Russian is rudimentary these days. That 'sort of a flash' was a photon explosion. It was the only way we could figure on being sure of getting you out alive. We thought of trying gas, but if they had had gas masks, they would have been able to kill you anyhow."

"I haven't actually seen any masks, but I'm sure they have them. There are traveling volcanic gas clouds in this part of the planet, they say; they must have evolved some absorption device—charcoal is well known here. Lucky we were so far underground, or we'd be blind, too, then. You people must be engineers."

"More or less," Amalfi agreed. "Strictly, we're miners and petroleum geologists, but we've developed a lot of side lines since we went aloft—like any Okie. On Earth we were a port city and did just about everything, but aloft you have to specialize. Here's our rocket—crawl in. It's rough, but it's transportation. How about you?"

"Agronomists. Our mayor thought there was a good field for it out here along the periphery—teaching the abandoned colonies and the offshoots how to work poisoned soil and manage low-yield crops without heavy machinery. Our side line was waxmans."

"What are those?" Amalfi said, adjusting the harness around the wasted body.

"Soil-source antibiotics. It was those the bindlestiff wanted—and got. The filthy swine. They can't bother to keep a reasonably sanitary city; they'd rather pirate some honest outfit for drugs when they have an epidemic. Oh, and they wanted germanium, too, of course. They blew us up when they found we didn't have any—we'd converted to a barter economy as soon as we got out of the last commerce lanes."

"What about your passenger?" Amalfi said with studied nonchalance.

"Doctor Beetle? Not that that was his name—I couldn't pronounce *that* even when I had my tongue. I don't imagine he survived. We had to keep him in a tank even in the city, and I can't quite see him living through a lifeship journey. He was a Myrdian—smart cookies all of them, too. That no-fuel drive of his——"

Outside, a shot cracked, and Amalfi winced. "We'd best take off—they're getting their eyesight back. Talk to you later. Hazleton, any incidents?"

"Nothing to speak of, boss. Everybody stowed?"

"Yep. Kick off."

There was a volley of shots, and then the rocket coughed, roared, and stood on its tail. Amalfi pulled a deep sigh loose from the acceleration and turned his head toward the rational man.

He was still securely strapped in and looked quite relaxed. A brass-nosed slug had come through the side of the ship next to him and had neatly removed the top of his skull.

Working information out of the madmen was a painfully long, anxious process. Even after the manic case had been returned to a semblance of rationality, he could contribute very little.

The lifeship had not come to He because of Hazleton's

Dirac warning, he said. The lifeship and the burned Okie had not had any Dirac equipment to the best of his knowledge. The lifeship had come to He, as Amalfi had predicted, because it was the only possible planetfall in the desert of the Rift. Even so, the refugees had had to use deep-sleep and strict starvation rationing to make it.

"Did you see the 'stiff again?"

"No, sir. If they heard your Dirac warning, they probably figured the police had spotted them and scrammed— or maybe they thought there was a military base or an advanced culture here on the planet."

"You're guessing," Amalfi said gruffly. "What happened to Doctor Beetle?"

The man looked startled. "The Myrdian in the tank? He got blown up with the city, I suppose."

"He wasn't put off in another lifeship?"

"Doesn't seem very likely. But I was only a pilot. Could be that they took him out in the mayor's gig for some reason."

"You don't know anything about his no-fuel drive?"

"First I heard of it."

Amalfi was far from satisfied; he suspected that there was still a short circuit somewhere in the man's memory. But that was all that could be gotten from him, and Amalfi had to accept the fact. All that remained to be done was to get some assessment of the weapons available to the bindlestiff; on this subject the ex-manic was ignorant, but the city's neurophysiologist said cautiously that something might be extracted from the catatonic within a month or two; thus far, he hadn't even succeeded in capturing the man's attention.

Amalfi accepted the estimate also, since it was the best he could get. With Moving Day for He coming near, he couldn't afford to worry overtime about another problem. He had already decided that the simplest answer to vulcanism, which otherwise would be inevitable when the planet's geophysical balance was changed, would be to reinforce the crust. At two hundred points on the surface of He, drilling teams were now sinking long, thin, slanting shafts, reaching toward the stress-fluid of the world's core. The shafts interlocked intricately, and thus far only one volcano had been created by the drilling. In general, the lava pockets which had been tapped had already been anticipated, and the flow had been bled off into many intersecting channels without ever reaching the surface. After the molten rock had hardened, the clogged channels were redrilled, with mesotron rifles set to the smallest possible dispersion.

None of the shafts had yet tapped the stress-fluid; the plan was to complete them all simultaneously. At that point, specific volcanic areas, riddled with channel intersections, would give way, and immense plugs would be forced up toward the crust, plugs of iron, connected by ferrous cantilevers through the channels between. The planet of He would wear a cruel corset, permitting only the slightest flexure—it would be stitched with threads of steel, steel that had held even granite in solution for geological ages.

The heat problem was tougher, and Amalfi was not sure whether or not he had hit upon the solution. The very fact of structural resistance would create high temperatures, and any general formation of shearplanes would cut the imbedded girders at once. The method being prepared to cope with that was rather drastic, and its aftereffects largely unknown.

On the whole, however, the plans were simple, and putting them into effect had seemed heavy but relatively uncomplicated labor. Some opposition, of course, had been expected from the local bandit towns.

But Amalfi had not expected to lose nearly 20 percent of his crews during the first month after the raid on Fabr-Suithe.

It was Miramon who brought the news of the latest work camp found slaughtered. Amalfi was sitting under a tree fern on high ground overlooking the city, watching a flight of giant dragonflies and thinking about heat transfer in rock.

"You are sure they were adequately protected?" Miramon asked cautiously. "Some of our insects——"

Amalfi thought the insects, and the jungle, almost disturbingly beautiful. The thought of destroying it all occasionally upset him. "Yes, they were," he said shortly. "We sprayed out the camp areas with dicoumarins and fluorine-substituted residuals. Besides—do any of your insects use explosives?"

"Explosives! There was dynamite used? I saw no evidence——"

"No. That's what bothers me. I don't like all those felled trees you describe; that sounds more like TDX than dynamite or high explosive. We use TDX ourselves to get a cutting blast—it has the property of exploding in a flat plane."

Miramon goggled. "Impossible. An explosion had to expand evenly in all directions that are open to it."

"Not if the explosive is a piperazohexynitrate built from polarized carbon atoms. Such atoms can't move in any direction but at right angles to the gravity radius. That's what I mean. You people are up to dynamite, but not to TDX."

He paused, frowning. "Of course some of our losses have just been to bandit raids, with missile weapons and ordinary bombs—your friends from Fabr-Suithe and their allies. But these camps where there was an explosion and no crater to show for it——"

He fell silent. There was no point in mentioning the gassed corpses. It was hard even to think about them. Somebody on this planet had a gas which was a regurgitant, a sternutatory, and a vesicant all in one. The men had been forced out of their masks—which had been designed solely to protect them from volcanic gases—to vomit, had taken the stuff into their lungs by convulsive sneezing, and had blistered into great sacs of serum inside and out. That, obviously, had been the multiple-benzene-ring gas Hawkesite; it had been very popular during the days of the warring stellar "empires," when it had been called "*polybathroomfloorine*" for no discoverable reason. But what was it doing on He?

There was only one possible answer, and for a reason which he did not try to understand, it made Amalfi breathe a little easier. All around him the jungle sighed and swayed, and humming clouds of gnats made rainbows over the dew-laden pinnae of the ferns. The jungle, almost always murmurously quiet, had never seemed like the real enemy—and now Amalfi knew that his intuition had been right. The real enemy had at last declared itself, stealthily, but with a stealth which was naïveté itself in comparison with the ancient guile of the jungle.

"Miramon," Amalfi said tranquilly, "we're in a spot. That criminal city I told you about—the bindlestiff—is already here. It must have landed even before my city arrived, long enough ago to hide itself very thoroughly. Probably it came down at night in some taboo area. The tramps in it have leagued themselves with Fabr-Suithe anyhow, that much is obvious."

A moth with a two-meter wingspread blundered across the clearing, piloted by a gray-brown nematode which had sunk its sucker above the ganglion between the glittering creature's pinions. Amalfi was in a mood to read parables into things, and the parasitism reminded him of how greatly he had underestimated the enemy. The bindlestiff evidently knew, and was skillful with, the secret of manipulating a new culture. A shrewd Okie never attempts to overwhelm a civilization by direct assault, but instead pilots it, as indetectably as possible, doing no apparent harm, adding no apparent burden, but turning history deftly and tyrannically aside at the crucial instant. . . .

Amalfi snapped the belt switch of his ultraphone. "Hazleton?"

"Here, boss." Behind the city manager's voice was the indistinct rumble of heavy mining. "What's up?"

"Nothing yet. Are you having any bandit trouble out there?"

"No. We're not expecting any, either, with all this artillery."

"Famous last words," Amalfi said. "The 'stiff's here, Mark—and it's no stranger, either."

There was a short silence. In the background, Amalfi could hear the shouts of Hazleton's crew. When the city manager's voice came in again, it was moving from word to word very carefully, as if it expected each one to break under its weight. "You imply that the 'stiff was already on He when our Dirac broadcast went out. Right? I'm not sure these losses of ours can't be explained some simpler way, boss; the theory . . . uh . . . lacks elegance."

Amalfi grinned tightly. "A heuristic criticism," he said.

"Go to the foot of the class, Mark, and think it over. Thus far they've outthought us six ways for Sunday. We may be able to put your old scheme about the women into effect still, but if it's to work, we'll have to smoke the 'stiff out into the open."

"How?"

"Everybody here knows that there's going to be a drastic change in the planet when we finish what we're doing, but we're the only ones who know exactly what we're going to do. The 'stiffs will have to stop us, whether they've got Doctor Beetle or not. So I'm forcing their hand. Moving Day is hereby advanced by one thousand hours."

"What! I'm sorry, boss, but that's flatly impossible."

Amalfi felt a rare spasm of anger. "That's as may be," he growled. "Nevertheless, spread it around; let the Hevians hear it. And just to prove that I'm not kidding, Mark, I'm turning the City Fathers back on at M plus 1100. If you're not ready to spin before then, you may well swing instead."

The click of the belt switch to the *off* position was unsatisfying. Amalfi would much have preferred to have concluded the interview with something really final—a clash of cymbals, for instance. He swung suddenly on Miramon.

"What are you goggling at?"

The Hevian shut his mouth, flushing. "Your pardon," he said. "I was hoping to understand your instructions to your assistant, in the hope of being of some use. But you spoke in such incomprehensible terms that it sounded like a theological dispute. As for me, I never argue about politics or religion." He turned on his heel and stamped off through the trees.

Amalfi watched him go, cooling off gradually. This would never do. He must be getting to be an old man. All during the conversation with Hazleton he had felt his temper getting the better of his judgment, yet he had felt sudden and inert, unwilling to make the effort of opposing the momentum of his anger. At this rate, the City Fathers would soon depose him and appoint some stable character to the mayoralty—not Hazleton, certainly, but some unpoetic youngster who would play everything by empirics. Amalfi was in no position to be threatening anyone else with liquidation, even as a joke.

He walked toward the grounded city, heavy with sunlight, sunk in reflection. He was now about nine hundred years old, give or take fifty; strong as an ox, mentally alert and active, in good hormone balance, all twenty-eight senses sharp, his own special psi faculty—orientation—still as infallible as ever, and all in all as sane as a compulsively peripatetic starman could be. The anti-agathics would keep him in this shape indefinitely, as far as anyone knew—but the problem of *patience* had never been solved.

The older a man became, the more quickly he saw answers to tough questions because the more experience he had to bring to bear on them; and the less likely he was to tolerate slow thinking among his associates. If he were sane, his answers were generally right answers—if he were unsane, they were not; but what mattered was the speed of the thinking itself. In the end, both the sane and the unsane became equally dictatorial, less and less ready to explain why they picked one answer over another.

It was funny: before death had been indefinitely postponed, it had been thought that memory would turn longevity into a Greek gift, because not even the human brain could remember a practical infinity of accumulated facts. Nowadays, however, nobody bothered to remember many facts. That was what the City Fathers and like machines were for: they stored data. Living men memorized nothing but processes, throwing out obsolete ones for new ones as invention made it necessary. When they needed facts, they asked the machines.

In some cases, even processes were wiped from human memory to make more room if there were simple, indestructible machines to replace them—the slide rule, for instance. Amalfi wondered suddenly if there was a single man in the city who could multiply, divide, take square root, or figure pH in his head or on paper. The thought was so novel as to be alarming—as novel as if an ancient astrophysicist had seriously wondered how many of his colleagues could run an abacus.

No, memory was no problem. But it was hard to be patient after a thousand years.

The bottom of an airlock drifted into his field of view, plastered with brown tendrils of mud. He looked up. The lock, drilled directly into the great granite disc which was the foundation of the city, was a severed end of what had been a subway line running out of Manhattan centuries ago; this one evidently had been the Astoria line of the BMT, a lock seldom used, since it was too far from both the Empire State and City Hall, the city's two present centers of control. It was certainly a long way around the perimeter from where Amalfi had expected to go back on board. Feeling like a stranger, he went in.

Inside, the corridor rang with bloodcurdling shrieks which echoed endlessly. It was as if somebody were flaying a live dinosaur, or, better, a pack of them. Underneath the noise there was a sound like water being expelled under high pressure, and someone was laughing hysterically. Alarmed, Amalfi ran up the nearest steps; the noise got louder. He hunched his bull shoulders and burst through the door behind which the butchery seemed to be going on.

Surely there had never been such a place in the city. It was a huge, steamy chamber, walled with some ceramic substance placed in regular tiles. The tiles were slimy and stained, hence, old—very old. On the floor, smaller hexagonal white tiles made an endlessly repeating mosaic, reminding Amalfi at once of the structural formula of Hawkesite.

Hordes of nude women ran aimlessly back and forth in the chamber, screaming, battering at the wall, dodging wildly, or rolling on the mosaic floor. Every so often a thick stream of water caught one of them, bowling her howling away. Overhead, long banks of nozzles sprayed needles of mist into the air; Amalfi was soaking wet almost at once. The laughter got louder.

The mayor bent quickly, threw off his muddy shoes, and stalked the laughter, his toes gripping the slippery tiles. The heavy column of water swerved toward him, then was warped away again.

"John! Do you need a bath so badly? Come join the party!"

It was Dee Hazleton. She was as nude as any of her victims, and was gleefully plying an enormous hose. She looked lovely; Amalfi turned his mind determinedly away from that thought.

"Isn't this fun? We just got a new batch of these creatures. I got Mark to have the old fire hose connected, and I've been giving them their first wash."

It did not sound much like the old Dee. Amalfi expressed his opinion of women who lost their inhibitions with such drastic thoroughness. He went on at some length, and Dee made as if to turn the hose on him again.

"No, you don't," he growled, wresting it from her. It proved extremely hard to manage. "What is this place, anyhow? I don't recall any such torture chamber in the plans."

"It was a public bath, Mark says. There's another one downtown, in the Baruch Houses district, and another one on Forty-first Street beside the Port Authority Terminal, and quite a few others. Mark says they must have been closed up when the city first went aloft. I've been using this one to sluice off these women before they're sent to Medical."

"With *city water?*" Even the thought of such waste made his hackles rise.

"Oh no, John, I know better than that. The water's pumped in from the river to the west."

"Water for bathing!" Amalfi said. "No wonder the ancients sometimes didn't have enough to drink. Still, I'd thought the static jet was older than that."

He surveyed the Hevian women, who, now that the water was turned off, were huddled in the warmest part of the echoing chamber. None of them shared Dee's gently curved ripeness, but, as usual, some of them showed promise. Hazelton was prescient, it had to be granted. Of course it had been expectable that the Hevians would turn out to be human. Only eleven nonhuman civilizations had ever been discovered, and of these, only the Lyrans and the Myrdians had any brains to speak of (unless one counted the Vegans; Earthmen did not think of them as human, but all the nonhuman cultures did; anyhow, they were extinct as a civilization).

But to have the Hevians turn over complete custody of their women to the Okies, without so much as a preliminary conference, at the first contact, had been a colossal break. Hazelton had advanced his proposal to use any possible women as bindlestiff-bait years before any Okie could have known that there were people on He at all.

Well, that was Hazleton's own psi gift: not true clairvoyance, but an ability to pluck workable plans out of logically insufficient data. Time after time only the seemingly miraculous working-out of some obvious flight of fancy had prevented Hazleton's being jettisoned by the blindly logical City Fathers.

"Dee, come to Astronomy with me," Amalfi said. "I've got something to show you. And for my sake, put on something, or the men will think I'm out to found a dynasty."

"All right," Dee said reluctantly. She was not yet used to the odd Okie standards of exposure, and sometimes appeared nude when it wasn't customary—a compensation, Amalfi supposed, for her Utopian upbringing, which had taught her that nudity had a deleterious effect upon the purity of one's politics. The Hevian women moaned and hid their heads while she put on her shorts. Most of them had been stoned for inadvertently covering themselves at one time or another, for in Hevian society women were not people but reminders of damnation, doubly evil for the slightest taint of secretiveness.

History, Amalfi thought, would be more instructive a teacher if it were not so stupefyingly repetitious. He led the way up the corridor, searching for a lift shaft, disturbingly conscious of Dee's wet soles padding cheerfully behind him.

In Astronomy, Jake was, as usual, peering wistfully at a galaxy somewhere out on the marches of nowhen, trying to turn spiral arms into elliptical orbits without recourse to the calculations section. He looked up as Amalfi and the girl entered.

"Hello," he said dismally. "Amalfi, I really need some help here. How can a man work without machines? If only you'd turn the City Fathers back on——"

"Shortly. How long has it been since you looked back the way we came, Jake?"

"Not since we started across the Rift. Why, should I have? The Rift is just a scratch in a saucer; you need real distance to work on basic problems."

"I know that. But let's take a look. I have an idea that we're not as alone in the Rift as we thought."

Resignedly, Jake went to his control desk and thumbed the buttons that moved his telescope. "What do you expect to find?" he demanded. "A haze of iron filings, or a stray meson? Or a fleet of police cruisers?"

"Well," Amalfi said, pointing to the screen, "those aren't wine bottles."

The police cruisers, so close that the light of He's star had begun to twinkle on their sides, shot across the screen in a brilliant stream, contrails of false photons striping the Rift behind them.

"So they aren't," Jake said, not much interested. "Now may I have my scope back, Amalfi?"

Amalfi only grinned. Cops or no cops, he felt young again.

Hazleton was mud up to the thighs. Long ribands of it trailed behind him as he hurtled up the lift shaft to the control room. Amalfi watched him coming, noting the set whiteness of the city manager's face as he looked up at Amalfi's bent head.

"What's this about cops?" Hazleton demanded while still in flight. "The message didn't get to me straight. We were raided, and all hell's broken loose everywhere. I nearly didn't get here straight myself." He sprang into the room, his boots shedding gummy clods.

"I saw some of the fighting," Amalfi said. "Looks like the Moving Day rumor reached the 'stiffs, all right."

"Sure. What's this about cops?"

"The cops are here. They're coming in from the northwest quadrant, already off overdrive, and should be ready to land day after tomorrow."

"Surely they're not still after us," Hazleton said. "And I can't see why they should come all this distance after the 'stiff. They must have had to use deep-sleep to make it. And we didn't say anything about the no-fuel drive in our alarm 'cast——"

"We didn't have to. They're after the 'stiff, all right. Someday I must tell you the parable of the diseased bee, but there isn't time now. Things are breaking too fast. We have to keep an eye on everything, and be ready to jump in any direction no matter which item on the agenda comes up first. How bad is the fighting?"

"Very bad. At least five of the local bandit towns are in on it, including Fabr-Suithe, of course. Two of them mount heavy stuff, about contemporary with the Hruntan Empire's in its heyday . . . ah, I see you know that already. Well, this is supposed to be a holy war on us. We're meddling with the jungle and interfering with their chances for salvation-through-suffering, or something—I didn't stop to dispute the point."

"That's bad. It will convince some of the civilized towns, too. I doubt that Fabr-Suithe really believes this is a jihad—they've thrown their religion overboard—but it makes wonderful propaganda."

"You're right there. Only a few of the civilized towns, the ones that have been helping us from the beginning, are putting up a stiff fight. Almost everyone else, on both sides, is sitting it out waiting for us to cut each other's throats. Our own handicap is that we lack mobility. If we could persuade all the civilized towns to come in on our side, we wouldn't need it, but so many of them are scared."

"The enemy lacks mobility, too, until the bindlestiff town is ready to take a direct hand," Amalfi said thoughtfully. "Have you seen any signs that the tramps are in on the fighting?"

"Not yet. But they won't wait much longer. And we don't even know where they are!"

"They'll be forced to locate themselves for us today or tomorrow, of that I'm certain. Right now it's time to muster all the rehabilitated women you have and get ready to plant them; as far as I can see, that whole scheme is going to pay off. As soon as I get a fix on the bindlestiff, I'll report the location of the nearest bandit town, and you can follow through from there."

Hazleton's eyes, very weary until now, began to glitter with gratification. "And how about Moving Day?" he said. "I suppose you know that not one of your stress-fluid plugs is going to hold with the work thus incomplete."

"I know it," Amalfi said. "I'm counting on it. We'll spin on the hour. If the plugs spring high, wide, and tall, I won't weep; as a matter of fact, I don't know how else we could hope to get rid of all that heat."

The radar watch blipped sharply, and both men turned to look at the screen. There was a fountain of green dots on it. Hazleton took three quick steps and turned the switch which projected the new butterfly grid onto the screen.

"Well, where are they?" Amalfi demanded. "That's got to be them."

"Right smack in the middle of the southwestern continent, in that vine jungle where the little chigger snakes nest—the ones that burrow under your fingernails. There's supposed to be a lake of boiling mud on that spot."

"There probably is. They could be under it, surrounded by a medium-light screen."

"All right, then we've got them placed. But what's this fountain effect the radar's giving us? What are the 'stiffs shooting up?"

"Mines, I suspect," Amalfi said. "On proximity fuses. Orbital."

"Mines? Isn't *that* dandy," Hazleton said. "They'll leave an escape lane for themselves, of course, but we'll never be able to find it. They've got us under a plutonium umbrella, Amalfi."

"We'll get out. And in the meantime, the cops can't land, either. Go plant your women, Mark. And—put some clothes on 'em first. They'll cause more of a stir that way."

"You bet they will," the city manager said feelingly. He stepped into the lift shaft and fell out of sight.

Amalfi went out onto the observation platform of the control tower. From there he could see all the rest of the city, including most of the perimeter, for the tower—it was still called, now and then, the Empire State Building—was the tallest structure in the city. There was plenty of battle noise rattling the garish tropical sunset along most of the northwest quadrant, and even an occasional tiny toppling figure. The city had adopted the local dodge of clearing and gelling the mud at its rim, and had returned the gel to the morass state at the first sign of attack, but the jungle men had broad skis, of some metal no Hevian could have machined so precisely, on which they slid over the muck. Discs of red fire marked bursting TDX shells, scything the air like death's own winnows. No gas was in evidence, but Amalfi knew that there would be gas before long with the bindlestiff directing the fighting.

The city's retaliatory fire was largely invisible, since it emerged below the top of the perimeter. There was a Bethé fender out, which would keep the rim from being scaled until one of the projectors was knocked out, and plenty of heavy rifles were being kept hot. But the city had never been designed for warfare, and many of its most efficient destroyers had their noses buried in the mud, since their intended function was only to clear a landing area. Using an out-and-out Bethé blaster was impossible where there was an adjacent planetary mass—fortunately, since the bindlestiff had such a blaster and Amalfi's city did not.

Amalfi sniffed the scarlet edges of the struggle appraisingly. The screen set up beside him did not show an intelligible battle pattern yet, but it seemed to be almost on the verge of making sense. Under Amalfi's fingers on the platform railing were three buttons which he had had placed there four hundred years ago, duplicating a set on the balcony of City Hall. They had set in motion different actions at different times. But each time they had represented choices of actions which he would have to make when the pinch came. He had never found any reason to have a fourth button installed on either railing.

Rockets shrilled overhead. Bombs fell from them, crepitating bursts of noise and smoke and flying metal. Amalfi did not look up. The very mild spindizzy screen would fend off anything moving that rapidly. Only slow-moving objects, like men, could sidle through a polarized gravitic field. He looked out toward the horizon, touching the three buttons very delicately.

Suddenly the sunset snuffed itself out. Amalfi, who had never seen a tropical sunset before coming to He, felt a vague alarm, but as far as he could tell, the abrupt darkness was natural, though startling. The fighting went on, the flying discs of TDX explosions much more lurid now against the blackness.

After a while there was a dogfight far aloft, identifiable

mostly by the exhaust traceries of rockets and missiles. Evidently Miramon's air force was tangling with Fabr-Suithe's. The jungle jammered derision and fury at Amalfi's city without any letup.

Amalfi stood, watching the screen so intently as to cut the rest of the world almost completely out of his consciousness. Understanding the emerging pattern was hard work, for he had never tried to grasp a situation at such close quarters before, and the blue-coded trajectory of every shell, sketched across the screen in glowing segments of ellipses, tried to capture his exclusive attention, as if they were all planets.

About an hour past midnight, at the height of the heaviest air raid yet, he felt a touch at his elbow.

"Boss——"

Amalfi heard the word as though it had been uttered at the bottom of the Rift. The still-ascending fountain of space mines the bindlestiff was throwing up had just come into the margin of the screen—meaning that O'Brian, the proxy chief, had just located the 'stiff with one of his flying robot bystanders—and Amalfi was trying to extrapolate the shape of the top of the fountain. Somewhere up there in the aeropause, the fountain flattened into a shell of orbits encompassing the whole of He, and it was important to know how high up that shell began.

But the utter exhaustion of the voice touched something deeper. He said, "Yes, Mark."

"It's done. We lost almost everybody in the party. But we planted the women in a clearing right where a 'stiff outpost could see them. . . . What a riot that caused." A ghost of animation stirred in the voice for a moment. "You should have been there."

"I'm almost there now. Just getting the picture from a proxy. Good work, Mark. . . . Better . . . get some rest."

"Now? But boss——"

Something very heavy described a searing parabola across the screen, and then the whole city turned to a scramble of magnesium-white and ink. As the light of the star-shell faded, the screen showed a formless dim-yellow spreading and crawling, as if someone had spilled paint in the innards of the machine. Amalfi had been waiting for it.

"Gas alarm, Mark," he heard himself saying. "Sure to be Hawkesite. Barium suits for everybody—that stuff's pure death-by-torture."

"Yes, right. Boss, have you been up here all this time? You'll kill yourself running things this way. You need rest more than I do."

Amalfi found that he did not have time to answer. O'Brian's proxy had come upon the town where Hazleton had dropped the women. There was certainly a riot there. Amalfi snapped a switch, backing the point of view off to another proxy which was hovering a mile up, scanning the whole battle area. From here he could see the black tendrils of movement which were files of soldiers moving through the jungle. Some which had been approaching Amalfi's city were now turning back. Furthermore, new tendrils were being put out from Hevian towns which up to now had taken no part in the fighting—the on-the-fence towns. Evidently they were no longer on the fence, but which side they had jumped to still remained to be seen.

He snapped the switch again, bringing back a close look at the lake of boiling mud which lay at the base of the mine fountain. Something new was going on there, too: The hot mud was flowing slowly, thickly, away from the center of the lake. Then there was a clear area in the center, as if the lake had suddenly developed a vortex. The clear area widened.

The bindlestiff city was rising to the surface. It came cautiously; half an hour went by before its periphery touched the lake shore. Then black tendrils stretched out into the tangled desolation of the jungle; the bindlestiff was at last risking its own men in the struggle. What they were after was plain enough, for the files were all moving in the direction of the town where Hazleton had dropped the women.

The bindlestiff city itself sat and waited. Even against the mass-pressure of the planet of He, Amalfi's sense of spatial orientation could pick up the unmistakable, slightly nauseating sensation of spindizzy field under medium drive, doming the seething mud.

Dawn was coming now. The riot around the town where the women had been dropped dwindled a little. Then one of the task forces from the bindlestiff reached it, and it flared all over again, worse than ever. The 'stiffs were fighting their own allies.

Abruptly there was no Hevian town in the center of the riot at all. There was only a mushrooming pillar of radioactive gas which made the screen race with interference patterns. The 'stiffs had bombed the town. What was left of the riot retreated slowly toward the lake of boiling mud; the 'stiffs had their women and were fighting a rear-guard action. The news, Amalfi knew, would travel fast.

Amalfi's own city was shrouded in sick orange mist, lit with flashes of no-color. The blistering gas could not pass the spindizzy screen in a body, but it diffused through, molecule by heavy molecule. The mayor realized suddenly that he had not heeded his own gas warning, and that there was probably some harm coming to him. He started and moved slightly, and discovered that he was completely encased. What . . .

Barium paste. Evidently Hazleton had known that Amalfi could not leave the platform, and instead had plastered him with the paste in default of trying to get a suit on him. Even his eyes were covered with a transparent visor, and a feeling of distension in his nostrils bespoke a Kolman barium filter.

So much for the gas. The heavy tensions in and around the bindlestiff city continued to gather; they would soon be unbearable. Above, just outside the shell of circling mines, the first few police cruisers were sidling down with great caution. The war in the jungle had already fallen apart into meaninglessness. The abduction of the women by the tramps had collapsed all Hevian rivalries. Bandits and civilized towns alike were bent now upon nothing but the destruction of Fabr-Suithe and its allies. Fabr-Suithe could hold them off for a long time, but it was clearly time for the bindlestiff to leave—time for it to make off with its pleased and wondering Hevian women, its anti-agathics, its germanium, and whatever else it had managed to garner— time for it to lose itself again in the Rift before the Earth police could invest the planet of He.

The gravitic field around the bindlestiff city knotted suddenly, painfully, in Amalfi's brain, and began to rise away from the lake of boiling mud. The 'stiff was taking off. In a moment it would be gone through the rent in the mine umbrella which only the tramps could see.

Amalfi pressed the button—the only one, this time, that had been connected to anything.

Moving Day began.

Moving Day began with six pillars of glaring white, forty miles in diameter, which burst through the soft soil at each compass point of He. Fabr-Suithe had sat directly over the site of one of them. The bandit town was nothing but a flake of ash in a split second, a curled black flake borne aloft on the top of a white-hot piston.

The pillars lunged, roaring, into the heavens, fifty, a hundred, two hundred miles, and burst at their tops like popcorn. The Hevian sky burned thermite-blue with steel meteors. Outside, the space mines, cut off from the world of which they had been satellites by the greatest spindizzy field in history, fled away into the Rift.

And when the meteors had burned away, the sun was growing.

The world of He was on spindizzy drive, its magnetic moment transformed into momentum. It was the biggest Okie "city" that had ever flown. There was no time to feel alarm. The sun flashed by and was dwindling to a point before the fact could be grasped. Then it was gone. The far wall of the Rift began to swell and separate into individual points of light.

The planet of He was crossing the Rift.

Appalled, Amalfi fought to understand the scale of speed. He failed. The planet of He was moving, that was all he could comprehend. It was moving at a proper cruising speed for a "city" of its size—a speed that gulped down light years as if they were gnats. Even to think of controlling such a flight was ridiculous.

Stars began to wink past He like fireflies. They had reached the other side of the Rift. The planet began to curve gradually away from the main cloud. Then the stars were all behind.

The surface of the saucer that was the galaxy began to come into view.

"Boss! We're going out of the galaxy! Look——"

"I know it. Get me a fix on He's old sun as soon as we're high enough above the Rift to see it again. After that it'll be too late."

Hazleton worked feverishly. It took him only half an hour, but during that time, the massed stars receded far enough to make plain the gray scar of the Rift as a long shadow on a spangled ground. At the end the Hevian sun was only a tenth-magnitude point in it.

"Got it, I think. But we can't swing the planet back. It'll take us thousands of years to cross to the next galaxy. We'll have to abandon He, boss, or we're sunk."

"All right. Get us aloft. Full drive."

"Our contract——"

"Fulfilled—take my word for it now. Spin!"

The city sprang aloft. The planet of He did not dwindle in the city's sky. It simply vanished, snuffed out in the intergalactic gap. Miramon, if he lived, would be the first of a totally new race of pioneers.

Amalfi moved then, back toward the controls, the barium casing cracking and falling off him as he came back to life. The air of the city still stank of Hawkesite, but the concentration of the gas already had been taken down below the harmful level by the city's purifiers. The mayor began to edge the city away from the vector of He's flight and the city's own, back toward the home lens.

Hazleton stirred restlessly.

"Your conscience bothering you, Mark?"

"Maybe," Hazleton said. "Is there some escape clause in our contract with Miramon that lets us desert him like this? If there is, I missed it, and I read the fine print pretty closely."

"No, there's no escape clause," Amalfi said abstractedly, shifting the space stick by a millimeter or two. "The Hevians won't be hurt. The spindizzy screen will protect them from loss of heat and atmosphere—their volcanoes will keep them warmer than they'll probably like, and their technology is up to producing all the light they'll need. But they won't be able to keep the planet well enough lit to satisfy the jungle. That will die. By the time Miramon and his friends reach the star that suits them in the

Andromedan galaxy, they'll understand the spindizzy well
enough to put their planet back into the proper orbit. Or
maybe they'll like roaming better by that time and will
decide to be an Okie planet. Either way, we licked the
jungle for them, just as we promised to do, fair and
square."

"We didn't get paid," the city manager pointed out.
"And it'll take a lot of fuel to get back to any part of our own
galaxy. The bindlestiff got off ahead of us, and got carried
way out of range of the cops in the process, right on our
backs—with plenty of germanium, drugs, women, the no-
fuel drive, everything."

"No, they didn't," Amalfi said. "They blew up the moment we moved He."

"All right," Hazleton said resignedly. "You could detect
that where I couldn't, so I'll take your word for it. But
you'd better be able to explain it!"

"It's not hard to explain. The 'stiffs had captured Doctor
Beetle. I was pretty sure they had; after all, they came to
He for no other reason. They needed the no-fuel drive,
and they knew Doctor Beetle had it because they heard
the agronomists' SOS, just as we did. So they snatched
Doctor Beetle when he was landed—do you remember
what a big fuss their bandit-city allies made about the
other agronomist lifeship, to divert us? It worked, too—
and in the meantime they cooked the secret out of him.
Probably in his own tank."

"So?"

"So," Amalfi said, "the tramps forgot that any Okie city
always has passengers like Doctor Beetle—people with big
ideas only partially worked out, ideas that need the finish-
ing touches that can only be provided by some other
culture. After all, a man doesn't take passage on an Okie
city unless he's a third-rater, hoping to make his everlasting fortune on some planet where the inhabitants know
much less than he does."

Hazleton scratched his head ruefully. "That's right. We
had the same experience with the Lyran invisibility machine. It never worked until we took Doc Schloss on
board."

"Exactly. The 'stiffs were in too much of a hurry. They

didn't carry their stolen no-fuel drive with them until they found some culture which could perfect it. They tried to use it right away. They were lazy. And they tried to use it inside the biggest spindizzy field ever generated. What happened? It blew up. I felt it happen—and the top of my head nearly came off then and there. If we hadn't left the 'stiffs parsecs behind in the first split second, Doctor Beetle's drive would have blown up He at the same time. It doesn't pay to be lazy, Mark."

"Who ever said it did?" Hazleton said. After a moment's more thought, he began to plot the point at which the city would probably reenter its own galaxy. That point turned out to be a long way away from the Rift, in an area that, after a mental wrench to visualize it backwards from the usual orientation, promised a fair population.

"Look," he said, "we'll hit about where the last few waves of the Acolytes settled—remember the Night of Hadjjii?"

Amalfi didn't, since he hadn't been born then, but he remembered the history, which was what the city manager had meant. He said, "Good. I want to take us to garage and get that Twenty-third Street machine settled for good and all. I'm tired of its blowing out in the pinches, and it's going sour for fair now. Hear it?"

Hazleton cocked his head intently. In the lull, Amalfi saw suddenly that Dee was standing in the doorway, still completely enswathed in her anti-gas suit except for the faceplate.

"Is it over?" she said.

"Well, our stay on He is over. We're still on the run, if that's what you mean. The cops never give up, Dee; you'll learn that sooner or later."

"Where are we going?"

She asked the question in the same tone in which she had once said, "What is a volt, John?" For an astonishing moment Amalfi was almost overwhelmed with an urge to send Hazleton from the room on some excuse, to return almost bodily to those days of her innocence, to relive all the previous questions that she had asked—the moments when he had known the answers better.

There was, of course, no real answer to this one. Where

would an Okie go? They were going, that was all. If there was a destination, no one could know what it was.

He endured the surge of emotion stoically. In the end, he only shrugged.

"By the way," he said, "what's the operational day?"

Hazleton looked at the clock. "M plus eleven twenty-five."

With a sidelong glance, Amalfi leaned forward, resumed the helmet he had cast aside on He, and turned on the City Fathers.

The helmet phones shrilled with alarm. "All right, all right," he growled. "What is it?"

"MAYOR AMALFI, HAVE YOU TIPPED THIS PLANET?"

"No," Amalfi said. "We sent it on its way as it was."

There was a short silence, humming with computation. It was probably just as well, Amalfi thought, that the machines had been turned off for a while; they had not had a rest in many centuries. They would probably emerge into consciousness a little saner for it.

"VERY WELL. WE MUST NOW SELECT THE POINT AT WHICH WE LEAVE THE RIFT. STAND BY FOR DETERMINATION."

Hazleton and Amalfi grinned at each other. Amalfi said, "We're coming in on the last Acolyte stars, and we'll need to decelerate far beyond spindizzy safety limits. We urgently need an overhaul on the Twenty-third Street driver. Give us a determination for the present social setup there, please——"

"YOU ARE MISTAKEN. THAT CLUSTER IS NOWHERE NEAR THE RIFT. FURTHERMORE, THE POPULACE THERE HAS A LONG RECORD OF MASS XENOPHOBIA AND HAD BEST BE AVOIDED. WE WILL GIVE YOU A DETERMINATION FOR THE FAR RIFT WALL. STAND BY."

Amalfi removed the headset gently.

"The Rift wall," he said, moving the microphone away from his mouth. "That was long ago—and far away."

CHAPTER FIVE: Murphy

A spindizzy going sour makes the galaxy's most unnerving noise. The top range of the sound is inaudible, but it eels like a multiple toothache. Just below that, there is a screech like metal tearing, which blends smoothly into a composite cataract of plate glass, slate, and boulders; this is the middle register. After that, there is a painful gap in the sound's spectrum, and the rest of the noise comes into one's ears again with a hollow round dinosaurian sob and plummets on down into the subsonics, ending in frequencies which induce diarrhea and an almost unconquerable urge to bite one's thumbs.

The noise was coming, of course, from the Twenty-third Street spindizzy, but it permeated the whole city. It was tolerable only so long as the hold which contained the moribund driver was kept sealed. Amalfi knew better than to open that hold. He surveyed the souring machine via instruments, and kept the audio tap prudently closed. The sound fraction which was thrumming through the city's walls was bad enough, even as far up as the control chamber.

Hazleton's hand came over his left shoulder, stabbing a long finger at the recording thermocouple.

"She's beginning to smoke now. Damned if I know how she's lasted this long. The model was two hundred years old when we took it aboard—and the repair job I did on He was only an emergency rig."

"What can we do?" Amalfi said. He did not bother to look around; the city manager's moods were his own second nature. They had lived together a long time—long enough to learn what learning is, long enough to know that, just as habit is second nature, so nature—the seven steps from chance to meaning—is first habit. The hand which rested upon Amalfi's right shoulder told him all he needed to know about Hazleton at this moment. "We can't shut her down."

"If we don't, she'll blow for good and all. That hold's hot already."

"Hot and howling. . . . Let me think a minute."

Hazleton waited. After another moment, Amalfi said, "We'll keep her shoving. If the City Fathers can push this much juice through her, maybe they can push just a little more. Maybe enough to get us down to a reasonable cruising speed. Besides—we couldn't jury-rig that spindizzy again. It's radiating all up and down the line. The City Fathers could shut her down if we ordered it, but it'd take human beings to repair her and retune the setup stages. And it's too late for that."

"It'll be a year before anything alive can go into that hold," Hazleton agreed gloomily. "All right. How's our velocity now?"

"Negligible, with reference to the galaxy as a whole. But as far as the Acolyte stars proper are concerned—we'd shoot through the whole cluster at about eight times the city's top speed if we stopped decelerating now. It's going to be damned tight, that's for sure, Mark."

"Excuse me," Dee's voice said behind them. She was hesitating just beyond the threshold of the lift shaft. "Is there something wrong? If you're busy——"

"No busier than usual," Hazleton said. "Just wondering about our usual baby."

"The Twenty-third Street machine. I could tell by the curvature of your spines. Why don't you have it replaced and get it over with?"

Amalfi and the city manager grinned at each other, but the mayor's grin was short-lived.

"Well, why not?" he said suddenly.

"My gods, boss, the cost," Hazleton said with incredulity. "The City Fathers would impeach you for suggesting it." He donned the helmet. "Treasury check," he told the microphone.

"They've never had to run her all by themselves under max overdrive before now. I predict that they'll emerge from the experience clamoring to have her replaced, even if we don't eat for a year to pay for it. Besides, we should have the money, for once. We dug a lot of germanium while we were setting up He to be de-wobbled. Maybe the time really has come when we can afford a replacement."

Dee came forward swiftly, motes of light on the move in her eyes. "John, can that be true?" she said. "I thought we'd lost a lot on the Hevian contract."

"Well, we're not rich. We would have been, I'm still convinced, if we'd been able to harvest the anti-agathics on a decent scale."

"But we didn't," Dee said. "We had to run away."

"We ran away. But in terms of germanium alone, we can call ourselves well off. Well enough off to buy a new spindizzy. Right, Mark?"

Hazleton listened to the City Fathers a moment more, and then took off the bone-mikes. "It looks that way," he said. "Anyhow, we can easily cover the price of an over-haul, or maybe even of a reconditioned second-hand machine of a later model. Depends on whether or not the Acolyte stars have a service planet, and what the garage fees are there."

"The fees should be low enough to keep us solvent," Amalfi said, thrusting his lower lip out thoughtfully. "The Acolyte area is a backwater, but it was settled originally by refugees from an anti-Earth pogrom in the Malar system—an aftermath of the collapse of Vega, as I recall. There's a record of the pogrom in the libraries of most planets—you reminded me of it, Mark: the Night of Hadjjii—which means that the Acolytes aren't far enough away from normal trading areas to be proper frontier stars."

He paused, and his frown deepened. "Now that I come to think of it, the Acolytes were an important minor source of power metals for part of this limb of the galaxy at one time. They'll have at least one garage planet, Mark, depend on it. They may even have work for the city to do."

"Sounds good," Hazleton said. "Too good, maybe. Actually, we've *got* to sit down in the Acolytes, boss, because that Twenty-third Street machine won't carry us beyond them at anything above a snail's pace. I asked the City Fathers that while I was checking the treasury. This is the end of the line for that gadget."

He sounded tired. Amalfi looked at him.

"That's not what's worrying you, Mark," he said. "We've always had that problem waiting for us somewhere in the future, and it isn't one that's difficult of solution. What's the real trouble? Cops, maybe?"

"All right, it's cops," Hazleton said, a little sullenly. "I know we're a long way away from any cops that know us by name. But have you any idea of the total amount of unpaid fines we're carrying? And I don't see how we can assume that any amount of distance is 'too great' for the cops to follow us if they really want us—and it seems that they do."

"Why, Mark?" Dee said. "After all, we've done nothing serious."

"It piles up," Hazleton said. "We haven't been called on our Violations docket in a long time. When we're finally caught, we'll have to pay in full, and if that were to happen now, we'd be bankrupt."

"Pooh," Dee said. Like anyone more or less recently naturalized, her belief in the capacities of her adopted city-state was as finite as it was unbounded. "We could find work and build up a new treasury. It might be hard going for a while, but we'd survive it. People have been broke before, and come through it whole."

"People, yes; cities, no," Amalfi said. "Mark is right on that point, Dee. According to the law, a bankrupt city must be dispersed. It's essentially a humane law, in that it prevents desperate mayors and city managers from taking bankrupt cities out again on long job-hunting trips, during which half of the Okies on board will die just because of the stubbornness of the people in charge."

"Exactly," Hazleton said.

"Even so, I think it's a bogey," Amalfi said gently. "I'll

grant you your facts, Mark, but not your extrapolation. The cops can't possibly follow us from He's old star to here. We didn't know ourselves that we'd wind up among the Acolytes. I doubt that the cops were even able to plot He's course, let alone our subsequent one. Isn't that so?"

"Of course. But——"

"And if the Earth cops alerted every *local* police force in the galaxy to every petty offender," Amalfi continued with quiet implacability, "no local police force would ever be able to do any policing. They'd be too busy, recording and filing and checking new alerts coming in constantly from a million inhabited planets. Their own local criminals would mostly go free, to become a burden upon the filing systems of every other inhabited area.

"So, believe me, Mark, the cops around here have never even heard of us. We're approaching a normal situation, that's all. The Acolyte cops haven't the slightest reason to treat us as anything but just another wandering, law abiding Okie city—and after all, that's really all we are."

"Good," Hazleton said, his chest collapsing to expel a heavy sigh.

Amalfi heard neither the word nor the sigh.

At the same instant, the big master screen, which had been showing the swelling, granulating mass of the Acolyte star cluster, flashed blinding scarlet over its whole surface, and the scrannel shriek of a police whistle made the air in the control room seethe.

The cops swaggered and stomped on board the Okie city, and into Amalfi's main office in City Hall, as if the nothingness of the marches of the galaxy were their personal property. Their uniforms were not the customary dress coveralls—actually, space-suit liners—of the Earth police, however. Instead, they were flashy black affairs, trimmed with silver braid, Sam Browne belt, and shiny boots. The blue-jowled thugs who had been jammed into these tight-fitting creations reminded Amalfi of a period which considerably antedated the Night of Jadjjii—or any other event in the history of space flight.

And the thugs carried meson pistols. These heavy, cum-

bersome weapons could be held in one hand, but two
hands were needed to fire them. They were very modern
side arms to find in a border star cluster. They were only
about a century out of date. This made them thoroughly
up-to-date as far as the city's own armament was concerned.

The pistols told Amalfi several other things that he
needed to know. Their existence here could mean only
one thing: that the Acolytes had had a recent contact with
one of those pollinating bees of the galaxy, an Okie city.
Furthermore, the probability was not high that it had
been the sole Okie contact the Acolytes had had for a long
time, as Amalfi might otherwise have assumed.

It took years to build up the technology to mass produce
meson pistols so that ordinary cops could pack them. It
took more years still, years spent in fairly frequent contact
with other technologies, to make adoption of the pistol
possible at all. The pistol, then, confirmed unusually frequent contact with other Okies, which, in turn, meant that
there was a garage planet here, as Amalfi had hoped.

The pistol also told Amalfi something else, which he did
not much like. The meson pistol was not a good antiper-
sonnel weapon.

It was much more suitable for demolition work.

The cops could still swagger in Amalfi's office, but they
could not stomp effectively. The floor was too thickly
carpeted. Amalfi never used the ancient, plushy office,
with its big black mahogany desk and other antiques,
except for official occasions. The control tower was his
normal on-duty habitat, but that was closed to noncitizens.

"What's your business?" the police lieutenant barked at
Hazleton. Hazleton, standing beside the desk, said nothing, but merely jerked his head toward where Amalfi was
seated and resumed looking at the big screen back of the
desk.

"Are you the mayor of this burg?" the lieutenant
demanded.

"I am," Amalfi said, removing a cigar from his mouth
and looking the lieutenant over with lidless eyes. He
decided that he did not like the lieutenant. His rump was
too big. If a man is going to be barrel-shaped, he ought to

do a good job of it, as Amalfi had. Amalfi had no use for top-shaped men.

"All right, answer the question, Fatty. What's your business?"

"Petroleum geology."

"You're lying. You're not dealing with some isolated, type Four-Q podunk now, Okie. These are the Acolyte stars."

Hazleton looked with pointedly vague puzzlement at the lieutenant, and then back to the screen, which showed no stars at all within any reasonable distance.

The by-play was lost on the cop. "Petroleum geology isn't a business with Okies," he said. "You'd all starve if you didn't know how to mine and crack oil for food. Now give me a straight answer before I decide you're a vagrant and get tough."

Amalfi said evenly, "Our business is petroleum geology. Naturally we've developed some side lines since we've been aloft, but they're mostly natural outgrowths of petroleum geology—on which subject we happen to be experts. We trace and develop petroleum sources for planets which need the material." He eyed the cigar judiciously and thrust it back between his teeth. "Incidentally, Lieutenant, you're wasting your breath threatening us with a vagrancy charge. You know as well as we do that vagrancy laws are specifically forbidden by article one of the Constitution."

"Consitution?" the cop laughed. "If you mean the Earth Constitution, we don't have much contact with Earth out here. These are the Acolyte stars, see? Next question: have you any money?"

"Enough."

"How much is enough?"

"If you want to know whether or not we have operating capital, our City Fathers will give you the statutory *yes* or *no* answer if you can give them the data on your system that they'll need to make the calculation. The answer will almost assuredly be yes. We're not required to report our profit pool to you, of course."

"Now look," the lieutenant said. "You don't need to play the space lawyer with me. All I want to do is get off this town. If you've got dough, I can clear you—that is, if you got it through legal channels."

"We got it on a planet called He, some distance from here. We were hired by the Hevians to rub out a jungle which was bothering them. We did it by regularizing their axis."

"Yeah?" the cop said. "Regularized their axis, eh? I guess that must have been some job."

"It was," Amalfi said gravely. "We had to setacetus on He's left-hand frannistan."

"Gee. Will your City Fathers show me the contract? Okay, then. Where are you going?"

"To garage; we've a bum spindizzy. After that, out again. You people look like you're well past the stage where you've much use for oil."

"Yeah, we're pretty modernized here, not like some of these border areas you hear about. These are the Acolyte stars." Suddenly it seemed to occur to him that he had somehow lost ground; his voice turned brusque again. "So maybe you're all right, Okie. I'll give you a pass through. Just be sure you go where you say you're going, and don't make stopovers, understand? If you watch your step, maybe I can lend you a hand here and there."

Amalfi said, "That's very good of you, Lieutenant. We'll try not to have to bother you, but just in case we do have to call on you, who shall we ask for?"

"Lieutenant Lerner, Forty-fifth Border Security Group."

"Good. Oh, before you go, I collect medal ribbons— every man to his hobby, you know. And that royal violet one of yours is quite unusual—I speak as a connoisseur. Would you consent to sell it? It wouldn't be like giving up the medal itself—I'm sure your corps would issue you another ribbon."

"I don't know," Lieutenant Lerner said doubtfully. "It's against regs——"

"I realize that, and naturally I'd expect to cover any possible fine you might incur. (Mark, would you call down for a check for five hundred Oc dollars?) No sum I could offer you would really be sufficient to pay for a medal for which you risked your life, but five hundred Oc is all our

City Fathers will allow me for hobbies this month. Could you do me the favor of accepting it?"

"Yeah, I guess so," the lieutenant said. He detached the bar of faded, dismal purple from over his pocket with clumsy eagerness and put it on the desk. A second later, Hazleton silently handed him the check, which he pocketed without seeming to notice it at all. "Well, be sure you keep a straight course, Okie. C'mon, you guys, let's get back to the boat."

The three thugs eased themselves tentatively into the lift shaft and slithered down out of sight through the friction-field wearing expressions of sternly repressed alarm. Amalfi grinned. Quite obviously the principle of molar valence, and frictionators and other gadgets using the principle, were still generally unknown.

Hazleton walked over to the shaft and peered down. Then he said, "Boss, that damn thing is a good-conduct ribbon. The Earth cops issued them by the tens of thousands about three centuries ago to any rookie who could get up out of bed when the whistle blew three days running. Since when is it worth five hundred Oc?"

"Never, until now," Amalfi said tranquilly. "But the lieutenant wanted to be bribed, and it's always wise to appear to be buying something when you're bribing someone. I put the price so high because he'll have to split it with his men. If I hadn't offered the bribe, I'm sure he'd have wanted to look at our Violations docket."

"I figured that; and ours is none too clean, as I've been pointing out. But I think you wasted the money, Amalfi. The Violations docket should have been the first thing he asked to see, not the last. Since he didn't ask for it at the beginning, he wasn't interested in it."

"That's probably exactly so," Amalfi admitted. He put the cigar back and pulled on it thoughtfully. "All right, Mark, what's the pitch? Suppose you tell me."

"I don't know yet. I can't square the maintenance of an alert guard, so many parsecs out from the actual Acolyte area, with that slob's obvious indifference to whether or not we might be on the shady side of the law—or even be bindlestiff. Hell, he didn't even ask *who* we were."

"That rules out the possibility that the Acolytes have been alerted against some one bindlestiff city."

"It does," Hazleton agreed. "Lerner was far too easily bribed, for that matter. Patrols that are really looking for something specific don't bribe, even in a fairly corrupt culture. It doesn't figure."

"And somehow," Amalfi said, pushing a toggle to *off*, "I don't think the City Fathers are going to be a bit of help. I had the whole conversation up to now piped down to them, but all I'm going to get out of them is a bawling out for spending money and a catechism about my supposed hobby. They never have been able to make anything out of voice tone. Damn! We're missing something important, Mark, something that would be obvious once it hit us. Something absolutely crucial. And here we are plunging on toward the Acolytes without the faintest idea of what it is!"

"Boss," Hazleton said.

The cold flatness of his voice brought Amalfi swiveling around in his chair in a hurry. The city manager was looking up again at the big screen, on which the Acolyte stars had now clearly separated into individual points. "What is it, Mark?"

"Look there—in the mostly dark area on the far side of the cluster. Do you see it?"

"I see quite a lot of star-free space there, yes." Amalfi looked closer. "There's also a spectroscopic double, with a red dwarf standing out some distance from the other components——"

"You're warm. Now look at the red dwarf."

There was also, Amalfi began to see, a faint smudge of green there, about as big as the far end of a pencil. The screen was keyed to show Okie cities in green, but no city could possibly be that big. The green smudge covered an area that would blank out an average Sol-type solar system.

Amalfi felt his big square front teeth beginning to bite his cigar in two. He took the dead object out of his mouth.

"Cities," he muttered. He spat, but the bitterness in his mouth did not seem to be tobacco juice after all. "Not one city. *Hundreds.*"

"Yes," Hazleton said. "There's your answer, boss, or part of it. It's a jungle."

"An Okie jungle."

Amalfi gave the jungle a wide berth, but he had O'Brian send proxies as soon as the city was safely down below top speed. Had he released the missiles earlier, they would have been left behind and lost, for they were only slightly faster than the city itself. Now they showed a fantastic and gloomy picture.

The empty area where the hobo cities had settled was well out at the edge of the Acolyte cluster, on the side toward the rest of the galaxy. The nearest star to the area, as Hazleton had pointed out, was a triple. It consisted of two type G_0 stars and a red dwarf, almost a double for the Soy-Alpha Centauri system. But there was one difference: The two G_0 stars were quite close to each other, constituting a spectroscopic doublet, separable visually only by the Dinwiddie circuits even at this relatively short distance; while the red dwarf had swung out into the empty area and was now more than four light years away from its companions.

Around this tiny and virtually heatless fire, more than three hundred Okie cities huddled. On the screen they passed in an endless, boundaryless flood of green specks, like a river of fantastic asteroids, bobbing in space and passing and repassing each other in their orbits around the dwarf star. The concentration was heaviest near the central sun, which was so penurious of its slight radiation that it had been masked almost completely by the Dinwiddie code lights when Hazleton first spotted the jungle. But there were latecomers in orbits as far out as three billion miles—spindizzy screens do not take kindly to being thrust into close contact with each other.

"It's frightening," Dee said, studying the screen intently. "I knew there were other Okie cities, especially after we hit the bindlestiff. But so many! I could hardly have imagined three hundred in the whole galaxy."

"A gross underestimate," Hazleton said indulgently. "There were about eighteen thousand cities at the last census, weren't there, boss?"

"Yes," Amalfi said. He was as unable to look away from the screen as Dee. "But I know what Dee means. It scares the hell out of me, Mark. Something must have caused an almost complete collapse of the economy around this part of the galaxy. No other force could create a jungle of that kind. These bastardly Acolytes evidently have been exploiting it to draw Okies here, in order to hire the few they need on a competitive basis."

"At the lowest possible wages, in other words," Hazleton said. "But what for?"

"There you have me. Possibly they're trying to industrialize the whole cluster, to make themselves self-sufficient before the depression or whatever it is hits them. About all we can be sure of at this juncture is that we'd better get out of here the moment the new spindizzy gets put in. There'll be no decent work here."

"I'm not sure I agree," Hazleton said, redeploying his lanky, apparently universal-jointed limbs over his chair. "If they're industrializing here, it could mean that the depression is *here*, not anywhere else. Possibly they've overproduced themselves into a money shortage, especially if their distribution setup is as creaking, elaborate, and unjust as it usually is in these backwaters. If they're using a badly deflated dollar, we'll be sitting pretty."

Amalfi considered it. It seemed to hold up.

"We'll have to wait and see," he said. "You could well be right. But one cluster, even at its most booming stage, could never have hoped to support three hundred cities. The waste of technology involved would be terrific—and you don't attract Okies *to* a money-short area, you draw them *from* one."

"Not necessarily. Suppose there's an oversupply outside? Remember back in the Nationalist Era on Earth, artists and such low-income people used to leave the big Hamiltonian state, I've forgotten its name, to live in much smaller states where the currency was softer?"

"That was different. They had mixed coinage then——"

"Boys, may I break in on this bull session?" Dee said hesitantly, but with a trace of mockery in her voice. "It's getting a little over my head. Suppose this whole end of this star-limb has had its economy wrecked. How, I'll leave to you two; on Utopia, our economy was frozen at a fixed rate of turnover, and had been for as long as any of us could remember; so maybe I can be forgiven for not understanding what you're talking about. But in any case, inflation or deflation, we can always leave when we have our new spindizzy."

Amalfi shook his head heavily. "That," he said, "is what scares me, Dee. There are a hell of a lot of Okies in that jungle, and they can't all be suffering from defects in their driving equipment. If there were someplace they could go where times are better, *why haven't they gone there?* Why do they congregate in a jungle in this Godforsaken star cluster, for all the universe as if there were no place else where they could find work? Okies aren't sedentary, or sociable, either."

Hazleton began drumming his fingers lightly on the arm of his chair, and his eyes closed slightly. "Money is energy," he said. "Still, I can't say that I like that any better. The more I look at it, the more I think this is one fix we won't get out of by any amount of cute tricks. Maybe we should have stuck with He."

"Maybe."

Amalfi turned his attention back to the controls. Hazleton was subtle; but one consequence of his subtlety was that he intended to expend unnecessary amounts of time speculating about situations the facts of which would soon become evident in any case.

The city was now approaching the local garage world, which bore the unlikely name of Murphy, and maneuvering among the close-packed stars of the cluster was a job delicate enough to demand the mayor's own hand upon the space stick. The City Fathers, of course, could have teetered the city through the conflicting gravitic fields to a safe landing on Murphy, but they would have taken a month at the job. Hazleton would have gone faster, but the City Fathers would have monitored his route all the way and snatched control from him at the slightest transgression of the margins of error they had calculated. They were not equipped to respect shortcuts.

Of course, they were also unequipped to appreciate the direct intuition of spatial distances and mass pressures which made Amalfi a master pilot. But over Amalfi they had no authority, except the ultimate authority of the revocation of his office.

As Murphy grew on the screen, technicians began to file into the control room, activating with personal keys desks which had been disconnected for more than three centuries—ever since the last new spindizzy had been brought on board. Readying the city's drive machinery for new equipment was a major project. Every other spindizzy on board would have to be retuned to the new machine. In the present case, the job would be further complicated by the radioactivity of the defective unit. While the garagemen should have special equipment to cope with that problem—de-gaussing, for instance, was the usual first step—no garage would know the machinery involved as well as the Okies who used it. Every city is unique.

Murphy, as Amalfi saw it on his own screen, was a commonplace enough world. It was just slightly above the size of Mars, but pleasanter to live on, since it was closer to its primary by a good distance.

But it looked deserted. As the city came closer, Amalfi could see the twenty-mile pockmarks which were the graving docks typical of a garage; but every one of those perfectly regular, machinery-ringed craters in the planet's visible hemisphere turned out to be empty.

"That's bad," he heard Hazleton murmur. It was certainly unpromising. The planet turned slowly under his eyes.

Then a city slid up over the horizon. Hazleton's breath sucked sharply through his teeth. Amalfi could also hear a soft stirring sound, and then footsteps—several of the technicians had come up behind him to peer over his shoulder.

"Posts!" he growled. The technicians scattered like leaves.

On the idle service world, the grounded city was startlingly huge. It thrust up from the ground like an invader—but a naked giant, fallen and defenseless, without its spindizzy screens. There was, of course, every good reason why the screens should not be up, but still, a city without them was a rare and disconcerting sight, like a flayed corpse in a tank. There seemed to be some activity at its perimeter. Amalfi could not resist thinking of that activity as bacterial.

"Doesn't that answer the question Dee's way?" Hazleton suggested at last. "There's an outfit that has dough for repairs, so money from outside the Acolyte area must still be good. It's having the repairs made, so it can't be quite hopeless—it thinks it has someplace to go from here. And it's a cinch to be a smart outfit, well worth consulting. It's prevented the Acolytes from fleecing it—and some form of Acolyte swindle is the only remaining explanation for the existence of the jungle. We'd best get in touch with it before we land, boss, and find out what to expect."

"No," Amalfi said. "Stick to your post, Mark."

"Why? Surely it can't do any harm."

Amalfi didn't answer. His own psi sense had already told him something that knocked Hazleton's argument into a cocked helmet, but that something showed on Hazleton's own instruments, if Hazleton cared to look. The city manager had allowed an extrapolation to carry him off in to Cloud-Cuckoo-Land.

Abruptly the board began to wink with directional signals. Automatic guides from the control tower on Murphy were waving the city to a readied dock. Amalfi shifted the space stick obediently, awaiting the orange blinker that would announce some living intelligence ready with an opinion as to the desirability of Okies on Murphy.

But neither opinion nor blinker had yet asked for his attention even when Amalfi had begun to float the city for its planting in the unpromising soil below. Evidently business was so poor on Murphy that the garage had lost most of its staff to more "going" projects. In that case, no entities but the automatics in the tower would be on hand to supervise an unexpected landing.

With a shrug, Amalfi cut the City Fathers back in. There was no need for a human being to land a city as long as the landing presented no problem in policy. There were more than enough human uses for human beings; routine operations were the proper province of the City Fathers.

"First planetfall since He," Hazleton said. He seemed to be brightening a little. "It'll feel good to stretch our legs."

"No leg-stretching or any other kind of calisthenics," Amalfi said. "Not until we get more information. I haven't gotten a yeep out of this planet yet. For all we know, we may be restricted to our own premises by the local customs."

"Wouldn't the tower have said so?"

"No tower would be empowered to deliver a message like that to all comers. It might scare off an occasional legitimate customer. But it could still be so, Mark; you should know that. Let's do some snooping first."

Amalfi picked up his mike. "Get me the perimeter sergeant . . . Anderson? This is the mayor. Arm ten good men from the boarding squad, and meet the city manager and me at the Cathedral Parkway lookout. Station your men at the adjacent sally ports, well out of sight of the localities, if there are any such around. . . . Yes, that'd be just as well, too. . . . Right."

Hazleton said, "We're going out."

"Yes. And, Mark—*this star cluster may well be the last stop that we'll ever make. Will you remember that?*"

"I'll have no difficulty remembering it," Hazleton said, looking directly at Amalfi with eyes as gray as ice, "seeing that it's exactly what I told you four days ago. I have my own notions of the proper way to cope with the possibility, and they probably won't jibe with yours. Four days ago you were explaining to me that I was being excessively defeatist. Now you've expropriated my conclusion because something has forced it on you—and I know you better than to expect you to tell me what that something is—and so now you're telling me to 'Remember Thor Five' again. You can't have it both ways, Amalfi."

For a second, the two men's glances remained locked, pupil with pupil.

"You two," Dee's voice said, "might just as well be married."

From the skywalk of the graving dock in which the city rested at last, a walk level with the main deck of the city, the world of Murphy presented to Amalfi the face of a desolate mechanical wilderness.

It was an elephant's graveyard of cranes, hoists, dollies, spur lines, donkey engines, cables, scaffolding, pallets, half-tracks, camel-backs, chutes, conveyors, bins, tanks, hoppers, pipelines, waldoes, spindizzies, trompers, breed-

ers, proxies, ehrenhafts, and half a hundred other devices
of as many ages which might at some time be needed in
servicing some city.

Much of the machinery was rusty, or fallen in upon
itself, or whole on the surface but forever dead inside,
with a spurious wholeness that so simple an instrument as
the dosimeter every man wore on his left wrist could
reveal as submicroscopic scandal. Much of it, too, was still
quite usable. But all of it had the look of machinery which
no one really expected to use.

On the near horizon, the other city, the one Amalfi had
seen from aloft, stood tall and straight. Tiny mechanisms
puttered about it.

And far below the skywalk, on the cluttered surface of
Murphy, in the shadow of the bulge of Amalfi's city, a tiny
and merely human figure danced and gesticulated.

Amalfi led the way down the tight spiral of the metal
staircase, Hazleton and Sergeant Anderson behind him.
Their steps were muffled in the thin air. He watched his
own carefully; on a low-gravity world it was just as well to
temper the use of one's muscles. The fact that one fell
slower on such worlds did not much lessen the thump at
the end of the fall, and Amalfi had found long ago that,
away from the unvarying one-G field of the city, his bull
strength often betrayed him even when he was being
normally careful.

The dancing doll proved to be a short, curly-haired
technie in a clean but mussed uniform. Possibly he had
slept in it; at least it seemed clear that he had never done
any work in it. He had a smooth, chubby face, dark of
complexion, greasy and stippled with clogged pores. He
glared at Amalfi truculently with eyes like beer-bottle ends.

"What the hell?" he said. "How'd you get here?"

"We swam, how else? When do we get some service?"

"I'll ask the questions, bum. And tell your sergeant to
keep his hand off his gun. He makes me nervous, and
when I'm nervous, there's no telling what I'll do. You're
after repairs?"

"What else?"

"We're busy," the garageman said. "No charity here.
Go back to your jungle."

"You're about as busy as a molecule at zero," Amalfi roared, thrusting his head forward. The garageman's shiny, bulbous nose retreated, but not by much. "We need repairs, and we mean to have 'em. We've got money to pay, and Lieutenant Lerner of your own local cops sent us here to get 'em. If those two reasons won't suit you, I'll have my sergeant put his gun hand to some use—he could probably draw and fire before you tripped over something in this junkyard."

"Who the hell are you threatening? Don't you know you're in the Acolyte stars now? We've broken up better —no, now wait a minute, sergeant, let's not be hasty. I've been dealing with bums until they're coming out of my ears. Maybe you're all right after all. You did say something about money—I heard you distinctly."

"You did," Amalfi said, remaining impassive with difficulty.

"Your City Fathers will vouch for it?"

"Sure. Hazleton—oh, hell, Anderson, what happened to the city manager?"

"He took a branching catwalk farther up," the perimeter sergeant said. "Didn't say where he was going."

It didn't, after all, pay to be too cautious, Amalfi thought wryly. If his brains hadn't been concentrating so exclusively on his feet, he would have detected the fact that only one other pair of feet was with him as soon as Hazleton had begun to catfoot it away.

"He'll be back—I hope," Amalfi said. "Look, friend, what we need is repair work. We've got a bad spindizzy in a hot hold. Can you haul it out and give us a replacement, preferably the newest model you've got?"

The garageman considered it. The problem seemed to appeal to him; his whole expression changed, so thoroughly that he looked almost friendly in his intimate ugliness.

"I've got a Six-R-Six in storage that might do, if you've got the refluxlaminated pediments to mount it on," he said slowly. "If you haven't, I've also a reconditioned B-C-Seven-Seven-Y that hums as sweetly as new. But I've never done any hot hauling before—didn't know spindizzies ever hotted up enough to notice. Anybody on board your burg that can give me a hand on decontamination?"

"Yes, it's all set up and ready to ride. Check the color of our money, and let's get on it."

"It'll take a little time to get a crew together," the garageman said. "By the way, don't let your men wander around. The cops don't like it."

"I'll do my best."

The garageman scampered away, dodging in and out among the idle, rust-tinted machines. Amalfi watched him go, marveling anew at how quickly the born technician can be gulled into forgetting who he's working for, let alone how his work is going to be used. First you mention money—since technies are usually underpaid; you then cap that with a tough and inherently interesting problem— and you have your man. Amalfi was always happy when he met a pragmatist in the enemy's camp.

"Boss——"

Amalfi spun. "Where the hell have you been? Didn't you hear me say that this planet is probably taboo to tourists? If you'd been on hand when you were needed, you'd have heard the 'probably' knocked out of that statement—to say nothing of speeding matters considerably!"

"I'm aware of that," Hazleton said evenly. "I took a calculated risk—something you seem to have forgotten how to do, Amalfi. And it paid off. I've been over to that other city, and found out something that we needed to know. Incidentally, the graving docks around here are a mess. This one, and the one the other city is in, must be the only ones in operation for hundreds of miles. All the rest are nearly full of sand and rust and flaked concrete."

"And the other city?" Amalfi said very quietly.

"It's been garnisheed; there's no doubt about it. It's shabby and deserted. Half of it is being held up by buttressing, and it's got huts pitched in the streets. It's nearly a hulk. There's a crew over there putting it in some sort of operating order, but they're in no hurry, and they aren't doing a damn thing to make the city habitable—all they want it to do is run. It's not the city's own complement, obviously. Where *they* are, I'm afraid to think."

"There's considerable thinking you haven't done," Amalfi said. "The original crew is obviously in debtor's prison. The garage is putting the city in order for some kind of

dirty job that they don't expect it to outlast—and that no
city still free could be hired to do at any price."

"And what would that be?"

"Setting up a planethead on a gas giant," said Amalfi.
"They want to work some low-density, ammonia-methane
world with an ice core, a Jupiter-type planet, that they
can't conquer any other way. It's my guess that they hope
to use such a planethead as an inexhaustible source of
poison gas."

"That's not your only guess," Hazleton said, his lips
thinned. "I expect to be disciplined for wandering off,
Amalfi, but I'm a big boy, and won't have rationalizations
palmed off on me just to keep the myth of your omni-
science going."

"I'm not omniscient," Amalfi said mildly. "I looked at
the other city on the way in. And I looked at the instruments. You didn't. The instruments alone told me that
almost nothing was going on in that city that was normal to
Okie operation. They also told me that its spindizzies were
being turned to produce a field which would burn them
out within a year, and they told me what that field was
supposed to do—what kind of conditions it was supposed
to resist.

"Spindizzy fields will bounce any fast-moving large ag-
gregate of molecules. They won't much impede the passage of gases by osmosis. If you so drive a field as to
exclude the smallest possible molecular exchange, even
under a pressure of more than a million atmospheres, you
destroy the machine. That set of conditions occurs only in
one kind of situation, a situation no Okie would ever
commit himself to for an instant: setting down on a gas
giant. Obviously then, since the city *was* being readied
for that kind of job, it had been garnisheed—it was now
state property, and nobody cares about wasting state
property."

"Once again," Hazleton said, "you might have told me
that in time to prevent my taking my side jaunt. However,
this time it's just as well you didn't, because I still haven't
come to the main thing I discovered. Do you know the
identity of that city?"

"No."

"Good for you for admitting it. I do. It's *the* city we heard about when it was in the building three centuries ago; the so-called all-purpose city. Even under all the junk and decay, the lines are there. These Acolytes are letting it rot where it makes a real difference, just to hot-rod it for one job only. We could take it away from them if we tried. I studied the plans when they were first published, and——"

He stopped. Amalfi turned toward where Hazleton was looking. The garageman was coming back at a dead run. He had a meson pistol in one hand.

"I'm convinced," Amalfi said swiftly. "Can you get over there again without being observed? This looks to me like trouble."

"Yes, I can. There's a——"

"'Yes' is enough for now. Tune our City Fathers to theirs, and set up Standard Situation *N* in both. Cue it to our 'spin' key—straight yes-no signal."

"Situation *N?* Boss, that's a——"

"I know what it is. I think we need it now. Our bum spindizzy prevents us from making any possible getaway without the combined knowledge of the two sets of City Fathers; we just aren't fast enough. Git, before it's too late."

The garageman was almost upon them, emitting screams of fury each time he hit the ground at the end of a leap, as if the sounds were jolted out of him by the impact. In the thin atmosphere of Murphy, the yells sounded like toots on a toy whistle.

Hazleton hesitated a moment more, then sprinted up the stairway. The garageman ducked around a trunnion and fired. The meson pistol howled at the sky and flew backwards out of his hand. Evidently he had never fired one before.

"Mayor Amalfi, shall I——"

"Not yet, sergeant. Cover him, that's all. Hey, you! Walk over here. Nice and slow, with your hands locked behind your head. That's it. . . . Now then: what were you firing at my city manager for?"

The dark-complected face was livid now. "You can't get away," he said thickly. "There's a dozen police squads on the way. They'll break you up for fair. It'll be fun to watch."

"Why?" Amalfi asked, in a reasonable one. "You shot at us first. We've done nothing wrong."

"Nothing but pass a bum check! Around here that's a crime worse than murder, brother. I checked you with Lerner, and he's frothing at the mouth. You'd damn well better pray that some other squad gets to you before his does!"

"A bum check?" Amalfi said. "You're blowing. Our money's better than anything you're using around here, by the looks of you. It's germanium—solid germanium."

"Germanium?" the dockman repeated incredulously.

"That's what I said. It'd pay you to clean your ears more often."

The garageman's eyebrows continued to go higher and higher, and the corners of his mouth began to quiver. Two fat, oily tears ran down his cheeks. Since he still had his hands locked behind his head, he looked remarkably like a man about to throw a fit.

Then his whole face split open.

"Germanium!" He howled. "Ho, haw, haw, haw! *Germanium!* What hole in the plenum have you been living in, Okie? Germanium—haw, *haw!*" He emitted a weak gasp and took his hands down to wipe his eyes. "Haven't you any silver, or gold, or platinum, or tin, or iron? Or something else that's worth something? Clear out, bum. You're broke. Take it from me as a friend, clear out; I'm giving you good advice."

He seemed to have calmed down a little, Amalfi said. "What's wrong with germanium?"

"Nothing," the dockman said, looking at Amalfi over his incredible nose with a mixture of compassion and vindictiveness, "It's a good, useful metal. But it just isn't money any more, Okie. I don't see how you could have missed finding that out. Germanium is trash now—well, no, it's still worth something, but only what it's *actually* worth, if you get me. You have to buy it; you can't buy other things with it.

"It's no good here as money. It's no good anywhere else, either. *Anywhere* else. The whole galaxy is broke. Dead broke.

"And so are you."

He wiped his eyes again. Overhead a siren groaned, softly but urgently.

Hazleton was ready, and had sighted the incoming cops.

Amalfi found it impossible to understand what happened when he closed the "spin" key. He did not hope to understand it at any time in the future, either; and it would do no good to ask the City Fathers, who would simply refuse to tell him—for the very good reason that they did not know. Whatever they had had in reserve for Standard Situation N—that ultimate situation which every Okie city must expect to face eventually, the situation wherein what is necessary to prevent total destruction is only and simply to *get away fast*—it was drastic and unprecedented. Or it had become so when the City Fathers had been given the chance to pool their knowledge with that of the City Fathers of the all-purpose city.

The city snapped from its graving dock on Murphy to a featureless coördinate-set space. The movement took no time and involved no detectable display of energy. One moment the city was on Murphy; Amalfi closed the key, and Murphy had vanished, and Jake was demanding to know where in space the city was. He was told to find out.

The cops had come up on Murphy in fair order, but they had not been given the chance to fire a single shot. When Jake had managed to find Murphy again, O'Brian sent a proxy out to watch the cops, who by that time were shooting back and forth across the planet's sky like belated actors looking for a crucial collar button.

An hour later, without the slightest preliminary activity, the all-purpose city snapped out of existence on Murphy. By the time the garagemen had recovered enough to sound another alarm, the cops were scattered in all directions, still hunting something that they had had no prior idea could turn up missing: Amalfi's own town. By the time they managed to reform their ranks sufficiently to trace the all-purpose city, it had stopped operating, and thus had become undetectable.

It was floating now in an orbit half a million miles away from Amalfi's city. Its screens were down again. If there had been any garagemen on it when it took off, they were dead now; the city was airless.

And the City Fathers honestly did not know how all this had been accomplished; or, rather, they no longer knew. Standard Situation *N* was keyed in by a sealed and self-blowing circuit. It had been set up that way long ago, to prevent incompetent or lazy city administrators from calling upon it at every minor crisis. It could never be used again.

And Amalfi knew that he had called it into use, not only for his own city, but for the other one as well, in a situation which had not really been the ultimate extreme, had not really been Situation *N*. He had squandered the final recourse of both cities.

He was still equally certain that neither city would ever need that circuit again.

The two cities, linked only by an invisible ultraphone tight-beam, were now floating free in the starless area three light years away from the jungle, and eight parsecs away from Murphy. The dim towers of the dead city were not visible to Amalfi, who stood alone on the belfry of City Hall; but they floated in his brain, waiting for him to tell them to come to life.

Whether or not his act of extreme desperation in the face of a not ultimately desperate situation had in actuality murdered that city was a question he could not decide. In the face of the galactic disaster, the question seemed very small.

He shelved it to consider what he had learned about his own bad check. Germanium never had had the enormous worth in real terms that it had had as a treasure metal. It did have properties which made it valuable in many techniques: the germanium lattice would part with an electron at the urging of a comparatively low amount of energy; the *p-n* boundary functioned as a crystal detector; and so on. The metal found its way into uncountable thousands of electronic devices—and, it was rare.

But not *that* rare. Like silver, platinum, and iridium before it, germanium's treasure value had been strictly artificial—an economic convention, springing from myths, jewelers' preferences, and the jealousy of statal monopolies. Sooner or later, some planet or cluster with a high technology—and a consequently high exchange rate—would capture enough of the metal to drive its competitors, or, more likely, its own treasury, off the germanium standard; or someone would learn to synthesize or transmute the element cheaply. It hardly mattered which had happened now.

What mattered was the result. The actual metallic germanium on board the city now had only an eighth of its former value at current rates of sale. Much worse, however, was the fact that most of the city's funds were not metal, but paper: Oc dollars, issued against government-held metal back on Earth and a few other administrative centers. This money, since it did not represent any metallic germanium that belonged to the city, was now unredeemable—valueless.

The new standard was a drug standard. Had the city come away from He with the expected heavy surplus of anti-agathics, it would now have been a multibillionaire. Instead, it was close to being a pauper.

Amalfi wondered how the drug standard had come about. To Okies, cut off for the most part from the main stream of history, such developments frequently seemed like the brainstorms of some unknown single genius; it was hard to think of them as evolving from a set of situations when none of the situations could now be intimately known. Still, however it had arisen, the notion had its point. Drugs can be graded exactly as to value by their therapeutic effect and their availability. Drugs that could be made synthetically in quantity at low cost would be the pennies and nickels of the new coinage—and those that could not, and were rare and always in heavier demand than the supply could meet, would be the hundred-dollar units.

Further, even expensive drugs could be diluted, which would make debt payment flexible; drugs could be as amenable to laboratory test for counterfeit as metal had been; and finally, drugs became outmoded rapidly enough to make for a high-velocity currency which could not be hoarded or cornered, even by the most predatory measures.

It was a good standard. Since it would be impossible to carry on real transactions in terms of fractions of a cubic centimeter of some chemical, just as it had been impractical to carry a ton and a half of germanium about in order to pay one's debts, there would still be a paper currency.

But on the drug standard, the city was poor. It had none of the new paper money at all, though it would, of course, sell all its metallic germanium at once to get a supply. Possibly its germanium-based paper money might also be sold, against Earth redemption, at about a fifth of the current market value of the metallic equivalent if the Acolytes cared to bother with redeeming it.

The actual drugs on board the city could not be traded against. They were necessary to maintain the life of the city. Amalfi winced to think of the size of the bite medical care was going to take out of every individual's budget under the new economy. The anti-agathics, in particular, would pose a terrifying dilemma: shall I use my anti-agathic credits now, as money, to relieve my current money miseries, or shall I continue to live in poverty in order to prolong my life? . . .

Remorselessly, Amalfi drove one consequence after another through the stony corridors of his skull, like a priest wielding the whip behind lowing sacrifices. The city was poor. It could find no work among the Acolyte stars at a rate which would make the work justifiable. It could look for work nowhere else without a new spindizzy.

That left only the jungle. There was no place else to go.

Amalfi had never set down in a jungle before, and the thought made him wipe the palms of his hands unconsciously upon his thighs. The word in his mind—it had always been there, he knew, lying next to the word "jungle"—was *never*. The city must always pay its own way, it must always come whole out of any crisis, it must always pull its own weight. . . .

Those emblems of conduct were now clichés, which *never* had turned out to be a time, like any other time—one that had implicit in it the inevitable timeword: *Now*.

Amalfi picked up the phone which hung from the belfry railing.

"Hazleton?"

"Here, boss. What's the verdict?"

"None yet," Amalfi said. "Supposedly we snitched the

city next door for some purpose; now we need to know what the chances are of abandoning ship at this point and getting out of here with it. Get some men in suits over there and check on it."

Hazleton did not answer for a moment. In that moment, Amalfi knew that the question was peripheral, and that the verdict was already in. A line by the Earth poet Theodore Roethke crept across the floor of his brain like a salamander: *The edge cannot eat the center*.

"Right," Hazleton's voice said.

Half an eternal hour later. it added: "Boss, that city is worse off than we are, I'm afraid. It's got good drivers still, but of course they're all tuned wrong. Besides, the whole place seems to be structurally unsound on a close look; the garagemen really did a thorough job of burrowing around in it. Among other things, the keel's cracked—the Acolytes must have landed it, not the original crew."

It would, of course, be impossible to claim foreknowledge of any of this, with Hazleton's present state of mind teetering upon the edge of some rebellion Amalfi hoped he did not yet understand. It was possible that Hazleton, despite all the mayor's precautions, had divined the load of emotional guilt which had been accumulating steadily upon Amalfi—or perhaps that suspicion was only the guilt itself speaking. In any event, Amalfi had allowed himself to be stampeded into stealing the other city by Hazleton, even in the face of the foreknowledge, to keep peace in the family. He said instead, "What's your recommendation, Mark?"

"I'd cast loose from it, boss. I'm only sorry I advocated snitching it in the first place. We have the only thing it had to give us that we could make our own: our City Fathers now know everything their City Fathers knew. We couldn't take anything else but a new spindizzy, and that's a job for a graving dock."

"All right. Give it a point thirty-four percent screen to clinch its present orbit, and come on back. Make sure you don't give it more than that, or those overtuned spindizzies will advertise its position to anyone coming within two parsecs of it, and interfere with our own operation to boot."

"Right."

And now there were the local cops to be considered. They had chalked up against Amalfi's city, not only the issuing of a bad check, but the theft of state property, and the deaths of Acolyte technicians on board the other city.

Only the jungle was safe, and even the jungle was safe only temporarily. In the jungle, at least for the time being, one city could lose itself among three hundred others—many of which would be better armed than Amalfi's city had ever been.

There might even be a chance, in such a salmon-pack of cities, that Amalfi would see at last with his own eyes the mythical Vegan orbital fort—the sole nonhuman construction ever to go Okie, and now the center of an enormous saga of exploits woven about it by the starmen. Amalfi was as fascinated by the legend as any other Okie, though he knew the meager facts well: the fort had circled Vega until the smashing of the Confederacy's home planet, and then—unexpectedly, since the Vegans had never been given to flying anything bigger than a battleship—had taken off for parts unknown, smashing its way through the englobement of police cruisers almost instantly. Nothing had ever been heard of it since, although the legend grew and grew.

The Vegans themselves had been anything but an attractive people, and it was difficult to say why the story of the orbital fort was so beloved with the Okies. Of course, Okies generally disliked the cops and said that they had no love for Earth, but this hardly explained why the legend of the fort was so popular among them. The fort was now said to be invulnerable and unlimited; it had done miracles in every limb of the galaxy; it was everywhere and nowhere; it was the Okies' Beowulf, their Cid, their Sigurd, Gawaine, Roland, Cuchulainn, Prometheus, Lemminkainen . . .

Amalfi felt a sudden chill. The thought that had just come to him was so outrageous that he had almost stopped thinking it in the middle, out of sheer instinct. The fort—probably it had been destroyed centuries ago. But if it did still exist, certain conclusions emerged implacably, and certain actions could be taken on them. . . .

Yes, it was possible. It was possible. And definitely worth trying. . . .

But if it actually worked . . .

Having made the decision, Amalfi put the idea resolutely aside. In the meantime, one thing was sure: as long as the Acolytes continued to use the jungle as a labor pool, their cops would not risk smashing things up indiscriminately only in order to search out one single "criminal" city. To the Acolyte's way of thinking, all Okies were lawbreakers, by definition.

Which, Amalfi thought, was quite correct as far as his own city was concerned. The city was not only a bum now, but a bindlestiff to boot—by definition.

The end of the line.

"Boss? I'm coming in. What's the dodge? We'll need to pull it soon, or——"

Amalfi looked up steadily at the red dwarf star above the balcony.

"There is no dodge," he said. "We're licked, Mark. We're going to the jungle."

CHAPTER SIX: The Jungle

The cities drifted along their sterile orbits around the little red sun. Here and there, a few showed up on the screen by their riding lights, but most of them could not spare even enough power to keep riding lights going. The lights were vital in such close-packed quarters, but power to maintain spindizzy screens was more important still.

Only one city glowed—not with its riding lights, which were all out, but by street lighting. That city had power to waste, and it wanted the fact known. And it wanted it known, too, that it preferred to waste the power in sheer bragging to the maintenance of such elementary legalities as riding lights.

Amalfi looked soberly at the image of the bright city. It was not a very clear image, since the bright city was in a preferred position close to the red dwarf, where that sun's natural and unboundable gravitational field strained the structure of space markedly. The saturation of the intervening area with the smaller screens of the other Okies made the seeing still worse, since Amalfi's own city had been unable to press through the pack beyond eighteen AU's from the sun, a distance about equivalent to that from Sol to Uranus. For Amalfi, consequently, the red dwarf was visually only a star of the tenth magnitude—the G_0 star four light years away seemed much closer.

But obviously, three hundred-odd Okie cities could not all huddle close enough to a red dwarf to derive any warmth from it. Somebody had to be on the outside. It was equally obvious, and expectable, that the city with the most power available to it should be the one drawn up the most cosily to the dull stellar fire, while those who most needed to conserve every erg shivered in the outer blackness.

What *was* surprising was that the bright city should be advertising its defiance of local law and common sense alike—while police-escorted Acolyte ships were shoving their way into the heart of the jungle.

Amalfi looked up at the screen banks. For the second time within the year, he was in a chamber of City Hall which was almost never used. This one was the ancient reception hall, which had been fitted with a screen system of considerable complexity about five hundred and eighty years ago, just after the city had first taken to space. It was called into service only when the city was approaching a heavily developed, highly civilized star system, in order to carry on the multiple negotiations with various diplomatic, legal, and economic officials which had to be gone through before an Okie could hope to deal with such a system. Certainly Amalfi had never expected to have any use for the reception hall in a jungle.

There was a lot, he thought grimly, that he didn't know about living in an Okie jungle.

One of the screens came alight. It showed the full-length figure of a woman in sober clothing of an old style, utilitarian in cut, but obviously made of perishable materials. The woman inside the clothes was hard-eyed, but not hard of muscle, an Acolyte trader, evidently.

"The assignment," the trader said in a cold voice, "is a temporary development project on Hern Six, as announced previously. We can take six cities there, to be paid upon a per-job basis."

"Attention, Okies."

A third screen faded in. Even before the image had stabilized in the locally distorted space-lattice, Amalfi recognized its outlines. The general topology of a cop can seldom be blurred by distortion of any kind. He was only mildly surprised to find, when the face came through, that the police spokesman was Lieutenant Lerner, the man whose bribe had turned to worthless germanium in his hands.

"If there's any disorder, nobody gets hired," Lerner said. "Nobody. Understand? You'll present your offers to the lady in proper fashion, and she'll take or leave your bids as she sees fit. Those of you who are wanted outside the jungle will be held accountable if you leave the jungle— we're offering no immunities this trip. And if there's any damn insolence——"

Lieutenant Lerner's image drew its forefinger across its throat in a gesture that somehow had never lost its specificity. Amalfi growled and switched off the audio; Lerner was still talking, as was the trader, but now another screen was coming on, and Amalfi had to know what words were to come from it. The speeches of the trader and the cop could be predicted almost positively in advance—as a matter of fact, the City Fathers had already handed Amalfi the predictions, and he had listened to the actual speeches only long enough to check them for barely possible unknowns.

But what the bright city near the red dwarf—the jungle's boss, the king of the hobos—would say . . .

Not even Amalfi, let alone the City Fathers, could know that in advance. Lieutenant Lerner and the trader worked their mouths soundlessly while the wavering shadow on the fourth screen jelled. A slow, heavy, brutally confident voice was already in complete possession of the reception hall.

"Nobody takes any offer less than sixty," it said. "The class *A* cities will ask one hundred and twenty-four for the Hern Six job, and grade *B* cities don't get to underbid them until the goddam trader has all the *A*'s she'll take. If she picks all six from the *A*'s, that's tough. No *C*'s are to bid at all on the Hern Six deal. We'll take care of anybody that breaks ranks, either right away . . ."

The image came through. Amalfi goggled at it.

" . . . or after the cops leave. That's all for now."

The image faded. The twisted, hairless man in the ancient metal-mesh cape stood in Amalfi's memory for quite a while afterwards.

The Okie King was a man made of lava. Perhaps he had been born at one time, but now he looked like a geological accident, a column of black stone sprung from a fissure and contorted roughly into the shape of a man.

And his face was shockingly disfigured and scarred by the one disease that still remained unconquered, unsolved, though it no longer killed.

Cancer.

A voice murmured inside Amalfi's head, coming from the tiny vibrator imbedded in the mastoid bone behind the mayor's right ear. "That's just what the City Fathers said he would say," Hazleton commented softly from his post uptown in the control tower. "But he can't be as naïve as all that. He's an old-timer; been aloft since back before they knew how to polarize spindizzy screens against cosmic radiation. Must be eight hundred years old at a minimum."

"You can lay up a lot of cunning in that length of time," Amalfi agreed in a similarly low voice. He was wearing throat mikes under a high military collar. As far as the screens were concerned, he was standing motionless, silent, and alone; though he was an expert at talking without moving his lips, he did not try to do so now, for the fuzziness of local transmission conditions made it unlikely that his murmuring would be detected. "It doesn't seem likely that he means what he says. But we'd best sit tight for the moment."

He glanced into the auxiliary battle tank, a three-dimensional chart in which color-coded points of lights moved, showing each city, the nearby sun, and the Acolyte vessels, not to scale, but in their relative positions. The tank was camouflaged as a desk and could be seen into only from behind; hence it was out of sight of any eye but Amalfi's. In it the Acolyte force showed itself to consist of one trader's ship and four police craft; one of the latter was a command cruiser, very probably Lerner's, and the others were light cruisers.

It was not much of a force, but then, there was no real

need for a full squadron here. With a minimum of organization, the Okies could run Lerner and his ward out of the jungle, even at some cost to their own numbers—but where would the Okies run to after Lerner had yelled for navy support? The question answered itself.

A string of twenty-three small "personal" screens came on now, high up along the curve of the far wall. Twenty-three faces looked down at Amalfi—the mayors of all but one of the class A cities in the jungle; Amalfi's own city was the twenty-fourth. Amalfi valved the main audio gain back up again.

"Are we ready to begin?" the Acolyte woman said. "I've got codes here for twenty-four cities, and I see you're all here. Small courage among Okies these days—twenty-four out of three hundred of you for a simple job like this! That's the attitude that made Okies of you in the first place. You're afraid of honest work."

"We'll work," the King's voice said. His screen, however, remained gray-green. "Look over the codes and take your pick."

The trader looked for the voice. "No insolence," she said sharply. "Or I'll ask for volunteers from the grade B's. It would save me money, anyhow."

There was no reply. The trader frowned and looked at the code list in her hand. After a moment, she called off three numbers, and then, with greater hesitation, a fourth. Four of the screens above Amalfi went blank, and in the tank, four green flecks began to move outward from the red dwarf star.

"That's all we need for Hern Six except for a pressure job," the woman said slowly. "There are eight cities listed here as pressure specialists. You there—who are you, anyhow?"

"Bradley-Vermont," one of the faces above Amalfi said.

"What would you ask for a pressure job?"

"One hundred and twenty-four," Bradley-Vermont's mayor said sullenly.

"O-ho! You've a high opinion of yourself, haven't you? You may as well float here and rot for a while longer, until you learn something more about the law of supply and demand. You—you're Dresden-Saxony, it says here. What's your price? Remember, I only need one."

Dresden-Saxony's mayor was a slight man with high cheekbones and glittering black eyes. He seemed to be enjoying himself, despite his obvious state of malnutrition; at least, he was smiling a little, and his eyes glittered over the dark shadows which made them look large.

"We ask one hundred and twenty-four," he said with malicious indifference.

The woman's lids slitted. "You do, eh? That's a coincidence, isn't it? And you?"

"The same," the third mayor said, though with obvious reluctance.

The trader swung around and pointed directly at Amalfi. In the very old cities, such as the one the King operated, it would be impossible to tell who she was pointing at, but probably most of the cities in the jungle had compensating tri-di. "What's your town?"

"We're not answering that question," Amalfi said. "And we're not pressure specialists anyhow."

"I know that, I can read a code. But you're the biggest Okie I've ever seen, and I'm not talking about your belly either; and you're modern enough for the purpose. The job is yours for one hundred—no more."

"Not interested."

"You're a fool as well as a fat man. You just came into this hellhole and there are charges against——"

"Ah, you know who we are. Why did you ask?"

"Never mind that. You don't know what a jungle is like until you've lived in it. You'd be smart to take the job and get out now while you can. You'd be worth one hundred and twelve to me if you could finish the job under the estimated time."

"You've denied us immunity," Amalfi said, "and you needn't bother offering it, either. We're not interested in pressure work for any price."

The woman laughed. "You're a liar, too. You know as well as I do that nobody arrests Okies on jobs. And you wouldn't find it difficult to leave the job once it's finished. Here now—I'll give you one hundred and twenty. That's my top offer, and it's only four less than the pressure experts are asking. Fair enough?"

"It may be fair enough," Amalfi said. "But we don't do pressure work; and we've already gotten in reports from the proxies we sent to Hern Six as soon as Lieutenant Lerner said that was where the job was. We don't like the look of it. We don't want it. We won't take it at one hundred and twenty, we won't take it at one hundred and twenty-four—and we won't take it at all. Understand?"

"Very well," the woman said with concentrated viciousness. "You'll hear from me again, Okie."

The King was looking at Amalfi with an unreadable, but certainly unfriendly, expression. If Amalfi's guess was right, the King thought Amalfi was somewhat overdoing Okie solidarity. It might also be occurring to him that the expression of so much independence might be a bid for power within the jungle itself. Yes, Amalfi was sure that that, at least, had occurred to the King.

The hiring of the class *B* cities was now all that remained, but nevertheless it took quite a while to get started. The woman, it emerged, was more than a trader; she was an entrepreneur of some importance. She wanted the cities, twenty of them, each for the same identical piece of dirty work: working low-grade carnotite lies on a small planet too near a hot star. Twenty mining cities working upon such a planet would reduce it to as small and sculptured a lump of trash as a meteorite before very many months. The method, obviously, was to get the work done fast without paying more than a pittance for it.

Then, startlingly, while the woman was still making up her mind, the voice came through. It was weak and indistinct, and without any face to go with it.

"We'll take the job. Take us."

There was a murmuring from the screens, and across some of the faces there the same shadow seemed to run. Amalfi checked the tank, but it told him little. The signal had been too weak. All that could be made certain was that the voice belonged to some city far out on the periphery of the jungle—a city desperate for energy.

The Acolyte woman seemed momentarily nonplussed. Even in a jungle, Amalfi thought grimly, some crude rules had to be observed; evidently the woman realized that to take on the volunteer before interviewing the others might be—resented.

"Keep out of this," the voice of the King said, so much more slowly and heavily than before that its weight was almost tangible upon the air. "Let the lady do her own picking. She's got no use for a class C outfit."

"We'll take the job. We're a mining town from way back, and we can refine the stuff, too, by gaseous diffusion, mass spectrography, mass chromatography, whatever's asked. We can handle it. And we've got to have it."

"So do the rest," the King said, coldly unimpressed. "Take your turn."

"We're dying out here! Hunger, cold, thirst, disease!"

"Others are in the same state. Do you think any of us like it here? Wait your turn!"

"All right," the woman said suddenly. "I'm sick of being told who I do and who I don't want. Anything to get this over with. File your coördinates, whoever that is out there, and——"

"File your coördinates and we'll have a Dirac torpedo there before you've stopped talking!" the King roared. "Acolyte, what are you paying for this rock-heaving? Nobody here works for less than sixty—that's flat."

"We'll go for fifty-five."

The woman smiled an unpleasant smile. "Apparently somebody in this pest area is glad of a chance to do some honest work for a change. Who's next?"

"Hell, you don't need to take a class C city," one of the rejected class A's blurted. "We'll go for fifty-five. What can we lose?"

"Then we'll take fifty," the outsider whispered immediately.

"You'll take a bolt in the teeth! As for you—you're Coquilhatville-Congo, eh?—you're going to be sorry you ever had a tongue to flap."

There was already a stir among the green dots in the tank. Some of the larger cities were leaving their orbits. The woman began to look vaguely alarmed.

"Hazleton!" Amalfi murmured quickly. "This is going to get worse before it gets better. Set us up, as fast as you can, to move into one of the vacated orbits close to the red star the moment I give the word."

"We won't be able to put on any speed——"

"I wouldn't want us to if we could. It'll have to be done slowly enough so that it won't be apparent in any tank that we're moving counter to the general tendency. Also, get me a fix on that outfit on the outside that broke ranks if you possibly can. If you can't do it without attracting attention, drop the project at once."

"Right."

"By Hadjjii's nightshirt you've got a lesson coming!" the woman was exclaiming. "The whole deal is off for today. No jobs, not for anybody. I'll come back in a week. Maybe by then you'll have some common sense back. Lieutenant, let's get the hell out of here."

That, however, proved to be a difficult assignment. There was a sort of wave front of heavy-duty cities between the Acolyte ships and open space, expanding outward into the darkness where the weaklings shivered. In that second frigid shell most of the class *C* cities were panicking; and, still farther out, the brilliant green sparks of the cities whose promised jobs had just been written off were plunging angrily back toward the main cloud.

The reception hall was a bedlam of voices, mostly those of mayors trying to establish that *they* had not been responsible for the break in the wage line. Somewhere several cities were still attempting to shout new bids to the Acolyte woman under cover of the confusion. Through it all the voice of the King whirled like a bull-roarer.

"Clear the sky!" Lerner shouted. "Clear it up out there, by——"

As if in response, the tank suddenly crackled with hairthin sapphire tracers. The static of the scattered mesotron rifle fire rattled audio speakers, cross-hatched the desperate, shouting faces on the screens. Terror, the terror of a man who finds suddenly that the situation he is in has always been deadly, turned Lieutenant Lerner's features rigid. Amalfi saw him reach for something.

"All right, Hazleton, *spin!*"

The defective spindizzy sobbed, and the city moved painfully. Lerner's elbow jerked back toward his midriff, and from his ship came the pale guide light of a Bethé blaster.

Seconds later, something went up in the white agony of a fusion explosion—something so far off from the center of the riot that Amalfi first thought, with a shock of fury, that Lerner had undertaken to destroy Okie cities unselectively, simply to terrorize. Then the look on Lerner's face told him that the shot had been fired at random. Lerner was as taken aback as Amalfi, and seemingly for much the same reasons, at the death of the unknown bystander.

The depth of the response surprised Amalfi anew. Perhaps there was hope for Lerner yet.

Some incredible fool of an Okie was firing on the cop now, but the shots fell short; mesotron rifles were not primarily military instruments, and the Acolytes had almost worked free of the jungle. For a moment Amalfi was afraid that Lerner would fling a few vindictive Bethé blasts back into the pack, but evidently the cop was recovering the residue of his good sense; at least, no more shots came from the command cruiser. It was possible that he had realized that any further exchange of fire would turn the incident from a minor brawl to a mob uprising which would make it necessary to call in the Acolyte navy.

Not even the Acolytes could want that, for it would end in cutting off their supply of skilled labor.

The city's spindizzies cut out. Lurid, smoky scarlet light leaked down the stone stairwell which led out of the reception hall to the belfry.

"We're parked near the stinking little star, boss. We're less than a million miles out from the orbit of the King's own city."

"Good work, Mark. Break out a gig. We're going calling."

"All right. Anything special in the way of equipment?"

"Equipment?" Amalfi said, slowly. "Well—no. But you'd best bring Sergeant Anderson along. And Mark——"

"Yes?"

"Bring Dee, too."

The center of government of the King's city was enormously impressive: ancient, stately, marmoreal. It was surrounded on a lower level by a number of lesser structures of equally heavy-handed beauty. One of these was a heavy, archaic cantilever bridge for which Amalfi could postulate no use at all; it spanned an enormously broad avenue which divided the city in two, an avenue which was virtually untraveled; the bridge, too, carried only foot traffic now, and not much of that.

He decided finally that the bridge had been retained only out of respect to history. These seemed to be no other sentiment which fitted it, since the normal mode of transportation in the King's city, as in every other Okie city, was by aircab. Like the City Hall, the bridge was beautiful; possibly that had spoken for its retention, too.

The cab rocked slightly and grounded. "Here we are, gentlemen," the Tin Cabby said. "Welcome to Buda-Pesht."

Amalfi followed Dee and Hazleton out onto the plaza. Other cabs, many of them, dotted the red sky, homing on the palace and settling near by.

"Looks like a conclave," Hazleton said. "Guests from outside, not just managerial people inside this one city; otherwise, why the welcome from the cabby?"

"That's my guess, too, and I think we're none too early for it, either. It's my theory that the King is in for a rough time from his subjects. This shoot-up with Lerner, and the loss of jobs for everybody, must have lowered his stock considerably. If so, it'll give us an opening."

"Speaking of which," Hazleton said, "where's the entrance to this tomb, anyhow? Ah—that must be it."

They hurried through the shadows of the pillared portico. Inside, in the foyer, hunched or striding figures moved past them toward the broad, ancient staircase, or gathered in small groups, murmuring urgently in the opulent dimness. This entrance hall was marvelous with chandeliers; they did not cast much light, but they shed glamour like a molting peacock.

Someone plucked Amalfi by the sleeve. He looked down. A slight man with a worn Slavic face and black eyes which looked alive with suppressed mischief stood at his side.

"This place makes me homesick," the slight man said, "although we don't go in for quite so much sheer mass on my town. I believe you're the mayor who refused all offers, on behalf of a city with no name. I'm correct, am I not?"

"You are," Amalfi said, studying the figure with difficulty in the ceremonial dimness. "And you're the mayor of Dresden-Saxony: Franz Specht. What can we do for you?"

"Nothing, thank you. I simply wanted to make myself known. It may be that you will need to know someone, inside." He nodded in the direction of the staircase. "I admired your stand today, but there may be some who resent it. Why is your city nameless, by the way?"

"It isn't," Amalfi said. "But we sometimes need to use our name as a weapon, or at least as a lever. We hold it in reserve as such."

"A weapon! Now that is something to ponder. I will see you later, I hope." Specht slipped away abruptly, a shadow among shadows. Hazleton looked at Amalfi with evident puzzlement.

"What's his angle, boss? Backing a long shot, maybe?"

"That would be my guess. Anyhow, as he says, we can probably use a friend in this mob. Let's go on up."

In the great hall, which had been the throne room of an empire older than any Okie, older even than space flight, there was already a meeting in progress. The King himself was standing on the dais, enormously tall, bald, scarred, terrific, as shining black as anthracite. Ancient as he was, his antiquity was that of some, featureless, eventless, an antiquity without history against the rich backdrop of his city. He was anything but an expectable mayor of Buda-Pesht; Amalfi strongly suspected that there were recent bloodstains on the city's log.

Nevertheless, the King held the rebellious Okies under control without apparent effort. His enormous gravelly voice roared down about their heads like a rockslide, overwhelming them all with its raw momentum alone. The occasional bleats of protest from the floor sounded futile and damned against it, like the voices of lambs objecting to the inevitable avalanche.

"So you're mad!" he was thundering. "You got roughed up a little and now you're looking for somebody to blame it on! Well, I'll tell you who to blame it on! I'll tell you what to do about it, too. And by God, when I'm through telling you, you'll *do* it, the whole pack of you!"

Amalfi pushed through the restive, close-packed mayors

and city managers, putting his bull shoulders to good use. Hazleton and Dee, hand in hand, tailed him closely. The Okies on the floor grumbled as Amalfi shoved his way forward; but they were so bound up in the King's diatribe, and in their own fierce, unformulated resistance to the King's battering-ram leadership tactics, that they could spare nothing more than a moment's irritation for Amalfi's passage among them.

"Why are we hanging around here now, getting pushed around by these Acolyte hicks?" the King roared. "You're fed with it. All right, I'm fed with it, too. I wouldn't take it from the beginning! When I came here, you guys were bidding each other down to peanuts. When the bidding was over, the city that got the job lost money on it every time. It was me that showed you how to organize. It was me that showed you how to stand up for your rights. It was me that showed you how to form a wage line, and how to hold one. And it's going to be me that'll show you what to do when a wage line breaks up."

Amalfi reached behind him, caught Dee's hand, and drew her forward to stand beside him. They were now in the front row of the crowd, almost up against the dais. The King saw the movement; he paused and looked down. Amalfi felt Dee's hand tighten spasmodically upon his. He returned the pressure.

"All right," Amalfi said. When he was willing to let his voice out, he could fill a considerable space with it. He let it out. "Show, or shut up."

The King, who had been looking directly down at them, made a spasmodic movement—almost as if he had been about to take one step backwards. "Who the hell are you?" he shouted.

"I'm the mayor of the only city that held the line today," Amalfi said. He did not seem to be shouting, but somehow his voice was no smaller in the hall than the King's. A quick murmur went through the mob, and Amalfi could see necks craning in his direction. "We're the newest—and the biggest—city here, and this is the first sample we've seen of the way you run this wage bidding. We think it stinks. We'll see the Acolytes in hell before we take their jobs at *any* of the prices they offer, let alone the low pay levels you set."

Someone nearby turned and looked at Amalfi slantwise. "Evidently you folks can eat space," the Okie said dryly.

"We eat food. We won't eat slops," Amalfi growled. "You up there on the platform—let's hear this great plan for getting us out of this mess. It couldn't be any worse than the wage-line system—that's a cinch."

The King began to pace. He whirled as Amalfi finished speaking, arms akimbo, feet apart, his shiny bald cranium thrust forward, gleaming blankly against the faded tapestries.

"I'll let you hear it," he roared. "You bet I'll let you hear it. Let's see what your big talk comes to after you know what it is. You can stay behind and try to work boom-time wages out of the Acolytes if you want; but if you've guts, you'll go with us."

"Where to?" Amalfi said calmly.

"We're going to march on Earth."

There was a brief, stunned silence. Then a composite roar began to grow in the hall.

Amalfi grinned. The sound of the response was not exactly friendly.

"Wait!" the King bellowed, "Wait, dammit! I ask you— what's the sense in our fighting the Acolytes? They're just local trash. They know just as well as we do that they couldn't get away with their slave-market tactics and their private militia and their shoot-ups if Earth had an eye on 'em."

"Then why don't we holler for the Earth cops?" someone demanded.

"Because they wouldn't come here. They can't. There must be Okies all over the galaxy that are taking stuff from local systems and clusters, stuff like what we're taking. This depression is everywhere, and there just aren't enough Earth cops to be all over the place at once.

"But we don't have to take it. We can go to Earth and demand our rights. We're citizens, every one of us—unless there are any Vegans here. You a Vegan, buddy?"

The scarred face stared down at Amalfi, smiling gruesomely. A nervous titter went through the hall.

"The rest of us can go to Earth and demand that the

government bail us out. What else is government for, anyhow? Who produces the money that kept the politicians fat all through the good centuries? What would the government have to govern and tax and penalize if it weren't for the Okies? Answer me that, you with the orbital fort under your belt!"

The laughter was louder and sounded more assured now. Amalfi, however, was quite used to gibes at his pod; such thrusts were for him a sure sign that his current opponent had run out of pertinent things to say. He returned coldly: "More than half of us had charges against us when we came here—not local charges, but violations of Earth orders of one kind or another. Some of us have been dodging being brought back on our Violations dockets for decades. Are you going to offer yourselves to the Earth cops on a platter?"

The King did not appear to be listening with more than half an ear. He had brought up a broad grin at the second wave of laughter, and had been looking back down at Dee for admiration.

"We'll send out a call on the Dirac," he said. "To all Okies, everywhere. 'We're all going back to Earth,' we'll say. 'We're going home to get an accounting. We've done Earth's heavy labor all over the galaxy, and Earth's paid us by turning our money into waste paper. We're going home to see that Earth does something about it'—we'll set a date—'and any Okie with starman's guts will follow us.' How does that sound, eh?"

Dee's grip on Amalfi's hand was now tighter than any pressure he would have believed she could exert. Amalfi did not speak to the King; he simply looked back at him, his eyes metallic.

From somewhere fairly far back in the throne room, a newly familiar voice called, "The mayor of the nameless city has asked a pertinent question. From the point of view of Earth, we're a dangerous collection of potential criminals at worst. At best we're discontented jobless people, and undesirable in large numbers anywhere near the home planet."

Hazleton pushed up to the front row, on the other side

of Dee, and glared belligerently up at the King. The King, however, had looked away again, over Hazleton's head.

"Anybody got a better idea?" the immense black man said dryly. "Here's good old Vega down here; he's full of ideas. Let's hear his idea. I'll bet it's colossal. I'll just bet he's a genius, this Vegan."

"Get up there, boss," Hazleton hissed. "You've got 'em!"

Amalfi released Dee's hand—he had some difficulty in being gentle about it—bounded clumsily but without real effort onto the dais, and turned to face the crowd.

"Hey there, mister," someone shouted. "You're no Vegan!"

The crowd laughed uneasily.

"Never said I was," Amalfi retorted. Hazleton's face promptly fell. "Are you all a pack of children? No mythical fort is going to bail you out of this. Neither is any fool mass flight on Earth. There isn't any easy way out. There *is* one tough way out, if you've got the guts for it."

"Let's hear it."

"Speak up!"

"Let's get it over with."

"All right," Amalfi said. He walked back to the immense throne of the Hapsburgs and sat down in it, catching the King flatfooted. Standing, Amalfi, despite his bulk, was a smaller man than the King, but on the throne he made the King look not only smaller but also quite irrelevant. From the back of the dais, his voice boomed out as powerfully as before.

"Gentlemen," he said, "our germanium is worthless now. So is our paper money. Even the work we do doesn't seem to be worthwhile now, on any standard. That's our trouble, and there isn't much that Earth can do about it—they're caught in the collapse, too."

"A professor," the King said, his seamed lips twisting.

"Shaddap. You asked me up here. I'm staying up here until I've had my say. The commodity we all have to sell is labor. Hand labor, heavy work, isn't worth anything. Machines can do that. But brainwork can't be done with anything but brains; art and pure science are beyond the compass of any machine.

"Now, we can't sell art. We can't produce it; we aren't

artists and aren't set up as such; there's an entirely different segment of galactic society that supplies that heed. But brainwork in pure science is something we can sell, just as we've always sold brainwork in applied sciences. If we play our cards right, we can sell it anywhere, for any price we ask, regardless of the money system involved. It's the ultimate commodity, and in the long run it's a commodity which no one but the Okies could merchandise successfully.

"Selling that commodity, we could take over the Acolytes or any other star system. We could do it better in a general depression than we could ever have done it before, because we can now set any price on it that we choose."

"Prove it," somebody called.

"That's easy. We have here around three hundred cities. Let's integrate and use their accumulated knowledge. This is the first time in history that so many City Fathers have been gathered together in one place, just as it's the first time that so many big organizations specializing in different sciences have ever been gathered together. If we were to consult with each other, pool our intellectual resources, we'd come out technologically at least a thousand years ahead of the rest of the galaxy. Individual experts can be bought for next to nothing now, but no individual expert—*nor any individual city or planet*— could match what we'd have.

"That's the priceless coin, gentlemen, the universal coin: human knowledge. Look now: there are eighty-five million undeveloped worlds in this galaxy ready to pay for knowledge of the *current* vintage, the kind we all share right now, the kind that runs about a century behind Earth on the average. But if we were to pool our knowledge, then even the most advanced planets, even Earth itself, would see their coinages crumble in the face of their eagerness to buy what we would have to offer."

"Question!"

"You're Dresden-Saxony back there, right?" Amalfi said. "Go ahead, Mayor Specht."

"Are you sure accumulated technology *is* the answer? You yourself said that straight techniques are the province of machines. The ancient Gödel-Church theorems show

Specht's voice said, "Buda-Pesht, you're trying to drum up a stampede. The question isn't closed yet."

"All right," the King agreed. "I'm willing to be reasonable. Let's take a vote."

"We aren't ready for a vote yet. The question is still open."

"Well?" said the King. "You there on the overstuffed potty—you got anything more to say? Are you as afraid of a vote as Specht is?"

Amalfi got up with deliberate slowness.

"I've made my points, and I'll abide by the voting," he said, "if it's physically possible for us to do so—our spindizzy equipment wouldn't tolerate an immediate flight to Earth if the voting goes that way. I've made my point. A mass flight to Earth would be suicide."

"One moment," Specht's voice cut in again. "Before we vote, I for one want to know who it is that has been advising us. Buda-Pesht we know. But—*who are you?*"

There was instant dead silence in the throne room.

The question was loaded, as everyone in the hall knew. Prestige among Okies depended, in the long run, upon only two things: time aloft and coups recorded by the interstellar grapevine. Amalfi's city stood high on both tallies; he had only to identify his city, and he would stand at least an even chance of carrying the voting. Even while nameless, for that matter, the city had earned considerable kudos in the jungle.

Evidently Hazleton thought so, too, for Amalfi could see the frantic covert hand signals he was making. *Tell 'em, boss. It can't miss. Tell 'em!*

After a long, suspended heartbeat, the mayor said, "My name is John Amalfi, Mayor Specht."

A single broad comber of contempt rolled through the hall.

"Asked and answered," the King said, showing his ragged teeth. "Glad to have you aboard, Mister Amalfi. Now if you'll get the hell off the platform, we'll get on with the voting. But don't be in any hurry to leave town, Mister Amalfi. I want to talk to you, man to man. Understand?"

"Yeah," Amalfi said. He swung his huge bulk lightly to

the floor of the hall, and walked back to where Dee and Hazleton were standing, hand in hand.

"Boss, why didn't you tell 'em?" Hazleton whispered, his face hard. "Or did you *want* to throw the whole show away? You had two beautiful chances, and you muffed 'em both!"

"Of course I muffed them. I came here to muff them. I came here to dynamite them, as a matter of fact. Now you and Dee had better get out of here before I have to give Dee to the King in order to get back to our city at all."

"You staged that, too, John," Dee said. It was not an accusation; it was simply a statement of fact.

"I'm afraid I did," Amalfi said. "I'm sorry, Dee; it had to be done, or I wouldn't have done it. I was also sure that I could fox the King on that point, if that's any consolation to you. Now move, or you will be sunk. Mark, make plenty of noise about getting away."

"What about you?" Dee said.

"I'll be along later. Git!"

Hazleton stared at Amalfi a moment longer. Then he turned and pushed back through the crowd, the frightened, reluctant girl at his heels. His method of being very noisy was characteristic of him: he was so completely silent that everyone within sight of him knew that he was making a getaway; even his footsteps made no sound at all. In the surging hall his noiselessness was as conspicuous as a siren in church.

Amalfi stood his ground long enough to let the King see that the principal hostage was still on hand, still obeying the letter of the King's order. Then, the moment the King's attention was distracted, he faded, moving with the local current in the crowd, bending his knees slightly to reduce his height, tipping his head back to point his conspicuous baldness away from the dias, and making only the normal amount of sound as he moved—becoming, in short, effectively invisible.

By this time the voting was in full course, and it would be five minutes at the least before the King could afford to interrupt it long enough to order the doors closed against Amalfi. After Hazleton's and Dee's ostentatiously alarmed exists, an emergency order in the middle of the voting would have made it painfully obvious what the King was after.

Of course, had the King had the foresight to equip himself with a personal transmitter before mounting the dais, the outcome might have been different. The King's failure to do so strengthened Amalfi's conviction that the King had not been mayor of Buda-Pesht long, and that he had not won the post by the usual processes.

But Dee and Hazleton would get out all right. So would Amalfi. On this limited subject, Amalfi had been six jumps ahead of the King all the way.

Amalfi drifted toward the part of the crowd from where, roughly, he estimated that the voice of the mayor of Dresden-Saxony had been coming. He found the worn, birdlike Slav without difficulty.

"You keep a tight holster-flap on your weapons," Specht said in a low voice.

"Sorry to disappoint you, Mayor Specht. You set it up beautifully. It might cheer you up a bit to know that the question *was* just the right one, all the same, and many thanks for it. In return I owe you the answer; are you good at riddles?"

"Riddles?"

"*Raetseln,*" Amalfi translated.

"Oh—conundrums. No, but I can try."

"What city has two names twice?"

Evidently Specht did not need to be good at riddles to come up with the answer to that one. His jaw dropped. "You're N——" he began.

Amalfi held up his hand in the conventional Okie FYI sign: "For your information *only.*" Specht gulped and nodded. With a grin, Amalfi drifted on out of the palace.

There was a lot of hard work still ahead, but from now on it should be all downhill. The "march" on Earth would be carried in the voting.

Nothing essential remained to be done now in the jungle but to turn the march into a stampede.

By the time he reached his own city, Amalfi found he was suddenly intensely tired. He berthed the second gig Hazleton had had the perimeter sergeant send for him and went directly to his room, where he ordered his supper sent up.

This last move, he was forced to conclude, had been a mistake. The city's stores were heavily diminished, and the table that was set for him—set, as it would have been for anyone else in the city, by the City Fathers with complete knowledge of his preferences—was meager and uninteresting. It included fuming Rigellian wine, which he despised as a drink for barbarians; such a choice could only mean that there was nothing else to drink in the city but water.

His weariness, the solitude, the direct transition from the audience hall of the Hapsburgs to his bare new room under the mast in the Empire State Building—it had been an elevator-winch housing until the city had converted to friction-fields—and the dullness of the meal combined to throw him into a rare and deep state of depression. What he thought he could see of the future of Okie cities did not exactly cheer him, either.

It was at this point that the door to his room irised open, and Hazleton stalked silently through it, hooking his chromoclav back into his belt.

They looked at each other stonily for a moment. Amalfi pointed to a chair.

"Sorry, boss," Hazleton said, without moving. "I've never used my key before except in an emergency, you know that. But I think maybe this is an emergency. We're in a bad way—and the way you're dealing with the problem strikes me as crazy. For the survival of the city, I want to be taken into your confidence."

"Sit down," Amalfi said. "Have some Rigel wine."

Hazleton made a wry face and sat down.

"You're in my confidence, as always, Mark. I don't leave you out of my plans except where I think you might shoot from the hip if I didn't. You'll agree that you've done that occasionally—and *don't* throw up the Thor Five situation again, because there I was on your side; it was the City Fathers that objected to that particular Hazleton gimmick."

"Granted."

"Good," Amalfi said. "Tell me what you want to know, then."

"Up to a point I understand what you're out to do," Hazleton said without preamble. "Your use of Dee as a safe-conduct in and out of the meeting was a shrewd trick. Considering the political threat we represented to the King, it was probably the only thing you could have done. Understand, I resent it personally and I may yet pay you off for it. But it was necessary, I agree."

"Good," the mayor said wearily. "But that's a minor point, Mark."

"Granted, except on the personal level. The main thing is that you threw away the whole chance you schemed so hard to get. The knowledge-pooling plan was a good one, and you had two major chances to put it across. First of all, the King set you up to claim we were Vegan—nobody has ever actually seen that fort, and physically you're enough unlike the normal run of humanity to pass for a Vegan without much trouble. Dee and I don't look Vegan, but we might be atypical, or maybe renegades.

"But you threw that one away. Then the mayor from Dresden-Saxony set you up to swing almost everybody our way by letting them know our name. If you'd followed through, you would have carried the voting. Hell, you'd probably have wound up king of the jungle to boot.

"And you threw that one away, too."

Hazleton took his slide rule out of his pocket and moodily pushed the slide back and forth in it. It was a gesture frequent enough with him, but ordinarily it preceded or followed some use of the rule. Tonight it was obviously just nervous play.

"But Mark, I didn't want to be king of the jungle," Amalfi said slowly. "I'd much rather let the present incumbent hold that responsibility. Every crime that's ever been committed, or will be committed in the near future, in this jungle, will be laid at his door eventually by the Earth cops. On top of that, the Okies here will hold him personally responsible for every misfortune that comes their way while they're in the jungle. I never did want that job; I only wanted the King to think that I wanted it. . . . Incidentally, did you try to raise that city out on the perimeter, the one that said it had mass chromatography?"

"Sure," Hazleton said. "They don't answer."

"Okay. Now, about this knowledge-pooling plan: it wouldn't work, Mark. First of all, you couldn't keep a pack of Okies working at it long enough to get any good out of it. Okies aren't philosophers, and they aren't scientists except in a limited way. They're engineers and merchants; in some respects they're adventurers, too, but they don't think of themselves as adventurers. They're *practical*—that's the word they use. You've heard it."

"I've used it," Hazleton said edgily.

"So have I. There's a great deal of meaning packed into it. It means, among other things, that if you get Okies involved in a major analytical project, they'll get restive. They want sets of applications of principles, not principles pure and useless. And it isn't in their natures to sit still in one place for long. If you convince them that they should, they'll try, and the whole thing will wind up in a terrific explosion.

"But that's only point one. Mark, have you any idea of the real scope of the knowledge-pooling project? I'm *not* trying to put you on the spot, believe me. I don't think anybody in that hall realized it. If they had, they'd have laughed me off the platform. There again, Okies aren't scientists, and their outlook is too impatient to let them carry a really long chain of reasoning to a conclusion."

"You're an Okie," Hazleton pointed out. "You carried it to a conclusion. You told them how long it would take."

"I'm an Okie. I told them it would take from two to five years to do even a scratch job. As an Okie, I'm an expert at half-truths. It would take from two to five years even to get the project set up! And the rest of the job, Mark, would take *centuries*."

"For a scratch job?"

"No such thing as a scratch job in this universe of discourse," Amalfi said, reaching for the fuming wine and reconsidering at the last minute. "Those cities out there represent the accumulated scientific knowledge of all the high-technical-level cultures they've ever encountered. Even allowing for the usual information gaps, that's about five thousand planets-full of data, at a minimum estimate. Sure, we could pool all that knowledge—just as I said at the meeting, the City Fathers could take it all in, and classify it, in only a little over an hour—*after we'd spent two to five years setting them up to do it*. And then we'd have to integrate it. And you've got to integrate it, Mark; you've got to know it thoroughly enough to be able to make it *do* something. You couldn't offer it for sale unless you did that. Would you like the job?"

"No," Hazleton said slowly, but at once. "But Amalfi, am I ever going to know what you're doing if you persist in proceeding like this? You didn't go to that meeting just to waste time; I can trust you that far. So I have to assume that the whole maneuver was a trick, designed to force the March on Earth, rather than to defeat it. You gave the cities a clearly defined, superficially sound, and less-attractive alternative. Once they had rejected the alternative, they had committed themselves to the King's tactics, without knowing it."

"That's quite right."

"If that's right," Hazleton said, looking up suddenly with a flat flash of almost-violet eyes, "I think it's stupid. I think it's stupid even though it was marvelously devious. There's such a thing as outsmarting yourself."

Amalfi said, "That could be. In any event, if the choice had been limited to marching on Earth versus staying in the jungle, the cities would have stayed in the jungle. Would it have been sensible to allow that?"

"We can't afford to stay in the jungle, anyhow."

"Of course we can't. And by the same token, we couldn't leave it by ourselves. The only way we could get free of this star cluster is in the middle of a mass movement. What else could I have been shooting for?"

"I don't know," Hazleton said. "But there's something else besides that in the back of your head."

"And your complaint is that you don't know about it in advance. I know why you don't know. You know, too."

"Dee?"

"Certainly," Amalfi said. "You weren't asking yourself the right question. You were emotionally driven to ask why I wanted Dee along. The question was pertinent enough, but it wasn't exactly central. If you had stood back a little further from the *whole* problem, you'd have seen why I wanted the March on Earth to go through, too."

"I'll keep trying," Hazleton said grimly. "Though I'd have preferred to be told. You and I are getting further apart every year, boss. It used to be that we thought very much alike; and it was then that you developed your habit of not telling me the whole story. It was a training device, I think now. The more I was made to worry about the total plan, the more I was required to think the thing out for myself—which meant trying to figure *you* out—the more training I got in thinking like you. And of course, to be a proper city manager, I had to think like you. You had to be sure that any decisions I made in your absence would be the decisions you would have made had you been around.

"All this hit me after our tangle with the Duchy of Gort. That incident was the first time that you and I had been out of touch with each other long enough for a situation of really major proportions to develop—a situation about which I knew very little until I could get back to the city from Utopia and get briefed.

"When I got back, I found that I was damn lucky *not* to have thought like you. My first failure to comprehend your whole plan—and your training method of leaving me to puzzle things out alone—apparently had doomed me in your mind. You had written me off, and you were training Carrel as my successor."

"All this is accurate reportage," Amalfi said. "If you mean to accuse me of keeping a hard school——"

"——a fool will learn in no other?"

"No. A fool won't learn at all. But I don't deny keeping a hard school. Go on."

"I haven't far to go, now. I learned in the Gort-Utopia system that thinking the way you think can sometimes be deadly for me. I got off Utopia by thinking *my* way, not yours. The confirmation came when we hit He; had I been thinking entirely like you in that situation, we'd still be on the planet."

"Mark, you still haven't made your point. I can tell. It's perfectly true that we often relied on your plans, and precisely because they come from a mind most unlike my own. What of it?"

"This of it. You're now out to rub out whatever trace of

originality I have. You used to value it, as you say. You used to use it for the city, and defend it against the City Fathers when they had an attack of conservatism. But now you've changed, and so have I.

"These days, I seem to be tending toward thinking more and more like a human being, with human concerns. I don't feel like Hazleton the master conniver any more, except in flashes. The opposite change is taking place in you. You're becoming more and more alienated from human concerns. When you look at people, you see—machines. After a little more of this, we won't be able to tell you from the City Fathers."

Amalfi tried to think about it. He was very tired, and he felt old. It was not yet time for his anti-agathic shot, not by more than a decade, but knowing that he would probably not get it made the centuries he had already traversed weigh heavily upon his back.

"Or maybe I'm beginning to think that I'm a god," he said. "You accused me of that on Murphy. Have you ever tried to imagine, Mark, how completely crippling it is to any man's humanity to be the mayor of an Okie city for hundreds of years? I suppose you have—your own responsibilities aren't lighter than mine, only a little different. Let me ask you this, then: isn't it obvious that this change in you dates from the day when Dee first came on board?"

"Of course it's obvious," Hazleton said, looking up sharply. "It dates from the Utopia-Gort affair. That's when Dee came on board; she was a Utopian. Are you about to tell me that *she's* to blame?"

"Shouldn't it also be obvious," Amalfi continued, with weary implacability, "that the converse change in me dates from the same event? Gods of all stars, Mark, *don't you know that I love Dee, too?*"

Hazleton froze and went white. He looked rigidly with suddenly blind eyes at the remains of Amalfi's miserable supper. After a long time, he laid his slide rule on the table as delicately as if it were made of spun sugar.

"I do know," he said, at long last. "I did know. But I didn't—want to know that I knew."

Amalfi spread his big hands in a gesture of helplessness

he had not had to use for more than half a century. The city manager did not seem to notice.

"That being the case," Hazleton resumed, his voice suddenly much tighter, "that being so, Amalfi, I——"

He stopped.

"You needn't rush, Mark. Actually it doesn't change things much. Take your time."

"Amalfi—I *want off*."

Each evenly spaced word struck Amalfi like the strokes of a mallet against a gong, the strokes which, timed exactly to the gong's vibration period, drive it toward shattering. Amalfi had expected anything but those three words. They told him that he had had no real idea of how helpless he had become.

I want off was the traditional formula by which a starman renounced the stars. The Okie who spoke them cut himself off forever from the cities, and from the long swooping lines of the ingeodesics that the cities followed through space-time. The Okie who spoke them became planet-bound.

And—it was entirely final. The words were seared into Okie law. *I want off* could never be refused—nor retracted.

"You have it," Amalfi said. "Naturally. I won't tax you with being hasty, since it's too late."

"Thanks."

"Well, where do you want it? On the nearest planet, or at the city's next port of call?"

These, too, were merely the traditional alternatives, but Hazleton didn't seem to relish either of them. His lips were white, and he seemed to be trembling slightly.

"That," he said, "depends on where you're planning to go next. You haven't yet told me."

Hazleton's disturbance disturbed Amalfi, too, more than he liked to recognize. Mechanically, it would almost surely be possible for the ex-city manager to withdraw his decision; and mechanically, it would be possible to make the suggestion to Hazleton. Those three words had been neither overheard nor recorded as far as Amalfi knew, except—a small chance—by the treacher, the section of the City Fathers which handled tablewaiting. Even there, however, the City Fathers wouldn't be likely to scan the treacher's memory bank more than once every five years.

The treacher had nothing interesting to remember but the eating preference patterns of the Okies, and such patterns change slowly and, for the most part, insignificantly. No, the City Fathers need not know that Hazleton had resigned, not for a while yet.

But allowing the city manager to back down did not even occur to Amalfi; the mayor was too thoroughly an Okie for that. Had it been proposed to him, Amalfi would have objected that the uttering of those three words had put Hazleton as totally under Amalfi's smallest command as was a private in the city's perimeter police; and he could have shown reasons why subservience of that kind was now required of Hazleton. He could also have shown that those three words could never be actually revoked, however closely they were kept a secret between Hazleton and himself; if pressed, he could have shown that he could never forget them, and that Hazleton couldn't either. He might have explained that, every time Amalfi decided against a plan of Hazleton's, the city manager would put it down to secret rancor against that smothered resignation. Or, being Amalfi, he might merely have noted that the conflict between the two men had already been deep-running, and that after Hazleton had said, "I want off," it would become outright pathological.

Actually, however, no one of these things entered his mind. Hazleton had said, "I want off." Amalfi was an Okie, and for an Okie, "I want off" is final.

"No," the mayor said, at once. "You've asked for off, and that's the end of it. You're no longer entitled to any knowledge of city policy or plans, except for what reaches you in the form of directives. Now's the time when you can use your training in thinking like me, Mark—obviously you'll have no difficulty in thinking like the City Fathers—because it'll be your only source of information on policy from now on."

"I understand," Hazleton said formally. He stood silent a moment longer. Amalfi waited.

"At the next port of call, then," Hazleton said.

"All right. Until then, you're outgoing city manager. Put Carrel back into training as your successor, and begin feeding the City Fathers predisposing data toward him now. I don't want any more fuss from them when the election is held than we had when you were elected."

Hazleton's expression became slightly more set. "Right."

"Secondly, get the city moving toward the perimeter to intersect the town you couldn't raise. I'll want an orbit that gives us logarithmic acceleration, with all the real drive concentrated at the far end. On the way, ready two work teams: one for a fast spindizzy assessment, the other to run up whatever's necessary on the mass chromatography equipment, whatever that may be. Include medium-heavy dismounting tools, below the graving dock size, but heavy enough to handle any job less drastic."

"Right."

"Also, ready Sergeant Anderson's squad, in case that city isn't quite as dead as it sounds."

"Right," Hazleton said again.

"That's it," Amalfi said.

Hazleton nodded stiffly, and made as if to turn. Then, astonishingly, his stiff face exploded into a torrential passion of speech.

"Boss, tell me this before I go," he said, clenching his fists. "Was all this to push me into asking for off? Couldn't you think of any way of keeping your plans to yourself but kicking me out—or making me kick myself out? I don't believe this love story of yours, damned if I do. You know I'll take Dee with me when I disembark. And the Great Renunciation is just slop, just pure fiction, especially coming from you. You aren't any more in love with Dee than I am with you——"

And then Hazleton turned so white that Amalfi thought for a moment that the man was about to faint.

"Score one for you, Mark," Amalfi said. "Evidently I'm not the only one who's staging a Great Renunciation."

"Gods of all stars, Amalfi!"

"There are none," Amalfi said. "I can't do anything more, Mark. I've said good-bye to you a hell of a lot of times, but this has to be the last time—not by my election, but by yours. Go and get the jobs done."

Hazleton said, "Right." He spun and strode out. The door reached full dilation barely in time.

Amalfi sighed as deeply as a sleeping child. Then he

flipped the treacher switch from *set* to *clear*. The treacher said, "Will that be all, sir?"

"What do you want to do, poison me twice at the same meal?" Amalfi growled. "Get me an ultraphone line."

The treacher's voice changed at once. "Communications," it said briskly.

"This is the mayor. Raise Lieutenant Lerner, Forty-fifth Acolyte Border Security Group. Don't give up too easily; that was his last address, but he's been upgraded since. When you get him, tell him you're speaking for me. Tell him also that the cities in the jungle are organizing for some sort of military action, and that if he can get a squadron in here fast enough, he can break it up. Got it?"

"Yes, sir." The Communications man read it back. "If you say so, Mayor Amalfi."

"Who else would say so? Be sure Lerner doesn't get a fix on us. Send it pulse-modulated if you can."

"Can't, boss. Mr. Hazleton just put us under way. But there's a powerful Acolyte AM ultraphone station somewhere near by. I can get our message into synch with it, and make the cop's detectors focus on the vector. Is that good enough?"

"Better, even," Amalfi said. "Hop to it."

"There's one other thing, boss. That big drone you ordered last year is finally finished, and the shop says that it has Dirac equipment mounted in it and ready to go. I've inspected it and it looks fine, except that it's as big as a lifeship and just as detectable."

"All right, good; but that can wait. Get the message out."

"Yes, sir."

The voice cut out entirely. The incinerator chute gaped suddenly, and the dishes rose from the table and soared toward the opening in solemn procession. The goblet of wine left behind a miasmic trail, like a miniature comet.

At the last minute, Amalfi jerked out of his reverie and made a wild grab in midair; but he was too late. The chute gulped down that final item and shut again with a satisfied slam.

Hazleton had left his slide rule upon the table.

*   *   *

The space-suited party moved cautiously and with grim faces through the black, dead streets of the city on the periphery. At the lead, Sergeant Anderson's hand torch flashed into a doorway and flicked out again at once.

No other lights whatsoever could be seen in the dark city, nor had there been any response to calls. Except for a weak spindizzy field, no power flowed in the city at all, and even the screen was too feeble to maintain the city's air pressure above four pounds per square inch—hence the space suits.

Inside Amalfi's helmet O'Brian's voice was saying, "The second phase is about to start in the jungle, Mr. Mayor. Lerner moved in on them with what looks from here like all of the Acolyte navy he dared to pull out of the cluster itself. There's an admiral's flagship in the fleet, but all the big brass is doing is relaying Lerner's suggestions in the form of orders; he seems to have no ideas of his own."

"Sensible setup," Amalfi said, peering ahead unsuccessfully in the gloom.

"As far as it goes, sir. The thing is, the squadron itself is far too big for the job. It's unwieldly, and the jungle detected it well in advance; we stood ready to give the alarm to the King as you ordered, but it didn't prove necessary. The cities are drawing up in a rough battle formation now. It's quite a sight, even through the proxies. First time in history, isn't it?"

"As far as I know. Does it look like it'll work?"

"No, sir," the proxy pilot said promptly. "Whatever organization the King's worked out, it's functioning only partially, and damn sloppily. Cities are too clumsy for this kind of work even under the best hand, and his is a long way from the best, I'd judge. But we'll soon see for ourselves."

"Right. Give me another report in an hour."

Anderson held up his hand and the party halted. Ahead was a huge pile of ultimately solid blackness, touched deceptively here and there with feeble stars where windows threw back reflections. Far aloft, however, one window glowed softly with its own light.

The boarding-squad men deployed quickly along opposite sides of the street while the technies took cover.

Amalfi sidled along the near wall to where the sergeant was crouching.

"What do you think, Anderson?"

"I don't like it, Mr. Mayor. It stinks of mousetraps. Maybe everybody's dead and the last man didn't have the strength to turn out the light. On the other hand, just *one* light left burning for that reason, in the whole city?"

"I see what you mean. Dulany, take five men down that side street where the facsimile pillar is, follow it until you're tangent to the corner of this building up ahead, and stick out a probe. Don't use more than a couple of microvolts, or you might get burned."

"Yessir." Dulany's squad—the man himself might best be described as a detector-detector—slipped away soundlessly, shadows among shadows.

"That isn't all I stopped us for, Mr. Mayor," Anderson said. "There's a grounded aircab just around the corner here. It's got a dead passenger in it. I wish you'd take a look at him."

Amalfi took the proffered torch, covered its lens with the mitten of his suit so that only a thin shred of light leaked through and played it for half a second through the cab's window. He felt his spine going rigid.

Wherever the light touched the flesh of the hunched corpse, it—glistened.

"Communications!"

"Yes, sir!"

"Set up the return port for decontamination. Nobody gets back on board our town until he's been boiled alive— understand? I want the works."

There was a brief silence. Then: "Mr. Mayor, the city manager already has that in the works."

Amalfi grimaced wryly in the darkness. Anderson said, "Pardon me, sir, but—how did Mr. Hazleton guess?"

"Why, that's not too hard to see, at least after the fact, sergeant. This city we're on was desperately poor. And being poor under the new money system means being low on drugs. The end result, as Mr. Hazleton saw, and I should have seen, is—plague."

"The sons of bitches," the sergeant said bitterly. The

epithet seemed intended to apply to every non-Okie in the universe.

At the same moment, a lurid scarlet glare splashed over his face and the front of his suit, and red lanes of light checkered the street. There was an almost-simultaneous flat crash, without weight in the thin air, but ugly-sounding.

"TDX!" Anderson shouted, involuntarily.

"Dulany? Dulany! Damn it all, I told the man to take it easy with that probe. Whoever survived on that squad, report!"

Underneath the ringing in Amalfi's ears, someone began to laugh. It was as ugly a sound as the TDX explosion had been. There was no other answer.

"All right, Anderson, surround this place. Communications, get the rest of the boarding squad and half the security police over here on the double."

The nasty laughter got louder.

"Whoever you are that's putting out that silly giggle, you're going to learn how to make another kind of noise when I get my hands on you," Amalfi added viciously. "Nobody uses TDX on my men, I don't care whether he's an Okie or a cop. Get me? Nobody!"

The laughter stopped. Then a cracked voice said, "You lousy damned vultures."

"Vultures, is it?" Amalfi snapped. "If you'd answered our calls in the first place, there'd have been no trouble. Why don't you come to your senses? Do you *want* to die of the pestilence?"

"Vultures," the voice repeated. It carried an overtone of sinister idiocy. "Eaters of carrion. The gods of all stars will boil your bones for soup." The cackling began again.

Amalfi felt a faint chill. He switched to tight-beam. "Anderson, keep your men at a respectable distance, and wait for the reinforcements. This place is obviously mined to the teeth, and I don't know what other surprises our batty friend has for us."

"I could lob a gas grenade through that window——"

"Don't you suppose they're wearing suits, too? Just ring the place and sit tight."

"Check."

Amalfi squatted down upon his hams behind the aircab,

sweating. There just might be enough power left in the accumulators here to put up a Bethé fender around the building, but that wasn't the main thing on his mind. This business of boarding another Okie city was easily the hardest operation he had ever had to direct. Every move went against the grain. The madman's accusation had hit him in his most vulnerable spot.

After what seemed like a whole week, his helmet ultraphone said, "Proxy room. Mr. Mayor, the jungle beat off Lerner's first wave. I didn't think they could do it. They got in one good heavy lick at the beginning—blew two heavy cruisers right out of the sky—and the Acolytes act scared green. The admiral's launch has run out completely, and left Lerner holding the bag."

"Losses?"

"Four cities definitely wiped out. We haven't enough proxies out to estimate cities damaged with any accuracy, but Lerner had a group of about thirty towns enfiladed when the first cruiser got it."

"You haven't got the big drone out there, have you?" the mayor said in sudden alarm.

"No, sir; Communications ordered that one left berthed. I'm waiting now to see when the next Acolyte wave gets rolling. I'll call you as——"

The proxy pilot's voice snapped off, and the stars went out.

There was a shout of alarm from some technie in the party. Amalfi got up cautiously and looked overhead. The single window in the big building which had shown a light was blacked out now, too.

"What the hell happened, Mr. Mayor?" Anderson's voice said quietly.

"A local spindizzy screen, at at least half-drive. Probably they've dropped their main screen entirely. Everybody keep to cover—there may be flares."

The laughter began again.

"Vultures," the voice said. "Little mangy vultures in a big tight cage."

Amalfi cut back in on the open radio band. "You're going to wreck your city," he said steadily. "And once you tear this section of it loose, your power will fail and your screen will go down again. You can't win, and you know it."

The street began to tremble. It was only a faint trembling now, but there was no telling how long the basic structure of the dead city could hold this one small area in place against the machine that was trying to fling it away into space. Hazleton, of course, would rush over a set of portable nutcrackers as soon as he had seen what had happened—but whether this part of the city would still be here when the nutcrackers arrived was an open question.

In the meantime, there was exactly nothing Amalfi could do about it. Even his contact with his own city was cut off.

"It isn't your city," the voice said, suddenly deceptively reasonable. "It's our city. You're hijacking us. But we won't let you."

"How were we supposed to know any of you were still alive?" Amalfi demanded angrily. "You didn't answer our calls. Is it our fault if you didn't hear them? We thought this town was open for salvage——"

His voice was abruptly obliterated by a new one, enormous yet familiar, which came slamming into his helmet as if it intended to drive him out of his suit entirely.

"EARTH POLICE AA EMERGENCY ACOLYTE CLUSTER CONDENSATION XIII ARM BETA," it thundered. "SYSTEM UNDER ATTACK BY MASS ARMY OF TRAMP CITIES. POLICE AID URGENTLY NEEDED. LERNER LIEUTENANT FORTY-FIFTH BORDER SECURITY GROUP ACTING COMMANDER CLUSTER DEFENSE FORCES. ACKNOWLEGE."

Amalfi whistled soundlessly through his teeth. There was evidently a Dirac transceiver in operation somewhere inside the close-drawn spindizzy screen, or his helmet phones wouldn't have caught Lerner's yell for help; Diracs were too bulky for the usual proxy, let alone for a space suit. By the same token, everybody else in the galaxy possessing Dirac equipment had heard that yell—it had been the instantaneous propagation of Dirac pulses that had dealt the death blow to the West's hypercomplex relativity theories millennia ago.

And if a Dirac sender was open inside this bubble . . .

"LERNER ACOLYTE DEFENSE FORCES YOUR MESSAGE IN.

SQUADRON ASSIGNED YOUR CONDENSATION ON WAY. HANG ON. BETA ARM COMMAND EARTH."

. . . then Amalfi could use it. He flipped the chest switch and shouted, "Hazleton, are your nutcrackers rolling?"

"Rolling, boss," Hazleton shot back instantly. "Another ninety seconds and——"

"Too late, this sector will tear loose before then. Tune up our own screen to twenty-four percent and hold——"

He realized suddenly that he was shouting into a dead mike. The Okies here had caught on belatedly to what was happening, and had cut the power to their Dirac. Had that last, crucial, incomplete sentence gotten through, even a fragment of it? Or . . .

Deep down under Amalfi's feet an alarming sound began to rise. It was part screech, part monstrous rockslide, part prolonged and hollow groan. Amalfi's teeth began to itch in their sockets, and his bowels stirred slightly. He grinned.

The message had gotten through—or enough of it to enable Hazleton to guess the rest. The one spindizzy holding this field was going sour. Against the combined power of the nearby drivers of Amalfi's city, it could no longer maintain the clean space-lattice curvature it was set for.

"You're sunk," Amalfi told the invisible defenders quietly. "Give up now, and you'll not be hurt. I'll skip the TDX incident—Dulany was one of my best men, but maybe there was some reason on your side, too. Come on over with us, and you'll have a city to call your own again. This one isn't any good to you any more, that's obvious."

There was no answer.

Patterns began to race across the close-pressing black sky. The nutcrackers—portable generators designed to heterodyne a spindizzy field to the overload point—were being brought to bear. The single tortured spindizzy howled with anguish.

"Speak up, up there," Amalfi said. "I'm trying to be fair, but if you force me to drive you out——"

"Vultures," the cracked voice sobbed.

The window aloft lit up with a searing glare and burst outward. A long tongue of red flame winnowed out over the street. The spindizzy screen went down at once, and with it the awful noise from the city's power deck; but it was several minutes before Amalfi's dazzled eyes could see the stars again.

He stared up at the exploded scar on the side of the building, outlined in orange heat swiftly dimming. He felt a little sick.

"TDX again," he said softly. "Consistent to the last, the poor sick idiots."

"Mr. Mayor?"

"Here."

"This is the proxy room. There's a regular stampede going on in the jungle. The cities are streaming away from the red star as fast as they can tune up. No discernible order—just a mob, and a panicky mob, too. No signs of anything being done for the wounded cities; and it looks to me like they're just being left for Lerner to break up as soon as he gets up enough courage."

Amalfi nodded to himself. "All right, O'Brian, launch the big drone now. I want that drone to go with those cities and stick with them all the way. Pilot it personally; it's highly detectable, and there'll probably be several attempts to destroy it, so be ready to dodge."

"I will, sir. Mr. Hazleton just launched her a moment ago; I'm giving her the gun right now."

For some reason this did not improve Amalfi's temper in the least.

The Okies set to work rapidly, dismounting the dead city's spindizzies from their bases and shipping them into storage on board their own city. The one which had been overdriven in that last futile defense had to be left behind, of course; like the Twenty-third Street machine, it was hot and could not be approached, except by a graving dock. The rest went over as whole units. Hazleton looked more and more puzzled as the big machines came aboard, but he seemed resolved to ask no questions.

Carrel, however, suffered under no such self-imposed restraints. "What are we going to do with all these dismounted drivers?" he said. All three men stood in a sally port at the perimeter of their city, watching the ungainly bulks being floated across.

"We're going to fly another planet," Hazleton said flatly.

"You bet we are," Amalfi agreed. "And pray to your star gods that we're in time, Mark."

Hazleton didn't answer.

Carrel said, "In time for what?"

"That I won't say until I have it right under my nose on a screen. It's a hunch, and I think it's a good one. In the meantime, take my word for it that we're in a hurry, like we've never been in a hurry before. What's the word on that mass chromatography apparatus, Hazleton?"

"It's a reverse-English on the zone-melting process for refining germanium, boss. You take a big column of metal—which metal doesn't matter, as long as it's pure—and contaminate one end of it with the stuff you want to separate out. Then you run a disc-shaped electric field up the column from the contaminated end, and the contaminants are carried along by resistance heating and separate out at various points along the bar. To get pure fractions, you cut the bar apart with a power saw."

"But does it work?"

"Nah," Hazleton said. "It's just what we've seen a thousand times before. Looks good in theory, but not even the guys who owned this city could make it go."

"Another Lyran invisibility machine—or no-fuel drive," the mayor said, nodding. "Too bad; a process like that would be useful. Is the equipment massive?"

"Enormous. The area it occupies is twelve city blocks on a side."

"Leave it there," Amalfi decided at once. "Obviously this outfit was bragging from desperation when it offered the technique for the Acolyte woman's job. If she'd taken them up on it, they wouldn't have been able to deliver—and I don't care to lead us into any such temptation."

"In this case the knowledge is as good as the equipment," Hazleton said. "Their City Fathers will have all the information we could possibly worry out of the apparatus itself."

"Would somebody give me the pitch on this exodus of cities from the jungle?" Carrel put in. "I wasn't along on your trip to the King's city, and I still think the whole idea of a March on Earth is crazy."

Amalfi remained silent. After a moment, Hazleton said, "It is and it isn't. The jungle doesn't dare stand up to a real Earth force and slug it out, and everybody knows now that there's an Earth force on its way here. The cities want to be somewhere else in a hurry. But they still have some hope of getting Earth protection from the Acolyte cops and similar local organizations if they can put their case before the authorities outside of a trouble area."

"That," Carrel said, "is just what I don't see. What hope do they have of getting a fair shuffle? And why don't they just contact Earth on the Dirac, as Lerner did, instead of making this long trip? It's sixty-three hundred or so light years from here to Earth, and they aren't organized well enough to make such a long haul without a lot of hardship."

"And they'll do all their talking with Earth over the Dirac even after they get there," Amalfi added. "Partly, of course, this march is sheer theatricalism. The King hopes that such a big display of cities will make an impression on the people he'll be talking to. Don't forget that Earth is a quiet, rather idyllic world these days—a skyful of ragged cities will create a lot of alarm there.

"As for getting a square shuffle: the King is relying on a tradition of at least moderately fair dealing that goes back many centuries. Don't forget, Carrel, that for the last thousand years the Okie cities have been the major unifying force in our entire galactic culture."

"That's news to me," Carrel said, a little dubiously.

"But it's quite true. Do you know what a bee is? Well, it's a little Earth insect that sucks nectar from flowers. While it's about it, it picks up pollen and carries it about; it's a prime factor in cross-fertilization of plants. Most habitable planets have similar insects. The bee doesn't know that he's essential to the ecology of his world—all he's out to do is collect as much honey as he can—but that doesn't make him any less essential.

"The cities have been like the bee for a long time. The governments of the advanced planets, Earth in particular, know it, even if the cities generally don't. The planets distrust the cities, but they also know that they're vital and must be protected. The planets are tough on bindlestiffs for the same reason. The bindlestiffs are diseased bees; the taint that they carry gets fastened upon innocent cities, cities that are needed to keep new techniques and other essential information on the move from planet to planet. Obviously, cities and planets alike have to protect themselves from criminal outfits, but there's the culture as a whole to be considered, as well as the safety of an individual unit; and to maintain that culture, the free passage of legitimate Okies throughout the galaxy has to be maintained."

"The King knows this?" Carrel said.

"Of course he does. He's eight hundred years old; how could he help but know it? He wouldn't put it like this, but all the same, it's the essence of what he's depending upon to carry through his March on Earth."

"It still sounds risky to me," Carrel said dubiously. "We've all been conditioned almost from birth to distrust Earth, and Earth cops especially——"

"Only because the cops distrust us. That means that the cops are conditioned to be strict with cities about the smallest violations; so, since small violations of local laws are inevitable in a nomadic life, it's smart for an Okie to steer clear of cops. But for all the real hatred that exists between Okies and cops, we're both on the same side. We always have been."

On the underside of the city, just within the cone of vision of the three men, the big doors to the main hold swung slowly shut.

"That's the last one," Hazleton said. "Now I suppose we go back to where we left the all-purpose city we stole from Murphy, and relieve it of its drivers, too."

"Yes, we do," Amalfi said. "And after that, Mark, we go on to Hern Six. Carrel, ready a couple of small fission bombs for the Acolyte garrison there—it can't be large enough to make us much trouble, but we've no time left to play patty-cake."

"Is Hern Six the planet we're going to fly?" Carrel said.

"It has to be," Amalfi said, with a trace of impatience. "It's the only one available. Furthermore, this time we're going to have to control the flight, not just let the planet scoot off anywhere its natural converted rotation wants it to go. Being carried clean out of the galaxy once is once too often for me."

"Then I'd better put a crack team to work on the control problem with the City Fathers," Hazleton said. "Since we didn't have them to consult with on He, we'll have to screen every scrap of pertinent information they have in stock. No wonder you've been so hot on this project for corralling knowledge from other cities. I only wish we could have gotten started on integrating it sooner."

"I haven't had this in mind quite that long," Amalfi said. "But, believe me, I'm not sorry now that it turned out this way."

Carrel said, "Where are we going?"

Amalfi turned away toward the airlock. He had heard the question before, from Dee, but this was the first time that he had had an answer.

"Home," he said.

CHAPTER SEVEN: Hern VI

Mounting Hern VI—as desolate and damned a slab of rock as Amalfi had ever set down upon—for guided spindizzy flight was incredibly tedious work. Drivers had to be spotted accurately at every major compass point, and locked solidly to the center of gravity of the planetoid; and then each and every machine had to be tuned and put into balance with every other. And there were not enough spindizzies to set up a drive for the planet as a whole which would be fully dirigible when the day of flight came. The flight of Hern VI, when all the work was finally done, promised to be giddy and erratic.

But at least it would go approximately where the master space stick directed it to go. That much responsiveness, Amalfi thought, was all that was really necessary—or all that he hoped would be necessary.

Periodically, O'Brian, the proxy pilot, reported on the progress of the March on Earth. The mob had lost quite a few stragglers along the way as it passed attractive-looking systems where work might be found, but the main body was still streaming doggedly toward the mother planet. Though the outsize drone was as obvious a body as a minor moon, so far not a single Okie had taken a potshot at it. O'Brian had kept it darting through and about the

179

marchers in a double-sine curve in three dimensions, at its top speed and with progressive modulations of the orbit. If the partial traces which it made on any individual city's radar screen were not mistaken for meteor tracks, predicting its course closely enough to lay a gun on it would keep any ordinary computer occupied full time.

It was a superb job of piloting. Amalfi made a mental note to see to it that the task of piloting the city itself was split off from the city manager's job when Hazleton stepped down. Carrel was not a born pilot, and O'Brian was obviously the man Carrel would need.

At the beginning of the Hern VI conversion, the City Fathers had placed E-Day—the day of arrival of the marchers within optical telescope distance of Earth—at one hundred fifty-five years, four months, twenty days. Each report which came in from the big drone's pilot cut this co-ordinate-set back toward the flying present as the migrating jungle lost its laggards and became more and more compact, more and more able to put on speed as a unit. Amalfi consumed cigars faster and drove his men and machines harder every time the new computation was delivered to his desk.

But a full year had gone by since installation had started on Hern VI before O'Brian sent up the report he had been dreading and yet counting upon to arrive sooner or later.

"The march has lost two more cities to greener pastures, Mr. Amalfi," the proxy pilot said. "But that's routine. We've gained a city, too."

"Gained one?" Amalfi said tensely. "Where'd it come from?"

"I don't know. The course I've got the drone on doesn't allow me to look in any one direction more than about twenty-five seconds at a time. I have to take a census every time I pass her through the pack. The last time I went around, there was this outfit on the screen, just as if it had been there all the time. But that isn't all. It's the damnedest looking city I've ever seen, and I can't find anything like it in the files, either."

"Describe it."

"For one thing, it's enormous. I'm not going to have to worry about anybody spotting my drone for a while. This outfit must have every detector in the jungle screaming blue bloody murder. Besides, it's closed up."

"What do you mean by that?"

"It's got a smooth hull all around, Mr. Mayor. It isn't the usual platform with buildings on it and a spindizzy screen around both. It's more like a proper spaceship, except for its size."

"Any communication between it and the pack?"

"About what you'd expect. Wants to join the march; the King gave it the okay. I think he was pleased; it's the very first answer he's had to his call for a general mobilization of Okies, and this one really looks like a top-notch city. It calls itself Lincoln-Nevada."

"It would," Amalfi said grimly. He mopped his face. "Give me a look at it, O'Brian."

The screen lit up. Amalfi mopped his face again.

"All right. Back your drone off a good distance from the march and keep that thing in sight from now on. Get 'Lincoln-Nevada' between you and the pack. It won't shoot at your drone; it doesn't know it doesn't belong there."

Without waiting for O'Brian's acknowledgment, Amalfi switched over to the City Fathers. "How much longer is this job going to take?" he demanded.

"ANOTHER SIX YEARS, MR. MAYOR."

"Cut it to four at a minimum. And give me a course from here to the Lesser Magellanic Cloud, one that crosses Earth's orbit."

"MR. MAYOR, THE LESSER MAGELLANIC CLOUD IS TWO HUNDRED AND EIGHTY THOUSAND LIGHT YEARS AWAY FROM THE ACOLYTE CLUSTER!"

"Thank you," Amalfi said sardonically. "I have no intention of going there, I assure you. All I want is a course with those three points on it."

"VERY WELL. COMPUTED."

"When would we have to spin, to cross Earth's orbit on E-Day?"

"FROM FIVE SECONDS TO FIFTEEN DAYS FROM TODAY, FIGURING FROM THE CENTER OF THE CLOUD TO EITHER EDGE."

"No good. We can't start within those limits. Give me a perfectly flat trajectory from here to there."

"THAT ARC INVOLVES NINE HUNDRED AND
FIFTY-EIGHT DIRECT COLLISIONS AND FOUR
HUNDRED ELEVEN THOUSAND AND TWO GRAZES
AND NEAR-MISSES."

"Use it."

The City Fathers were silent. Amalfi wondered if it
were possible for machinery to be stunned. He knew that
the City Fathers would never use the crow-flight arc,
since it conflicted with their most ineluctable basic directive: *Preserve the city first.* This was all right with the
mayor. He had given that instruction with an eye to the
tempo of building on Hern VI; he had a strong hunch that
it would go considerably faster after that stunner.

And as a matter of fact, it was just fourteen months later
when Amalfi's hand closed on the master space stick for
Hern VI, and he said:

"Spin!"

The career of Hern VI from its native Acolyte cluster
across the center of the galaxy made history—particularly
in the field of instrumentation. Hern VI was a tiny world,
considerably smaller than Mercury, but nevertheless it
was the most monstrous mass ever kicked past the speed
of light within the limits of the inhabited galaxy. Except
for the planet of He, which had left the galaxy from its
periphery and was now well on its way toward Messier 31
in Andromeda, no such body had ever before been flown
under spindizzy or any other drive. Its passage left permanent scars in the recording banks of every detecting instrument within range, and the memories of it graven into
the brains of sentient observers were no less drastic.

Theoretically, Hern VI was following the long arc laid
out for it by Amalfi's City Fathers, an arc leading from the
fringe of the Acolyte cluster all the way across the face of
the galaxy to the center of the Lesser Magellanic Cloud.
(Its mass center, of course; both clouds had emerged too
recently from the galaxy as a whole to have developed the
definite orbital dead centers characteristic of "spiral" nebulae.) The mean motion of the flying planet followed that
arc scrupulously.

But at the speed at which Hern VI was traveling—a

velocity which could not be expressed comfortably even in multiples of C, the old arbitrary velocity of light—the slightest variation from that orbit became a careening side jaunt of horrifying proportions before even the microsecond reactions of the City Fathers could effect the proper corrections.

Like other starmen, Amalfi was accustomed enough to traveling at transphotic speeds—in space, a medium ordinarily without enough landmarks to make real velocity very apparent. And, like all Okies, he had traveled on planets in creeping ground vehicles which seemed to be making dangerous speed simply because there were so many nearby reference points to make that speed seem great. Now he was finding out what it was like to move among the stars at a comparable velocity.

For at the velocity of Hern VI, the stars became almost as closely spaced as the girders beside a subway track—with the added hazard that the track frequently swerved enough to place two or three girders in a row between the rails. More than once Amalfi stood frozen on the balcony in the belfry of City Hall, watching a star that had been invisible half a second before cannoning directly at his head, swelling to fill the whole sky with glare——

Blackness.

Amalfi felt irrationally that there should have been an audible *whoosh* as Hern VI passed that star. His face still tingled with the single blast of its radiation which had bathed him, despite the planet's hard-driven and nearly cross-polarized spindizzy screen, at that momentary perihelion.

There was nothing the matter, of course, with the orbit corrections of the City Fathers. The difficulty was simply that Hern VI was not a responsive enough space craft to benefit by really quick orbital corrections. It took long seconds for the City Fathers' orders to be translated into enough vector thrust to affect the flight of the dead planet over parsecs of its shambling, paretic stride. And there was another, major reason: when all of Hern VI's axial rotation had been converted to orbital motion, all of a considerable axial libration had also been converted, and there was nothing that could be done about the kinks this put in the planet's course.

Possibly, had Amalfi spotted his own city's spindizzies over the surface of the planet, as he had those of the all-purpose city and the plague city, Hern VI might have been more sensitive to the space stick; at the very least, the libration could have been left as real libration, for it wouldn't have mattered had the planet heeled a little this way and that as long as it kept a straight course. But Amalfi had left the city's drivers undisturbed for the most cogent of all reasons: for the survival of the city. Only one of the machines was participating at all in the flight of Hern VI, that being the big pivot spindizzy at Sixtieth Street. The others, including the decrepit but now almost cool Twenty-third Street machine, rested.

". . . *calling the free planet, calling the free planet* . . . *is* there anybody alive on that thing? . . . *EPSILON CRUCIS, HAVE YOU SUCCEEDED IN RAISING THE BODY THAT JUST PASSED YOU? . . . CALLING THE FREE* PLANET! YOU'RE ON COLLISION COURSE WITH US—HELL AND *DAMNATION! . . . CALLING ETA PALINURI, THE FREE PLANET JUST GAVE US A HAIRCUT AND IT'S HEADING* for you. It's either dead or out of control . . . Calling the free *planet, calling the free pla*——"

There was no time to answer such frantic calls, which poured into the city from outside like a chain of spring freshets as inhabited systems were bypassed, skirted, over-shot, fringed, or actually penetrated. The calls could have been acknowledged but acknowledgment would demand that some explanation be offered, and Hern VI would be out of ultraphone range of the questioner before more than a few sentences could he exchanged. The most pan-icky inquiries might have been answered by Dirac, but that had two drawbacks: the minor one, that there were too many inquiries for the city to handle, and no real reason to handle them; the major one, that Earth and one other important party would be able to hear the answer.

Amalfi did not care too much about what the Earth heard—Earth was already hearing plenty about the flight of Hern VI; if Dirac transmission could be spoken of as jammed, even in metaphor (and it could, for an infinite number of possible electron orbits in no way presupposes a Dirac transmitter tuned to each one), then Earth Dirac boards were jampacked with the squalls of alarmed planets along Hern VI's arc.

But about the other party, Amalfi cared a great deal.

O'Brian kept that other party steadily in the center of his drone's field of vision, and a small screen mounted on the railing of the belfry showed Amalfi the shining, innocuous-looking globe whenever he cared to look at it. The newcomer to the Okie jungle—and to the March on Earth—had made no untoward or even interesting motion since it had arrived in the Okies' ken. Occasionally it exchanged chitchat with the King of the jungle; less often, it talked with other cities. Boredom had descended on the jungle, so there was now a fair amount of intercity touring; but the newcomer was not visited as far as O'Brian or Amalfi could tell, nor did any gigs leave it. This, of course, was natural: Okies are solitary by preference, and a refusal to fraternize, providing that it was not actively hostile in tone, would always be understood in any situation. The newcomer, in short, was giving a very good imitation of being just another member of the hegira—just one more Birnam tree on the way to Dunsinane. . . .

And if anyone in the jungle had recognized it for what it was, Amalfi could see no signs of it.

A fat star rocketed blue-white over the city and Dopplered away into the black, shrinking as it faded out. Amalfi spoke briefly to the City Fathers. The jungle would be within sight of Earth within days—and the uproar on the Dirac was now devoted more and more to the approach of the jungle, less and less to Hern VI. Amalfi had considerable faith in the City Fathers, but the terrifying flight of stars past his head could not fail to make him worry about overshooting E-Day, or undershooting it, however accurate the calculations seemed to be.

But the City Fathers insisted doggedly that Hern VI would cross the solar system of Earth on E-Day, and Amalfi had to be as content as he could manage with the answer. On this kind of problem, the City Fathers had never been known to be wrong. He shrugged uneasily and phoned down to Astronomy.

"Jake, this is the mayor. Ever heard of something called 'trepidation'?"

"Ask me a hard one," the astronomer said testily.

"All right. How do I go about introducing some trepidation into this orbit we're following?"

The astronomer sounded his irritating chuckle. "You don't," he said. "It's a condition of space around suns, and you haven't the mass. The bottom limit, as I recall, is one and five-tenths times ten to the thirtieth power kilograms, but ask the City Fathers to be sure. My figure is of the right order of magnitude, anyhow."

"Damn," Amalfi said. He hung up and took time out to light a cigar, a task complicated by the hurtling stars in the corner of his eye; somehow the cigar seemed to flinch every time one went by. He lit the nervous cheroot and called Hazleton next.

"Mark, you once tried to explain to me how a musician plays the beginning and the end of a piece a little bit faster than normal so that he can play the middle section a little bit slower. Is that the way it goes?"

"Yes, that's *tempo rubato*—literally, 'robbed time.'"

"What I want to do is introduce something like that into the motion of this rock pile as we go across the solar system without any loss in total transit time. Any ideas?"

There was a moment's silence. "Nothing occurs to me, boss. Controlling that kind of thing is almost purely intuitional. You could probably do it better by personal control than O'Brian could set it up in the piloting section."

"Okay. Thanks."

Another dud. Personal control was out of the question at this speed, for no human pilot, not even Amalfi, had reflexes fast enough to handle Hern VI directly. It was precisely because he wanted to be able to handle the planet directly for a second or so of its flight that he wanted the trepidation introduced; and even then he would be none too sure of his ability to make the one critical, razor-edged alteration in her course which he knew he would need.

"Carrel? Come up here, will you?"

The boy arrived almost instantly. On the balcony, he watched the hurtling passage of stars with what Amalfi suspected was sternly repressed alarm.

"Carrel, you began with us as an interpreter, didn't you? You must have had frequent occasion to use a voice-writer, then."

"Yes, sir, I did."

"Good. Then you'll remember what happens when the carriage of the machine returns and spaces for another line. It brakes a little in the middle of the return, so it won't deform the carriage stop by constantly slamming into it; isn't that right? Well, what I want to know is: How is that done?"

"On a small machine, the return cable is on a cam instead of a pulley," Carrel said, frowning. "But the big multiplex machines that we use at conclaves are electronically controlled by something called a klystron; how *that* works, I've no idea."

"Find out," Amalfi said. "Thanks, Carrel, that's just what I was looking for. I want such an apparatus cut into our present piloting circuit, so as to give us the maximum braking effect as we cross Earth's solar system that's compatible with our arriving at the cloud on time. Can it be done?"

"Yes, sir, that sounds fairly easy." He went below without being dismissed; a second later, a swollen and spotted red giant sun skimmed the city, seemingly by inches.

The phone buzzed. "Mr. Mayor—O'Brian here. The cities are coming up on Earth. Shall I put you through?"

Amalfi started. Already? The city was still megaparsecs away from the rendezvous; it was literally impossible to conceive of any speed which would make arrival on time possible. The mayor suddenly began to find the subway-pillar flashing of the stars reassuring.

"Yes, O'Brian, hook up the big helmet and stand by. Give me full Dirac on all circuits, and have our alternate course ready to plug in. Has Mr. Carrel gotten in touch with you yet?"

"No, sir," the pilot said. "But there's been some activity from the City Fathers in the piloting banks which I assumed was by your orders or one of the city manager's. Apparently we're to be out of computer control at opposition."

"That's right. Okay, O'Brian, put me through." Amalfi donned the big helmet . . .

. . . and was back in the jungle.

The entire pack of cities, decelerating heavily now, was entering the "local group"—an arbitrary sphere with a radius of fifty light years, with Earth's sun at its center. This was the galaxy's center of population still, despite the outward movement which had taken place for the past centuries, and the challenges which were now ringing around the heads of the Okies were like voices from history: 40 Eridani, Procyon, Kruger 60, Sirius, 61 Cygni, Altair, RD-4°4048, Wolf 359, Alpha Centauri . . . to hear occasionally from Earth itself was no novelty, but these challenges were almost like being hailed by ancient Greece or the Commonwealth of Massachusetts.

The jungle King had succeeded by now in drumming the hobo cities into a roughly military formation: a huge cone, eighteen million miles along its axis. The cone was pointed by smaller towns unlikely to possess more than purely defensive armament. Just behind the point, which was actually rounded into a paraboloid like the head of a comet, the largest cities rode in the body of the cone. These included the King's own town, but did not include the "newcomer," which, despite its size, was flying far behind, roughly on the rim of the cone—it was this positioning which made it possible for Amalfi's drone to see almost the entire cone in the first place, for O'Brian's orders were to keep the big sphere in view regardless of how much of the jungle he had to sacrifice.

The main wall of the cone was made up mostly of medium-sized heavy-duty cities, again unlikely to be heavily armed, but having the advantage of mounting spindizzy equipment which could be polarized to virtual opacity to any attack but that of a battleship.

All in all, Amalfi thought, a sensible organization of the materials at hand. It suggested power in reserve, plus considerable defensive ability, without at the same time advertising any immediate intention to attack.

He settled the heavy viewing helmet more comfortably on his shoulders and laid one hand on the balcony railing near the space stick. Simultaneously, a voice rang in his ears.

"Earth Security Center calling the Cities," the voice said heavily. "You are ordered to kill your velocity and remain where you are pending an official investigation of your claims."

"Not bloody likely," the King's voice said.

"You are further warned that current Rulings in Council forbid any Okie city to approach Earth more closely than ten light years. Current Rulings also forbid gatherings of Okie cities in any numbers greater than four. However, we are empowered to tell you that this latter Ruling will be set aside for the duration of the investigation, provided that the approach limit is not crossed."

"We're crossing it," the King said. "You're going to take a good look at us. We're not going to form another jungle out here—we didn't come this far for nothing."

"Under such circumstances," the speaker at Earth Security continued, with the implacable indifference of the desperate bureaucrat operating by the book, "the law prescribes that participating cities be broken up. The full penalty will be applied in this case as in all cases."

"No it won't, either, any more than it is in ninety-four cases out of a hundred. We're not a raiding force and we aren't threatening Earth with anything but a couple of good loud beefs. We're here because we couldn't hope for a fair deal any other way. All we want is justice."

"You've been warned."

"So have you. You can't attack us. You don't dare to. We're citizens, not crooks. We want justice done us, and we're coming on in to see that it gets done."

There was a sudden *click* as the City Fathers' Dirac scanner picked up a new frequency. The new voice said: "Attention Police Command Thirty-two, Command HQ speaking for Vice Admiral MacMillan. Blue alert; blue alert. Acknowledge."

Another click, this time to the frequency the King used to communicate with the jungle.

"Pull up, you guys," the King said. "Hold formation, but figure to make camp fifteen degrees north of the ecliptic, in the orbit of Saturn but about ten degrees ahead

of the planet. I'll give you the exact coördinates later. If
they won't dicker with us there, we'll move on to Mars
and *really* throw a scare into them. But we'll give them a
fair chance."

"How do you know they'll give *us* a fair chance?" someone asked petulantly.

"Go back to the Acolytes if you can't take it here.
Damned if I care."

Click.

"Hello Command HQ. Command Thirty-two acknowledging blue alert, for Commander Eisenstein. Command
Thirty-two blue alert."

Click.

"Hey, you guys at the base of the cone, pull up! You're
piling up on us."

"Not in our tanks, Buda-Pesht."

"Look again, dammit. I'm getting a heavy mass-gain
here——"

Click.

"Attention Police Command Eighty-three, Command
HQ speaking for Vice Admiral MacMillan. Blue alert, blue
alert. Acknowledge. Attention Police Command Thirty-
two, red alert, red alert. Acknowledge."

"Eisenstein, Command Thirty-two, red alert acknowledged."

Click.

"Calling Earth; Prosperine Two station calling Earth
Security. We are picking up some of the cities. Instructions?"

("Where the hell is Prosperine?" Amalfi asked the City
Fathers.)

("PROSPERINE IS A GAS GIANT, ELEVEN THOU-
SAND MILES IN DIAMETER, OUTSIDE THE ORBIT
OF PLUTO AT A DISTANCE OF——"

("All right. Shut up.")

"Earth Security. Keep your nose clean, Prosperine Two.
Command HQ is handling this situation. Take no action."

Click.

"Hello Command HQ. Command Eighty-three acknowledging blue alert for Lieutenant Commander Fiorelli. Command Eighty-three blue alert."

Click.

"Buda-Pesht, they're bracketing us!"

"I know it. Make camp like I said. They don't dare lay a finger on us until we commit an actual aggression, and they know it. Don't let a show of cops bluff you now."

Click.

"Pluto station. We're picking up the vanguard of the cities."

"Sit tight, Pluto."

"You won't get them again until they've made camp— we're in opposition with Prosperine, but Neptune and Uranus are out of the line of flight entirely——"

"Sit tight."

Earth's sun grew gradually in Amalfi's view, growing only with the velocity of the drone, which was the velocity of the jungle. Earth's sun was still invisible from the city itself. In the helmet it was a yellow spark, without detectable disc, like a carbon arc through a lens-system set at infinity.

But it was, inarguably, the home sun. There was a curious thickness in Amalfi's throat as he looked at it. At this moment, Hern VI was screeching across the center of the galaxy, that center where there was no condensation of stars, such as other galaxies possessed, visible from Earth because of the masking interstellar dust clouds; the hurtling planet had just left behind it a black nebula in which every sun was an apparition, and every escape from those a miracle. Ahead was the opposite limb of the Milky Way, filled with new wonder.

Amalfi could not understand why the tiny, undistinguished yellow spark floating in front of him in the helmet made his eyes sting and water so intolerably.

The jungle was almost at a halt now, already down to interplanetary speeds, and still decelerating. In another ten minutes, the cities were at rest with reference to the sun; and from the drone, Amalfi could see, not very far away as he was accustomed to think of spatial distance, something else he had seen only once before: the planet Saturn.

No Earthly amateur astronomer with a new, uncertain, badly adjusted home reflector ever could have seen the ringed giant with fresher eyes. Amalfi was momentarily stupefied. What he saw was not only incredibly beautiful, but obviously impossible. A gas giant with rigid rings! Why had he ever left the Sol system at all, with a world so anomalous in his very backyard? And the giant had another planet circling it, too—a planet more than 3,000 miles through—in addition to the usual family of satellites of Hern VI's order of size.

Click.

"Make camp," the King was saying. "We'll be here for a while. Dammit, you guys at the base are still creeping on us a little. We're going to have to stop here—can't I pound that into your heads?"

"We're decelerating in good order, Buda-Pesht. It's the new city, the big job, that's creeping. He's in some kind of trouble, looks like."

From the drone, the diagnosis seemed accurate. The enormous spherical object had separated markedly from the main body of the jungle, and was now well ahead of the trailing edge of the cone. The whole sphere was wobbling a little as it moved, and every so often it would go dim as if under unexpected and uncontrollable polarization.

"Call him and ask if he needs help. The rest of you, take up orbits."

Amalfi barked, "O'Brian—time!"

"Course time, sir."

"How do I know when this space stick comes alive again?"

"It's alive now, Mr. Mayor," the pilot said. "The City Fathers cut out as soon as you touch it. You'll get a warning buzzer five seconds before our deceleration starts into the deep part of its curve, and then a beep every half second after that to the second inflection point. At the last beep, it's all yours, for about the next two and a half seconds. Then the stick will go dead and the City Fathers will be back in control."

Click.

"Admiral MacMillan, what action do you plan to take now—if any?"

Amalfi took an instant dislike to the new voice on the Dirac. It was flat, twangy, and as devoid as a vodeur of emotion, except perhaps for a certain self-righteousness tinged with *Angst*. Amalfi decided at once that in a face-to-face meeting the speaker would always look somewhere else than into the face of the man to whom he was speaking. The owner of that voice could not possibly be anywhere on the surface of the Earth, looking aloft for besiegers or going doggedly about his business; he was instead almost surely crouched in some subcellar.

"None, sir, at the moment," said the cops' Command HQ. "They've stopped, and appear to be willing to listen to reason. I have assigned Commander Eisenstein to cover their camp against any possible disturbance."

"Admiral, these cities have broken the law. They're here in defiance of our approach limits, and the very size of their gathering is illegal. Are you aware of that?"

"Yes, Mr. President," Command HQ said respectfully. "If you wish me to order individual arrests——"

"No, no, we can't jail a whole pack of flying tramps. I want action, Admiral. These people need to be taught a lesson. We can't have fleets of cities approaching Earth at will—it's a bad precedent. It indicates a decline of interstellar morality. Unless we return to the virtues of the pioneers, the lights will go out all over Earth, and grass will grow in the space lanes."

"Yes, sir," said Command HQ. "Well spoken, if you will permit me to say so. I stand ready for your orders, Mr. President."

"My orders are to do something. That camp is a festering sore on our heavens. I hold you personally responsible."

"Yes, sir." The Admiral's voice was very crisp. "Commander Eisenstein, proceed with Operation A. Command Eighty-two, red alert; red alert."

"Command Eighty-two acknowledging red alert."

"Eisenstein calling Command HQ."

"Command HQ."

"MacMillan, I'm taping my resignation over to you. The President's instructions don't specify Operation A. I won't be responsible for it."

"Follow orders, Commander," Command HQ said pleasantly. "I will accept your resignation—when the maneuver is completed."

The cities hung poised tensely in their orbits. For seconds, nothing happened.

Then pear-shaped, bumpy police battleships began springing out of nothingness around the jungle. Almost instantly, four cities raved into boiling clouds of gas.

The Dinwiddie pickup in the proxy backed itself hurriedly down the intensity scale until it could see again through the glare. The cities were still hanging there, seemingly stunned—as was Amalfi, for he had not imagined that Earth could have come to such a pass. Only an ideal combination of guilt and savagery could have produced so murderous a response; but evidently the president and MacMillan made up between them the necessary combination. . . .

Click.

"Fight!" the King's voice roared. "Fight, you lunkheads! They're going to wipe us out! Fight!"

Another city went up. The cops were using Bethé blasters; the Dinwiddie circuit, stopped down to accommodate the hydrogen-helium explosions, could not pick up the pale guide beams of the weapons; it would have been decidedly difficult to follow the King's order effectively.

But the city of Buda-Pesht was already sweeping forward out of the head of the cone, arcing toward Earth. It spat murder back at the police ships, and actually caught one. The mass of incandescent, melting metal appeared as a dim blob in Amalfi's helmet, then faded out again. A few cities followed the King; then a larger number; and then, suddenly, a great wave.

Click.

"MacMillan, stop them! I'll have you shot! They're going to invade——"

New police craft sprang into being every second. A haze gradually began to define the area of the Okie encampment: a planetary nebula of gas molecules, dust, and condensations of metal and water vapor. Through it the Bethé guide beams played, just on the edge of visibility now, but the sun, too, was acting on the cloud, and the whole mass was beginning to re-radiate, casting a deepening luminous veil over the whole scene, about which the Dinwiddie circuit could do very little. The whole spectacle reminded

Amalfi of NGC 1435 in Taurus, with exploding cities substituting novas for the Pleiades.

But there were more novas than the cities could account for, novas outside the cone of the encampment. The police craft, Amalfi noted with amazement, were beginning to burst almost as fast as they appeared. The swarming, disorganized cities were fighting back; but their inherent inefficiency as fighting machines ruled them out as the prime causes of such heavy police losses. Something else, something new was happening—something utterly deadly was loose among the cops . . .

"Command Eighty-two, Operation A sub *a*—on the double!"

A police monitor blew up with an impossible, soundless flare.

The cities were winning. Any police battleship could handle any three cities without even beginning to breathe hard, and there had been at least five battleships per city when the pogrom had started. The cities hadn't had a chance.

Yet they were winning. They streamed on toward Earth, boiling with rage, and the police ships, with their utterly deadly weapons, exploded all over the sky like milkweed.

And, a little bit ahead of the maddened cities, an enormous silver sphere wallowed toward Earth, apparently out of control.

Amalfi could now see Earth herself as the tiniest of blue-green dots. He did not try to see it any better, though it was growing to a disc with fantastic speed. He did not want to see it. His eyes were already fogged enough with sentimental tears at the sight of the home sun.

But his eyes kept coming back to it. At its pole he caught the shine of ice . . .

. . . *beep* . . .

The sound shocked him. The buzzer had already sounded, without his having heard it. The city would cross the solar system within the next two and a half seconds—*or less,* for he had no idea how many beeps had probed at his ears without response during his hypnotic struggle with the blue-green planet.

He could only guess, with the fullest impact of his intuition, that *now* was the time . . .

Click.

"PEOPLE OF EARTH. US THE CITY OF SPACES CALLS UPON YOU . . ."

He moved the space stick out and back in a flat loop about three millimeters long. The City Fathers instantly snatched the stick out of his hand. Earth vanished. So did Earth's sun. Hern VI began to accelerate rapidly, regaining the screeching velocity across the face of the galaxy for which two Okie cities had died.

". . . YOUR NATURAL MASTERS TO OKAY, THE MANS OF STARS, WHO THE UNIVERSE-UNDERSTANDING LONG-LIFE-UNDERSTANDING INHERITORS, THE INFERIOR HOMESTAYING DECADENT EARTH PEOPLES THEREOVER, THE NEW RULERS OF, ARE ABOUT TO BE BECOMING. US INSTRUCTS YOU SOON TO PREPARE——"

The mouthy voice abruptly ceased to exist. The blue fleck of light which had been Amalfi's last sight of his ancestral planet had already been gone for long seconds.

The whole of Hern VI lurched and rang. Amalfi was thrown heavily to the floor of the balcony. The heavy helmet fell askew on his head and shoulders, cutting off his view of the battle in the jungle.

But he didn't care. That impact, and the death of that curious voice, meant the real end of the battle in the jungle. It meant the end of any real threat that might have existed for Earth. And it meant the end of the Okie cities—not just those in the jungle, but all of them, as a class, including Amalfi's own.

For that impact, transmitted to the belfry of City Hall through the rock of Hern VI, meant that Amalfi's instant of personal control had been fair and true. Somewhere on the leading hemisphere of Hern VI there was now an enormous white-hot crater. That crater, and the traces of metal salts which were dissolved in its molten lining, held the grave of the oldest of all Okie legends:

The Vegan orbital fort.

It would be forever impossible now to know how long the summated, distilled, and purified power of the Vegan military, conquered once only in fact, had been bowling through the galaxy, awaiting this one unrepeatable clear lane to a strike. Certainly no answer to that question could be found on the degenerate planets of Vega itself; the fort was as much a myth there as it had been anywhere else in the galaxy.

But it had been real all the same. It had been awaiting its one chance to revenge Vega upon Earth, not, certainly, in the hope of reasserting the blue-white glory of Vega over every other star, but simply to smash the average planet of the average sun which had so inexplicably prevailed over Vega's magnificence. Not even the fort could have expected to prevail against Earth by itself—but in the confusion of the Okies' March on Earth, and under the expectation that Earth would hesitate to burn down its own citizen-cities until too late, it had foreseen a perfect triumph. It had swung in from its long, legend-blurred exile, disguised primarily as a city, secondarily as a fable, to make its last bid.

Residual tremors, T-waves, made the belfry rock gently. Amalfi got to his feet, steadying himself on the railing.

"O'Brian, cast us off. The planet goes on as she is. Switch the city to the alternate orbit."

"To the Greater Magellanic?"

"That's right. Make fast any quake damage; pass the word to Mr. Hazleton and Mr. Carrel."

"Yes, sir."

The Vegan fortress had nearly won, at that; only the passage of a forlorn and outcast-piloted little world had defeated it. But the Earth would never know more than a fraction of that, only the fraction which was the passage of Hern VI across the solar system. All the rest of the evidence was now seething and amalgamating in a cooling crater on the leading hemisphere of Hern VI; and Amalfi meant to see to it that Hern VI would be lost to Earth forever. . . .

As the Earth was lost to Okies, from now on.

Everyone was in the old office of the mayor: Dee, Hazleton, Carrel, Dr. Schloss, Sergeant Anderson, Jake, O'Brian, the technies; and, by extension, the entire population of the city, through a city-wide, two-way P.A. hookup;

even the City Fathers. It was the first such gathering since the last election; that election having been the one which put Hazleton into office, few present now remembered the occasion very well, except for the City Fathers—and they would be the least likely of all to be able to apply that memory fruitfully to the present meeting. Undertones were not their forte.

Amalfi began to speak. His voice was gentle, matter-of-fact, impersonal; it was addressed to everyone, to the city as an organism. But he was looking directly at Hazleton.

"First of all," he said, "it's necessary for everyone to understand our gross physical and astronomical situation. When we cut loose from Hern VI a while back, that planet was well on its way toward the Lesser Magellanic Cloud, which, for those of you who come from the northerly parts of the galaxy, is one of two small satellite galaxies moving away from the main galaxy along the southern limb. Hern Six is still on its way there, and unless something unlikely happens to it, it will go right on to the Cloud, through it, and on into deep intergalactic space.

"We left on it almost all the equipment we had accumulated from other cities while we were in the jungle because we had to. We hadn't the room to take much of it on board our own city; and we couldn't stick with Hern VI because Earth will almost certainly chase the planet, either until the planet leaves the galaxy, or until they're sure we aren't on it any longer."

"Why, sir?" several voices from the G.C. speaker said, almost simultaneously.

"For a long list of reasons. Our flying the planet across the face of the solar system—as well as our flying it through a number of other systems and across main interstellar traffic areas—was a serious violation of Earth laws. Furthermore, Earth has us chalked up as having sideswiped a city as we went by; they don't know the real nature of that 'city.' And incidentally, it's important that they never find out, even if keeping it a secret results in our being written up in the history books as murderers."

Dee stirred protestingly. "John, I don't see why we shouldn't take the credit. Especially since it really was a pretty big thing we did for the Earth."

"Because we're not through doing it yet. To you, Dee, the Vegans are an ancient people you first heard about only three centuries ago. Before that, on Utopia, you were cut off from the main stream of galactic history. But the fact is that Vega ruled much of the galaxy before Earth did, and that the Vegans always were, and have just shown us that they still are, dangerous people to get involved with. That fort didn't just exist in a vacuum. It had to touch port now and then, just as we do. And being a military machine, it needed more service and maintenance than it could take care of by itself.

"Somewhere in the galaxy there is a colony of Vega which is still dangerous. That colony must be kept in utter ignorance of what happened to its major weapon. It must be made to live on faith; to believe that the fort failed on its first attempt but may some day be back for another try. It must not know that the fort is destroyed, or it will build another one.

"The second one will succeed where the first one failed. The first one failed because of the nature of the nomadic kind of culture on which Earth has been depending up to now; the Okies defeated it. We happened to have been the particular city to do the job, but it was no accident that we were on hand to do it.

"But for quite a while to come, Okies are not going to be effective or even welcome factors in the galaxy as a whole; and the galaxy, Earth in particular, is going to be as weak as a baby all during that period because of the depression. If the Vegans hear that their fort did strike at Earth, and came within a hair's breadth of knocking it out, they'll be building another fort the same day they get the news. After that . . .

"No, Dee, I'm afraid we'll have to keep the secret."

Dee, still a little rebellious, looked at Hazleton for support; but he shook his head.

"Our own situation, right now, is neither good nor bad," Amalfi continued. "We still have Hern VI's velocity. It's enough slower than the velocity we hit when we flew the planet of He to make us readily maneuverable, even though clumsily, especially since we're so much less massive than a planet. We will be able to make any port of call which is inside the cone our trajectory would describe if we rotated it. Finally, Earth has figures only on the path of Hern VI; it has none on the present path of the city.

"Cast up against that the fact that our equipment is old and faltering, and will never carry us anywhere again under our own steam. When we land at the next port of call, we will be landed for good. We have no money to buy new equipment; without new equipment, we can't make money. So it will pay us to pick our next stop with great care. That's why I've asked everybody to sit in on this conference."

One of the technies said, "Boss, are you sure it's as bad as all that? We should be able to make some kind of repairs——"

"THE CITY WILL NOT SURVIVE ANOTHER LAND-ING," the City Fathers said flatly. The technie swallowed and subsided.

"Our present orbit," Amalfi said, "would lead us eventually out into the greater of the two Magellanic clouds. At our present velocity, that's about twenty years' journey away still. If we actually want to go there, we'll have to plan on that period stretching on by another six years, since the clip at which we're traveling now is so great that we'd blow out every driver on board if we undertook normal deceleration.

"I propose that the Greater Magellanic Cloud is exactly where we want to go."

Tumult.

The whole city roared with astonishment. Amalfi raised his hand; those actually in the room quieted slowly, but elsewhere in the city the noise went on for quite a while. It did not seem to be a sound of general protest, but rather the angry buzzing of large numbers of people arguing among themselves.

"I know how you feel," Amalfi said when he could be sure most of them could hear him again. "It's a long way to go, and though there are supposed to be one or two colonies on the near side of the Cloud, there can be no real interstellar commerce there, and certainly no commerce with the main body of the galaxy. We would have to settle down—maybe even take to dirt farming; it would be a matter of giving up being an Okie, and giving up being a starman. That's a lot to give up, I know.

"But I want you all to remember that there's no longer any work, or any hope of work, for us anywhere in the main body of the galaxy, even if by some miracle we manage to put our beat-up old city back into good order again. We have no choice. We *must* find a planet of our own to settle down on, a planet we can claim as our own."

"ESTABLISH THIS POINT," the City Fathers said.

"I'm prepared to do so. You all know what has happened to the galactic economy. It's collapsed completely. As long as the currency was stable in the main commerce lanes, there was some pay we could work for; but that doesn't exist any longer. The drug standard which Earth has rigged up now is utterly impossible for the cities, because the cities have to use those drugs *as drugs*, not as money, in order to stay alive long enough to do business at all. Entirely aside from the possibility of plague—and you'll remember, I think, what we saw of that not so long ago—there's the fact that we live, literally, on longevity. We can't trade on it, too.

"And that's only the beginning. The drug standard will collapse, and sooner and more finally than the germanium standard did. The galaxy's a huge place. There will be new monetary standards by the dozens before the economy gets back onto some stable basis. And there will be thousands of local monetary systems in operation before that happens. The interregnum will last at least a century——"

"AT LEAST THREE CENTURIES."

"Very well, three centuries. I was being optimistic. In either case, it's plain that we can't make a living in an economy which isn't at least reasonably stable, and we can't afford to sweat out the waiting period before the galaxy jells again. Especially since we don't know whether the eventual stabilization will have any corner in it for Okies or not.

"Frankly, I don't think the Okies have a prayer of surviving. Earth will be especially hard on them after this 'march,' which I took pains to encourage all the same because I was pretty sure we could suck in the Vegans with it. But even if there had been no march, the Okies would have been made obsolete by the depression. The histories of depressions show that a period of economic chaos is invariably followed by a period of extremely rigid economic controls—during which all the variables, the only partially controllable factors like commodity speculation, unlimited credit, free marketing, and competitive wages get shut out.

"Our city represents nearly the ultimate in competitive labor. Even if it lasts through the interregnum—which it can't—it will be an anachronism in the new economy. It will almost surely be *forced* to berth down on some planet selected by the government. My own proposition is simply that we select our *own* berth, long before the government gets around to enforcing its own selection; that we pick a place hundreds of parsecs away from the outermost boundary-surface that government will think to claim; a place which is retreating steadily and at good speed from the center of that government and everything it will eventually want to claim; and that once we get there, we dig in. There's a new imperialism starting where we used to be free; to stay free, we'll have to go out beyond any expectable frontier and start our own little empire.

"But let's face it. *The Okies are through.*"

Nobody said anything. Stunned faces scanned stunned faces.

Then the City Fathers said calmly, "THE POINT IS ESTABLISHED. WE ARE NOW MAKING AN ANALYSIS OF THE SELECTED AREA, AND WILL HAVE A REPORT FROM THE ASSIGNED SECTION IN FOUR TO FIVE WEEKS."

Still the silence persisted in the big chamber. The Okies were testing it—almost tasting it. No more roaming. A planet of their own. A city at rest, and a sun to come up and go down over it on a regular schedule; seasons; a quietness free of the eternal whirling of gravity fields. No fear, no fighting, no defeat, no pursuit; self-sufficiency— and the stars only points of light forever.

A planetbound man presented with a similar revolution in his habits would have rejected it at once, terrified. The Okies, however, were used to change; change was the only stable factor in their lives. It is the only stable factor in the

life of a planetbound man, too, but the planetbound man
has never had his nose rubbed in it.

Even so, had they not been in addition virtually immortal—had they been, like the people of the old times before
space travel, pinned like insects on a spreading-board to a
lifespan of less than a century—Amalfi would have been
afraid of the outcome. A short lifespan leads to restless-
ness; somewhere within the next few years, there has to
be some El Dorado for the ephemerid. But the conquest
of age had almost eliminated that Faustian frenzy. After
three or four centuries, people grew tired of searching for
the unnamable; they learned—they began to think of the
future not as holding a haven of placidity and riches, but
simply as the realm of things that had not happened yet.
They became interested in the budding, the unfolding
present, and thought about the future only with an attitude of indifferent acceptance toward whatever catastrophe it might bring. They no longer burned out their lives
seeking catastrophe, under the name of "security."

In short, they grew a little more realistic, and more than
a little tired.

Amalfi waited with calm confidence. The smallest objections, he knew, would come first. He was not anxious to
have to cope with them, and the silence had lasted so
much longer than he had expected that he began to wonder if his argument had become too abstract toward the
end. If so, a note of naïve practicality at this point should
be proper. . . .

"This solution should satisfy almost everyone," he said
briskly. "Hazleton has asked to be relieved of his post, and
this will certainly relieve him of it most effectively. It
takes us out of the jurisdiction of the cops. It leaves Carrel
as city manager if he still wants the post, but it leaves him
manager of a grounded city, which satisfies *me*, since I've
no confidence in Carrel as a pilot. It——"

"Boss, let me interrupt a minute."

"Go ahead, Mark."

"What you say is all very well, but it's too damned
extreme. I can't see any reason why we have to go so far
afield. Granted that the Greater Magellanic is off the
course Hern VI is following; granted that it's pretty re-

mote, granted that even if the cops do go looking for us
there, it's too big and unpopulated and complex for them
to hope to find us. But couldn't we accomplish the same
thing without leaving the galaxy? Why do we have to take
up residence in a cloud that's moving away from the galaxy
at some colossal speed——"

"THREE HUNDRED AND FORTY-FOUR MILES PER
SECOND."

"Oh, shut up. All right, so that's not very fast. Still and
all, the Cloud is a long way away—and if you give me the
exact figures, I'll bust all your tubes—and if we ever want
to get back to the galaxy again, we'll have to fly another
planet to do it."

"All right," Amalfi said. "What's your alternative?"

"Why don't we hide out in a big cluster in our own
galaxy? Not a picayune ball of stars like the Acolyte cluster, but one of the big jobs like the Great Cluster in
Hercules. There must be at least one such in the cone of
our present orbit; there might even be a Cepheid cluster
where spindizzy navigation would be impossible for anybody who didn't know the local space strains. We'd be just
as unlikely to be traced by the cops, but we'd still be on
hand inside our own galaxy if conditions began to look
up."

Amalfi did not choose to contest the point. Logically, it
should be Carrel, who was being deprived of the effective
command of a flying city, who should be raising this objection. The fact that the avowed retired Hazleton had brought
it up first was enough for Amalfi.

"I don't care if conditions ever do look up," Dee said,
unexpectedly. "I like the idea of our having a planet of our
own, and I'd want it to be as far away from the cops as we
could possibly make it. If that planet really does become
ours, would it make any difference to us whether Okie
cities become possible again two or three centuries from
now? We wouldn't need to be Okies any longer."

"You'd say that," Hazleton said, "because you haven't
lived more than two or three centuries yet, and because
you're still used to living on a planet. Some of the rest of
us are older; some of the rest of us like wandering. I'm not
speaking for myself, Dee, you know that. I'll be happy to

get off this junk pile. But this whole proposition has a faint smell to me. Amalfi, are you sure you aren't forcing us to set down simply to block a change of administration? It won't, you know."

Amalfi said, "Of course, I know. I'm submitting my resignation along with yours the moment we touch ground. Right now I'm still an officer of this city, and I'm doing the job I've been assigned to do."

"No, I didn't mean that. Let it go. What I still want to know is why we have to go all the way out to the Greater Magellanic."

"Because it'll be ours," Carrel said abruptly. Hazleton swung on him, obviously astonished; but Carrel's rapt eyes did not see the older man. "Not only our planet—whichever one we choose—but our galaxy. Both the Magellanics are galaxies in little. I know; I'm a southerner, I grew up on a planet where the Magellanics went across the night sky like tornadoes of sparks. The Greater Magellanic even has its own center of rotation; I couldn't see it from my home planet because we were too close, but from Earth it has a distinct Milne spiral. And both clouds are moving away, taking on their own independence from the main galaxy. Hell, Mark, it isn't a matter of one planet. That's nothing. We won't be able to fly the city, but we can build spaceships. We can colonize. We can settle the economy to suit ourselves. Our own galaxy! What more could you want?"

"It's too easy," Hazleton said stubbornly. "I'm used to fighting for what I want. I'm used to fighting for the city. I want to use my head, not my back; your spaceships, your colonization, those things are going to be preceded by a lot of plain and simple weeding and plowing. There's the core of my objection to this scheme, Amalfi. It's wasteful. It commits us to a situation where most of what we'll have to do will be outside of our experience."

"I disagree," Amalfi said quietly. "There are already colonies in the Greater Magellanic. They weren't set up by spaceships. They were set up by cities. No other mechanism could have made the trip at all in those days."

"So?"

"So there's no chance that we'll be able to settle down placidly and get out our hoes. We'll have to fight to make any part of the Cloud our own. It's going to be the biggest fight we've ever had, because we'll be fighting Okies— Okies who probably have forgotten most of their history and their heritage, but Okies all the same, Okies who had this idea long before we did and who are going to defend their patent."

"As they have a right to do. Why should we poach on them when a giant cluster would serve us just as well? Or nearly as well?"

"Because they are poachers themselves—and worse. Why would a city go all the way to the Greater Magellanic in the old days, when cities were solid citizens of the galaxy? Why didn't *they* settle down in a giant cluster? Think, Mark! They were bindlestiffs. Cities who had to go to the Greater Magellanic because they had committed crimes that made every star in the main galaxy their enemies. You could name one such city yourself and one you know must be out there in that cloud: the Interstellar Master Traders. And not only because Thor Five still remembers it, but because every sentient being in the galaxy burns for the blood of every last man on board it. Where else could it have gone but the Greater Magellanic, even though it starved itself for fifty years to make the trip?"

Hazleton began kneading his hands, slowly, but with great force. His knuckles went alternately white and red as his fingers ground over them.

"Gods of all stars," he said. His lips thinned. "The Mad Dogs. Yes, they went there if they went any place. Now there's an outfit I'd like to meet."

"Bear in mind that you might not, Mark. The Cloud's a big place."

"Sure, sure. And there may be a few other bindlestiffs, too. But if the Mad Dogs are out there, I'd like to meet them. I remember being taken for one of them on Thor Five; that's a taste I'd like to get out of my mouth. I don't care about the others. Except for them, the Greater Magellanic is ours, as far as I'm concerned."

"A galaxy," Dee murmured, almost soundlessly. "A galaxy with a home base, a home base that's ours."

"An Okie galaxy," Carrel said.

The silence sifted back over the city. It was not a

contentious silence now. It was the silence of a crowd in which each man is thinking for and to himself.

"HAVE MESSRS. HAZLETON AND CARREL ANY FURTHER ADDITIONS TO THEIR PLATFORMS?" the City Fathers blared, their vodeur-voice penetrating flatly into every cranny of the hurtling city. As Amalfi had expected, the extended discussion of high policy had convinced the City Fathers that the election was for the office of mayor, rather than for that of city manager. "IF NOT, AND IF THERE ARE NO ADDITIONAL CANDIDATES, WE ARE READY TO PROCEED WITH THE TABULATION."

For a long instant, everyone looked very blank. Then Hazleton too recognized the mistake the City Fathers had made. He began to chuckle.

"No additions," he said. Carrel said nothing; he simply grinned, transported.

Ten seconds later, John Amalfi, Okie, was the mayor-elect of an infant galaxy.

CHAPTER EIGHT: IMT

The city hovered, and then settled silently through the early morning darkness toward the broad expanse of heath which the planet's Proctors had designated as its landing place. At this hour, the edge of the misty acres of diamonds which were the Lesser Magellanic Cloud was just beginning to touch the western horizon; the whole cloud covered nearly 35° of the sky. The cloud would set at 0512; at 0600 the near edge of the home galaxy would rise, but during the summer, the suns rose earlier.

All of which was quite all right with Amalfi. The fact that no significant amount of the home galaxy could begin to show in the night sky for months to come was one of the reasons why he had chosen this planet to settle on. The situation confronting the dying city now, and its citizens, too, posed problems enough without its being recomplicated by an unsatisfiable homesickness.

The city grounded, and the last residual hum of the spindizzies stopped. From below there came a rapidly rising and more erratic hum of human activity, and the clank and roar of heavy equipment getting under way. The geology team was losing no time, as usual.

Amalfi, however, felt no disposition to go down at once. He remained on the balcony of City Hall looking at the

thickly set night sky. The star density in the Greater
Magellanic was very high, even outside the clusters—often,
the distances between stars were matters of light months
rather than light years. Even should it prove impossible to
move the city itself again—which was inevitable, considering that the Sixtieth Street spindizzy had just followed the
Twenty-third Street machine into the junk pit—it should
be possible to set interstellar commerce going here by
cargo ship. The city's remaining drivers, ripped out and
remounted on a one-per-hull basis, would provide the
nucleus of quite a respectable little fleet.

It would not be much like cruising among the far-
scattered, various civilizations of the Milky Way had been,
but it would be commerce of a sort, and commerce was
the Okies' oxygen.

He looked down. The brilliant starlight showed that the
blasted heath extended all the way to the horizon in the
west; in the east it stopped about a mile away and gave
place to land regularly divided into tiny squares. Whether
each of these minuscule fields represented an individual
farm he could not tell, but he had his suspicions. The
language the Proctors had used in giving the city permission to land had had decidedly feudal overtones.

While he watched, the black skeleton of some tall structure erected itself swiftly nearby, between the city and
the eastern stretch of the heath. The geology team already
had its derrick in place. The phone at the balcony's rim
buzzed, and Amalfi picked it up.

"Boss, we're going to drill now," the voice of Hazleton
said. "Coming down?"

"Yes. What do the soundings show?"

"Nothing very hopeful, but we'll know for sure shortly.
This does look like oil land, I must say."

"We've been fooled before," Amalfi grunted. "Start boring; I'll be right down."

He had barely hung up the phone when the burring
roar of the molar drill violated the still summer night,
echoing calamitously among the buildings of the city. It
was almost certainly the first time any planet in the Greater
Magellanic had heard the protest of collapsing molecules,

though the technique had been a century out of date back
in the Milky Way.

Amalfi was delayed by one demand and another all the
way to the field, so that it was already dawn when he
arrived. The test bore had been sunk and the drill was
being pulled up again; the team had put up a second
derrick, from the top of which Hazleton waved to him.
Amalfi waved back and went up in the lift.

There was a strong, warm wind blowing at the top,
which had completely tangled Hazleton's hair under the
earphone clips. To Amalfi, it could make no such difference, but after years of the city's precise air-conditioning,
it did obscure things to his emotions.

"Anything yet, Mark?"

"You're just in time. Here she comes."

The first derrick rocked as the long core sprang from the
earth and slammed into its side girders. There was no
answering black fountain. Amalfi leaned over the rail and
watched the sampling crew rope in the cartridge and
guide it back down to the ground. The winch rattled and
choked off, its motor panting.

"No soap," Hazleton said disgustedly. "I knew we
shouldn't have trusted the damned Proctors."

"There's oil under here somewhere all the same," Amalfi
said. "We'll get it out. Let's go down."

On the ground, the senior geologist had split the cartridge and was telling his way down the boring with a
mass-pencil. He shot Amalfi a quick reptilian glance as the
mayor's blocky shadow fell across the table.

"No dome," he said succinctly.

Amalfi thought about it. Now that the city was permanently cut off from the home galaxy, no work that it could
do for money would mean a great deal to it; what was
needed first of all was oil, so that the city could eat. Work
that would yield good returns in the local currency would
have to come much later. Right now the city would have
to work for payment in drilling permits.

At the first contact that had seemed to be easy enough.
This planet's natives had never been able to get below the
biggest and most obvious oil-domes, so there should be
plenty of oil left for the city. In turn, the city could throw

up enough low-grade molybdenum and wolfram as a byproduct of drilling to satisfy the terms of the Proctors.

But if there was no oil to crack for food . . .

"Sink two more shafts," Amalfi said. "You've got an oil-bearing till down there, anyhow. We'll pressure jellied gasoline into it and split it. Ride along a Number Eleven gravel to hold the seam open. If there's no dome, we'll boil the oil out."

"Steak yesterday and steak tomorrow," Hazleton murmured. "But never steak today."

Amalfi swung upon the city manager, feeling the blood charging upward through his thick neck. "Do you think you'll get fed any other way?" he growled. "This planet is going to be home for us from now on. Would you rather take up farming like the natives? I thought you outgrew *that* notion after the raid on Gort."

"That isn't what I meant," Hazleton said quietly. His heavily space-tanned face could not pale, but it blued a little under the taut, weathered bronze. "I know just as well as you do that we're here for good. It just seemed funny to me that settling down on a planet for good should begin just like any other job."

"I'm sorry," Amalfi said, mollified. "I shouldn't be so jumpy. Well, we don't know yet how well off we are. The natives never have mined this planet to anything like pay-dirt depth, and they refine stuff by throwing it into a stewpot. If we can get past this food problem, we've still got a good chance of turning this whole Cloud into a tidy corporation."

He turned his back abruptly on the derricks and began to walk slowly away from the city. "I feel like a walk," he said. "Like to come along, Mark?"

"A walk?" Hazleton looked puzzled. "Why—sure. Okay, boss."

For a while they trudged in silence over the heath. The going was rough; the soil was clayey and heavily gullied, particularly deceptive in the early morning light. Very little seemed to grow on it: only an occasional bit of low, starved shrubbery, a patch of tough, nettlelike stalks, a few clinging weeds like crab grass.

"This doesn't strike me as good farming land," Hazleton said. "Not that I know a thing about it."

"There's better land farther out, as you saw from the city," Amalfi said. "But I agree about the heath. It's blasted land. I wouldn't even believe it was radiologically safe until I saw the instrument readings with my own eyes."

"A war?"

"Long ago, maybe. But I think geology did most of the damage. The land was let alone too long; the topsoil's all gone. It's odd, considering how intensively the rest of the planet seems to be farmed."

They half-slid into a deep arroyo and scrambled up the other side. "Boss, straighten me out on something," Hazleton said. "Why did we adopt this planet, even after we found that it had people of its own? We passed several others that would have done as well. Are we going to push the local population out? We're not too well set up for that, even if it were legal or just."

"Do you think there are Earth cops in the Greater Magellanic, Mark?"

"No," Hazleton said. "But there are Okies, and if I wanted justice, I'd go to Okies, not to cops. What's the answer, Amalfi?"

"We may have to do a little judicious pushing," Amalfi said, squinting ahead. The double suns were glaring directly in their faces. "It's all in knowing where to push, Mark. You heard the character some of the outlying planets gave this place when we spoke to them on the way in."

"They hate the smell of it," Hazleton said, carefully removing a burr from his ankle. "It's my guess that the Proctors made some early expeditions unwelcome. Still—"

Amalfi topped a rise and held out one hand. The city manager fell silent almost automatically, and clambered up beside him.

The cultivated land began only a few meters away. Watching them were two—creatures.

One, plainly, was a man—a naked man, the color of chocolate, with matted blue-black hair. He was standing at the handle of a single-bladed plow, which looked to be made of the bones of some large animal. The furrow that he had been opening stretched behind him beside its fellows, and farther back in the field there was a low hut. The man was standing, shading his eyes, evidently looking across the dusky heath toward the Okie city. His shoulders were enormously broad and muscular, but bowed even when he stood erect, as now.

The figure leaning into the stiff leather straps which drew the plow also was human—a woman. Her head hung down, as did her arms, and her hair, as black as the man's but somewhat longer, fell forward and hid her face.

As Hazleton froze, the man lowered his head until he was looking directly at the Okies. His eyes were blue and unexpectedly piercing. "Are you the men from the city?" he said.

Hazleton's lips moved. The serf could hear nothing; Hazleton was speaking into his throat mikes, audible only to the receiver imbedded in Amalfi's right mastoid process.

"English, by the gods of all stars! The Proctors speak Interlingua. What's this, boss? Was the Cloud colonized *that* far back?"

Amalfi shook his head. "We're from the city," the mayor said aloud, in the same tongue. "What's your name, young fella?"

"Karst, lord."

"Don't call me 'lord.' I'm not one of your Proctors. Is this your land?"

"No, lord. Excuse—I have no other word——"

"My name is Amalfi."

"This is the Proctors' land, Amalfi. I work this land. Are you of Earth?"

Amalfi shot a swift sidelong glance at Hazleton. The city manager's face was expressionless.

"Yes," Amalfi said. "How did you know?"

"By the wonder," Karst said. "It is a great wonder, to raise a city in a single night. IMT itself took nine men of hands of thumbs of suns to build, the singers say. To raise a second city on the Barrens overnight—such a thing is beyond words."

He stepped away from the plow, walking with painful, hesitant steps, as if all his massive muscles hurt him. The woman raised her head from the traces and pulled the hair back from her face. The eyes that looked forth at the Okies were dull, but there were phosphorescent stirrings of alarm behind them. She reached out and grasped Karst by the elbow.

"It—is nothing," she said.

He shook her off. "You have built a city over one of night," he repeated. "You speak the Engh tongue, as we do on feast days. You speak to such as me, with words, not with the whips with the little tags. You have fine clothes, with patches of color of fine-woven cloth."

It was beyond doubt the longest speech he had ever made in his life. The clay on his forehead was beginning to streak with the effort.

"You are right," Amalfi said. "We are from Earth, though we left it long ago. I will tell you something else, Karst. You, too, are of Earth."

"This is not so," Karst said, retreating a step. "I was born here, and all my people. None claim Earth blood——"

"I understand," Amalfi said. "You are of this planet. But you are an Earthman. And I will tell you something else. I do not think the Proctors are Earthmen. I think they lost the right to call themselves Earthmen long ago, on another planet, a planet named Thor Five."

Karst wiped his callused palm against his thighs. "I want to understand," he said. "Teach me."

"Karst!" the woman said pleadingly. "It is nothing. Wonders pass. We are late with the planting."

"Teach me," Karst said doggedly. "All our lives we furrow the fields, and on the holidays they tell us of Earth. Now there is a marvel here, a city raised by the hands of Earthmen, there are Earthmen in it who speak to us——" He stopped. He seemed to have something in his throat.

"Go on," Amalfi said gently.

"Teach me. Now that Earth has built a city on the Barrens, the Proctors cannot hold knowledge for their own any longer. Even when you go, we will learn from your empty city before it is ruined by wind and rain. Lord Amalfi, if we are Earthmen, teach us as Earthmen are taught."

"Karst," said the woman. "It is not for us. It is a magic of the Proctors. All magics are of the Proctors. They mean to take us from our children. They mean us to die on the Barrens. They tempt us."

The serf turned to her. There was something indefinably gentle in the motion of his brutalized, crackle-skinned, thick-muscled body.

"You need not go," he said, in a slurred Interlingua patois which was obviously his usual tongue. "Go on with the plowing, does it please you. But this is no thing of the Proctors. They would not stoop to tempt slaves as mean as we are. We have obeyed the laws, given our tithes, observed the holidays. This is of Earth."

The woman clenched her horny hands under her chin and shivered. "It is forbidden to speak of Earth except on holidays. But I will finish the plowing. Otherwise our children will die."

"Come, then," Amalfi said. "There is much to learn."

To his complete consternation, the serf went down on both knees. A second later, while Amalfi was still wondering what to do next, Karst was up again, and climbing up onto the Barrens toward them. Hazleton offered him a hand, and was nearly hurled like a flat stone through the air when Karst took it; the serf was as solid and strong as a pile driver, and as sure on his stony feet.

"Karst, will you return before night?"

Karst did not answer. Amalfi began to lead the way back toward the city. Hazleton started down the far side of the rise after them, but something moved him to look back again at the little scrap of farm. The woman's head had fallen forward again, the wind stirring the tangled curtain of her hair. She was leaning heavily into the galling traces, and the plow was again beginning to cut its way painfully through the stony soil. There was now, of course, nobody to guide it.

"Boss," Hazleton said into the throat mike. "Are you listening, or are you too busy playing Messiah?"

"I'm listening."

"I don't think I want to snitch a planet from these people. As a matter of fact, I'm damned if I will!"

Amalfi didn't answer; he knew well enough that there was no answer. The Okie city would never go aloft again. This planet was home. There was no place else to go.

The voice of the woman, crooning as she plowed, dwindled behind them. Her song droned monotonously over unseen and starving children: a lullaby. Hazleton and Amalfi had fallen from the sky to rob her of everything but the stony and now unharvestable soil.

The city was old—unlike the men and women who manned it, who had merely lived a long time, which is quite a different thing. And like any old intelligence, its past sins lay very near the surface, ready for review either in nostalgia or in self-accusation at the slightest cue. It was difficult these days to get any kind of information out of the City Fathers without having to submit to a lecture, couched in as high a moral tone as was possible to machines whose highest morality was survival.

Amalfi knew well enough what he was letting himself in for when he asked the City Fathers for a review of the Violations docket. He got it, and in bells—big bells. The City Fathers gave him everything, right down to the day six hundred years ago when they had discovered that nobody had dusted the city's ancient subways since the managership of deFord. That had been the first time the younger Okies had heard that the city had ever had any subways.

But Amalfi stuck to the job, though his right ear ached with the pressure of the earphone. Out of the welter of minor complaints and wistful recollections of missed opportunities, certain things came through clearly and urgently.

Amalfi sighed. In the end, it appeared that the Earth cops would remember Amalfi's city for two things only. *One:* The city had a long Violations docket, and still existed to be brought to book on it. *Two:* The city had gone out toward the Greater Magellanic, just as a far older and blacker city had done centuries before—the city which had perpetrated the massacre on Thor V, the city whose memory still stank in the nostrils of cops and surviving Okies alike.

Amalfi shut off the City Fathers in mid-reminiscence and removed the phone from his aching ear. The control boards of the city stretched before him, still largely useful, but dead forever in one crucial bloc—the bank that had once flown the city from star to new star. The city was grounded; it had no choice now but to accept, and then win, this one poor planet for its own.

If the cops would let it. The Magellanic clouds were, of course, moving steadily and with increasing velocity away from the home galaxy. It would take the cops time to decide that they should make that enormously long flight in pursuit of one miserable Okie. But in the end they would make that decision. The cleaner the home galaxy became of Okies—and there was no doubt but that the cops had by now broken up the majority of the space-faring cities—the greater the urge would become to track down the last few stragglers.

Amalfi had no faith in the ability of a satellite star cloud to outrun human technology. By the time the cops were ready to cross from the home lens to the Greater Magellanic, they would have the techniques with which to do it, and techniques far less clumsy than Amalfi's city had used. If the cops wanted to chase the Greater Magellanic, they would find ways to catch it. If . . .

Amalfi put the earphone on again. "Question," he said. "Will the need to catch us be urgent enough to produce the necessary techniques in time?"

The City Fathers hummed, drawn momentarily from their eternal mulling over the past. At last they said:

"YES, MAYOR AMALFI. BEAR IN MIND THAT WE ARE NOT ALONE IN THIS CLOUD. REMEMBER THOR FIVE."

There it was: the ancient slogan that had made Okies hated even on planets that had never seen an Okie city, and could never expect to. There was only the smallest chance that the city which had wrought that atrocity had made good its escape to this Cloud; it had all happened a long time ago. But even the narrow chance, if the City Fathers were right, would bring the cops here sooner or later to destroy Amalfi's own city in expiation of that still-burning crime.

Remember Thor V. No city would be safe until that raped and murdered world could be forgotten. Not even out here, in the virgin satellites of the home lens.

"Boss? Sorry, we didn't know you were busy. But we've

got an operating schedule set up, as soon as you're ready to look at it."

"I'm ready right now, Mark," Amalfi said, turning away from the boards. "Hello, Dee. How do you like your planet?"

The girl smiled. "It's beautiful," she said simply.

"For the most part, anyway," Hazleton agreed. "This heath is an ugly place, but the rest of the land seems to be excellent—much better than you'd think it from the way it's being farmed. The tiny little fields they break it up into here just don't do it justice, and even I know better cultivation methods than these serfs do."

"I'm not surprised," Amalfi said. "It's my theory that the Proctors maintain their power partly by preventing the spread of any knowledge about farming beyond the most rudimentary kind. That's also the most rudimentary kind of politics, as I don't need to tell you."

"On the politics," Hazleton said evenly, "we're in disagreement. While that's ironing itself out, the business of running the city has to go on."

"All right," Amalfi said. "What's on the docket?"

"I'm having a small plot on the heath, next to the city, turned over and conditioned for some experimental plantings, and extensive soil tests have already been made. That's purely a stop gap, of course. Eventually we'll have to expand onto good land. I've drawn up a tentative contract of lease between the city and the Proctors, which provides for us to rotate ownership geographically so as to keep displacement of the serfs at a minimum, and at the same time opens a complete spectrum of seasonal plantings to us—essentially it's the old Limited Colony contract, but heavily weighed in the direction of the Proctors' prejudices. There's no doubt in my mind but that they'll sign it. Then——"

"They won't sign it," Amalfi said. "They can't even be shown it. Furthermore, I want everything you've put into your experimental plot here on the heath yanked out."

Hazleton put a hand to his forehead in frank exasperation. "Oh, hell, boss," he said. "Don't tell me that we're *still* not at the end of the old squirrel-cage routine—intrigue, intrigue, and then more intrigue. I'm sick of it, I'll tell you that directly. Isn't a thousand years enough for you? I thought we had come to this planet to settle down!"

"We did. We will. But as you reminded me yourself yesterday, there are other people in possession of this planet at the moment—people we can't legally push out. As matters stand right now, we can't give them the faintest sign that we mean to settle here; they're already intensely suspicious of that very thing, and they're watching us for evidence of it every minute."

"Oh no," Dee said. She came forward swiftly and put a hand on Amalfi's shoulder. "John, you promised us after the March was over that we were going to make a home here. Not necessarily on this planet, but somewhere in the Cloud. You promised, John."

The mayor looked up at her. It was no secret to her, or to Hazleton either, that he loved her; they both knew, as well, the cruelly just Okie law—and the vein of iron loyalty in Amalfi that would have compelled him to act by that law even if it had never existed. Until the crisis in the jungle had forced Amalfi to reveal to Hazleton the existence of that love, neither of the two youngsters had more than suspected it over a period of nearly three centuries.

But Dee was comparatively new to Okie mores, and was, in addition, a woman. Only to know that she was loved had been unable to content her long. She was already beginning to put the knowledge to work.

She was certainly not old enough yet to realize that the crisis had passed, leaving behind only a residuum of devotion useless to her and to Amalfi alike. She could not know that the person who had replaced her in Amalfi's mind was Karst; that Amalfi was now hearing from the lips of the serf the innocent and vastly touching questions which Dee had once asked; that Amalfi had realized that his thousand years of adult life had fitted him to answer not one question, but a thousand. Had anyone suggested to her that Amalfi was only just now coming into his full maturity, she would not have understood; possibly, she might have laughed. Amalfi had himself smiled when the realization had come to him.

"Of course I promised," he said. "I've delivered on my promises for a millennium now, and I'll continue to do so.

220

This planet will be our home if you'll give me just the minimum of help in winning it. It's the best of all the planets we passed on the way in, for a great many reasons— including a couple that won't begin to show until you see the winter constellations here, and a few more that won't become evident for a century yet. But there's one thing I certainly can't give you, and that's immediate delivery."

"All right," Dee said. She smiled. "I trust you, John, you know that. But it's hard to be patient."

"Is it?" Amalfi said, not much surprised. "Come to think of it, I remember when the same thought occurred to me, back on He. In retrospect the problem doesn't seem large."

"Boss, you'd better give us some substitute courses of action," Hazleton cut in, a little coldly. "With the possible exception of yourself, every man, woman, and alley cat in the city is ready to spread out all over the surface of this planet the moment the starting gun is fired. You gave us every reason to think that that would be the way it would happen. If there's going to be a delay, you have a good many idle hands to put to work."

"Use straight work-contract procedure all the way down the line. No exploiting of the planet that we wouldn't normally do during the usual stopover for a job. That means no truck gardens or any other form of local agriculture; just refilling the oil tanks, re-breeding the *Chlorella* strains from local sources for heterosis, making up our water losses, and so on. The last I heard, we were still using the Tx 71105 strain of *Chlorella pyrenoidosa;* that's too high-temp an alga for a planet with a winter season, like this one."

"That won't work," Hazleton said. "It may fool the Proctors, Amalfi, but how can you fool your own people? What are you going to do with the perimeter police, for instance? Sergeant Anderson's whole crew knows that it won't ever again have to make up a boarding squad or defend the city or take up any other military duty. Nine-tenths of them are itching to throw off their harness for good and all and start dirt farming. What am I going to tell them?"

"Send 'em out to your experimental patch on the heath,"

Amalfi said, "on police detail. Tell 'em to pick up everything that grows."

Hazleton started to turn toward the lift shaft, holding out his hand to Dee. Then, characteristically, he had a third thought and turned back.

"But why, boss?" he said plaintively. "What makes you think the Proctors suspect us of squatting? And what could they do about it if we did?"

"The Proctors have asked for the standard work contract," Amalfi said. "They knew what it was, they got it, and they insist upon its observation, to the letter—*including* the provision that the city must be off this planet by the date of termination. As you know, that's impossible; we can't leave this planet at all. But we'll have to pretend that we're going to leave up to the last possible minute."

Hazleton looked stubborn. Dee took his hand reassuringly, but it didn't seem to register.

"As for what the Proctors themselves can do about it," Amalfi said, picking up the earphones again, "I don't know. I'm trying to find out. But this much I do know:

"The Proctors have *already* called the cops."

Under the gray, hazy light in the schoolroom, neutral light which seemed cast like a cloak along the air rather than to illuminate it, voices and visions came thronging even into the conscious and prepared mind of the visitor, pouring from the memory cells of the City Fathers. Amalfi could feel their pressure, just below the surface of his mind; it was vaguely unpleasant, partly because he already knew what they sought to impart, so that the redoubled impressions tended to shoulder forward into the immediate attention, nearly with the vividness of immediate experience.

He waved a hand before his eyes in annoyance and looked for a monitor, found one standing at his elbow, and wondered how long he had been there—or, conversely, how long Amalfi himself had been lulled into the learning trance.

"Where's Karst?" he said brusquely. "The first serf we brought in? I need him."

"Yes, sir. He's in a chair toward the front of the room."

The monitor—whose function combined the duties of classroom supervisor and nurse—turned away briefly to a nearby wall treacher, which opened and floated out to him a tall metal tumbler. The monitor took it, and led the way through the room, threading his way among the scattered couches. Usually most of these were unoccupied, since it took less than 500 hours to bring the average child through tensor calculus and hence to the limits of what he could be taught by passive inculcation alone. Now, however, every couch was occupied, and few of them by children.

One of the counterpointing, sub-audible voices was murmuring: "Some of the cities which turned bindlestiff did not pursue the usual policy of piracy and raiding, but settled instead upon faraway worlds and established tyrannical rules. Most of these were overthrown by the Earth police; the cities were not efficient fighting machines. Those which withstood the first assault sometimes were allowed to remain in power for various reasons of policy, but such cases were invariably barred from commerce. Some of these involuntary empires may still remain on the fringes of Earth's jurisdiction. Most notorious of these recrudescences of imperialism was the reduction of Thor Five, the work of one of the earliest of the Okies, a heavily militarized city which had already earned itself the popular nickname of 'the Mad Dogs.' The epithet, current among other Okies as well as planetary populations, of course referred primarily . . ."

"Here's your man," the monitor said in a low voice. Amalfi looked down at Karst. The serf had already undergone a considerable change. He was no longer a distorted and worn caricature of a man, chocolate colored with sun, wind, and ground-in dirt, so brutalized as to be almost beyond pity. He was, instead, rather like a fetus as he lay curled on the couch, innocent and still perfectable, as yet unmarked by any experience which counted. His past—and there could hardly have been much of it, for although he had said that his present wife, Eedit, had been his fifth, he was obviously scarcely twenty years old—had been so completely monotonous and implacable that, given the chance, he had sloughed it off as easily and totally as one throws away a single garment. He was, Amalfi realized, much more essentially a child than any Okie infant would ever be.

The monitor touched Karst's shoulder and the serf stirred uneasily, then sat up, instantly awake, his intense blue eyes questioning Amalfi. The monitor handed him the anodized aluminum tumbler, now beaded with cold, and Karst drank from it. The pungent liquid made him sneeze, quickly and without seeming to notice that he had sneezed, like a cat.

"How's it coming through, Karst?" Amalfi said.

"It is very hard," the serf said. He took another pull at the tumbler. "But once grasped, it seems to bring every-thing into flower at once. Lord Amalfi, the Proctors claim that IMT came from the sky on a cloud. Yesterday I only believed that. Today I think I understand it."

"I think you do," Amalfi said. "And you're not alone. We have serfs by scores in the city now, learning—just look around you and you'll see. And they're learning more than just simple physics or cultural morphology. They're learning freedom, beginning with the first one—freedom to hate."

"I know that lesson," Karst said, with a profound and glacial calm. "But you awakened me for something."

"I did," the mayor agreed grimly. "We've got a visitor we think you'll be able to identify: a Proctor. And he's up to something that smells damned funny to me and Hazleton both, but we can't pin down what it is. Come give us a hand, will you?"

"You'd better give him some time to rest, Mr. Mayor," the monitor said disapprovingly. "Being dumped out of hypnopaedic trance is a considerable shock; he'll need at least an hour."

Amalfi stared at the monitor incredulously. He was about to note that neither Karst nor the city had the hour to spare when it occurred to him that to say so would take ten words where one was plenty. "Vanish," he said.

The monitor did his best.

Karst looked intently at the judas. The man on the screen had his back turned; he was looking into the big operations tank in the city manager's office. The indirect light beamed on his shaved and oiled head. Amalfi watched over Karst's left shoulder, his teeth sunk firmly in a new cigar.

"Why, the man's as bald as I am," the mayor said. "And he can't be much past his adolescence, judging by his skull; he's forty-five at the most. Recognize him, Karst?"

"Not yet," Karst said. "All the Proctors shave their heads. If he would only turn around—ah. Yes. That's Heldon. I have seen him myself only once, but he is easy to recognize. He is young, as the Proctors go. He is the stormy petrel of the Great Nine—some think him a friend of the serfs. At least he is less quick with the whip than the others."

"What would he be wanting here?"

"Perhaps he will tell us." Karst's eyes remained fixed upon the Proctor's image.

"Your request puzzles me," Hazleton's voice said, issuing smoothly from the speaker above the judas. The city manager could not be seen, but his expression seemed to modulate the sound of his voice almost specifically: the tiger mind masked behind a pussycat purr as behind a pussycat smile. "We're glad to hear of new services we can render to a client, of course. But we certainly never suspected that antigravity mechanisms even existed in IMT."

"Don't think me stupid, Mr. Hazleton," Heldon said. "You and I know that IMT was once a wanderer, as your city is now. We also know that your city, like all Okie cities, would like a world of its own. Will you allow me this much intelligence, please?"

"For discussion, yes," Hazleton's voice said.

"Then let me say that it's quite evident to me that you're nurturing an uprising. You have been careful to stay within the letter of the contract, simply because you dare not breach it, any more than we; the Earth police protect us from each other to that extent. Your Mayor Amalfi was told that it was illegal for the serfs to speak to your people, but unfortunately it is illegal only for the serfs, not for your citizens. If we cannot keep the serfs out of your city, you are under no obligation to do it for us."

"A point you have saved me the trouble of making," Hazleton said.

"Quite so. I'll add also that when this revolution of yours comes, I have no doubt that you'll win it. I don't know what kinds of weapons you can put into the hands of our serfs, but I assume that they are better than anything we can muster. We haven't your technology. My fellows disagree with me, but I am a realist."

"An interesting theory," Hazleton's voice said. There was a brief pause. In the silence, a soft pattering sound became evident. Hazleton's fingertips, Amalfi guessed, drumming on the desk top, as if with amused impatience. Heldon's face remained impassive.

"The Proctors believe that they can hold what is theirs," Heldon said at last. "If you overstay your contract, they will go to war against you. They will be justified, but unfortunately Earth justice is a long way from here. You will win. My interest is to see that we have a way of escape."

"Via spindizzy?"

"Precisely." Heldon permitted a stony smile to stir the corners of his mouth. "I'll be honest with you, Mr. Hazleton. If it comes to war, I will fight as hard as any other Proctor to hold this world of ours. I come to you only because you can repair the spindizzies of IMT. You needn't expect me to enter into any extensive treason on that account."

Hazleton, it appeared, was being obdurately stupid. "I fail to see why I should lift a finger for you," he said.

"Observe, please. The Proctors will fight because they believe that they must. It will probably be a hopeless fight, but it will do your city some damage all the same. As a matter of fact, it will cripple your city beyond repair, unless your luck is phenomenal. Now then: none of the Proctors except one other man and myself know that the spindizzies of IMT are still able to function. That means that they won't try to escape with them; they'll try to knock you out instead. But with the machines in repair, and one knowledgeable hand at the controls——"

"I see," Hazleton said. "You propose to put IMT into flight while you can still get off the planet with a reasonably whole city. In return you offer us the planet and the chance that our own damages will be minimal. Hmm.

It's interesting, anyhow. Suppose I take a look at your spindizzies and see if they're in operable condition. It's been a good many years, without doubt, and untended machinery has a way of gumming up. If they can still be operated at all, we'll talk about a deal. All right?"

"It will have to do," Heldon grumbled. Amalfi saw in the Proctor's eyes a gleam of cold satisfaction which he recognized at once, from having himself looked out through it often—though never concealing it so poorly. He shut off the screen.

"Well?" the mayor said. "What's he up to?"

"Trouble," Karst said slowly. "It would be very foolish to give or trade him any advantage. His stated reasons are not his real ones."

"Of course not," Amalfi said. "Whose are? Oh, hello, Mark. What did you make of our friend?"

Hazleton stepped out of the lift shaft, bouncing lightly once on the resilient concrete of the control-room floor. "He's a dummox," the city manager said, "but he's dangerous. He knows that there's something he doesn't know. He also knows that we don't know what he's driving at, and he's on his home grounds. It's a combination I don't care for."

"I don't like it myself," Amalfi said. "When the enemy starts giving away information, look out! Do you think the majority of the Proctors really don't know that IMT has operable spindizzies?"

"I am sure they do not," Karst offered tentatively. Both men turned to him. "The Proctors do not even believe that you are here to capture the planet. At least, they do not believe that that is what you intend, and I'm sure they don't care, one way or the other."

"Why not?" Hazleton said. "I would."

"You have never *owned* several million serfs," Karst said, without rancor. "You have serfs working for you, and you are paying them wages. That in itself is a disaster for the Proctors. And they cannot stop it. They know that the money you are paying is legal, with the power of the Earth behind it. They cannot stop us from earning it. To do so would cause an uprising at once."

Amalfi looked at Hazleton. The money the city was

handing out was the Oc dollar. It was legal here—but back in the galaxy it was just so much paper. It was only germanium-backed. Could the Proctors be that naïve? Or was IMT simply too old to possess the instantaneous Dirac transmitters which would have told it of the economic collapse of the home lens?

"And the spindizzies?" Amalfi said. "Who else would know of them among the Great Nine?"

"Asor, for one," Karst said. "He is the presiding officer, and the religious fanatic of the group. It is said that he still practices daily the full thirty yogas of the Semantic Rigor, even to chinning himself upon every rung of the Abstraction Ladder. The prophet Maalvin banned the flight of men forever, so Asor would not be likely to allow IMT to fly at this late date."

"He has his reasons," Hazleton said reflectively. "Religions rarely exist in a vacuum. They have effects on the societies they reflect. He's probably afraid of the spindizzies, in the last analysis. With such a weapon it takes only a few hundred men to make a revolution—more than enough to overthrow a feudal setup like this. IMT didn't dare keep its spindizzies working."

"Go on, Karst," Amalfi said, raising his hand impatiently at Hazleton. "How about the other Proctors?"

"There is Bemajdi, but he hardly counts," Karst said. "Let me think. Remember, I have never seen most of these men. The only one who matters, it seems to me, is Larre. He is a dour-faced old man with a pot belly. He is usually on Heldon's side, but seldom travels with Heldon all the way. He will worry less about the money the serfs are earning than will the rest. He will contrive a way to tax it away from us—perhaps by declaring a holiday, in honor of the visit of Earthmen to our planet. The collection of tithes is a duty of his."

"Would he allow Heldon to put IMT's spindizzies in shape?"

"No, probably not," Karst said. "I believe Heldon was telling the truth when he said that he would have to do that in secret."

"I don't know," Amalfi said. "I don't like it. On the surface, it looks as though the Proctors hope to scare us off the planet as soon as the contract expires, and then collect all the money we've paid the serfs—with the cops to back them up. But when you look closely at it, it's crazy. Once the cops find out the identity of IMT—and it won't take long—they'll break up both cities and be glad of the chance."

Karst said. "Is this because IMT was the Okie city that did—what was done—on Thor Five?"

Amalfi suddenly found that he was having difficulty in keeping his Adam's apple where it belonged. "Let that pass, Karst," he growled. "We're not going to import that story into the Cloud. That should have been cut from your learning tape."

"I know it now," Karst said calmly. "And I am not surprised. The Proctors never change."

"Forget it. Forget it, do you hear? Forget everything. Karst, can you go back to being a dumb serf for a night?"

"Go back to my land?" Karst said. "It would be awkward. My wife must have a new man by now——"

"No, not back to your land. I want to go with Heldon and look at his spindizzies as soon as he says the word. I'll need to take some heavy equipment, and I'll need some help. Will you come along?"

Hazleton raised his eyebrows. "You won't fool Heldon, boss."

"I think I will. Of course he knows that we've educated some of the serfs, but that's not a thing he can actually see when he looks at it; his whole background is against it. He just isn't accustomed to thinking of serfs as intelligent. He knows we have thousands of them here, and yet he isn't really afraid of that idea. He thinks we may arm them, make a mob of them. He can't begin to imagine that a serf can learn something better than how to handle a sidearm—something better, and far more dangerous."

"How can you be sure?" Hazleton said.

"By analogue. Remember the planet of Thetis Alpha called Fitzgerald, where they used a big beast called a horse for everything—from pulling carts to racing? All right: suppose you visited a place where you had been told that a few horses had been taught to talk. While you're working there, somebody comes to give you a hand, dragging a spavined old plug with a straw hat pulled down over its ears and a pack on its back. (Excuse me, Karst, but business is business.) You aren't going to think of that horse as one of the talking ones. You aren't accustomed to thinking of horses as being able to talk at all."

"All right," Hazleton said, grinning at Karst's evident discomfiture. "What's the main strategy from here on out, boss? I gather that you've got it set up. Are you ready to give it a name yet?"

"Not quite," the mayor said. "Unless you like long titles. It's still just another problem in political pseudomorphism."

Amalfi caught sight of Karst's deliberately incurious face and his own grin broadened. "Or," he said, "the fine art of tricking your opponent into throwing his head at you."

CHAPTER NINE: Home

IMT was a squat city, long rooted in the stony soil, and as changeless as a forest of cenotaphs. Its quietness, too, was like the quietness of a cemetery, and the Proctors, carrying the fanlike wands of their office, the pierced fans with the jagged tops and the little jingling tags, were much like friars moving among the dead.

The quiet, of course, could be accounted for very simply. The serfs were not allowed to speak within the walls of IMT unless spoken to, and there were comparatively few Proctors in the city to speak to them. For Amalfi, there was also the imposed silence of the slaughtered millions of Thor V blanketing the air. He wondered if the Proctors themselves could still hear that raw silence.

He got his answer almost at once. The naked brown figure of a passing serf glanced furtively at the party, saw Heldon, and raised a finger to its lips in what was evidently an established gesture of respect. Heldon barely nodded. Amalfi, necessarily, took no overt notice at all, but he thought: *Shh, is it? I don't wonder. But it's too late, Heldon. The secret is out.*

Karst trudged behind them, shooting an occasional wary glance at Heldon from under his tangled eyebrows. His caution was wasted on the Proctor. They passed through a decaying public square, in the center of which was an almost-obliterated statuary group, so weatherworn as to have lost any integrity it might ever have had. Integrity, Amalfi mused, is not a common characteristic of monuments. Except to a sharp eye, the mass of stone on the old pedestal might have been nothing but a moderately large meteor, riddled with the twisting pits characteristic of siderites.

Amalfi could see, however, that the spaces sculpted out of the interior of that block of black stone, after the fashion of an ancient Earth sculptor named Moore, had once had meaning. Inside the stone there had once stood a powerful human figure, with its foot resting upon the neck of a slighter figure; both surrounded by matter, but cut into space.

Heldon, too, stopped and looked at the monument. There was some kind of struggle going on inside of him. Amalfi did not know what it was, but he had a good guess. Heldon was a young man; hence, as a Proctor, he was probably recently elected. Karst's testimony had made it clear that most of the other members of the Great Nine—Asor, Bemajdi, and the rest—had been members of the Great Nine from the beginning. They were, in short, not the descendants of the men who had ravaged Thor V, but those very same men, preserved by a jealous hoarding of anti-agathics right down to the present.

Heldon looked at the monument. The figures inside it made it clear that once upon a time IMT had actually been proud of the memory of Thor V, and the ancients of the Great Nine, while they might not still be proud, were still guilty. Heldon, who had not himself committed that crime, was choosing whether or not to associate himself with it in fact, as he had already associated himself by implication, by being a Proctor at all. . . .

"Ahead is the Temple," Heldon said suddenly, turning away from the statue. "The machinery is beneath it. There should be no one of interest in it at this hour, but I had best make sure. Wait here."

No one of interest: that meant the serfs. Heldon had decided; he was of the Proctors; he had taken Thor V into his pigeon's bosom.

"Suppose somebody notices us?" Amalfi said.

"This square is usually avoided. Also, I have men posted

around it to divert any chance traffic. If you don't wander away, you'll be safe."

The Proctor gathered in his shirts and strode away toward the big domed building, where he disappeared abruptly down an alleyway. Behind Amalfi, Karst began to sing, in an exceedingly scratchy voice, but very softly—a folk tune of some kind, obviously. The melody, which once had had to do with a town named Kazan, was too many thousands of years old for Amalfi to recognize it, even had he not been tune deaf. Nevertheless, the mayor abruptly found himself listening to Karst, with the intensity of a hooded owl sonar-tracking a field mouse. Karst chanted:

"Wild on the wind rose the righteous wrath of Maalvin,
 Borne like a brand to the burning of the Barrens.
 Arms of hands of rebels perished then,
 Stars nor moons bedecked that midnight.
 IMT made the sky
 Fall!"

Seeing that Amalfi was listening to him, Karst stopped with an apologetic gesture. "Go ahead, Karst," Amalfi said at once. "How does the rest go?"

"There isn't time. There are hundreds of verses; every singer adds at least one of his own to the song. It is always supposed to end with this one:

"Black with their blood was the brick of that barrow,
 Toppled the tall towers, crushed to the clay.
 None might live who flouted Maalvin,
 Earth their souls spurned spaceward, wailing,
 IMT made the sky
 Fall!"

"That's great," Amalfi said grimly. "We really are in the soup—just about in the bottom of the bowl, I'd say. I wish I'd heard that song a week ago."

"What does it tell you?" Karst said wonderingly. "It is only an old legend."

"It tells me why Heldon wants his spindizzies fixed. I knew he wasn't telling me the straight goods, but that old

Laputa gag never occurred to me—more recent cities aren't strong enough in the keel to risk it. But with all the mass this burg packs, it can squash us flat—and we'll just have to sit still for it!"

"I don't understand——"

"It's simple enough. Your prophet Maalvin used IMT like a nutcracker. He picked it up, flew it over the opposition, and let it down again. The trick was dreamed up away before space flight, as I recall. Karst, stick close to me; I may have to get a message to you under Heldon's eye, so watch for . . . Sst, here he comes."

The Proctor had been uttered by the alleyway like an untranslatable word. He came rapidly toward them across the crumbling flagstones.

"I think," Heldon said, "that we are now ready for your valuable aid, Mayor Amalfi."

Heldon put his foot on a jutting pyramidal stone and pressed down. Amalfi watched carefully, but nothing happened. He swept his flash around the featureless stone walls of the underground chamber, then back again to the floor. Impatiently, Heldon kicked the little pyramid.

This time, there was a protesting rumble. Very slowly, and with a great deal of scraping, a block of stone perhaps five feet long by two feet wide began to rise, as if pivoted or hinged at the far end. The beam of the mayor's flash darted into the opening, picking out a narrow flight of steps.

"I'm disappointed," Amalfi said. "I expected to see Jules Verne come out from under it—or Dean Swift. All right, Heldon, lead on."

The Proctor went cautiously down the steps, holding his skirts up against the dampness. Karst came last, bent low under the heavy pack, his arms hanging laxly. The steps felt cold and slimy through the thin soles of the mayor's sandals, and little trickles of moisture ran down the close-pressing walls. Amalfi felt a nearly intolerable urge to light a cigar; he could almost taste the powerful aromatic odor cutting through the humidity. But he needed his hands free.

He was almost ready to hope that the spindizzies had been ruined by all this moisture, but he discarded the idea

even as it was forming in the back of his mind. That would
be the easy way out, and in the end it would be disastrous.
If the Okies were ever to call this planet their own, IMT
had to be made to fly again.

How to keep it off his own city's back, once IMT was
aloft, he still was unable to figure. He was piloting, as he
invariably wound up doing in the pinches, by the seat of
his pants.

The steps ended abruptly in a small chamber so small,
chilly, and damp that it was little more than a cave. The
flashlight's eyes roved, came to rest on an oval doorway
sealed off with dull metal—almost certainly lead. So IMT's
spindizzies ran "hot"? That was already bad news; it back-
dated them far beyond the year to which Amalfi had
tentatively assigned them.

"That it?" he said.

"That is the way," Heldon agreed. He twisted an incon-
spicuous handle.

Ancient fluorescents flickered into bluish life as the
valve drew back, and glinted upon the humped backs of
machines. The air was quite dry here—evidently the big
chamber was kept sealed—and Amalfi could not repress a
fugitive pang of disappointment. He scanned the huge
machines, looking for control panels or homologues thereof.

"Well?" Heldon said harshly. He seemed to be under
considerable strain. It occurred to Amalfi that Heldon's
strategy might well be a personal flyer, not an official
policy of the Great Nine, in which case it might go hard
with Heldon if his colleagues found him in this particular
place of all places with an Okie. "Aren't you going to make
any tests?"

"Certainly," Amalfi said. "I was a little taken aback at
their size, that's all."

"They are old, as you know," said the Proctor. "Doubtless they are built much larger nowadays."

That, of course, wasn't so. Modern spindizzies ran less
than a tenth the size of these. The comment cast new
doubt upon Heldon's exact status. Amalfi had assumed
that the Proctor would not let him touch the spindizzies
except to inspect; that there would be plenty of men in
IMT capable of making repairs from detailed instructions;

that Heldon himself, and any Proctor, would know enough physics to comprehend whatever explanations Amalfi might proffer. Now he was not so sure—and on this question hung the amount of tinkering Amalfi would be able to do without being detected.

The mayor mounted a metal stair to a catwalk which ran along the tops of the generators, then stopped and looked down at Karst. "Well, stupid, don't just stand there," he said. "Come on up, and bring the stuff."

Obediently Karst shambled up the metal steps, Heldon at his heels. Amalfi ignored them to search for an inspection port in the casing, found one, and opened it. Beneath was what appeared to be a massive rectifying circuit, plus the amplifier for some kind of monitor—probably a digital computer. The amplifier involved more vacuum tubes than Amalfi had ever before seen gathered into one circuit, and there was a separate power supply to deliver DC to their heaters. Two of the tubes were each as big as his fist.

Karst bent over and slung the pack to the deck. Amalfi drew out of it a length of slender black cable and thrust its double prongs into a nearby socket. A tiny bulb on the other end glowed neon-red.

"Your computer's still running," he reported. "Whether it's still sane or not is another matter. May I turn the main banks on, Heldon?"

"I'll turn them on," the Proctor said. He went down the stairs again and across the chamber.

Instantly Amalfi was murmuring through motionless lips into the inspection port. The result to Karst's ears must have been rather weird. The technique of speaking without moving one's lips is simply a matter of substituting consonants which do not involve lip movement, such as y, for those which do, such as w. If the resulting sound is picked up from inside the resonating chamber, as it is with a throat mike, it is not too different from ordinary speech, only a bit more blurred. Heard from outside the speaker's nasopharyngeal cavity, however, it has a tendency to sound like Japanese Pidgin.

"Yatch Heldon, Karst. See yhich syitch he kulls, an' nenorize its location. Got it? Good."

The tubes lit. Karst nodded once, very slightly. The

Proctor watched from below while Amalfi inspected the lines.

"Will they work?" he called. His voice was muffled, as though he were afraid to raise it as high as he thought necessary.

"I think so. One of these tubes is gassing, and there may have been some failures here and there. Better check the whole lot before you try anything ambitious. You do have facilities for testing tubes, don't you?"

Relief spread visibly over Heldon's face, despite his obvious effort to betray nothing. Probably he could have fooled any of his own people without effort, but for Amalfi, who, like any Okie mayor, could follow the parataxic "speech" of muscle interplay and posture as readily as he could spoken dialogue, Heldon's expression was as clear as a signed confession.

"Certainly," the Proctor said. "Is that all?"

"By no means. I think you ought to rip out about half of these circuits, and install transistors wherever they can be used; we can sell you the necessary germanium at the legal rate. You've got two or three hundred tubes to a unit here, by my estimate, and if you have a tube failure in flight—well, the only word that fits what would happen then is *blooey!*"

"Will you be able to show us how?"

"Probably," the mayor said. "If you'll allow me to inspect the whole system, I can give you an exact answer."

"All right," Heldon said. "But don't delay. I can't count on more than another half-day at most."

This was better than Amalfi had expected—miles better. Given that much time, he could trace at least enough of the leads to locate the master control. That Heldon's expression failed totally to match the content of his speech disturbed Amalfi profoundly, but there was nothing that he could do that would alter that now. He pulled paper and stylus out of Karst's pack and began to make rapid sketches of the wiring before him.

After he had a fairly clear idea of the first generator's setup, it was easier to block in the main features of the second. It took time, but Heldon did not seem to tire.

The third spindizzy completed the picture, leaving Amalfi

wondering what the fourth one was for. It turned out to be a booster, designed to compensate for the losses of the others wherever the main curve of their output failed to conform to the specs laid down for it by the crude, overall regenerative circuit. The booster was located on the backside of the feedback loop, behind the computer rather than ahead of it, so that all the computer's corrections had to pass through it; the result, Amalfi was sure, would be a small but serious "base surge" every time any correction was applied. The spindizzies of IMT seemed to have been wired together by Cro-Magnon Man.

But they would fly the city. That was what counted.

Amalfi finished his examination of the booster generator and straightened up painfully, stretching the muscles of his back. He had no idea how many hours he had consumed. It seemed as though months had passed. Heldon was still watching him, deep blue circles under his eyes, but still wide awake and watchful.

And Amalfi had found no point anywhere in the underground chamber from which the spindizzies of IMT could be controlled. The control point was somewhere else; the main control cable ran into a pipe which shot staight up through the roof of the cavern.

. . . IMT made the sky/ Fall . . .

Amalfi yawned ostentatiously and bent back to fasten the plate over the booster-generator's observation port. Karst squatted near him, frankly asleep, as relaxed and comfortable as a cat drowsing on a high ledge. Heldon watched.

"I'm going to have to do the job for you," Amalfi said. "It's really major; might take weeks."

"I thought you would say so," Heldon said. "And I was glad to give you the time to find out. But I don't think we'll make any such replacements."

"You need 'em."

"Possibly. But obviously there is a big factor of safety in the apparatus, or we would never have been able to fly the city at all." (Not, Amalfi noticed, "our ancestors," but "we"; Heldon had identified himself with the crime. He would pay.) "You will understand, Mayor Amalfi, that we cannot risk your doing something to the machines that we can't do ourselves, on the unlikely assumption that you're increasing their efficiency. If they will run as they are, that will have to be good enough."

"Oh, they'll run," Amalfi said. He began, methodically, to pack up his equipment. "For a while. I'll tell you flatly that they're not safe to operate, all the same."

Heldon shrugged, and went down the spiral metal stairs to the floor of the chamber. Amalfi rummaged in the pack a moment more. Then he ostentatiously kicked Karst awake—and kicked hard, for he knew better than to playact with a born overseer for an audience—and motioned the serf to pick up the bundle. They went down after Heldon.

The Proctor was smiling, and it was not a nice smile. "Not safe?" he said. "No, I never supposed that they were. But I think now that the dangers are mostly political."

"Why?" Amalfi demanded, trying to moderate his breathing. He was suddenly almost exhausted; it had taken—how many hours? He had no idea.

"Are you aware of the time, Mayor Amalfi?"

"About morning, I'd judge," Amalfi said dully, jerking the pack more firmly onto Karst's drooping left shoulder. "Damn late, anyhow."

"Very late," Heldon said. He was not disguising his expression now. He was openly crowing. "The contract between your city and mine expired at noon today. It is now nearly an hour after noon; we have been here all night and morning. And your city is still on our soil, in violation of the contract, Mayor Amalfi."

"An oversight——"

"No; a victory." Heldon drew a tiny silver tube from the folds of his robe and blew into it. "Mayor Amalfi, you may consider yourself a prisoner of war."

The little silver tube had made no audible sound, but there were already ten men in the room. The mesotron rifles they carried were of an ancient design, probably pre-Kammerman, like the spindizzies of IMT.

But, like the spindizzies, they looked as though they would work.

Karst froze; Amalfi unfroze him by jabbing him surreptitiously in the ribs with a finger, and began to unload the contents of his own small pack into Karst's.

"You've called the Earth police, I suppose?" he said.

"Long ago. That way of escape will be cut off by now. Let me say, Mayor Amalfi, that if you expected to find down here any controls that you might disable—and I was quite prepared to allow you to search for them—you expected too much stupidity from me."

Amalfi said nothing. He went on methodically repacking the equipment.

"You are making too many motions, Mayor Amalfi. Put your hands up in the air and turn around very slowly."

Amalfi put up his hands and turned. In each hand he held a small black object about the size and shape of an egg.

"I expected only as much stupidity as I got," he said conversationally. "You can see what I'm holding up there. I can and will drop one or both of them if I'm shot. I may drop them anyhow. I'm tired of your back-cluster ghost town."

Heldon snorted. "Explosives? Gas? Ridiculous; nothing so small could contain enough energy to destroy the city; and you have no masks. Do you take me for a fool?"

"Events prove you one," Amalfi said steadily. "The possibility was quite large that you would try to ambush me, once you had me in IMT. I could have forestalled that by bringing a guard with me. You haven't met my perimeter police; they're tough boys, and they've been off duty so long that they'd love the chance to tangle with your palace crew. Didn't it occur to you that I left my city without a bodyguard only because I had less cumbersome ways of protecting myself?"

"Eggs," Heldon said scornfully.

"As a matter of fact, they *are* eggs; the black color is an analine stain, put on the shells as a warning. They contain chick embryos inoculated with a two-hour alveolytic mutated Terrestrial rickettsialpox—a new airborne strain developed in our own BW lab. Free space makes a wonderful laboratory for that kind of trick; an Okie town specializing in agronomy taught us the techniques a couple of centuries back. Just a couple of eggs—but if I were to drop them, you would have to crawl on your belly behind me all the way back to my city to get the antibiotic shot that's specific for the disease; we developed that ourselves, too."

Cities in Flight

There was a brief silence, made all the more empty by the hoarse breathing of the Proctor. The armed men eyed the black eggs uneasily, and the muzzles of their rifles wavered out of line. Amalfi had chosen his weapon with great care; static feudal societies classically are terrified by the threat of plague—they have seen so much of it.

"Impasse," Heldon said at last. "All right, Mayor Amalfi. You and your slave have safe-conduct from this chamber——"

"From the building. If I hear the slightest sound of pursuit up the stairs, I'll chuck these down on you. They burst hard, by the way—the virus generates a lot of gas in chick-embryo medium."

"Very well," Heldon said, through his teeth. "From the building, then. But you have won nothing, Mayor Amalfi. If you can get back to your city, you'll be just in time to be an eyewitness of the victory of IMT—the victory you helped make possible. I think you'll be surprised at how thorough we can be."

"No, I won't," Amalfi said, in a flat, cold, and quite merciless voice. "I know all about IMT, Heldon. This is the end of the line for the Mad Dogs. When you die, you and your whole crew of Interstellar Master Traders, *remember Thor Five*."

Heldon turned the color of unsized paper, and so, surprisingly, did at least four of his riflemen. Then the color began to rise in the Proctor's plump, fungoid cheeks. "Get out," he croaked, almost inaudibly. Then, suddenly, at the top of his voice: "Get out; *Get out!*"

Juggling the eggs casually, Amalfi walked toward the lead radiation lock. Karst shambled after him, cringing as he passed Heldon. Amalfi thought that the serf might be overdoing it, but Heldon did not notice; Karst might as well have been—a horse.

The lead plug swung to, blocking out Heldon's furious, frightened face and the glint of the fluorescents on the ancient spindizzies. Amalfi plunged one hand into Karst's pack, depositing one egg in the siliconefoam nest from which he had taken it, and withdrew the hand again grasping an ugly Schmeisser acceleration pistol. This he thrust into the waistband of his breeches.

"Up the stairs, Karst. Fast. I had to shave it pretty fine.

Go on, I'm right behind you. Where would the controls for those machines be, by your guess? The control lead went up through the roof of that cavern."

"On the top of the Temple," Karst said. He was mounting the narrow steps in huge bounds, but it did not seem to cost him the slightest effort. "Up there is Star Chamber, where the Great Nine meets. There isn't any way to get to it that I know."

They burst up into the cold stone antechamber. Amalfi's flash roved over the floor, found the jutting pyramid; Karst kicked it. With a prolonged groan, the tilted slab settled down over the flight of steps and became just another block in the floor. There was certainly some way to raise it again from below, but Heldon would hesitate before he used it; the slab was noisy in motion, noisy enough to tell Amalfi that he was being followed. At the first such squawk, Amalfi would lay a black egg, and Heldon knew it.

"I want you to get out of the city, and take every serf that you can find with you," Amalfi said. "But it's going to take timing. Somebody's got to pull that switch down below that I asked you to memorize, and I can't do it; I've got to get into Star Chamber. Heldon will guess that I'm going up there, and he'll follow me. After he's gone by, Karst, you have to go down there and open that switch."

Here was the low door through which Heldon had first admitted them to the Temple. More stairs ran up from it. Strong daylight poured under it.

Amalfi inched the old door open and peered out. Despite the brightness of the afternoon, the close-set, chunky buildings of IMT turned the alleyway outside into a confusing multitude of twilights. Half a dozen leaden-eyed serfs were going by, with a Proctor walking behind them, half asleep.

"Can you find your way back into that crypt?" Amalfi whispered, leaving the door ajar.

"There's only one way to go."

"Good. Go back, then. Dump the pack outside the door here; we don't need it anymore. As soon as Heldon's crew goes on up these stairs, get back down there and pull that switch. Then get out of the city; you'll have about four minutes of accumulated warm-up time from all those tube stages: don't waste a second of it. Got it?"

"Yes, but——"

Something went over the Temple like an avalanche of gravel and dwindled into some distance. Amalfi closed one eye and screwed the other one skyward. "Rockets," he said. "Sometimes I don't know why I insisted on a planet as primitive as this. But maybe I'll learn to love it. Good luck, Karst."

He turned toward the stairs.

"They'll trap you up there," Karst said.

"No, they won't. Not Amalfi. But me no *buts*, Karst. Git."

Another rocket went over, and far away there was a heavy explosion. Amalfi charged like a bull up the new flight of stairs toward Star Chamber.

The staircase was long and widely curving, as well as narrow, and both its risers and its treads were infuriatingly small. Amalfi remembered that the Proctors did not themselves climb stairs; they were carried up them on the forearms of serfs. Such pussy-ant steps made for sure footing, but not for fast transit.

As far as Amalfi was able to compute, the steps rose gently along the outside curvature of the Temple's dome, following a one-and-a-half helix to the summit. Why? Presumably, the Proctors didn't require themselves to climb long flights of stairs for nothing, even with serfs to carry them. Why couldn't Star Chamber be under the dome with the spindizzies, for instance, instead of atop it?

Amalfi was not far past the first half-turn before one good reason became evident. There was a rustle of voices jostling its way through the chinks in the dome from below; a congregation, evidently, was gathering. As Amalfi continued to mount the flat spiral, the murmuring became more and more discreet, until individual voices could almost be separated out from it. Up there at what mathematically would be the bottom of the bowl, where the floor of Star Chamber was, the architect of the Temple evidently had contrived a whispering gallery—a vault to which a Proctor might put his ear and hear the thinnest syllable of conspiracy in the crowd of suppliants below.

It was ingenious, Amalfi had to admit. Conspirators on

church-bearing planets generally tend to think of churches as safe places for quiet plotting. In Amalfi's universe any planet which sponsored churches probably had a revolt coming to it.

Blowing like a porpoise, he scrambled up the last arc of the long Greek-spiral staircase. A solidly-closed double door, worked all over with phony-Byzantine scrolls, stood looking down at him. He didn't bother to stop to admire it; he hit it squarely under the paired, patently synthetic sapphires just above its center, and hit it hard. It burst.

Disappointment stopped him for a moment. The chamber was an ellipse of low eccentricity, monastically bare and furnished only with a heavy wooden table and nine chairs, now drawn back against the wall. There were no controls here, nor any place where they could be concealed. The chamber was windowless.

The lack of windows told him what he wanted to know. The other, the compelling reason why Star Chamber was on top of the Temple dome was that it harbored, somewhere, the pilot's cabin of IMT. And that, in as old a city as IMT, meant that visibility would be all-important—requiring a situation atop the tallest structure in the city, and as close to 360° visibility as could be managed. Obviously, Amalfi was not yet up high enough.

He looked up at the ceiling. One of the big stone slabs had a semicircular cup in it, not much bigger than a large coin. The flat edge was much worn.

Amalfi grinned and looked under the wooden table. Sure enough, there it was—a pole with a hooked bill at one end, rather like a halberd, slung in clips. He yanked it out, straightened, and fitted the bill into the opening in the stone.

The slab came down easily, hinged at one end as the block down below over the generator room had been. The ancestors of the Proctors had not been much given to varying their engineering principles. The free end of the slab almost touched the tabletop. Amalfi sprang onto the table and scrambled up the tilted face of the stone; as he neared the top, the translating center of gravity which he represented actuated a counterweighting mechanism somewhere, and the slab closed, bearing him the rest of the way.

This was the control cabin, all right. It was tiny and packed with panels, all of which were thick in dust. Bull's-eyes of thick glass looked out over the city at the four compass points, and there was one set overhead. A single green light was glowing on one of the panels. While he walked toward it, it went out.

That had been Karst, cutting the power. Amalfi hoped that the peasant would get out again. He had grown to like him. There was something in his weathered, unmovable, shockproof courage, and in the voracity of his starved intelligence, that reminded the mayor of someone he had once known. That that someone was Amalfi as he had been at the age of twenty-five, Amalfi did not know, and there was no one else alive who would be able to tell him.

Spindizzies in essence are simple; Amalfi had no difficulty in setting and locking the controls the way he wanted them, or in performing sundry small tasks of highly selective sabotage. How he was to conceal what he had done, when every move left huge smears in the heavy dust, was a tougher problem. He solved it at length in the only possible way: he took off his shirt and flailed it at all of the boards. The result made him sneeze until his eyes watered, but it worked.

Now all he had to do was get out.

There were already sounds below in Star Chamber, but he was not yet worried about a direct attack. He still had a black egg, and the Proctors knew it. Furthermore, he also had the pole with the hooked bill, so that in order to open up the control room at all, the Proctors would have to climb on each other's shoulders. They weren't in good physical shape for gymnastics, and besides, they would know that men indulging in such stunts could be defeated temporarily by nothing more complicated than a kick in the teeth.

Nevertheless, Amalfi had no intention of spending the rest of his life in the control room of IMT. He had only about six minutes to get out of the city altogether.

After thinking very rapidly for approximately four seconds, Amalfi stood on the stone slab, overbalanced it, and slid solemnly down onto the top of the table in Star Chamber.

After a stunned instant, half a dozen pairs of hands grabbed him at once. Heldon's face, completely unrecognizable with fury and fear, was thrust into his.

"What have you done? Answer, or I'll order you torn to pieces."

"Don't be a lunkhead. Tell your men to let go of me. I still have your safe-conduct—and in case you're thinking of repudiating it, I still have the same weapon I had before. Cast off, by God, or——"

Heldon's guards released him before he had finished speaking. Heldon lurched heavily up onto the tabletop and began to claw his way up the slab. Several other robed, bald-headed men jostled after him—evidently Heldon had been driven by a greater fear to tell some of the Great Nine what he had done. Amalfi walked backwards out of Star Chamber and down two steps. Then he bent, deposited his remaining black egg carefully on the threshold, thumbed his nose at the furious soldiery, and took off down the spiral stairs at a dead run.

It would take Heldon a while, perhaps as much as a minute after he switched on the controls, to discover that the generators had been cut out while he was chasing Amalfi; and another minute, at best, to get a flunky down into the basement to turn them on again. Then there would be a warm-up time of four minutes. After that—IMT would go aloft.

Amalfi shot out into the alleyway and thence into the street, caroming off an astounded Proctor. A shout rose behind him. He doubled over and kept running.

The street was nearly dark in the twilight of the twin suns. He kept in the shadows and made for the nearest corner. The cornice of the building ahead of him abruptly turned lava-white, then began to dim through the red. He never did hear the accompanying scream of the mesotron rifle. He was concentrating on something else.

Then he was around the corner. The quickest route to the edge of the city, as well as he could recall, was down the street he had just quitted, but that was now out of the question; he had no desire to be burned down. Whether or not he could get out of IMT in time by any alternate route remained to be seen.

Doggedly, he kept running. He was fired on once more, by a man who did not really know on whom he was firing. Here, Amalfi was just a running man who failed to fit the categories; any first shot at him would be a reflex of disorientation, and aimed accordingly badly. . . .

The ground shuddered, ever so delicately, like the hide of a monster twitching at flies in its sleep. Somehow Amalfi managed to run still faster.

The shudder came again, stronger this time. A long, protracted groan followed it, traveling in a heavy wave through the bedrock of the city. The sound brought Proctors and serfs alike boiling out of the buildings.

At the third shock, something toward the center of the city collapsed with a sullen roar. Amalfi was caught up in the aimless, terrified eddying of the crowd, and fought with hands, teeth, and bullet head. . . .

The groaning grew louder. Abruptly, the ground bucked. Amalfi pitched forward. With him went the whole milling mob, falling in wind-rows like stacked grain. There was frantic screaming everywhere, but it was worst inside the buildings. Over Amalfi's head a window shattered explosively, and a woman's body came twisting and tumbling through the shuddering air.

Amalfi heaved himself up, spitting blood, and ran again. The pavement ahead was cracked in great, irregular shards, like a madman's mosaic. Just beyond, the blocks were tilted all awry, reminding Amalfi irrelevantly of a breakwater he had seen on some other planet, in some other century. . . .

He was clambering over them before he realized that these could only mark the rim of the original city of IMT. There were still more buildings on the other side of the huge, rock-filled trench, but the trench itself showed where the perimeter of the ancient Okie city had been sunk into the soil of the planet. Fighting for air with saw-edged rales, he threw himself from stone to stone toward the far edge of the trench. This was the most dangerous ground of all; if IMT were to lift now, he would be ground as fine as mincemeat in the tumbling rocks. If he could just reach the marches of the Barrens. . . .

Behind him, the groaning rose steadily in pitch, until it

sounded like the tearing of an endless sheet of metal. Ahead, across the Barrens, his own city gleamed in the last rays of the twin suns. There was fighting around it; little bright flashes were sputtering at its edge. The rockets Amalfi had heard, four of them, were arrowing across the sky, and black things dropped from them. The Okie city responded with spouts of smoke.

Then there was an unbearably bright burst. After Amalfi could see again, there were only three rockets. In another few seconds there wouldn't be any: the City Fathers never missed.

Amalfi's lungs burned. He felt sod under his sandals. A twisted runner of furze lashed across his ankle, and he fell again.

He tried to get up and could not. The seared turf, on which an ancient rebel city once had stood, rumbled threateningly. He rolled over. The squat towers of IMT were swaying, and all around the edge of the city, huge blocks and clods heaved and turned over, like surf. Impossibly, a thin line of light, intense and ruddy, appeared above the moiling rocks. The suns were shining *under the city* . . .

The line of light widened. The old city took the air with an immense bound, and the rending of the long-rooted foundations was ear-splitting. From the sides of the huge mass, human beings threw themselves desperately toward the Barrens; most of them, Amalfi saw, were serfs. The Proctors, of course, were still trying to control the flight of IMT. . . .

The city rose majestically. It was gaining speed. Amalfi's heart hammered. If Heldon and his crew could figure out in time what Amalfi had done to the controls, Karst's old ballad would be reenacted, and the crushing rule of the Proctors made safe forever.

But Amalfi had done his work well. The city of IMT did not stop rising. With a profound, visceral shock, Amalfi realized that it was already nearly a mile up, and still accelerating. The air would be thinning up there, and the Proctors had forgotten too much to know what to do. . . .

A mile and a half.

Two miles.

It grew smaller. At five miles it was just a wavery inkblot, lit on one side. At seven miles it was a point of dim light.

A bristle-topped head and a pair of enormous shoulders lifted cautiously from a nearby gully. It was Karst. He continued to look aloft for a moment, but IMT at ten miles was invisible. He looked down to Amalfi.

"Can—can it come back?" he said huskily.

"No," Amalfi said, his breathing gradually coming under control. "Keep watching, Karst. It isn't over yet. Remember that the Proctors had called the Earth cops——"

At that same moment, the city of IMT reappeared—in a way. A third sun flowered in the sky. It lasted for three or four seconds. Then it dimmed and died.

"The cops were warned," Amalfi said softly, "to watch for an Okie city trying to make a getaway. They found it, and they dealt with it. Of course they got the wrong city, but they don't know that. They'll go home now—and now we're home, and so are you and your fellow men. Home on Earth, for good."

Around them, there was a murmuring of voices, hushed with disaster, and with something else, too—something so old, and so new, that it hardly had a name on the planet that IMT had ruled. It was called *freedom*.

"On Earth?" Karst repeated. He and the mayor climbed painfully to their feet. "What do you mean? This is not Earth——"

Across the Barrens, the Okie city glittered—the city that had pitched camp to mow some lawns. A cloud of stars was rising behind it.

"It is now," Amalfi said. "We're all Earthmen, Karst. Earth is more than just one little planet, buried in another galaxy than this. Earth is much more important than that.

"Earth isn't a place. It's an idea."

THE TRIUMPH
OF TIME

To Lester and Evelyn del Rey

Bismillahi 'rrahmani 'rrahim
When the day that must come shall have come
suddenly,
None shall treat that sudden coming as a lie:
Day that shall abase! Day that shall exalt!
When the earth shall be shaken with a shock,
And the mountains shall be crumbled with a
crumbling,
And shall become scattered dust,
And into three bands shall ye be divided: . . .
    Before thee have we granted to a man a life
    that shall last forever:
If thou then die, shall they live forever?
    Every soul shall taste of death: . . .
    But it shall come on them suddenly and shall
    confound them; and they shall not be able to
    put it back, neither shall they be respited.

—The Koran;
Sura LVI, Sura XXI

PROLOGUE

. . . Thus we have seen that Earth, a planet like other
civilized worlds, having a score of myriads of years of
atmosphere-bound history behind her, and having begun
manned local spaceflight in approximately her own year
1960, did not achieve importance on a galactic scale until
her independent discovery of the gravitron polarity generator in her year 2019. Her colonials made first contact with
the Vegan Tyranny in 2289, and the antagonism between
the two great cultures, one on its way down, the other
rapidly developing, culminated in the Battle of Altair in
2310, the first engagement of what has come to be known
as the Vegan War. Some 65 years later, Earth launched
the first of the fleet of space-cruising cities, the "Okies," by
which it was eventually to dominate the galaxy for a long
period, and in 2413 the long struggle with the Vegans
came to an end with the investment of Vega itself, and the
Battle of the Forts. The subsequent scorching of the Vegan
system by the Third Colonial Navy, under Admiral Alois
Hrunta, prompted Earth proper to indict its admiral *in
absentia* for atrocities and attempted genocide. The case
was tried, also *in absentia*, by the Colonial Court; Hrunta
was found guilty, but refused to submit to judgment. An
attempt to bring him in by force brought home for the first
time the fact that the Third Colonial Navy had defected to

him almost *en masse* and resulted in 2464 in the Battle of
BD 40°4048'. Both sides suffered heavy losses, but there
was no other outcome, and Hrunta subsequently declared
himself Emperor of Space—the first of many such gimcrack "empires" which were to spawn on the fringes of
Earth's jurisdiction during the so-called Empty Years. This
period officially began in 2522 with the collapse of local
government on Earth—the Bureaucratic State, dating from
2105—which after a brief police interregnum allowed the
now large numbers of Okie cities to develop in effectual
anarchy, a condition very well suited to their proliferation
of trade routes throughout the known and unknown galaxy.

We have already discussed the collapse under its own
weight of the Hruntan Empire and the final reduction of
the fragments by the recrudescent Earth police during the
period 3545–3602. We have stressed this relatively minor
aspect of Earth history not because it was at all unusual,
but because it was typical of the balkanization of Earth's
official power during the very period when its actual power
was greatly on the rise. Our discussion of the history of
one of the Okie cities, New York, N. Y., which began its
space-flying career in 3111 and thus overlapped much of
the history of the Hruntan Empire, may be compared to
illustrate the difference in the treatment accorded by Earth
to her two very different children, empires and Okies, and
history shows the wisdom of the choice; for it was the
wide-ranging Okies who were to make the galaxy an or-
chard for Earth for a relatively long period, as such periods go in galactic history.

Customs and cultures pronounced officially dead have,
however, a way of stirring again long after their supposed
interment. In some instances, of course, this is simply a
reflex twitch; for example, though the grandiose collapse
of the Earth culture certainly can be said to have begun
during the Battle of the Jungle in the Acolyte cluster in
3905, we find only five years later the Acolyte-Regent, a
Lt. Lerner, proclaiming himself Emperor of Space; but
the Acolyte fleet, already considerably cut up by its encounter with the Okies in the jungle, was annihilated by
the Earth police on their arrival a year later, and Emperor
Lerner died that same year in a slum on a tenthrate

Acolyte planet named Murphy from an overdose of wisdomweed. On a larger scale, the Battle of Earth in 3975, in which Earth found herself pitted against her own Okie cities, was marked also by an unexpected resurrection of the Vegan Tyranny, whose secretly constructed and long-wandering orbital fort chose this moment to make its last bid for galactic power. Its failure was a repetition in miniature of the failure of the entire Vegan Tyranny, despite superior force of arms, in any conflict with the Earthmen, who were far better chessmasters; the Vegans characteristically left prediction to computers, which lack the ability to make long intuitive leaps, as well as the decisiveness to act upon them.

The Okie city which had outplayed the Vegan orbital fort in the game of thinking ahead, our type-city New York, was far enough ahead of its own culture to have left the galaxy by 3978 for the Greater Magellanic Cloud. It left behind an Earth which in 3976 cut its own throat as a galactic power with the passage of the so-called anti-Okie Bill. Though the Magellanic planet which New York colonized in 3998 was in 3999 christened New Earth, the earlier date of 3976 marks the passing of Earth from the stellar stage. Already there were reaching out from one of the galaxy's largest and most beautiful star-clusters the first tentative strands of that strange culture called the Web of Hercules, which was destined to become the Milky Way's IVth great civilization. And yet once more a civilization which from every historical point of view had to be pronounced dead refused to stay entirely buried. The creeping, inexorable growth of the Web of Hercules through the heart of the galaxy was destined to be interrupted by that totally revolutionary, totally universal physical cataclysm now known as the Ginnangu-Gap; and though it is due entirely to the Web of Hercules that we still have records of galactic history before that cataclysm, and thus a continuity with the universe's past surely unprecedented in all the previous cycles, we must note, with more than a little awe, the sudden and critical reappearance of Earthmen in this timeless moment of chaos and creation, and the drastic and fruitful exeunt which they wrote for themselves into the universal drama.

—ACREFF-MONALES: *The Milky Way: Five Cultural Portraits*

CHAPTER ONE: New Earth

In these later years it occasionally startled John Amalfi to be confronted by evidence that there was anything in the universe that was older than he was, and the irrationality of his allowing himself to be startled by such a truism startled him all over again. This crushing sensation of age, of the sheer dead weight of a thousand years bearing down upon his back, was in itself a symptom of what was wrong with him—or, as he preferred to think of it, of what was wrong with New Earth.

He had been so startled while prowling disconsolately through the grounded and abandoned hulk of the city, itself an organism many millennia older than he was, but—as befitted such an antiquity—now only a corpse. It was, indeed, the corpse of a whole society; for nobody on New Earth now contemplated building any more space-cruising cities or in any other way resuming the wandering life of the Okies. Those of the original crew on New Earth, spread very thin among the natives and their own children and grandchildren, now looked back on that entire period with a sort of impersonal, remote distaste, and would certainly recoil from the very idea of returning to it, should anyone have the bad manners to broach such a notion. As for the second and third generations, they knew

of the Okie days only as history, and looked upon the hulk
of the flying city that had brought their parents to New
Earth as a fantastically clumsy and outmoded monster,
much as the pilot of an ancient atmospheric liner might
have regarded a still more ancient quinquireme in a
museum.

No one except Amalfi even appeared to take any interest in what might have happened to the whole of Okie
society back in the home lens, the Milky Way galaxy of
which the two Magellanics were satellites. To give them
credit, finding out what had happened would in any event
have been an almost impossible task; all kinds of broad-
casts—literally millions of them—could be picked up easily from the home lens if anyone cared to listen, but so
much time had elapsed since the colonization of New
Earth that sorting these messages into a meaningful picture would require years of work by a team of experts, and
none could be found who would take any interest in so
fruitless and essentially nostalgic a chore. Amalfi had in
fact come into the city with the vague notion of turning
the task over to the City Fathers, that enormous bank of
computing and memory-storage machines to which had
been intrusted all the thousands of routine technical, operational, and governmental problems of the city when it had
been in flight. What Amalfi would do with the information
when and if he got it he had no idea; certainly there was
no possibility of interesting any of the other New Earthmen in it, except in the form of half an hour's idle chatter.

And after all, the New Earthmen were right. The Greater
Magellanic Cloud was drawing steadily away from the
home lens, at well over 150 miles per second—a trifling
velocity in actuality, only a little greater than the diameter
of the average solar system per year, but symbolic of the
new attitude among the New Earthmen; people's eyes
were directed outward, away from all that ancient history.
There was considerably more interest in a nova which had
flared into being in intergalactic space, somewhere beyond
the Lesser Magellanic, than there was in the entire pano-
ply of the home lens, visibly though the latter dominated
the night sky from horizon to horizon during certain seasons of the year. There was, of course, still space flight, for

trade with other planets in the little satellite galaxy was a necessity; the trade was conducted for the most part in large cargo hulls, and there were a number of larger units such as mobile processing plants which still needed to be powered by gravitron-polarity generators or "spindizzies"; but for the most part the trend was toward the development of local, self-sufficient industries.

It was while he was setting up the City Fathers for the problem in analysis of the million-fold transmission from the home lens, alone in what had once been his Mavor's Office, that Amalfi had suddenly had thrown at him the fragment from the writings of a man dead eleven centuries before Amalfi had been born. Possibly the uttering of the unexpected fragment had been simply an artifact of the warming-up process—like most computers of their age and degree of complexity, it took the City Fathers two to three hours to become completely sane after they had been out of service for a while—or perhaps Amalfi's fingers, working with sure automatism even after all these years, had been wiser than his head, and without the collusion of Amalfi's consciousness had built into the problem elements of what was really troubling him: the New Earthmen. In either event, the quotation was certainly apposite:

"If this be the whole fruit of victory, we say: if the generations of mankind suffered and laid down their lives; if prophets and martyrs sang in the fire, and all the sacred tears were shed for no other end than that a race of creatures of such unexampled insipidity should succeed, to protract *in saecula saeculorum* their contented and inoffensive lives—why, at such a rate, better lose than win the battle, or at all events better ring down the curtain before the last act of the play, so that a business that began so importantly may be saved from so singularly flat a winding-up."

"What was *that?*" Amalfi barked into the microphone.

"AN EXTRACT FROM '*THE WILL TO BELIEVE,*' BY WILLIAM JAMES, MR. MAYOR."

"Well, it's irrelevant; get your bottles and firecrackers back on the main problem. Wait a minute—is this the Librarian?"

"YES, MR. MAYOR."

"What's the date of the work you quoted?"

"1897, MR. MAYOR."

"All right. Switch out and hook into the analytical side of the loop; you've no business at the output end for this problem."

A flowmeter needle bobbed upward as the drain of the library machine on the circuit was discontinued for a moment, then dipped again. He did not proceed with the project for a while, however, but instead simply sat and thought about the fragment that the machines had offered him. There were, he supposed, a few unreconstructed Okies still alive on New Earth, though the only one that he knew personally was John Amalfi. He himself had no special nostalgia *qua* nostalgia for all the history he had outlived, for he could hardly forget that it had been by his foreplanning that New Earth had been founded. And for a period of perhaps four years there had been plenty to occupy his mind: the discovery that the planet, then unnamed, was at once the refuge and the feudal fief of a notorious pack of bindlestiffs calling itself Interstellar Master Traders—better known in the home lens simply as "the Mad Dogs"—had raised a considerable obstacle to colonization, the solution of which obviously needed to be drastic, and was. But the destruction of IMT in 3948 in the Battle of the Blasted Heath had left Amalfi at long last without problems and without function, and he had subsequently found himself utterly unable to become used to living in a stable and ordered society. The James quotation almost perfectly summarized his feelings about the Okie citizens who had once been his charges, and their descendants; he had of course to excuse the natives, who knew no better and were finding the problems of self-government an unprecedented challenge after their serfdom under "the Mad Dogs."

Local space travel, he knew very well, was no solution for him; one planet in the Cloud was very like another, and the Cloud itself was only 20,000 light years in diameter—a fact which made the Cloud extremely convenient to organize from one administrative center, but a fact of no significance whatsoever to a man who had once shepherded his city across 280,000 light years in a single flight. What he missed, after all, was not space, but instability itself, the feeling of being on the way to an unknown destination, unable to predict what outlandish surprises might be awaiting him at the next planetfall.

The fact of the matter was that longevity now hung on him like a curse. An indefinitely prolonged life span had been a prerequisite for an Okie society—indeed, until the discovery of the anti-agathic drugs early in the 21st Century, interstellar flight even with the spindizzy had been a physical impossibility; the distances involved were simply too great for a short-lived man to compass at any finite speed—but to be a virtually immortal man in a stable society was to be as uninteresting to one's self, for Amalfi at least, as an everlasting light bulb; he felt that he had simply been screwed into his socket and forgotten.

It was true that most of the other former Okies had seemed able to make the changeover—the youngsters in particular, whose experience of star-wandering had been limited, were now putting their long life expectancies to the obvious use: launching vast research or development projects the fruition of which could not be expected in under five centuries or more. There was, for example, an entire research team now hard at work in New Manhattan on the overall problem of antimatter. The theoretical brains of the project were being supplied largely by Dr. Schloss, an ex-Hruntan physicist who had boarded the city back in 3602 as a refugee during the reduction of the Duchy of Gort, a last surviving polyp of the extinct Hruntan Empire; administration of the project was in the hands of a comparative youngster named Carrel, who not so long ago had been the city's copilot and ranking understudy to the City Manager. The immediate objective of the project, according to Carrel, was the elucidation of the theoretical molecular structures possible to antimaterial atoms, but it was no secret that most of the young men in the group, with the active support of Schloss himself, were hoping in a few centuries to achieve the actual construction, not only of simple chemical compounds—that might come about in a matter of decades—of this radical type, but a visible, macroscopic artifact composed entirely of anti-matter. Upon the unthinkably explosive object they would no doubt paint, Amalfi surmised, had they by that time also composed an antimaterial paint and something to keep it in, the warning *Noli me tangere*.

That was all very well; but it was equally impossible for Amalfi, who was not a scientist, to participate. It was, of course, perfectly possible for him to end his life; he was not invulnerable, nor even truly immortal; immortality is a meaningless word in a universe where the fundamental laws, being stochastic in nature, allow no one to bar accidents, and where life no matter how prolonged is at bottom only a local and temporary discontinuity in the Second Law of Thermodynamics. The thought, however, did not occur to Amalfi; he was not the suicidal type. He had never felt less tired, less used-up, less despairing than he felt today; he was simply snarlingly bored, and too confirmed in his millennia-old patterns of thought and emotion to be able to settle for a single planet and a single social order, no matter how utopian; his thousand years of continuous translation from one culture to another had built up in him an enormous momentum which now seemed to be bearing him irresistibly toward an immovable inertial wall labeled, NO PLACE TO GO.

"Amalfi! So it's you. I might have guessed."

Amalfi shot the "hold" switch closed convulsively and swung around on his stool. He had, however, recognized the voice at once from centuries of familiarity. He had heard it often since somewhere around 3500, when the city had taken its owner on board as chief of the astronomy section: a testy and difficult little man with a deceptively mild manner who had never been precisely the chief astronomer that the city needed, but who had come through in the pinches often enough to prevent the City Fathers from allowing him to be swapped to another Okie city during the period when such swaps were still possible for Amalfi's town.

"Hello, Jake," Amalfi said.

"Hello, John," the astronomer said, peering curiously at the set-up board. "The Hazletons told me I might find you prowling around this old hulk, but I confess I'd forgotten about it by the time I decided to come over here. I wanted to use the computation section, but I couldn't get in—the machines were all shuttling back and forth on their tracks and coupling and uncoupling like a pack of demented two-hundred-ton ballet dancers. I thought maybe one of the kids had wandered in up here in the control room and was fooling with the boards. What are you up to?"

It was an extremely pointed question which, up to now, Amalfi had not asked himself. Even to consider answering Jake by describing the message-analysis project was to reject it; not that Jake would care one way or the other, but to Amalfi's inner self the answer would be an obvious blind. He said:

"I don't quite know. I had an urge to look around the place again. I hate to see it going to rust; I keep thinking it must still be good for something."

"It is, it is," Jake said. "After all, there are no computers quite like the City Fathers anywhere else on New Earth, let alone anywhere else in the Magellanics. I call on them pretty frequently when there's anything really complicated to be worked on; so does Schloss, I understand. After all, the City Fathers know a great deal that nobody else around here can know, and old though they are, they're still reasonably fast."

"I think there must be more to it than that," Amalfi said. "The city was powerful, is powerful still; the central pile is good for a million years yet at a minimum, and some of the spindizzies must still be operable—providing that we ever again find anything big enough to need all the lifting power we've got concentrated down below in the hold."

"Why should we?" the astronomer said, obviously not very much interested. "That's all past and done with."

"But is it? I keep thinking that no machine of the sophistication and complexity of the city can ever go quite out of use. And I don't mean just marginal uses, like occasionally consulting the City Fathers, or tapping the pile for some fraction of its total charge. This city was meant to fly, and by God it ought to be flying still."

"What for?"

"I don't know, exactly. Maybe for exploration, maybe for work, the kind of work we used to do. There must be some jobs in the Cloud for which nothing less than a machine of this size is suitable—though obviously we haven't hit such a job yet. Maybe it would be worth cruising and looking for one."

"I doubt it," Jake said. "Anyhow, she's gotten pretty tumbledown since we had our little difference with IMT, what with all those rocket bombs they threw at us—and letting her be rained on steadily ever since hasn't helped, either. Besides, I seemed to remember that that old 23rd St. spindizzy blew for good and all when we landed here. I hardly think she'd stir at all now if you tried to lift her, though no doubt she'd groan a good deal."

"I wasn't proposing to pick up the whole thing, anyhow," Amalfi said. "I know well enough that that couldn't be done. But the city's *over*-sophisticated for a field of action as small as the Cloud; there's a lot you could leave behind. Besides, we'd have a great deal of difficulty in scaring up anything more than a skeleton crew, but if we could rehabilitate only a part of her, we might still get her aloft again—"

"Part of her?" Jake said. "How do you propose to section a city with a granite keel? Particularly one composed as a unit on that keel? You'd find that many of the units that you most needed in your fraction would be in the outlying districts and couldn't be either cut off or transported inward; that's the way she was built, as a piece."

This of course was true. Amalfi said, "But supposing it could be done? How would you feel about it, Jake? You were an Okie for nearly five centuries; don't you miss it, a little, now?"

"Not a bit," the astronomer said briskly. "To tell you the truth, Amalfi, I never liked it. It was just that there was no place else to go. I thought you were all crazy with your gunning around the sky, your incessant tangles with the cops, and your wars, and the periods of starvation and all the rest, but you gave me a floating platform to work from and a good close look at stars and systems I could never have seen as well from a fixed observatory with any possible telescope, and besides, I got fed. So I was reasonably satisfied. But do it again, now that I have a choice? Certainly not. In fact, I only came over here to get some computational work done on this new star that's cropped up just beyond the Lesser Cloud; it's behaving outrageously—in fact, it's the prettiest theoretical problem I've encountered in a couple of centuries. I wish you'd let me

know when you're through with the boards: I really do
need the City Fathers, when they're available."

"I'm through now," Amalfi said, getting off the stool. As
an afterthought, he turned back to the boards and cleared
the instruction circuits of the problem he had been setting
up, a problem which he now knew all too well to be a
dummy.

He left Jake humming contentedly as he set up his nova
problem, and wandered without real intention or direction
down into the main body of the city, trying to remember it
as it had been as a living and vibrant organism; but the
empty streets, the blank windows, the flat quiet of the
very air under the blue sky of New Earth, was like an
insult. Even the feeling of gravity under his feet seemed in
these familiar surroundings a fleeting denial of the causes
and values to which he had given most of his life; a smug
gravity, so easily maintained by sheer mass, and without
the constant distant sound of spindizzies which always
before—since his distant, utterly unrememberable youth—
had signified that gravity was a thing made by man, and
maintained by man.

Depressed, Amalfi quit the streets for the holds of the
city. There, at least, his memory of the city as a live entity
would not be mocked by the unnaturally natural day. But
that in the long run proved to be no better. The empty
granaries and cold-storage bins reminded him that there
was no longer any need to keep the city stocked for trips
that might last as much as a century between planet-falls;
the empty crude-oil tanks rang hollowly, not to his touch,
but simply to his footfall as he passed them; the empty
dormitories were full of those peculiar ghosts which not
the dead, but the living leave behind when they pass, still
living, to another kind of life; the empty classrooms, which
were, as was quite usual with Okie cities, small, were
mocked by the memory of the myriads of children which
the Okies were now farrowing on their own planet, New
Earth, no longer bound by the need to consider how many
children an Okie city needs and can comfortably provide
for. And down at the threshold of the keel itself, he
encountered the final sign and signal of his forthcoming
defeat: the fused masses of two spindizzies ruined beyond

repair by the landing of 3944 on the Blasted Heath. New spindizzies, of course, could be built and installed, the old yanked out; but the process would take a long time; there were no graving docks suitable for the job on New Earth, since the cities were extinct. As was the spirit.

Nevertheless, in the cold gloom of the spindizzy hold, Amalfi resolved to try.

"But what on earth do you expect to gain?" Hazleton said in exasperation, for at least the fifth time. "I think you're out of your mind."

There was still no one else on New Earth who would have had the temerity to speak to Amalfi quite like that; but Mark Hazleton had been Amalfi's city manager ever since 3301 and knew his former boss very well. A subtle, difficult, lazy, impulsive and sometimes dangerous man, Hazleton had survived many blunders for which the City Fathers would have had any other city manager shot—as, indeed, they had had his predecessor shot—and there had survived, too, his often unwarranted assumption that he could read Amalfi's mind.

There was surely no other ex-Okie on New Earth who might be as likely to understand Amalfi's present state of mind, but Hazleton was not at the moment giving a very good demonstration of this. For one thing, he and his wife Dee—the girl from a planet called Utopia who had boarded the city about the same time that Dr. Schloss had, during the reduction of the Duchy of Gort—had perhaps forgotten that an Okie tradition forbade the mayor of an Okie city to marry or have children, and that Amalfi as the mayor of New York since 3089 was conditioned beyond redemption to this state of mind; and in particular would not welcome being surrounded by the children and grandchildren of his city manager at any time, and particularly not when what he most urgently needed was advice from someone who remembered the traditions well enough to understand why another man might still be clinging to them.

It was one of Mark's virtues, however, that at his best he tended to react more like a symbiote than a truly separate entity. When the children made graceful exits soon after dinner, Amalfi knew that it was at Hazleton's behest. He also knew it was not because Hazleton even faintly suspected his friend's discomfiture in the presence of so many fruits of the settling-down process; it was just that the city manager had intuited Amalfi's need for a conference and had promptly set one up, scuttling Dee's social timetable without a qualm.

The children charged their unseasonably early departure to the grandchildren's impending bedtimes, although Amalfi knew that when the whole clan came to dinner they customarily made a great occasion of it, and all stayed the night in the adjoining building, a beehive of bedrooms where the Hazletons had raised their numerous family; the current Hazleton dwelling consisted mostly of the huge social room where they had just dined. Now that the meal was over, Amalfi just barely kept from fidgeting while all the procession of big and little Hazletons made their manners. Even the youngest had each to make his farewell speech to the great man, identifying his inconsiderable self; their parents had long since learned in their own childhoods that the busy Mr. Mayor would not trouble himself to remember which was which.

It never occurred to Amalfi to admire the children's concealment of their disappointment at leaving so precipitately, since he did not realize that they were disappointed. He simply listened without listening. One middle-sized boy caught his attention mainly because from the moment he had arrived Amalfi had noticed that the child had kept his eyes riveted on the guest of honor. It was disconcerting. Amalfi suspected he had forgotten to don some essential garment or to doff some trace of his party preparations. When the child who had caused him to rub his chin and smooth his eyebrows and finger his ears to see if there were still soapsuds in them spoke up, Amalfi paid attention.

"Webster Hazleton, sir, and I hope to be seeing you again on a matter of the greatest importance," the boy said. He said it as if he had been rehearsing it for weeks, with a ringing conviction that almost impelled Amalfi to fix an appointment then and there.

Instead, he growled, "Webster, eh?"

"Yes, sir. I was put on the Great List to be born when Webster wanted off."

Amalfi was considerably jolted. So long ago as that! Webster had been the pile engineer who had elected to leave the city before the landing on Utopia, around 3600. Of course it had taken a long time to fill up the gaps in the city's roster after the murderous attempt of the bandit cities to prevent fulfillment of their contract on He, and the considerable losses in boarding the plague city in the Acolyte jungle; and then there had been so many girls born at first. Webster had been an unconscionably long time in coming, though. He could not be more than fourteen, from the looks of him.

Dee intervened. "Actually, John, Web arrived a long time after the Great List was abandoned. It pleases him to have his patron citizen, that's all, just like in the old days."

The boy turned his clear brown eyes on Dee briefly, and then, as if dismissing her from their male universe, he said, "Good night, sir." Amalfi bridled a little. Nobody could write Dee off, not even Amalfi; he knew; once he had tried.

The procession continued while he lapsed back into inattention, and eventually he found himself closeted with Dee and Mark—if closeted was the word in a room so large and echoing with so many strong personalities. The aura of furious domesticity remained behind on the Hazleton hearth, and came between Amalfi and what he was trying to say, so that his exposition was unwontedly stumbling; and it was then that Hazleton had asked him what he expected to gain.

"Gain?" Amalfi said. "I don't expect to gain anything. I'd just like to be aloft again, that's all."

"But, John," Dee said. "Think about it a minute. Suppose you do succeed in persuading a few people from the old days to go in with you. It all doesn't have any meaning anymore. You'll just turn yourself into a sort of Flying Dutchman, sailing under a curse, going nowhere and doing nothing."

"Maybe so," Amalfi said. "The picture doesn't frighten me, Dee. As a matter of fact, it gives me a sort of perverse satisfaction, if you must know. I shouldn't mind becoming a legend; at least that would fit me back into history again—give me a role to play comparable to roles I've played in the past. And besides, I'd be aloft again, which is the important thing. I'm beginning to believe that nothing else is important to me anymore."

"Does it matter what's important to us?" Hazleton said. "For one thing, such a venture would leave the Cloud without a mayor. I don't know how important that is to you anymore—I seem to remember that it was pretty important to you back when we were on our way here—but whether it matters to you anymore or not, you ran for the job, you connived for it, you even rigged the election—Carrel and I were supposed to be the only candidates, and the office we were running for was city manager, but you had the City Fathers hornswoggled into believing that it was a mayoralty election, so of course they elected you."

"Do you want the job?" Amalfi said.

"Gods of all stars, no! I want you to keep it. You exercised considerable ingenuity to get it, and I'm not alone in expecting you to hold it down now that you've got it. Nobody else is bidding for the job; they expect you to handle it, as you undertook to do."

"Nobody else is running for it because they wouldn't know what to do with it after they got it," Amalfi said steadily. "I don't know what to do with it myself. The office of mayor is an anachronism in this Cloud. Nobody has asked me to do anything or to say anything or to appear anywhere or to be in any other way useful in I don't know how many years. I occupy an honorary office, and that's all. As everybody knows, you are the man that is actually running this Cloud, and that's as it should be. It's high time you took over in name, as well as in fact. I've given everything I could give to the initial organizing job, and my talents are unsuitable to the situation as it now stands; everybody on New Earth knows that, and it would be healthier if they'd put a name to it. Otherwise, Mark, how long could I be allowed to go on in the job? Apparently forever, under your present assumptions. This is a new society; suppose I should go right on being its titular leader for another thousand years, as is entirely possible? A thousand years during which a new society continues to give lip-service to the same old set of attitudes and ideas that I represented when they meant something? That would be insane; and you know it. No, no, it's high time you took over."

Hazleton was silent for quite a long time. At last he said: "I can see that. In fact, I've thought of it several times myself. Nevertheless, Amalfi, I have to say that this whole proposition distresses me a good deal. I suppose the matter of the mayoralty would settle itself out almost automatically; that wasn't a real objection. What bothers me is the exit you're contriving for yourself, not only because it's dangerous—which it is, but that wouldn't make any difference to you and I suppose it shouldn't make any difference to me—but because it's dangerous to no purpose."

"It suits my purposes," Amalfi said. "I don't see that there are any other purposes to be suited, at this juncture. If I did, I wouldn't go, Mark; you know that; but it seems to me that I am now, for the first time in all my life, a free agent; hence I may now do what I will do."

Hazleton shrugged convulsively. "And so you may," he said. "I can only say that I wish you wouldn't."

Dee bowed her head and said nothing.

And the rest was left unsaid. That Dee and Mark would be personally bereaved if Amalfi persisted on his present course, for their different reasons, was an obvious additional argument which they might have used, but they came no closer to it than that; it was the kind of argument which Hazleton would regard as pure emotional blackmail, precisely because it was unreasonably powerful, and Amalfi was grateful to him for not bringing it to bear. Why Dee had not was more difficult to fathom; there had been a time when she would have used it without a moment's hesitation; and Amalfi thought he knew her well enough to suspect that she had good reasons for wanting to use it now. She had been waiting for the founding of New Earth for a long time, indeed, almost since she had come on board the city, and anything that threatened it now that she had children and grandchildren should provoke her into using every weapon at her command; yet, she was silent. Perhaps she was old enough now to realize that not even John Amalfi could steal from her an entire satellite galaxy; at any event, if that was what was on her mind, she gave no inkling of it, and the evening in Hazleton's house ended with a stiff formality which, cold though it was, was far from the worst that Amalfi had expected.

The whole of the residential area to Amalfi's eyes swarmed with pets. Those to whom freedom to run was paramount, frisked and scuttered, in the wide lanes. Few of them ventured onto the wheelways, and those who did were run down instantly, but four-footed animals were a constant and undignified hazard to walkers. By day raffish dogs stopped just short of bowling strangers over, but leaped to brace forepaws on the shoulders of anyone they knew—and everyone, including, seemingly, all the dogs of New Manhattan, knew Amalfi. An occasional svengali from Altair IV—originally a rare specimen in the flying city's zoo, but latterly force-budded in New Earth labs during the full-fertility program of 3950, when every homesteader's bride had her option of a vial of trilby water or a gemmate svengali and frequently wound up with both among the household lares and penates; the half-plant, half-animal, even nowadays a not infrequent pet—took the breeze and hunted in the half-light of dawn or dusk. A svengali lay bonelessly in mid-lane and fixed its enormous eyes on any moving object until something small enough and gelid enough to ingest might blunder near. Nothing suitable ever did, on New Earth. The two-legged victim tended to drift helplessly into that hypnotic stare until the starer got stepped on; then the svengali turned mauve and exuded a protective spray which might have been nauseating on Altair IV, but on New Earth was only euphoric. Sudden friendships, bursts of song, even a brief and deliriously happy crying jag might ensue, after which the shaken svengali would undulate back indoors to rest up and be given, usually, a bowl of jellied soup.

By night in the walkways of New Manhattan, it was cats, catching with sudden claw at floating cloak or fashionable sandal-streamer. Through the air of the town sizable and brightly colored creatures flew and glided: singing birds, squawking birds, talkers and mutes, but pets every last one of them. Amalfi loathed them all.

When he walked anywhere—and he walked almost everywhere. now that the city's aircabs were no more—he more than half-expected to have to free himself from the embraces of a burbling citizen or a barking dog before he got where he was going. The half-century-old fad for household pets had arisen after the landing, and after his effectual abdication. What time-wasting quirk had moved so many pioneers' descendants to adopt the damnable svengalis as pets was beyond Amalfi.

He made it home from the Hazletons' without any such encounter; instead, it rained. He wrapped his cloak more tightly around him and hastened, muttering, for his own square uncompromising box of a dwelling before the full force of the storm should be let loose; his house and grounds were sheltered by a 0.02 percent spindizzy field— the New Earthmen called the household device a "spindilly," a name which Amalfi loathed but put up with for the sake of, as Dee had once put it, "not knowing enough to come out of the rain." He had growled at her so convincingly for that that she had never brought up the subject again, but she had put her finger on it all the same.

Amalfi reached his entrance lane and laid his palm on the induction switch which softened the spindilly field just enough to let him through in a spatter of glistening drops, and noted with the grim dissatisfaction that was becoming natural to him that the storm had slacked off and would be over in minutes. Inside, he made a drink and stood, rubbing his hands, looking about him. If his house was an anachronism, well, he liked it that way, insofar as he liked anything on New Earth.

"What's wrong with me?" he thought suddenly. "People's pets are their own business, after all. If practically everybody else likes weather, what difference does it make if I don't? If Jake doesn't even take an interest, nor Mark either for that matter—"

He heard the distant, endlessly comforting murmur of the modified spindizzy under his feet alter momentarily; someone else had chosen to come in out of the rain. His visitor had never been there at that hour before, and had indeed never been there before alone, but he knew without a moment's doubt who had followed him home.

CHAPTER TWO: Nova Magellanis

"You'll have to make me more welcome than that, John," Dee said.

Amalfi said nothing. He lowered his head like a bull contemplating a charge, spread his feet slightly, and clasped his hands behind him.

"Well, John?" Dee insisted gently.

"You don't want me to go," he said baldly. "Or, you suspect that if I do go, Mark just may throw up the managership and New Earth along with it and take off with me."

Dee walked slowly all the way across the room and stood, hesitating, beside the great deep cushion. "Wrong, John, on both counts. I had something else altogether in mind. I thought—well, I'll tell you later what I thought. Right now, may I have a drink?"

Amalfi was forced to abandon his position, which by being so firm had imparted a certain strength to his desire to oppose her, in order to play host. "Did Mark send you, then?"

She laughed. "King Mark sends me on a good many errands, but this wouldn't be a very likely one for him." She added bitterly, "Besides, he's so wrapped up in Gifford Bonner's group that he ignores me for months on end."

Amalfi knew what she meant: Dr. Bonner was the teacher-leader of an informal philosophical group called the Stochastics; Amalfi hadn't bothered to inform himself in detail on Bonner's tenets, but he knew in general that Stochasticism was the most recent of many attempts to construct a complete philosophy, from esthetics to ethics, using modern physics as the metaphysical base. Logical positivism had been only the first of those; Stochasticism, Amalfi strongly suspected, would be far from the last.

"I could see something had been keeping his mind off the job lately," he said grimly. "He might do better to study the doctrines of Jorn the Apostle. The Warriors of God control no less than fifteen of the border planets right now, and the faith doesn't lack for adherents right here on New Earth. It appeals to the bumpkin type—and I'm afraid we've been turning out a lot of those lately."

If Dee recognized this as in part a shaft at the changes in New Earth's educational system which she had helped to institute, she showed no sign of it.

"Maybe so," she said. "But I couldn't persuade him, and I wonder if you could either. He doesn't believe there's any real threat; he thinks that a man simpleminded enough to be a Fundamentalist is too simpleminded to hold together an army."

"Oh? Mark had better ask Bonner to tell about Godfrey of Bouillon."

"Who was—?"

"The leader of the First Crusade."

She shrugged. Possibly only Amalfi, as the only New Earthman who had actually been born and raised on Earth, could ever have heard of the Crusades; doubtless they were unknown on Utopia.

"Anyhow, that isn't what I came here to talk about, either."

The wall treacher opened and floated the drinks out. Amalfi captured them and passed one over silently, waiting.

She took her glass from him but, instead of sinking down with it as he had half-pictured her doing, she walked nervously back to the door and took her first sip as if she might put it aside and be leaving at any moment.

He discovered that he did not want her to go. He

wanted her to walk some more. There was something about the gown she was wearing—

That there were fashions again was a function of being earthbound. One simple utilitarian style had sufficed both men and women all their centuries aloft when there had been the unending demands of the city's spaceworthiness to keep all hands occupied. Now that the ex-Okies were busily fulfilling Franklin's law that people will breed to the point of overpopulating any space available to them, they were also frittering away their time with pets and flower-gardens and fashions that changed every time a man blinked. Women were floating around time year of 3995 in diaphanous creations that totaled so much yardage a man might find himself treading on their skirts. Dee, however, was wearing a simple white covering above and a clinging black tubular affair below that was completely different. The only diaphanous part of her outfit was a length of something gossamer and iridescent that circled her throat under a fold of the white garment and hung down between her still delicate, still gently rounded breasts, as girlish in appearance as the day Utopia had sent her out to New York, in a battleship, to ask for help.

He had it. "Dee, you looked just as you look now when I first saw you!"

"Indeed, John?"

"That black thing—"

"A sheath-skirt," she interpolated helpfully.

"—I noticed it particularly when you came aboard. I'd never seen anything like it. Haven't seen anything like it since." He refrained from telling her that during all the centuries he had loved her, he had pictured her in that black thing, turning to him instead of Hazleton. Would the course of history have been any different, had she done so? But how could he have done anything but reject her?

"It took you long enough to notice it tonight," she said. "I had it made up especially for this evening's dinner. I've been tired of all this float and flutter for a year. Essentially I'm still a product of Utopia, I guess. I like stern clothes and strong men and a reasonably hard life."

She was certainly trying to tell him something, but he

was still adrift. The situation was impossible, on the face of it. He was not in the habit of discussing fashion with his best and oldest friend's wife at an hour when all sensible planet-bound pioneers were abed. He said, "It's very pretty."

To his astonishment, she burst into tears. "Oh, *don't* be stuffy, John!" She put the glass down and reached for her cloak.

"All right, Dee." Amalfi put the cloak out of her reach. "Your 'King Mark' sounds reasonably stern and hard. Suppose you sit down and tell me what this is all about."

"I want to go with you, John. You won't be the mayor of New York, you won't be bound by the old rules, if you take the city aloft now. I want—I want to—"

It was weeks before he got her to state that ultimate desire. They had talked without ceasing after that blundering beginning. When it finally penetrated his cautious bald head that the message all his senses had been clamoring from the moment of her arrival was not another daydream from the chilly past, but warm actuality, he had folded her in his arms and they had been silent for a time. But then the flow of words began again and could not be checked. They had reminisced endlessly and how-it-might-have-beens and even of certain ways it had been. He was amazed to discover that she had taken into her household however briefly every companion whose bed he had honored during the officially celibate years; in her position as First Lady of New Earth, during the intensive family years, she could have installed twenty nursemaids simultaneously without attracting undue notice, just as she launched every new fashion and many of the fads that made New Earth what it was. That Dee had been cruelly bored had simply never occurred to him.

But she told him the full tale of that discontent, more indeed than he wanted to hear. They quarreled like giddy young lovers—except that their first and worst quarrel followed a complaint he could have wept to hear wrung from her.

"John," she said, "aren't you ever going to take me to bed?"

He spread his hands in exasperation. "I'm not at all sure

I want to take Mark's wife to bed. Besides," he added, knowing he was being cruel, "you've already had it. You've pumped every woman I resorted to in half a thousand years. I should think I would bore you in actuality as much as everything else does."

Their reconciliations were not much like those of young love; they were more and more like the creeping home of a rebellious daughter to her father's arms. And still he held off. Now that he had for the taking what he had only dreamed of wanting for so many years, he made the Adamic discoveries all over again: there is wanting the unobtainable, and there is the obtaining of desire, and the greatest of these is the wanting. Especially since the object of desire always turns out to exist only in some other universe, to be mocked by actuality.

"You don't believe me, John," she said bitterly. "But it's true. When you go, I want to go with you—all the way, don't you understand? I want to—I want to bear you a child."

She looked at him through a film of tears—somehow he had never, in all the centuries of fancy, imagined or seen her in tears, but the actuality wept as predictably as New Earth's skies—and waited. She had shot her bolt, he saw. This was the supreme thing that Dee Hazleton wanted to give him.

"Dee, you don't know what you're saying! You can't offer me your girlhood all over again—that's irretrievably Mark's, and you know it. Besides, I don't want—"

He stopped. She was weeping again. He had never wanted to hurt her, although he knew he had done so unintentionally more times than he would ever know.

"Dee, I've *had* a child."

Now she was listening, wide-eyed, and he winced as he saw pity take the place of resentment. He laid the encysted pain bare like a surgeon before her. "When the population balance shifted after the landing and there were all those excess females—remember? Do you also remember the artificial insemination program? They asked me to contribute. The good old argument against it was supposed to be bypassed by the assurance that I'd never know which children carried my genes—only the doctors supervising the program would know. But there was an unprecedented wave of miscarriages and stillbirths—and some survivors that shouldn't have survived, all with the same set of . . . disadvantages. I was told about it; as mayor, I had to decide what was to be done with them."

"John," she whispered. "No. Stop."

"We were taking over the Cloud," he continued implacably. Presenting him with a wizened, squalling, scarlet, normal baby boy was one favor she could not do him, and there was no way to tell her so but this. "We couldn't afford bad genes. I ordered the survivors . . . dealt with; and I had a brief conference with the genetics team. They had planned not to tell me—they were going to keep up the farce, like good-hearted dolts. But I'd been in space too long; my germ plasm is damaged beyond hope; I am no longer a contributor. Do you understand me, Dee?"

Dee tried to draw his head down on her breast. Amalfi moved violently away. It irritated him unreasonably that she still thought she had anything to give him.

"The city was yours," she said tonelessly. "And now it's grown up and gone away and left you. I saw you grieving, John, and I couldn't bear it—oh, I don't mean that I was pretending. I love you, I think I always have. But I should have known that the time for us had gone by. There's nothing at all left for me to give you that you haven't had in full measure."

She bowed her head, and he stroked her hair awkwardly, wishing it had never begun, since it had to end like this. "And what now?" he said. "Now that life with father has turned out to be nothing more than that? Can you leave home again and go to Mark?"

"Mark? He doesn't even know I've been . . . away. As his wife, I'm dead and buried," she said in a low voice. "Living seems to be a process of continually being born again. I suppose the trick is to learn how to make that crucial exit without suffering the trauma each time. Goodbye, John."

She didn't look as if she were being too successful at mastering the trick, but he made no move to help her. She was going to have to find her own way back; she was beyond his aid now.

He thought that what she had said was probably the truth—for a woman. For a man, he knew, life is a process of dying, again and again; and the trick, he thought, is to do it piecemeal, and ungenerously.

For the first time in weeks, he walked the streets of New Manhattan again. He had never felt so utterly done with the purpose he had sowed in his people. Now that it was coming to fruition, he urgently needed to be seeking some purpose far removed from theirs.

Inevitably, he found himself leaving cats, birds, svengalis, dogs and Dee for the dilapidated streets of the Okie city. He was almost all the way down to the banks of the City Fathers, when a suspicion that he was again being followed turned into a certainty. For a panic moment he feared it might be Dee, spoiling both her exit and his; but it was not.

"All right, who is it?" he said. "Stop skulking and name yourself."

"You wouldn't remember me, Mr. Mayor," a frightened voice said in several registers at once.

"Remember you? Of course I do. You're Webster Hazleton. Who's your friend? What are you doing here in the old city? It's off limits for children."

The boy drew himself up to his full height.

"This is Estelle. She and I are in this together." Web appeared to have some difficulty in going on. "There's been talk—I mean, Estelle's father, he's Jake Freeman, kind of hinted about it—that is, if the city's really going up again. Mr. Mayor—"

"Maybe it is. I don't know yet. What of it?"

"If it is, *we want on*," the boy said in a rush.

Amalfi had had no further plans to try and convert Jake, who certainly appeared to be as lost a cause as Hazleton himself; but the Freeman-Hazleton partnership represented by Web and Estelle meant that he would have to broach the subject again to Jake sooner or later. Of course it was out of the question that the children should be allowed to go—and yet it was not within the bounds of fairness to forbid them out of hand, without knowing what their elders thought of it. Children had gone adventuring on Okie cities many a time before; but of course that had been back in the old days, when the cities had been as well equipped as any earthbound community to take good care of them, at least most of the time. Every thread he touched these days, it seemed to Amalfi, had knots in it.

Temporarily, however, the fates allowed him to shelve that part of the problem; for Jake was waiting for him again in the computation section, in a state of excitement so febrile that the sight of his daughter and Web tagging behind Amalfi barely raised his eyebrows.

"You're just in time," he said as though there had been some prior appointment. "You recall the nova I was talking to you about? Well, it isn't a nova at all, and at this point it's no longer an astronomical problem; in fact, it's your problem."

"What do you mean?" Amalfi said. "If it isn't a nova, what is it?"

"Just what I was asking myself," Jake said. One of his more irritating failings was his inability to get to a point by any but a preselected route. "I have a remarkable collection of spectrographs for this thing; if you looked at them without any clue as to what they were, you'd think they represented a stellar catalogue, rather than a single object— and a catalogue containing stars from all over the Russell diagram, too. On top of which, all of them show a blue shift in the absorption lines, particularly in the lines contributed by New Earth's own atmosphere, which made no sense whatsoever, up to now."

"It still doesn't make any sense to me," Amalfi admitted.

"All right," Jake said, "try this on for size; when the spectra turned out to be far too dim for an object of the apparent magnitude of this thing—remember, it's been getting brighter all the time—I asked Schloss and his crew to neglect anti-matter long enough to do a wave-trap analysis of the incoming light. It turns out to be about seventy-five percent false photons; the thing must be leaving behind a tremendous contrail, if we were only in a position to see it—"

"Spindizzies!" Amalfi shouted. "And under damn near

full deceleration! But how could an object that size—no, wait a minute; do you actually know the size yet?"

The astronomer chuckled, a noise which from Jake never failed to remind Amalfi of a demented parrot. "I think we have the size, and all the rest of the answers, at least as far as astronomy is concerned," he said. "The rest, as I said, is your problem. The thing is a planetary body, roughly seventy-five hundred miles in diameter, and much closer than we thought it was—right now, in fact, it's actually inside the Greater Magellanic, and coming our way, directly for the system of New Earth. The change in spectra simply means that it's shining by the reflected light of the different suns it's passing, and the blue shift in the Frauenhofer lines strongly suggests an atmosphere very much like ours. I don't know offhand what that reminds you of, but I know what it should remind you of—and the City Fathers agree with me."

Web Hazleton could contain himself no longer. "I know, I know! It's the planet He! It's coming home! Isn't that it, Mr. Mayor?"

The boy knew his city history well; nobody from the old days could have been confronted with such a set of data as Jake had just trotted out without responding with the same wild surmise. The planet He had been one of the city's principal jobs of work, the outcome of which, for very complicated reasons, had entailed the installation on the planet itself of a number of spindizzies sufficient to rip He from her orbit around her home sun and send her careening, wholly out of control, out of the galaxy and into intergalactic space. The city had been carried a considerable distance with her, enabling it to reenter the galaxy far away from any area where New York, N. Y., was being actively sought by the cops, but it had been a near thing. She, herself, presumably, had been hurtling toward the Andromeda galaxy ever since that moment in 3850 when she and the city had parted company, each vanishing to the other as abruptly and finally as a blownout candleflame.

"Let's not jump to conclusions," Amalfi said. "The tipping of He took place only a century and a half ago—and at that time the Hevians didn't have the technology or the resources to master controlled spindizzy flight; in fact, they weren't very far from being savages. Smart savages, I grant you, but still savages. Is this planet that's coming our way truly dirigible, or don't you know yet?"

"It looks that way," Jake said. "That's what first tipped me off that there was something unnatural about the object. It kept changing velocity and line of flight erratically—in fact, in a totally irrational way, unless one assumed that the changes were in fact rational. Whoever they are, they know enough to prevent that world of theirs from zigging when they want to zag. And they're headed our way, Amalfi."

"Have you made any attempt to get in touch with them, whoever they are?" Amalfi said.

"No, indeed. In fact, I haven't even told anybody else about it yet. Not even Mark. Somehow it struck me as peculiarly your baby."

"That was just a waste of pussyfooting, Jake. Dr. Schloss isn't an idiot; surely he can read his own figures as well as you can and draw obvious conclusions from the very question you asked him; he must have told Mark by now, and a good thing, too. Mark is probably calling your object right now; let's go directly up to the control room and find out."

They made an oddly assorted procession through the haunted streets of the Okie city: the bald-headed keg-chested mayor with his teeth deeply sunk in a dead cigar, the bird-like and slightly crestfallen astronomer, the bright-eyed skipping youngsters now darting ahead of them, then falling behind to wait to be shown the way. Their eagerness moved Amalfi unexpectedly, bringing home to him the realization that their dream of the city back in flight had always been, like this, a very fragile one; and that this incoming dirigible planet, whatever else it might portend, would probably put the quietus to it, serious business and the dull cold morning light it thrived in being immemorially fatal to dreams.

On an impulse, he stopped at a station that he knew and called for an aircab, partly, he assured himself, to see whether or not the City Fathers still considered that service worth maintaining at this stage in the city's long death. In due course one came, to the obvious delight of the children, leaving Amalfi with the rueful realization that his had not been a fair test; a million years from now, with the last ergs of energy remaining in the pile, the City Fathers would of course still send a cab for the mayor; if he wanted to know whether or not the entire garage was still alive, he would have to ask the City Fathers directly.

But Web and Estelle were so delighted at soaring through the silent canyons of the city in the metal and crystal bubble, and in exploring the limited and very respectful repartee of the Tin Cabby, that they fell entirely off their precarious adolescent dignity with squeals of laughter, alternating with gasps of not very real alarm as the cab cut around corners and came close to grazing the structures of the city which familiarity had worn smooth to the point of contempt inside the Tin Cabby's flat little black box of a brain. It was, in a way, a shame that the youngsters were unable to make out, even had they known where to look for it, the graven letters of the city's ancient motto—MOW YOUR LAWN, LADY?—if only for the sense it might have given them of the reason why Okie cities once flew; but the motto had become unreadable a long time ago, as its meaning had become obliterated soon after. Only the memory remained to remind Amalfi that were the city ever to go aloft again—which, suddenly, he did not even believe—it would not be for the purpose of mowing lawns for hire; there were no more; that was all over and done with.

The control room in City Hall muted the children considerably, as well it might, for no one much below the age of a century had ever been allowed in it before, and the many screens which lined its walls had seen events in a history unlikely to be matched for drama (or even simple interest) in any imaginable future saga of New Earth. In this dim stagnant-smelling room the very man who was with them now had watched the rise and fall of a galaxy-dominating race—of which, to be sure, these children were genetically a part, but whose inheritors they could never be; history had passed them by.

"And don't touch anything," Amalfi said. "Everything in this room is alive, more or less. We've never had the time to disarm the city totally; I'm not even sure we'd know how to go about it now. That's why it's off limits. You'd better come stand behind me. Web and Estelle, and watch what I do; it'll keep you out of reach of the boards."

"We won't touch anything," Web said fervently.

"I know you won't, intentionally. But I don't want any accidents. Better you learn how to run the board from scratch; come stand right here—you too, Estelle—and call your grandfather's house for me. Touch the clear plastic bar—that's it, now wait for it to light up. That lets the City Fathers know that you want to talk to somebody outside the city; that's very important; otherwise they'd give you a long argument, believe you me. Now you see the five little red buttons just above the bar; the one you touch is number two; four and five are ultraphone and Dirac lines, which you don't need for a local call. One and three are inside trunk lines, which is why they're not lit up. Go ahead, push it."

Web touched the glowing red stud tentatively. Over his head, a voice said: "Communications."

"Now it's my turn," Amalfi said, picking up the microphone. "This is the mayor. Get me the city manager, crash priority." He lowered the microphone and added, "That requires the Communications section to scan for your grandfather along all of the channels on which he's known to be available, and send him a 'call-in' signal wherever he may be; New Earth Hospital has much the same call-in system for its doctors."

"Can we hear him being called?" Estelle said.

"Yes, if you like," Amalfi said. "Here, take the microphone, and put your finger on the two-button as Web did. There."

"Communications," the invisible speaker again said briskly.

"Say, 'Reprise, please,' " Amalfi whispered.

"Reprise, please," the girl said.

Immediately the air of the ancient room was filled with a series of twittering pure tones and chords, as though every shadow hid a bird with a silver throat. Estelle almost dropped the microphone; Amalfi took it from her gently.

"Machines don't call for people by name," he explained. "Only very complicated machines, like the City Fathers, are able to speak at all; a simple computer like the Communications section finds it easier to use musical tones. If you listen a while, you'll begin to hear a kind of melody; that's the code for Web's grandfather; the harmonies represent the different places where the computer is looking for him."

"I like it," Estelle said. At the same instant the pipings of the invisible birds came to an end with a metallic snap, and Mark Hazleton's voice said in the middle of the air: "Boss, are you looking for me?"

Amalfi lifted the microphone back to his lips with a grim smile, the children instantly forgotten.

"You bet I am. Are you on top of this dirigible planet which seems to be heading for us?"

"Yes; I didn't know you were interested. In fact I didn't know that it was a planet instead of a star until yesterday, when Schloss and Carrel came in to see me about it." Amalfi threw Jake a meaningful glance. "I gather you're calling me from the city; what do the City Fathers think?"

"I don't know, I haven't talked to them," Amalfi said. "But Jake is here, and he's come to the obvious conclusion, as I'm sure you have. What I want to know is, have you or Carrel made any attempt to communicate with this object?"

"Yes, but I can't say that it's been very fruitful," Hazleton's voice said. "We've called them four or five times on the Dirac, but if they've answered us, it's gotten lost in the general babble of Dirac 'casts we're surrounded with from the home galaxy. It puzzles me a little bit; they do seem to be homing on us, without any question, but it's hard to imagine what kind of signal from us they could be using to guide on."

"Do you really think that this is He come back again?" Amalfi said cautiously.

"Yes, I think I do," Hazleton said, with apparent equal caution. "I don't see what other conclusion one could come to with the data as they stand now."

"Then use your head," Amalfi said. "If this really is He, you'll never be able to reach it with a Dirac 'cast. While we were on He, we never even let the Hevians hear a Dirac 'cast, or see a Dirac transmitter; they had no reason to suspect that any such universal transmitter even existed, or could exist. And if by the same token this is *not* He, but some exploring vessel coming in toward us for the first time from another galaxy, and out of an entirely different culture than any we know, then it's obvious that they cannot have the Dirac, otherwise they would have heard every one of the millions of Dirac messages which have gone out from our galaxy since the day they found the device. Try the ultraphone instead."

"He didn't have the ultraphone either, when last we saw it," Hazleton's voice said amusedly. "And if we don't know how to drive an ultraphone carrier through a spindizzy screen, I very much doubt that they do. If we're going to go all the way back to methods of communications as primitive as that, shouldn't we first try wigwagging?"

"I think probably there is an ultraphone message from that planet on its way here," Amalfi said. "It would be the part of common sense to precede such a flight as that planet is conducting into so densely populated an area as the Greater Magellanic Cloud with a general identification signal, which you could hardly do with a Dirac signal in any event; a signal which is received uniformly everywhere simultaneously with its being sent is not a proper beacon signal. It doesn't matter whether this is He or a visitor coming to us from the entirely unknown; they will be sending some sort of pip in advance, which they would absolutely have to do by ultraphone, there being no other way to do it, and if this requires them to work out a way to punch an ultraphone signal through a spindizzy screen, then they will have done so and you should be listening for it; and you can put a return signal through the same hole." He took a deep breath. "At the very least, Mark, stop wasting my time telling me it's impossible before you've even tried it."

"I tell *you*," Webster Hazleton said under his breath and turned a bright scarlet. Behind him, Estelle's father chortled alarmingly on the edge of his metaphorical crackerbarrel.

The riot act, however, had been becoming less and less effective with Hazleton in the past few decades, as Amalfi knew well; perhaps it dated from Hazleton's new preoccu-

pation with the Stochastics, about which Amalfi had not
known until Dee had brought it up; or perhaps—though
this was a much less attractive possibility—from an aware-
ness in Hazleton, paralleling Amalfi's own, of Amalfi's
growing impotence on New Earth. "Nevertheless," Hazleton
said gravely, "I will raise one further objection, boss, if I
may. Even supposing that they are putting out an ultraphone
beam we can tie to, they're still roughly fifty light-years
away; by the time they hear anything we say to them by
ultraphone and get a message back to us the same way,
we'll be seventy-five years into the next millennium."

"True," Amalfi admitted. "Which means we'll have to
send a ship. I'm all for taking ten years or so to make full
contact, anyhow, since we really have no idea what it is
we're confronted with, and we may need to lay in some
armaments. But you'd better tell Carrel to stand ready to
fly me out there no later than the beginning of next week,
and in the meantime, try to eavesdrop on whatever transmission our visitor is broadcasting. I'll attend to the answering part later from shipboard."

"Right," Hazleton said, and switched out.

"Can we go too?" Web demanded immediately.

"What do you say to that, Jake? These kids were all for
going with me on board the city, too."

The astronomer smiled and shrugged. "Wherever she
gets the taste for spaceflight from, it can't be from me," he
said. "But I knew she was going to ask sooner or later. It's
an experience she'll have to have behind her before she's
very much older, and I don't know of any commander in
two galaxies that she'd be safer with. I think my wife will
concur—though she's as uneasy about it as I am."

Web cheered; but Estelle only said, in a tone of utmost
practicality:

"I'll go home and get my svengali."

CHAPTER THREE: The Nursery of Time

Even from half a million miles out, it was already plain to Amalfi that the planet of He had undergone a vast transformation since he had last seen it, back in 3850. The Okies had first encountered that planet six years earlier, the only fertile offspring of a wild star then swimming alone in a vast starless desert, not one of the normal starfree areas between spiral arms of the galaxy, but a temporary valley called the Rift, the mechanics of whose origin lay shrouded impenetrably in the origins of the universe itself.

Even at first sight, it had been apparent that the history of He had been more than ordinarily complicated. It had then been an emerald-green world, covered with rank jungle from pole to pole, a jungle which had almost completely swamped out what had obviously been a high civilization not many years before. The facts as they emerged after landing turned out to be complex in the extreme; it was highly probably that there was not another planet in the galaxy which had undergone so many fatal and unlikely accidents. The Hevians had fought them all doggedly, but by the time the Okies had arrived they had realized that nothing less than a miracle could help them now.

For Hevian civilization, the Okies had been that miracle, giving the Hevians mastery over their own local and considerable banditry, and killing off the planetwide jungle, in the only way possible: by abruptly and permanently changing the climate of He. That this geological revolution had had to be accomplished by putting the whole planet into uncontrolled flight out of the galaxy was perhaps unfortunate, but Amalfi did not think so at the time. He had formed a high opinion of the shrewdness and latent technological ability underlying the Hevian ceremonial paint and feathers, and did not doubt that the Hevians would learn the necessary techniques for preserving their planet as an abode of life well before the danger point would be reached. After all, the Hevians had been great once, and even after the long battle with the jungle and each other they had still had such sophistications as radio, rockets, missile weapons and supersonics when the Okies had first encountered them; and during the brief period that the Okies had been in contact with them, they had snapped up such Middle Ages and Early Modern techniques as nuclear fission and chemotherapy. Besides, there had been the spindizzies, some from the city, some new-built, but all necessarily left behind and in full operation; studied with the eye of intelligence, they could not but provide the Hevians with clues to many potent disciplines which they would have little difficulty putting to work once the jungle was gone; in the meantime, the machines would maintain the atmosphere of the planet and its internal heat even in the most frigid depths of intergalactic space; it would be the darkness of those gulfs, which the Hevians could mitigate but could hardly abolish, which would kill off the jungle.

Nevertheless, Amalfi had hardly expected to see the return of He, under wholly controlled spindizzy drive, in barely a century and a half, still faintly, patchily blue-green with cultivation under cloud-banks which glared a brilliant white in the light of a nearby Cepheid variable star. That the wandering body was He had been settled back home on New Earth as soon as Hazleton had been able to identify the wanderer's advance ultraphone beacon, as Amalfi had predicted; and hardly five minutes after Carrel had brought his ship out of spindizzy drive within hailing distance of the new planet, Amalfi had himself spoken to Miramon, the very same Hevian leader with whom the Okies had dealt one hundred and fifty years ago—to the mutual astonishment of each that the other was still alive.

"Not that I myself should have been surprised," Miramon said, from the head of his great council table of black, polished, oily wood. "After all, I myself am still alive, to an age beyond the age of all the patriarchs in our recorded history; which in turn is only a small fraction of the age you gave us to understand you had attained when first we met you. But old habits of thought die hard. We were able to isolate and purify only a few of the anti-agathics produced by our jungle, acting on the hints you had given us, before the jungle died off and the plants which produced those drugs did not prove cultivatable under the new conditions, so we had no choice but to search for ways to synthesize these compounds. We were forced to work very fast, and happily the search was successful by the third generation, but in the meantime the existing supply had sufficed to keep only a few of us alive beyond what we still think of as our normal lifespans. Hence to most of our population, Mayor Amalfi, you are now only a legend, an immortal man of infinite wisdom from beyond the stars, and I have been unable to prevent myself from coming to think of you in much the same way."

Though he still wore in his topknot the great black barbaric saw-toothed feather of his authority, the Miramon before Amalfi today bore little resemblance to the lithe, supple, hard-headedly practical semi-savage who had once squatted on the floor in Amalfi's presence, because chairs were the uncomfortable prerogatives of the gods. His skin was still firm and tanned, his eyes bright and darting, but, though his abundant hair was now quite white, he had settled into that period of life, neither youth nor age, characteristic of the man who goes on anti-agathics only when somewhat past "natural" middle age. His councillors—including Retma, of Fabr-Suithe, which in Amalfi's time had been a bandit town which had been utterly destroyed during the last struggle before He took flight, but which now, rebuilt in ceremonial pink marble, was the second city of all He—mostly wore this same look. There were one or two who obviously had not been allowed access to the death-curing drugs until they had been in their "natural" seventies, bringing to the council table the probably spurious appearance of sagacity conferred by many wrinkles, an obvious physical fragility, and a sexual neutrality which was both slightly repellent and covertly enviable at the same time—a somatotype which for mankind as a whole had long ago lost its patent as the physiological stamp of hard-won wisdom, but which here among these recent immortals still exerted a queer authority, even upon Amalfi.

"If you managed to synthesize even one of the antiagathics, you've proven yourselves better chemists than anyone else in human history," Amalfi said. "They're far and away the most complicated molecules ever found in nature; certainly we've never heard of anyone who was able to synthesize even one."

"One is all we managed to synthesize," Miramon admitted. "And the synthetic form has certain small but undesirable side-effects we've never been able to eliminate. Several others turned out to be natural sapogenins which we could raise in our artificial climate, and modify into anti-agathics by two or three subsequent fermentation steps. Finally there are four others, of very broad usefulness, which we produce by fermentation alone, using micro-organisms grown in nutrient solutions in deep tanks, into which we feed comparatively simple and cheap precursors."

"We have one like that, the first, in fact, that was ever discovered: ascomycin," Amalfi said. "I think I will stick to my original judgment. As chemists you people could obviously give all the rest of us cards and spades."

"Then it is fortunate for us, and perhaps for every sentient being everywhere, that it is not as chemists that we come seeking you," Retma said, a trifle grimly.

"Which brings me to my main question," Amalfi said. "Just why did you turn back? I can't imagine that you would have been seeking me personally, you had no reason to believe that I was anywhere within thousands of parsecs of this area; we last parted company on the other side of the home galaxy. Obviously you must have looped back toward home as soon as you were sure you had centralized control over your spindizzy installation long before you were much past halfway to the Andromeda galaxy. What I want to know is, what turned you back?"

"There you are both right and wrong," Miramon said, with a trace of what could have been pride; it was hard to tell, for his face was extremely solemn. "We obtained reasonably close control of the antigravity machines only about thirty years after you and I parted company, Mayor Amalfi. When the full implications of what we had found were borne in upon us, we were highly elated. Now we had a real planet, in the radical meaning of the word, a real wanderer which could go where it chose, settling in one solar system or another and leaving it again when we so decided. By that time we were almost self-sufficient, there was obviously no need for us to become migrant workers, as your city and its enemies had been. And since we were well on the way to the second galaxy in any event, and since there seemed to be absolutely no limit to the velocities we could mount with the huge mass of our planet on which to operate, we chose to go on and explore."

"To the Andromeda galaxy?"

"Yes, and beyond. Of course we saw very little of that galaxy, which is as vast as our home; we think that it is not inhabited by any widespread, space-cruising race such as yours and mine, but in the brief sampling of its stars that we were able to take we might well simply have missed hitting upon an inhabited or colonized system. By that time, in any event, we had made the discovery which was to become the basis of our lives and purposes from then onward, and knew that we should have to return home very shortly. We left the Andromeda nebula for its satellite, the one that you identified for us as M-33 on our old star-tapestries from the Great Age, and thence took the million and a half light-year leap to the Lesser Magellanic Cloud. It was during our transition from the Lesser to the Greater Cloud that you detected us. That was, to be sure, an accident; we had intended to go directly through into the home galaxy and onward to Earth, where, our experience with you had given us good reason to believe, we might find a reservoir of knowledge great enough to cope with what we had discovered. That our own knowledge was insufficient was never for a moment in doubt.

"But it is an accident of the greatest good omen that we should have been found again by you as we were returning home, Mayor Amalfi. Surely the gods must have arranged such an accident, which otherwise is impossibly unlikely; for if there is any man not on Earth itself who can help us, you are that man."

"You were not once such a believer in the gods, as I recall," Amalfi said, smiling tightly.

"Opinions change with age; otherwise what is age for?"

"So does history," Amalfi said. "And, whether I can help you or not, it is a lucky accident that you stopped here before carrying on into the home lens. Earth is no longer dominant there. We've had considerable difficulty in understanding what actually is going on, the messages that we get from there came pouring in to us in such an enormous garble; but of one thing I'm sure: there's a huge new imperialism on the rise there, on its way to becoming as powerful as Earth once was, and as Vegas was before Earth. It calls itself the Web of Hercules, and what remains of Earth's interstellar empire doesn't appear to be putting up much of a resistance against it. If you want my advice, I would suggest that you stay out of the home galaxy entirely, or you may well be gobbled down whole."

There was a long silence around the Hevian council table. At last, Miramon said:

"This leaves us with little recourse indeed. It may well be that there is no answer, as we have often suspected. Or it may be that the gods have indeed brought us back to the one source of wisdom that we need."

"We will know soon enough," Retma said quietly. "If in that instant there will be time enough to know anything. Or enough of time left thereafter to remember it."

"I shall probably be unable to advise you so long as I don't know what you're talking about," Amalfi said, impressed in spite of himself by the tone of high seriousness with which the Hevians spoke. "Just what was the discovery that turned you back? What is the forthcoming event that you seem to dread?"

"Nothing less," Retma said evenly, "than the imminent coming to an end of time itself."

For a while, even after they had explained it to him, Amalfi was so unable to believe that the Hevians had meant what they said that he was prepared to dismiss it as one of those superstitions with which He had been riddled, like many another provincial planet, when the Okies had first made contact with it. That time must have a stop was a proposition that nothing in all his long life had prepared him to accept even for an instant. Even after it became reluctantly clear to him that what Miramon and the Hevians had found in the intergalactic deeps had been a real event with real implications, and one which Amalfi's own people—particularly Schloss' group—were prepared to document, event and implication alike, he continued to be unable to do more with it than dismiss it out of hand.

He said so, at a conference on shipboard which included Miramon, Retma, Dr. Schloss, Carrel, and—by Dirac— Jake and Dr. Gifford Bonner, the latter the leader of that group of New Earth philosophers which Hazleton had recently joined, called the Stochastics. "If what you say is true," he said, "there's nothing to be done about it anyhow. Time will come to an end, and that's that. But the end of the world has been predicted often before, I seem to remember from history, and here we all are still; I can't credit that so vast a process as the whole physical universe could possibly come to an end in the flicker of an eyelash, and since I can't believe it, I'm not suddenly going to start behaving as if I did. No more do I see why anyone else should."

"Amalfi, you're quite right! You don't understand," Dr. Schloss said. "Of course the end of the universe has been predicted often before. It's one of those two-pronged choices that any philosopher has to make: either you hold that the universe will at some time come to an end, or else you arrive at the position that it never can; there are intermediate guesses that you can make, that's where we get our cyclical theories, but essentially they're simply hedges. If you decided that the universe has a limited lifetime, then you must begin to think about when that life will come to an end, on the basis of whatever data are available to you. We have been agreed for millennia that the universe cannot last forever, however we've hedged the agreement, so that leaves us nothing to quarrel about but the date at which we fixed the end. And sooner or later, too, the time was going to come when we had enough data to fix even the date without doubt. The Hevians have brought us sufficient facts to do that now; the date is fixed, whatever it proves to be, without cavil or quibble. If we are to talk about the matter intelligently at all, there is a fixed fact with which we must begin. It is not open to agreement. It is a fact.

"I think," Amalfi said in a voice of steel, "that you have gone quietly insane. You should listen to the City Fathers for a while on this subject, as I have; if you like, I can give you a Dirac line to them from right here aboard ship, and you can hear some of the memories that they have stored up—some of them dating back long before spaceflight; our city is very old. You should hear particularly the stories about the end of the world which emerge as inevitably as a plant from a seed every time someone takes it into his head to believe that he has a direct wire to the Almighty. Some of the stories, of course, are just jokes like the many predictions of the end of the world which were made by a man named Voliva, who *knew* that the Earth was flat; or the predictions of Armageddon that came repeatedly from an Earthly sect called the Believers, which was riding high on Earth during the very decade when both the spindizzy and the anti-agathics were discovered. But high intelligence doesn't prevent you from falling into this kind of apocryphal madness, either; seven centuries before space flight on Earth, the greatest scientist of that time, a man named Bacon, was predicting the imminent arrival of Anti-Christ simply because he was unable to persuade his contemporaries to adopt scientific method, which he had just invented. Furthermore, I may add, in the decade just before spaceflight on Earth, all the best minds of the age saw no future for the human race, and all other air-breathing life on Earth, but complete obliteration in a worldwide thermonuclear war, which over a period of eight years could have broken out within any given twenty-minute period. And in that, Dr. Schloss, they were quite right; their world really could have ended during any one of these twenty-minute periods; the physical possibilities were there, but somehow the world managed to last until spaceflight became only a specter, burned out by starlight, as the ghosts of night-bound peoples evaporate from their mythologies as soon as they're able to produce light even at midnight simply by tripping a switch."

He looked around at the faces of the men drawn up at the ship's chart table. Few of them would meet his eyes; most of them were looking down at the table itself, or at their own hands. Their expressions were those of men who had been listening to a mass murderer attempting to enter a plea of insanity.

"Amalfi," Jake's voice said abruptly from the Dirac, "the time for forensics is past. This question does not have two sides, except for the right side and the wrong side, and we are going to have to shuck you off as a brilliant advocate for the wrong side. You have done your magnificent best, but since the right side does not need an advocate, you have been wasting your breath. Let me ask the rest of this conference: What shall we do now? Does it appear that, as the Hevians think, there is anything at all that we can do? I am inclined to doubt it."

"So am I," Dr. Schloss said, though there was nothing in his manner to suggest the gloom inherent in his conclusion; he seemed rather to be as intensely interested as Amalfi had ever seen him in his life. "For temporal creatures to hope to survive the end of time is surely as futile as a fish hoping to survive being thrown into a sun. The paradox is immediate, on the surface, and quite inescapable."

"No technical problem is ever that insoluble," Amalfi said in exasperation. "Miramon, if you will pardon me for passing such a judgment—and I don't care if you don't—I think you are suffering from the same syndrome as Dr. Freeman and Dr. Schloss: you have grown old before your time. You've lost your sense of adventure."

"Not entirely," Miramon said, regarding Amalfi with an expression of grave and hurt disappointment. "We, at least, are not yet convinced that there is no answer; if we do not find it here, we have every intention of continuing to travel in the hope of finding someone with whom we can combine forces, someone who may have some solution to suggest. If we find no one, then we shall continue to seek that solution ourselves."

"Good for you," Amalfi said fiercely. "And by God I'll go with you. We can't very well reenter our own galaxy, but the next one is NGC 6822, that's about a million light-years from here—for you, that's only a hop. And at least we'd be in motion; we wouldn't be sitting around here with folded hands waiting for the blow to fall."

"That would be motion without purpose," Miramon said solemnly. "I agree with you that it would be dangerous and unwise to risk any entanglement with the Web of Hercules, whatever that may be; but I can see no better point in cruising from one galaxy to another solely in the bare hope of encountering a high civilization which might be able to help us, and all the rest of the universe with us. We have that hope, but it cannot be the final goal of our journey; our ultimate destination must be the center of the metagalaxy, the hub of all the galaxies of space-time. It is only there, where all the forces of the universe lie in dynamic balance, that anyone can hope to take any action to escape or to modify the end which is coming. There is, after all, not much time left before that moment is due. And above all, Mayor Amalfi, it is not simply a technical problem; it is an ending which was written organically into the fundamental structure of the universe itself, written in the beginning by what hands we know not; all that we can know now is that it was foreordained."

And from this conclusion, though Amalfi's own psyche had been fighting against its acceptance since the moment that he himself had realized it was so, there was really no escape. Conceptually, the universe had been a reasonably comfortable place to live in, in primitive atomic theory which offered the assurance that everything, earth, air, fire or water, steel and oranges, man or star, was ultimately composed of submicroscopic vortices called protons and electrons leavened a little with neutrons and neutrinos which had no charge, and bound together by a disorderly but homely family of mesons. The type case was the hydrogen atom, one proton sitting cosily on the hearth, contentedly positive in charge, while about it wove one electron, surrounded by its negative field like crackling cat's fur. That was the simple case; but one was assured that even in the heaviest and most complicated atoms, even those man-made ones like plutonium, one need only add more and heavier logs to the fire, and more cats would come droning about it; it would be hard to tell one cat from another, but this is the customary penalty the owner of hundreds pays.

The first omen that there was something wrong with this chromo of submicroscopic and universal domesticity appeared, as all good omens should, in the skies. Back on Earth, nearly half a century before space flight, some astronomer whose name is quite lost had noticed that two or three of the millions of meteors that entered Earth's atmosphere every day exploded at a height and with a violence which could not be accounted for by an eccentricity of orbit or velocity; and in one of those great flights of fancy which account in the long run for every new link in the great chain of understanding, he had a dream of something which he called "contra-terrene" matter—a matter made of fire with cat's fur, which would be circled by cats in flames: matter in which the fundamental hydrogen atom would have a nucleus which would be an anti-proton, with the mass of a proton but carrying a negative charge, around which would orbit an anti-electron, with the negligible mass of an electron, but carrying a positive charge. A meteor of atoms constructed on this model, he reasoned, would explode with especial violence at the first contact with even the faintest traces of Earth's normal-matter atmosphere; and such meteors would suggest that somewhere in the universe there were whole planets, whole suns, whole galaxies composed of such matter, whose barest touch would be more than death—would be ultimate and complete annihilation, each form of matter converting the other wholly into energy in a flaming and total embrace.

Curiously, the contra-terrene meteors died out of the theory shortly thereafter, while the theory itself survived. The exploding meteors were found to be easier to explain in more conventional terms, but anti-matter survived, and by the middle of the Twentieth Century experimental

physicists were even able to produce the stuff a few atoms
at a time. Those topsy-turvy atoms proved to be nonviable
beyond a few millionths of a micro-second, and it gradually
became clear that even in this short lifetime the time in
which they lived was running backwards. The particles of
which they were made were born, in the great clumsy
bevatrons of that age, some micro-seconds in the future,
and their assembly into atoms of anti-matter in the present
time of the observers was in fact the moment of their
death. Obviously anti-matter was not only theoretically
possible, but could exist; but it could not exist in this
universe in any assemblage so gross as a meteor; if there
were worlds and galaxies made of anti-matter, they existed
only in some unthinkable separate continuum where time
and the entropy gradient ran backwards. Such a continuum would require at least four extra dimensions, at a
minimum, in addition to the conventional four of experience.

As the universe of normal matter expanded, unwound
and ran down toward its inevitable heat-death, somewhere
nearby and yet in a "somewhere" unimaginable by man, a
duplicate universe as vast and complex was contracting,
winding up, approaching the supernal concentration of
mass and energy called the monobloc. As complete dispersion, darkness and silence was to be the fate of the universe in which the arrow of time pointed down the entropy
gradient, so in the anti-matter universe the end was to be
mass beyond mass, energy beyond energy, raw glare and
fury to the ultimate power raging in a primeval "atom" no
bigger across than the orbit of Saturn. And out of one
universe might come the other; in the universe of normal
matter the monobloc was the beginning, but in the universe of anti-matter it would be the end; in a universe of
normal entropy, the monobloc is intolerable and must
explode; in a universe of negative entropy, the heat-death
is intolerable and must condense. In either case, the command is: *Let there be light.*

What the visible, tangible universe had been like before
the monobloc was, however, agreed to be forever unknowable. The classic statement had been made many
centuries earlier by St. Augustine, who, when asked what
God might have been doing before He created the uni-

verse, replied that He was constructing a hell for persons who asked such questions; thus "pre-Augustinean time" came to be something that a historian could know all about, but a physicist, by definition, nothing.

Until now; for if the Hevians were right, they had lifted that curtain a little way and caught an instant's glimpse of the unknowable.

To have looked it full in the face could have been no more fatal.

During the course of their exultant drive upon the Andromeda galaxy, the Hevians had discovered that one of their spindizzies—oddly, it was one of the machines which had been new-built for the project, not one of the old and somewhat abused drivers which had been dismounted from the Okie city—was beginning to run somewhat hot. This was a problem which was then brand new to them, and rather than take chances on the to them unknown effects which might be produced by such a machine were it to run really wild, they shut down their entire spindizzy network while repairs were made, leaving behind only a 0.02 percent screen necessary to protect the planet's atmosphere and heat budget.

And it was then and there, in the utter silences of intergalactic space, that their instruments detected for the first time in human history the whispers of continuous creation: the tiny *ping* of new atoms of hydrogen being born, one by one, out of nothing at all.

This would alone and in itself have been a sobering enough experience for any man of a thoughtful cast of mind, even one who lacked the Hevians' history of preoccupation with religious questions; no one could view the birth of the raw material from which the whole known universe was built, out of what was demonstrably nothingness, without being shaken by the conviction that there must also be a Creator, and that He must be in the immediate vicinity of where His work was proceeding. Those tiny pings and pips in the Hevians' instruments seemed at first to leave no room in the long arguments of cosmogony and cosmology for any cyclical theory of the universe, any continuous and eternal systole diastole from monobloc to heat-death and back again, with a Creator

required only at the remote inception of the rhythmic
process, or not at all. Here was creation in process: the
invisible Finger touched nothingness, and from nothing
came something; the ultimate absurdity, which, because it
was ultimate, could be nothing else but divine.

Yet the Hevians were sophisticated enough to be suspicious. Historically, fundamental discoveries were dependa-
bly ambiguous; this discovery, which on the face of it
seemed to provide a flat answer to 25,000 years of theological speculation, and in effect to bring God into inarguable
being for the first time since He had been postulated by
some Stone Age sun-worshipper or mushroom-eating mystic, could not be as simple as it seemed. It had been won
too easily; too much else is implied by the continual creating existence of a present God to make it tenable that that
existence should be provable by so simple and single a
physical datum, arrived at by what could honestly only be
described as ordinary accident.

Gifford Bonner was later to remark that it had been
fortunate beyond belief that it had been the Hevians, a
people only recently winning back to some degree of
scientific sophistication, but which had never lost its sense
of the continuity and the overwhelming complexity of
theology in a scientific age, who had first been allowed to
hear these tiny birth-cries in the nursery of time. The
typical Earthman of the end of the Third Millennium, with
his engineer's bias, philosophically webbed in about equal
measure to a sentimentally hard-headed "common sense"
and a raw and naive mystique of Progress (it was at about
this point in Bonner's analysis that Amalfi had felt a slight
impulse to squirm), might easily have taken the datum at
face value and walked the plank on it directly into a
morass of telepathy, the racial unconscious, personal rein-
carnation or any of a hundred other traps which await the
scientifically oriented man who does not know that he too
is as thorough-going a mystic as a fakir lying on a bed of
nails.

The Hevians were suspicious; they questioned the discovery first of all only on the subject of what it said it was
saying. Theology could wait. If continuous creation was a
fact, then primarily that ruled out that there should ever

have been a monobloc in the history of the universe, or that they should ever be a heat-death; instead, it would always go along like this, world without end. Therefore, if the discovery was as fundamentally ambiguous as all such discoveries before had proved to be, it should in the same breath be implying exactly the opposite; as if *that* question, and see what it says.

This singularly tough-minded approach paid off at once, though the further implications which it offered for inspection proved in no way easier to digest than the first and contrary set had been. Taking a long chance with the still largely unfamiliar machines, and with the precarious life of their entire planet, the Hevians shut down their spindizzies entirely and listened more intently.

In that utmost of dead silences, the upsetting whisper of continuous creation proved to have two voices. Each pinging birth-pang was not a single note, but a duo. As each atom of hydrogen leapt into being from nowhere into the universe of experience, a sinister twin, a hydrogen atom of anti-matter, came there in that instant to die, from . . . somewhere else.

And there it was. Even what had seemed to be fundamental, ineluctable proof of one-way time and continuous creation could also be regarded as inarguable evidence for a cyclical cosmology. In a way, to the Hevians, it was satisfying; this was physics as they knew it to be, an idiot standing at a crossroads shouting "God went thataway!" and managing to point down all four roads at once. Nevertheless, it left them a legacy of dread. This single many-barbed burr of a datum, which could have been obtained under no other circumstances, was also sufficient in itself to endorse the existence of an entire second universe of anti-matter, congruent point for point with the universe of experience of normal matter, but opposite to it in sign. What appeared to have been the birth of a hydrogen atom of anti-matter, simultaneous with the birth of the normal hydrogen atom, was actually its death; there was now no doubt that time ran backwards in the anti-matter universe, and so did the entropy gradient, one being demonstrably a function of the other.

The concept, of course, was old—so old, in fact, that

Amalfi had difficulty in remembering just when in his lifetime it had become so familiar to him that he had forgotten about it entirely. Its revival here by the Hevians struck him at first as an exasperating anachronism, calculated only to get in the way of the real work of practical men. He was in particular rather scornful of the notion of a universe in which negative entropy could be an operating principle; under such circumstances, his rustily squeaking memory pointed out, cause and effect would not preserve even the rough statistical associations which they were allowed in the universe of experience; energy would accumulate, events would undo themselves, water would run uphill, old men would clump into existence out of the air and soil and unlearn their profitless ways back toward their mothers' wombs.

"Which is what they do in any event," Gifford Bonner had said gently. "But actually, I doubt that it's that paradoxical, Amalfi. Both of these universes can be regarded as unwinding, as running down, as losing energy with each transaction. The fact that from our point of view the antimatter universe seems to be gaining energy is simply a bias built into the way we're forced to look at things. Actually these two universes probably are simply unwinding in opposite directions, like two millstones. Though the two arrows of time seem to be pointing in opposite directions, they probably both point downhill, like fingerboards at the crest of a single road. If the dynamics of it bother you, bear in mind that both are four dimensional continua and from that point of view both are wholly static."

"Which brings us to the crucial question of contiguity," Jake said cheerfully. "The point is, these two four-dimensional continua are intimately related, as the twin events the Hevians observed make very plain; which I suppose must mean that we must allow for a total of at least sixteen dimensions to contain the whole system. Which is no particular surprise in itself; you need at least that many to accommodate the atomic nucleus of average complexity comfortably. What is surprising is that the two continua are approaching each other; I agree with Miramon that the observations his people made can't be interpreted any other way; up to now, the fact that gravitation in the two universes is also opposite in sign seems to have kept them apart, but that repulsion or pressure or whatever you want to call it is obviously growing steadily weaker. Somewhere in the future, the near future, it will decline to zero, there will be a Pythagorean point-for-point collision between the two universes as a whole—"

"—and it's hard to imagine how any physical framework, even one that allows sixteen dimensions of elbowroom, will be able to contain the energy that's going to be released," Dr. Schloss said. "The monobloc isn't even in the running; if it ever existed, it was just a wet firecracker by comparison."

"Translation: *blooey*," Carrel said.

"It's perfectly possible that a rational cosmology is going to have to accommodate all three events," Gifford Bonner said. "I mean by that the monobloc, the heat death, and this thing—this event that seems to fall midway between the two. Curious; there are a number of myths, and ancient philosophical systems, that allow for such a break or discontinuity right in the middle of the span of existence; Giordano Bruno, Earth's first relativist, called it the period of Interdestruction, and a compatriot of his named Vico allowed for it in what was probably the first cyclical theory of ordinary human history; and in Scandanavian mythology it was called the Ginnangu-Gap. But I wonder, Dr. Schloss, if the destruction is going to be quite as total as you suggest. I am nobody's physicist, I freely confess, but it seems to me that if these two universes are opposite in sign *at every point*, as everyone at this meeting has been implying, then the result cannot be *only* a general transformation of the matter on both sides into energy. There will be energy transformed into matter, too, on just as large a scale, after which the gravitational pressure should begin to build up again and the two universes, having in effect passed through each other and exchanged hats, will begin retreating from each other once more. Or have I missed something crucial?"

"I'm not sure that the argument is as elegant as it appears on the surface," Retma said. "That awaits Dr. Schloss's mathematical analysis, of course; but in the meantime I cannot help but wonder why, for instance, if this simultaneous creation-interdestruction-destruction cycle is truly cyclical, it should have this ornamental waterspout of continuous creation attached to it? A machinery of creation which involves no less than three universal cataclysms in each cycle should not need to be powered by a sort of continuous drip; either the one is too grandiose, or the other is insufficient. Besides, continuous creation implies a steady state, which is irreconcilable."

"I don't know about that," Jake said. "It doesn't sound like anything the Milne transformations couldn't handle; it's probably just a clock function."

"Defined, as I recall, as a mathematical expression about the size of a bottle of aspirin," Carrel said ruefully.

"Well, there's one thing I'm perfectly certain of," Amalfi growled, "and that is that it's damned unlikely anybody is going to be around to care about the exact results of the collision after it happens. At least not at the rate this hassle is going. Is there actually anything useful that we can do, or would we be better off spending all this time playing poker?"

"That," Miramon said, "is exactly what we know least about. In fact it would appear that we know nothing about it whatsoever."

"Mr. Miramon—" Web Hazleton's voice spoke from the shadows and stopped. Obviously he was waiting to be told that he was breaking his promise not to interrupt, but it was as plain to Amalfi as it was to the rest of the group that he was interrupting nothing now; his voice had broken only a dead and despairing silence.

"Go ahead, Web," Amalfi said.

"Well, I was just thinking. Mr. Miramon came here looking for somebody to help him do something he doesn't know how to do himself. Now he thinks we don't know how to do it either. But what was it?"

"He's just said that he doesn't know," Amalfi said gently.

"That isn't what I mean," Web said hesitantly. "What I mean is, what would he *like* to do, even if he doesn't know how to do it? Even if it's impossible?"

Bonner's voice chuckled softly in the still shipboard air. "That's right," he said, "the ends determine the means. A hen is only an egg's device for producing another egg. Is that Hazleton's grandson? Good for you, Web."

"There are a good many experiments that ought to be performed, if only we knew how to design them," Miramon admitted thoughtfully. "First of all, we ought to have a better date for the catastrophe than we have now; 'the near future' is a huge block of time under these conditions, almost as shapeless a target as 'sometime'; we would need it defined to the millisecond just to begin with. I applaud the young Earthman's brilliant common sense, but I refuse to delude myself by asking for more than that; even that seems hopeless."

"Why?" Amalfi said. "What would you need to calculate it from? Given the data, the City Fathers can handle the calculations; they were designed to handle any mathematical operation once the parameters were filled, and in a thousand years I've never known them to fail to come through on that kind of thing, usually within two or three minutes; never as long as a day."

"I remember your City Fathers," Miramon said, with a brief ironical motion of his eyebrows which was perhaps a last vestigial tremor of his old savage awe at the things which were the city and of the city. "But the major parameter that needs to be filled here is a precise determination of the energy level of the other universe."

"Why, that shouldn't be so very difficult," Dr. Schloss said, in dawning astonishment. "That can't be anything but a transform of energy level in our own universe; the mayor's right, the City Fathers could give you that almost before you could finish stating the problem to them; t-tau transforms are the fundamental stuff of faster-than-light space travel—I'm astonished that you've been able to get along without them."

"Not so," Jake said. "No doubt the t-tau relationships are congruent on both sides of the barrier, I don't doubt that for a minute, but you're dealing in sixteen dimensions here; along what axis are you going to impose the congruency? Are you going to assume that t-time and tau-time apply uniformly and transformably along all sixteen axes? You can't do that, unless you're willing to involve the total system in such a double, which in t-time involves a monobloc for the whole apparatus; that's hopeless. At least it's hopeless for us, in the time we have left; we'd be frittering away our days in chase of endlessly retreating decimals. You might just as well set the City Fathers to work giving you a final figure for *pi*."

"I stand corrected," Dr. Schloss said, his tone halfway between wry humor and stiff embarrassment. "You're quite right, Miramon; there's a discontinuity here which we can't read from theory. How inelegant."

"Elegance can wait," Amalfi said. "In the meantime, why is it so impossible to get an energy-level reading from the other side? Dr. Schloss, your research group used to talk about their hopes of constructing an anti-matter artifact. Couldn't we use such a thing as an exploratory missile to the other side?"

"No," Dr. Schloss said promptly. "You forget that such an object would be on the other side—it would be on our side. We would have to work out some way of assembling it in the future of the experiment; by the time we were first able to see it, in the present of the experiment, it would be in an advanced state of decay, to say the least, and would then evolve only to the condition in which we assembled it. No reading that we got from it would tell us anything but how anti-matter behaves in our universe; it would tell us nothing about any universe in which anti-matter is normal."

After a moment, he added thoughtfully, "And besides, that would be a project hard to realize in anything under a century. I'd be more inclined to say it would take two; under the circumstances I too would rather be playing poker."

"Well, I wouldn't," Jake said unexpectedly. "I think Amalfi may be right in principle. Difficult though the problem is, there ought to be some sort of probe that we could extend across the discontinuity. Mind you, I agree that the anti-matter artifact is the wrong approach entirely; the thing would have to be absolutely immaterial, a construct made entirely out of what we could pick up in No-Man's-Land. But seeing across long distances under great odds is the discipline I was trained in. I don't think we should count this an impossible problem. Schloss, how do you feel about this? If you and your group are willing to give up your anti-matter artifact for poker, would you be willing to work with me on this a while? I'll need your background, but you'll need my point of view; between us we just might devise the instrument and get the message. Mind you, Miramon, I hold out no hope, but—"

"—except the hope you hold out," Miramon said, his eyes shining. "Now I am hearing from you what I hoped to hear. This is the voice of the Earth of memory. We will give you everything you need that is within our power to give; we give you our planet, to begin with; but the universe, the twin universes, the unthinkable meta-universe you must take for yourselves. We remember you now; you have always had that boundless ambition." His voice darkened suddenly. "And we shall be your disciples; that, too, is as it has always been. Only begin; that is all we ask."

Amalfi gathered the consensus of the present eyes around the chart table. Such agreement as he needed from the listeners on New Earth he was able to gather almost as well from the silence.

"I think," he said slowly, "that we have begun already."

CHAPTER FOUR: Fabr-Suithe

It was hot on the Hevian hillside in the post-noon glare of the great Cepheid about which the planet was now orbiting at the respectful distance of thirty-five astronomical units—thirty-five times the distance of old Earth from the Sun. At this distance the star, which had a mean absolute magnitude of plus one, was barely tolerable at the peak of its eight-day cycle; at the bottom of the cycle, when the star's radiation had dropped by a factor of 25, it got cold enough on He to nip one's ears—far from an ideal situation for a predominantly agricultural planet, but the Hevians did not expect to remain in the vicinity for as long as one growing season.

Web and Estelle lay in the long grass of the hillside under the hot regard of that swollen star and slowly got their breaths back. Web in particular was glad for the recess. The morning had begun in sober exploration of Fabr-Suithe, He's greatest monument to its own past, and He's present center of pure philosophy; thus far it was the only place they had found on He which they were allowed to explore by themselves, by both the adult Hevians and their own people. This morning, however, this freedom had had an unexpected but logical consequence: they had found that Fabr-Suithe was also one of the few cities on

He where Hevian children were free to roam. Elsewhere there were far too many machines vital to the life of the planet as a whole; the Hevians could not afford the chance that children might get into the works, nor, with their sparse population, could they afford the loss of even a single life.

Web and Estelle had changed into the chiton-like Hevian costume the moment they had been told that they would be allowed to explore the city, albeit in very limited terms, but it did not take the Hevian youngsters long to penetrate this disguise, since Web and Estelle spoke their language only in a most rudimentary way. This language block was in part a nuisance—for although most adult Hevians spoke the mixture of English, Interlingua and Russian which was the *bêche-de-mer* of deep space, learned long ago from the Okies, none of the children did—but it was also a blessing, since it precluded any extensive inter-rogation of Web and Estelle about their own world, culture and background. Shortly, instead, they found themselves involved in an elaborate chase game called Matrix, rather like run-sheep-run combined with checkers except that it was three-dimensional, for it was played in a twelve-story building with transparent floors so that one could always see the position of the other players, and with strategically placed spindizzy and friction-field shafts for fast transit from one floor to another. Web was the first to develop the suspicion that the building had either been designed for the game or had been totally abandoned to it, for the transparent floors were appropriately ruled, and the structure otherwise did not seem to contain anything or to be used for any other purpose.

Web had found the game itself exhilarating at first, but rather baffling too, and he was generally the first player to be eliminated. Had it not been for an impromptu change in the rules, he would have been It in nearly every new round, and even under the aegis of the new rules he did not make a very brave showing. Estelle, on the other hand, took to Matrix as though she had been born in the game, and within half an hour her lanky-legged, slender figure, as bosomless and hipless as any of the boys', was darting in and out of the kaleidoscope of running figures

with inordinate grace and swiftness. When time was called
for lunch, Web's laboring lungs and bruised ego more than
welcomed the chance to escape from the city entirely for
the hot stillness of the fallow hills.

"They're nice; I like them," Estelle said, rising to one
elbow to attack, meditatively, a gourd-shaped green and
silver melon which one of the Hevian boys had given her,
apparently as a prize. At the first bite, there was a low but
prolonged hiss, and the air around them became impreg-
nated with a fragrance so overwhelmingly spicy that
Estelle had to sneeze five times in quick succession. Web
began to laugh, but the laughter ended abruptly in a
paroxysmal sneeze of his own.

"They *love* us," he said, wiping his eyes. "You're so
good at their game, they've given you a sneeze-gas bomb
to keep you from playing it any longer."

The odor diminished gradually, carried off by what little
breeze there was. After a while Estelle cautiously put two
thumbs into the wound she had made and broke the
melon open. Nothing else happened; the odor was now
tolerable, and then abruptly became both barely detectable and overpoweringly mouth watering. Estelle handed
him half. He bit into the crisp white pulp more deeply
than he had intended. The result made him close his eyes;
it tasted like quick-frozen music.

They finished it in reverent silence and, wiping their
mouths on their chitons, lay back. After a while, Estelle
said:

"I wish we could talk to them better."

"Miramon can talk to *us* well enough," Web said som-
nolently. "He didn't have to learn our language the hard
way, either. They do it here by machine, like we used to
do it when we were Okies. I wish we still did it that way."

"Hypnopaedia?" Estelle said. "But I thought that was all
dead and done for. You didn't really *learn* anything that
way; just facts."

"That's right, just facts. It didn't teach you to relate. For
that you have to have a tutor. But it was good for learning
things like 1 X 1 = 10, or the tables in the back of the
book, or the 850 words you most need to know in a new
language. It used to take only five hundred hours to cram

all that stuff into you, by EEG feedback, flicker, oral repetition, and I don't know what all else—and the whole time, you were under hypnosis."

"It sounds too easy," Estelle said sleepily.

"The easy parts of things ought to be easy," Web said. "What's the point of having to learn them by rote? That takes too much time. You know yourself that something you can learn in ten repetitions, or five, it takes some kids thirty repetitions to learn. So you have to sit around through twenty or twenty-five repetitions that you don't need. If there's anything I hate about school, it's drill—all that time wasted that you could actually be doing something with."

Suddenly Web became conscious of a peculiar flopping sound at the crest of the hill behind him. He knew well enough that there were no dangerous animals left on He, but he realized that he had been hearing the sound for some time while he was talking; and the notion occurred to him that his definition of a dangerous animal might not necessarily make a good match with that of a Hevian. Anyhow, he could hope; he could use a tiger to best, along about now. He twisted quickly to his hands and knees.

"Don't be silly," Estelle said, without moving or even opening her eyes. "It's only Ernest."

The svengali appeared over the crest of the hill and came humping itself through the tall grass in a symphony of desperate disorganization. It gave Web only the briefest of glances, and then bent upon Estelle the reproachful stare of an animal utterly betrayed, but still—it hoped you noticed—firm in the true faith. Web stiffed his impulse to laugh, for in fact he could hardly blame the poor creature; since it was as brainless as it was sexless—despite its name—it had been able to contrive no better way of keeping up with Estelle than to follow her through her every move in the Matrix game, a discipline for which it was so magnificently unequipped that it had only just now finished. It was lucky that the children had not counted it as a player, or poor Ernest would have been It to—Web thought with unfocussed uneasiness—the end of time.

"We could sign up for it here," Web said abruptly.

"For what? Hypnopaedia? Your grandmother wouldn't let us."

Web turned around and sat up, plucking a long hollow blade of the bamboo-like grass and sinking his grinding teeth thoughtfully into the woody butt end. "But she isn't here," he said.

"No, but she will be," Estelle said. "And she's a school officer on the New Earth. I used to hear her fighting about it with my father when I was a child. She used to tell him he was out of his mind. She would say, 'Why do kids need all this calculus and history now? What good is it to somebody who's going to have to go out and hoe a virgin planet?' She used to make poor Dad stutter something awful."

"But she isn't here," Web repeated, with a little unwilling exasperation. He had just realized that Estelle's face with its closed eyes, so perfectly in repose in the blue-white light of this one-day-long summer, was lovelier than anything he had ever seen before. He found that he could not go on.

At the same moment, the svengali felt rested enough to take a consensus among the scattered ganglia which served it, however badly, for a brain, and concluded that its long soulful stare at Estelle was doing it no good at all. Simultaneously one of its limbs, which had the whole time been inching in the direction of one of the melon rinds, suddenly passed a threshold and telegraphed back to the rest of the animal the implications of that now faint spicy odor. All the rest of Ernest flowed eagerly into that arm and bunched itself around the rind; and then the polyp was rolling helplessly down the hill, curled into a ball, with the melon rind clutched firmly in the middle. As it rolled, it emitted a small thrilling whistle of alarm which made Web's back hairs stir—it was the first time he had ever heard a svengali make a sound—but it would not let go of its prize; it came to rest in the middle of a rivulet in the valley and was washed gently downstream out of sight, still faintly protesting and avidly digesting.

"There goes Ernest," Web said.

"I know. I heard him. He's such a stupid. But he'll be back. Your grandmother will be here too. Once the Mayor and Miramon and Dr. Schloss and the rest decided to stay on He, because of all the work they have to do here, they had to send home for somebody to take care of us. They don't think we can take care of ourselves. They wouldn't let us go knocking all around a strange planet all by ourselves."

"Maybe not," Web said reluctantly. He tested the proposition; it seemed to hold water. "But why would it have to be grandmother?"

"Well, it wouldn't be Daddy, because he has to stay on New Earth and work on the New Earth part of the problem that we're working on here," Estelle said. "And it wouldn't be your grandfather because he has to stay home on New Earth and be mayor while Mayor Amalfi's here. It wouldn't be my mother because they're not scientists or philosophers and would just clutter up He even more than we're doing. If they're going to fly anyone out here to oversee us, it has to be your grandmother."

"I suppose so," Web said. "That'll put a crimp in us, for sure."

"It'll do more than that," Estelle said tranquilly. "She'll send us home."

"She wouldn't do that!"

"Yes she would. That's the way they think. She'll be practical about it."

"That's not being practical," Web protested. "It's treachery, that's what it is. She can't come all the way here to take care of us on He, just as an excuse to take us off He."

Estelle did not reply. After a moment Web opened his eyes, belatedly realizing that a shadow had fallen across his face. The Hevian boy who had given Estelle the melon was standing above them, deferentially, respecting their silence, but obviously poised to renew the game when they were ready. Behind him, the heads of the other Hevian children bobbed over the hill, obviously wondering what the strangers and their boneless odd-smelling pet would do next, but leaving the initiative to their spokesman.

"Hello," Estelle said, sitting up again.

"Hello," the tall boy said hesitantly. "Yes?"

For a moment he seemed baffled; then, making the best

of the situation, he sat down and went on in as simple a Hevian as he could contrive.

"You are rested. Yes? Shall we play another game?"

"No more for me," Web said, almost indignantly. "Then play Matrix yesterday, tomorrow sometime day. Yes?"

"No, no," the Hevian boy said. "Not Matrix. This is another game, a resting game. You play it sitting down. We call it the lying game."

"Oh. How works it?"

"Everyone takes turns. Each tells a story. It must be a real story, without any truth in it. The other players are the jury. You gain a point for everything in the story that is clearly true. The low score wins."

"I lost about five key words in there somewhere," Estelle said to Web. "How does it go again?"

Web explained quickly. Although his spoken command of the Hevian language was limited to the tenses of past indictable, present excitable and future irredeemable, his vocabulary a thoroughly unbotanical mixture of stems and roots, and his declensions one massive disinclination to decline, he found that he was developing a fair facility at understanding the language, at least when it was being spoken this slowly. It was quite probable that he too had lost five words in the course of the Hevian boy's speech, but he had picked up their meaning from context; Estelle apparently was still trying to translate word by word, instead of striving first to catch the total import of the sentence.

"Oh, I see," Estelle said. "But how do they rate one truth over another? If in my story the sun rises in the morning, and I also say I'm wearing this whatever-it-is, this chiton, do I get docked one point for each?"

"I'll try to ask," Web said doubtfully. "I'm not sure I have all the nouns I need."

He put the question to the Hevian boy, finding it necessary to be rather more abstract than he wished; but the boy grasped not only the sense of what he was trying to say, but worked his way back to the concrete nouns with impressive insight.

"The jury will decide," the boy said. "But there are rules. A dress is only a little truth, and costs only one point. Sunrise on a captive planet, like New Earth, is a natural law, that may cost you fifty. On a free planet like He, it may be only partly true and cost you ten. Or it may be a flat lie and cost you nothing. That is why we have the jury."

Web had to have this restated to him in increasingly simpler terms before he chanced explaining it in turn to Estelle; but at last he was reasonably sure that both the New Earth players understood the rules of the game. To make assurance doubly sure, he asked the Hevians to begin, so that he and Estelle could become familiar with the kinds of lies which were most admired and the way the jury of players penalized each inadvertent truth.

The first two stories came close to convincing him that he was being overcautious. At the very least it seemed plain, both from the terms in which the game had been described and the stories as they were told, that the Hevians as a race had little talent for fiction. The third player, however, a girl of about nine who obviously had been bursting with impatience for her turn to come around, stunned him completely. The moment she was called upon, she began:

"This morning I saw a letter, and the address on it was Four. The letter had feet, and the feet had shoes on them. It was delivered by missile, but it walked all the way. Though it is Four for four, it's triple treble trouble," she wound up triumphantly.

There was a short, embarrassed silence.

"That doesn't sound like a lie at all," Estelle said to Web, relapsing into her own language. "It sounds more like a riddle."

"That was not fair," the Hevian leader was telling the nine-year-old at the same time in a stern voice. "We hadn't explained the rules of the coup." He turned to Web and Estelle. "Another part of the game is to try to tell a story which is entirely true, but sounds like a lie. In the coup, the jury penalizes you for lying if it can catch you. If you aren't caught, you have told a perfect truth, which wins the round even over a perfect lie. But it was unfair of Pyla to try for a coup before we'd explained it to you."

"I challenge once," Web said gravely. "Is really this morning was? If, then we had had knowed; but we haven't."

"This morning," Pyla insisted, determinedly defending her coup in the face of the group's obvious disapproval. "You weren't there then. I saw you leave."

"How do you know about all these?" Web said.

"I hung around," the girl said. Abruptly, she giggled. "And I heard you two talking, too, behind the hill."

Since the whole of her answer was offered in a fluent, though heavily accented Okie *bêche-de-mer*, there were obviously no further questions to be asked.

Web was feeling just barely civil toward females, but he offered Pyla his politest smile. "In that case," he said formally, "you win. We thank you from our heartmost bottom. This is good news."

He never did quite make up his mind whether his imperfect knowledge of Hevian made this polite speech come out as "Pullup hellup yiz are ninety" or "Why do I am alook alike a poss of porterpease?", or whether he managed to say exactly what he thought he was saying, but to his great astonishment, Pyla burst into tears.

"Oh, oh, oh," she wailed. "That would have been my very first coup. And you beat me, you beat me."

The jury was already in a huddle. A few moments later Silvador, the leader, stroked Pyla gently on the temples and said, "Hush now. On the contrary, our Web-friend must be penalized for lying."

His eyes twinkling, he offered Estelle his arm, and she came to her feet in one sinuous unravelling of the knot she had tied herself into during the lying game.

"The penalty must include our Estelle-friend too," he added portentously. "You must both come with us, directly to the city, and be—" he struck an executioner's pose— "put to sleep for a while."

"No," Web said. "We have to go." He clambered stiffly to his feet.

"Please," Silvador said. "We don't really mean to punish. You wanted to sleep-learn. We can take you to the sleep-learner. Is that not what you asked this morning? Pyla has two hours coming to her this afternoon. We were going to give it to you; you could learn Hevian and talk to us!"

"But how did we lie?" Estelle said, her eyes dancing.

"Web said it was good news," Silvador said solemnly, "that his Dee-friend was already here. He told a flat lie about an accomplished fact; that costs 50 points."

The two New Earth children looked at each other. "Oh, algae and gravity," Web said suddenly. "Let's go do it. We'll see Dee soon enough."

Dee blew her top.

"What on Earth were you thinking of, John?" she demanded. "How do you know what they teach in hypnopedia here? How could you let children run around a strange planet without knowing what these savages might do to them?"

"They didn't do anything to us—" Web said.

"They're not savages—" Amalfi said.

"I know what they are. I was here the first time, when you were. And I think it's criminally irresponsible to let savages tamper with a child's mind. Or any civilized mind."

"How would you recognize a civilized mind?" Amalfi demanded. But he knew that it was certainly a fruitless question, and possibly a spiteful one. He could see well enough that she was the same girl he had met during the Utopia-Gort affair, the same woman he had loved, the same bright physical image he would cherish to the nearing end of time; but she was getting old, and how do you tell a woman that? The Hevians and the children alike were approaching the end of the world as a new experience, but Dee, and Amalfi, and Mark, and indeed the whole of New Earth were approaching it from age, with the two forms of matter subsequent to the impact; Dee no thought but to stave off new experience, to dwell safely in accomplished fact. He himself would not accept that such a thing was to happen; Dee would not let the children learn a new language; they were exhibiting all the stigmata of the onset of old age, and so was their culture. The drugs still worked; physically they were still young; but age was with them nonetheless, and for good. In the long run there was no cheating time and the entropy gradient, nor any hope but that of putting one's hope into Hevians and other children. The cancer-scarred giant King of Buda-Pesht and the Acolyte jungle had been as old as Amalfi was now when Amalfi had met and bested him, and he had even then settled into an *idée fixe;* he had been still physically arrested, but mentally he was already used up.

There were only two ways to go toward death; you accept that you are going to die, or you refuse to believe it. To deny that the problem is there is childish, or senile; it lacks the fluidity of adjustment which is that process called maturity; and when children and savages are more fluid at this than you are, you must see that curfew has struck for you and go gracefully. Otherwise, they will bury you, their titular leader, nominally alive.

Dee had not, of course, bothered to answer the question; she simply looked grim. The aborted argument had been conducted mostly *sotto voce* anyhow, for the rest of the Hevian council-room was deeply embroiled in an attempt to quanticize the amount of gamma radiation which would be produced when the two universes passed through each other, and its degree of convertibility into either of the two forms of matter subsequent to the impact; Dee had been forced to push her way into the meeting to find Web and Estelle, who by now had become accepted silent partners at such skull-sessions.

"I'm not content with that at all," Retma was saying. "Dr. Schloss is assuming that a substantial part of this energy will go off as sheer noise, as though the meeting of the two universes were analogous to the clashing of cymbals. To allow that, one has to assume that Planck's Constant holds true in Hilbert space, for which we haven't a shred of evidence. One can't superimpose an entropy gradient at right angles to a reaction which itself involves entropies of opposite sign on each side of the equation."

"But why can't you?" Dr. Schloss said. "That's what Hilbert space is for: to provide a choice of axes for just such an operation. If you have such a choice, the rest is only a simple exercise in projective geometry."

"I don't deny that," Retma said, somewhat stiffly. "I'm questioning its applicability. We have no data which suggest that handling the problem in this way would be anything *more* than an exercise—so whether it would be a simple exercise or a complex exercise is not to the point."

"I think we'd better go," Dee said. "Web, Estelle, please come along; we're only interrupting, and there's a lot we have to do."

Her penetrating stage whisper rasped across the discussion more effectively than any speech at normal conversational volume could have done. Dr. Schloss's face pinched with annoyance. For a moment, the faces of the Hevians went politely blank; then Miramon turned and looked first at Dee, and then at Amalfi, slightly raising one eyebrow. Amalfi nodded, a little embarrassed.

"Do we have to go, grandmother?" Web protested. "I mean, all this is what we're here for. And Estelle's good at math; now and then Retma and Dr. Schloss want her to match up Hevian names for terms with ours."

Dee thought about it. "Well," she said, "I suppose it can't do any harm."

This was exactly and expectably the wrong answer, though Web could have had no way of anticipating it. He did not know, as Amalfi knew very well by direct memory, that women on He had once been much worse than slaves, that in fact they had been regarded as a wholly loathesome though necessary cross between a demon and a lower animal; hence he was unequipped to see that Hevian women today were still crucially subordinate to their men, and far from welcome in a situation of this kind. Nor did Amalfi see any present opportunity to explain to Web—or to Estelle, either—why both children must now go. The explanation would require more knowledge of Dee than either of the children had; they would need to know, for instance, that in Dee's eyes the women of He had been emancipated but not enfranchised, and that for Dee this abstract distinction carried a high emotional charge—all the more so because the Hevian women themselves were obviously quite content to have it that way.

Miramon settled his papers, arose and walked smoothly toward them, his face grave. Dee watched him approach with an expression of smouldering, resolute suspicion with which Amalfi could not help but sympathize, funny though he found it.

"We are delighted to have you with us, Mrs. Hazleton," Miramon said, bowing his head. "Much of what we are today, we owe to you. I hope you will allow us to express our gratitude; my wife and her ladies await to do you honor."

"Thanks, but I don't—I really mean—"

She had to stop, obviously finding it impossible to summon up in a split second the memory of what she had meant so many years ago, when she had been, whether she was yet aware of it or not, another person. Back then, she had in fact been one of the prime movers in the emancipation of the women of He, and Amalfi had been glad of her vigorous help, particularly since it had turned out to be crucial in a bloody power-struggle on the planet, and hence crucial to the survival of the city—the latter a formula which then had been as magical and beyond critical examination as the will to live itself, and now was as meaningless a slogan and one as far gone in time as "Remember the Bastille," "Mason, Dixon, Nixon and Yates," or "The Stars Must Be Ours!" Dee's first encounter with Hevian women had been in the days when they had been stinking unwashed creatures kept in ceremonial cages; something about Miramon's present mode of address to her apparently reminded her of those days, perhaps even made her feel the bars and the dirt falling into place about her own person; yet the time gap was too great, and the politeness too intensive, to permit her to take offense on those grounds, if indeed she was aware of them. She looked quickly at Amalfi, but his face remained unchanged; she knew him well enough to be able to see that there would be no help from that quarter.

"Thank you," she said helplessly. "Web, Estelle, it's time we left."

Web turned to Estelle, as if for help, in unconscious burlesque of Dee's unspoken appeal to Amalfi, but Estelle was already rising. To Amalfi's eyes the girl looked amused and a little contemptuous. Dee was going to have trouble with that one. As for Web, anyone could see plainly that he was in love, so *he* would require no special handling.

"What I suggest is this," Estelle's father's voice said, way up in the middle of the air. "Suppose we assume that there is no thermodynamic crossover between the two universes until the moment of contact. If that's the case, there's no possibility of applying symmetry unless we assume that the crossover point is actually a moment of complete neutrality, no matter how explosive it seems to somebody on one side or the other of the equivalence sign. That's a reasonable assumption, I think, and it would enable us to get rid of Planck's Constant—I agree with Retma that in a situation like this that's only a bugger factor—and handle the opposite signs in terms of the old Schiff neutrino-antineutrino theory of gravitation. That can be quanticized equally well, after all."

"Not in terms of the Grebe numbers," Dr. Schloss said.

"But that's exactly the point, Schloss," Jake said excitedly. "Grebe numbers don't cross over; they apply in our universe, and probably they apply on the other side too, *but they don't cross.* What we need is a function that does cross, or else some assumption that fits the facts, that frees us of crossover entirely. That's what Retma was saying, if I understood him correctly, and I think he's right. If you don't have a crossover expression which is perfectly neutral anywhere in Hilbert space, then you're automatically making an assumption about a real No-Man's-Land. What we're forced to start with here is *No.*"

Estelle stopped at the door and turned to look toward the invisible source of the voice.

"Daddy," she said, "that's just like translating Hevian math into New Earth math. If it's No-Man's-Land you have to deal with, why don't you start with the bullets?"

"Come, dear," Dee said. The door closed.

There was a very long silence in the room after that.

"You are letting those children go to waste, Mayor Amalfi," Miramon said at last. "Why do you do it? If only you would fill their brains with the facts that they need—and it is so easy, as you well know, you taught us how to do it—"

"It's no longer so easy with us," Amalfi said. "We are older than you are; we no longer share your preoccupation with the essences of things. It would take too long to explain how we came to that pass. We have other things to think about now."

"If that is true," Miramon said slowly, "then indeed we must hear no more about it. Otherwise I shall be tempted to feel sorry for you; and that must not happen, otherwise we all are lost."

"Not so," Amalfi said, smiling tightly. "Nothing is ever that final. Where were we? This is only the beginning of the end."

"Were the universe to last forever, Mayor Amalfi," Miramon said, "I should never understand you."

And so the betrayal was complete. Web and Estelle never heard the stiff and bitter exchange between Amalfi and Hazleton, across the trillions and trillions of miles of seethingly empty space between He and the New Earth, which resulted in Hazleton's being forced to call his wife home before she antagonized the Hevians any further; nor did they know precisely why Dee's recall had to mean their recall. They simply went, mute and grieving, willy-nilly, expressing by silence—the only weapon that they had—their revolt against the insanities of adult logic. In their hearts they knew that they had been denied the first real thing that they had ever wanted, except for each other.

And time was running out.

CHAPTER FIVE: Jehad

That conversation had been unusually painful for Amalfi, too, despite his many centuries of experience at having differences of opinion with Hazleton, ending ordinarily in enforcement of Amalfi's opinion if there was no other way around it. There had been something about this quarrel which had been tainted for Amalfi, and he knew very well what it was: the abortive, passionless and fruitless autumnal affair with Dee. Sending her home to Mark now, necessary though he believed it to be, was too open to interpretation as an act of revenge upon the once-beloved for being no longer loved. Such things happened between lovers, as Amalfi knew very well.

But there was so much to be done that he managed to forget about it after Dee and the children had left on the recall ship. He was not, however, allowed to forget about it for long—only, in fact, for three weeks.

The discussion of the forthcoming catastrophe had at last entered the stage where it was no longer possible to avoid coming to grips with the contrary entropy gradients, and hence had entered an area where words alone no longer sufficed—in fact, could seldom be called upon at all. This had had the effect of driving those participants who were primarily engineers or administrators or both, like Miramon and Amalfi, or primarily philosophers, like Gifford Bonner, into the stance of bystanders; so that the discussions now had been shifted to Retma's study. Amalfi stuck with them whenever he could, for he never knew when Retma, Jake or Schloss might drop back out of the symbolic strato-sphere and say something he could comprehend and use.

It was being heavy weather in the study today, however. Retma was saying:

"The problem as I see it is that time in our experience is not retrodictable. We write a diffusion equation like this, for instance." He turned to his blackboard—the immemorial "research instrument" of theoretical physicists everywhere—and wrote:

$$\frac{d^2G}{dx^2} + \frac{d^2G}{dy^2} + \frac{d^2G}{dz^2} = a^2\frac{dG}{dt}$$

Over Retma's head, for Jake's benefit, a small proxy fixed its television eye on the precise chalk marks. "In this situation a-squared is a real constant, so it is predictive only for a future time t, but not for an earlier time t, because the retrodictive expression diverges."

"An odd situation," Schloss agreed. "It means that in any thermodynamic situation we have better information about the future than we do about the past. In the anti-matter universe it has to be the other way around—but only from *our* point of view; a hypothetical observer living under their laws and composed of their energies, I as-sume, couldn't tell the difference."

"Can we write a convergent retrodictive equation?" Jake's voice said. "One which describes what their situation is as we would see it, if we could? If we can't, I don't see how we can design instruments to detect any difference."

"It can be done," Retma said. "For instance." He turned to the blackboard and the symbols flowed squeakily:

$$\frac{d^2G}{dx^2} + \frac{d^2G}{dy^2} + \frac{d^2G}{dz^2} = \frac{4\pi m}{ih}\frac{dG}{dt}$$

"Ah-*ha*," Schloss said. "Thus giving us an imaginary constant in place of a real one. But your second equation isn't a mirror of your first; parity is not conserved. Your first equation is an equalization process, but this one is oscillatory. Surely the gradient on the other side doesn't pulsate!"

"Parity is not conserved anyhow in these weak reactions," Jake said. "But I think the objection may be well taken all the same. If Equation Two describes anything at all, it can't be the other side. It has to be *both* sides—the whole vast system, providing that it is cyclical, which we don't know yet. Nor do I see any way to test it, it's as ultimately and finally unprovable as the Mach Hypothesis—"

The door opened quietly and a young Hevian beckoned silently to Amalfi. He got up without too much reluctance; the boys were giving him a hard time today, and he found that he missed Estelle. It had been her function to remind the group of possible pitfalls in Retma's notation: here, for instance, Retma was using the d which in Amalfi's experience was an increment in calculus, as simply an expression for a constant; he was using the G which to Amalfi was the gravitational constant, to express a term in thermodynamics Amalfi was accustomed to seeing written with the greek capital letter Ψ; and could Schloss be sure that Retma's i was equivalent to the square root of minus one, as it was in New Earth math? Doubtless Schloss had good reason to feel that agreement on that very simple symbol had been established between the New Earthmen and Retma long since, but without Estelle it made Amalfi feel uncomfortable. Besides, though he knew intellectually that all the important battles against a problem in physics are won in such blackboard sessions as this, he was not temperamentally fitted to them. He liked to see things happening.

They began to happen forthwith. As soon as the door was decently closed on the visible and invisible physicists, the young Hevian said:

"I am sorry to disturb you, Mr. Amalfi. But there is an urgent call for you from New Earth. It is Mayor Hazleton."

"Helleshin!" Amalfi said. The word was Vegan; no one now alive knew what it meant. "All right, let's go."

"Where is my wife?" Hazleton demanded without pre-

amble. "And my grandson, and Jake's daughter? And where
have you been these past three weeks? Why didn't you
call in? I've been losing my mind, and the Hevians gave
me the Force Four blowaround before they'd let me through
to you at all—"

"What are you talking about, Mark?" Amalfi said. "Stop
sputtering long enough to let me know what this is all
about."

"That's what *I* want to know. All right. I'll begin again.
Where is Dee?"

"I don't know," Amalfi said patiently. "I sent her home
three weeks ago. If you can't find her, that's your problem."

"She never got here."

"She didn't? But—"

"Yes, but. That recall ship never landed. We never
heard from it at all. It just vanished, Dee, children and all.
I've been phoning you frantically to find out whether or
not you ever sent it; now I know that you did. Well, we
know what *that* means. You'd better give up dabbling in
physics, Amalfi, and get back here on the double."

"What can I do?" Amalfi said. "I don't know any more
about it than you do."

"You can damn well come back here and help me out of
this mess."

"What mess?"

"What have you been doing the past three weeks?"
Hazleton yelled. "Do you mean to tell me that you haven't
heard what's been happening?"

"No," Amalfi said. "And stop yelling. What did you
mean, 'We know what *that* means'? If you think you know
what's happened, why aren't you doing something about
it, instead of jamming the Dirac raising me? You're the
mayor; I've got work of my own to do."

"I'll be the mayor about two days longer, if my luck
holds," Hazleton said in a savage voice. "And you're directly responsible, so you needn't bother trying to duck.
Jorn the Apostle began to move two weeks ago. He has a
navy now, though where he raised it is beyond me. His
main body's nowhere near New Earth, but he's about to
take New Earth all the same—the whole planet is swarming with farm kids with fanatical expressions and dismounted

spindillies. As soon as they get to me, I'm going to surrender out of hand—you know as well as I do what one of those machines can do, and the farmers are using them as side arms. I'm not going to sacrifice tens of thousands of lives just to maintain my administration; if they want me out, they can have me out."

"And this is my fault? I once told you the Warriors of God were dangerous."

"And I didn't listen. All right. But they'd never have moved if it hadn't been for the fact that you and Miramon didn't censor what you're up to. It's given Jorn his cause; he's telling his followers that you're meddling with the preordained Armageddon and jeopardizing their chances of salvation. He's proclaimed a jehad against the Hevians for instigating it, and the jehad includes New Earth because we're working with the Hevians—"

Over the phone came four loud, heavy strokes of fist upon metal.

"Gods of all stars, they're here already," Hazleton said. "I'll leave the line open as long as I can—maybe they won't notice. . . ." His voice faded. Amalfi hung on grimly, straining to hear every sound.

"Sinner Hazleton," a young and desperately frightened voice said, almost at once, "you have been found out. By the Word of Jorn, you—you are ordered to corrective discipline. Are you gone-tuh—will you submit humbly?"

"If you fire that thing in here," Hazleton's voice said, quite loudly—he was obviously projecting for the benefit of the mike—"you'll uproot half the city. What good will that do you?"

"We will die in the Warriors," the other voice said. It was still tense, but now that it spoke of dying it seemed more self-assured. "You will go to the flames."

"And all the other people—?"

"Sinner Hazleton, we do not threaten," a deeper, older voice said. "We think there is some good in everyone. Jorn commands us to redeem, and that we will do. We have hostages for your good conduct."

"Where are they?"

"They were picked up by the Warriors of God," the deep voice said. "Jorn in his blessedness was kind enough to grant us a *cordon sanitaire* for this Godless world. Will you yield, for the salvation of this woman and these two helpless children? I advise you, Sinner—hey, what the hell, that phone's open! Jody, smash that switch, and fast! What did I ever do to be saddled with a cadre of lousy yokels—"

The speaker began a thin howl and went dead before the cry was properly born.

For a moment, Amalfi sat stunned. He had gotten too much information too fast; and he was much older now than he had been on like occasions in the past. He had never expected that such an occasion would arise again— but here it was.

A jehad against He? No, not likely—at least, not directly. Jorn the Apostle would be wary of tackling a world so completely mysterious to him, especially with forces more mob than military. But New Earth was wholly vulnerable; it was a logical first step to invest that planet. And now Jorn had Dee and the children.

Move!

How to move was another matter; it needed to be done in a vessel which no possible Warrior cordon would have the strength to attack, but no such vessel existed on He. The only other alternative was a very small, very fast ship with a low detectability index; but that was equally impossible across so long a distance, since there is a minimum size for even one spindizzy. Or was there? Carrel was on He, and Carrel had had considerable experience in designing relatively small spindizzy-powered proxies; one such had followed the March of Earth all the way, without anybody's paying the slightest attention to it. Of course the proxy had been magnificently, noisily detectable by ordinary standards, and only Carrel's piloting of it had kept the massed cities from distinguishing between the traces that it made and the traces that were made adventitiously by ordinary interstellar matter. . . .

"Can you do that again, Carrel? Remember that this time you won't have a flock of massive cities to confuse the issue. The gamut you'll have to run will be one thin shell of orbiting warships, around one planet—and we don't know how many of them there are, what arms they mount, how careful a watch they keep—"

"Assume the worst," Carrel said. "They caught the re-call ship, after all, and they didn't even know we'd sent it. I can do it, Mr. Amalfi, if you'll let me do the maneuvering when the chips are down; otherwise I think you'll be caught, no matter how small the ship is."

"Helleshin!" But there was no way around it; Amalfi would have to subject himself to at least two days of Carrel's violent evasive-confusive maneuvers, without once touching the space stick himself. It was going to be a rough do for an old man, but Carrel was quite right, there was no other available course.

"All right," he said. "Just make sure I'm alive when I touch down."

Carrel grinned. "I've never lost a cargo," he said. "Providing it's been properly secured. Where do you want to land?"

That was not an easy question either. In the long run, Amalfi settled for a landing in Central Park, in the heart of the old Okie city. This was perhaps dangerously close to the Warriors' center of operations, but Amalfi did not want to be forced to trek across a thousand miles of New Earth just for a meeting with Hazleton; and there was a fair chance that the old city would be taboo for the bumpkins, or at least avoided instinctively. Jorn the Apostle would not have overlooked patrolling such an obvious rallying-point for the ousted, but presumably Jorn was somewhere at the other end of the Cloud with his main body.

Since there is, even with spindizzies, a limit to the amount of power that can be stored in a small hull, the trip was more than long enough for Amalfi to catch up, via ultraphone, on the Cloud events he had closeted himself away from on He. The picture Mark had given him had been accurate, if perhaps a little distorted in emphasis. Jorn the Apostle's real concerns were still far away from New Earth, and his jehad had been announced against unbelievers everywhere, not just against the Hevians. The Hevians were simply the article in the indictment which applied specifically to New Earth—that, and New Earth's unannounced but unconcealed intention of plumbing the

end of time, which was blasphemy. It was Amalfi's guess
that the uprising on New Earth and the seizure of the
central government there had been an unplanned byproduct
of the proclamation of which Jorn was unprepared to take
full advantage. Had he been planning on it, or militarily
able to capitalize on it, he would have rushed in his main
body on the double; as matters stood he had only—and
belatedly—set up a token blockade. If his followers' coup
stuck, all well and good; if it did not, he would withdraw
the blockade in a hurry, to save ships and men for another, more auspicious day.

Or so Amalfi reasoned; but he was uncomfortably aware
that in Jorn the Apostle he was for the first time dealing
with an enemy whose thought-processes might be utterly
unlike his, from first to last.

The ship shifted abruptly from spindizzy to ion-blast
drive. Amalfi stopped thinking entirely and just hung on.

Once in the atmosphere, the craft was back in Amalfi's
hands; back on He, Carrel had relinquished his remote
Dirac control over the space stick. Amalfi was able to
make a thistledown nightside landing in south Central
Park, in a broad irregular depression which legend said
had once been a lake. The landing was without incident;
apparently it had been undetected. In the morning the
abandoned proxy might be spotted by a Warrior flyer, but
the old city was littered with such ambiguous mechanical
objects; one had to be a student of the city, as knowledgeable as Schliemann was about the nine Troys, to know
which was new and which was not. Amalfi was confident
enough of this to leave the proxy behind without an attempt to camouflage it.

Now the problem was, How to get in touch with Mark?
Presumably he was still under arrest, or the next thing to
it; "corrective discipline" was what the Warrior voice Amalfi
had overheard had said. Did that mean that they were
going to make the lazy, cerebral Hazleton make beds,
sweep floors and pray six hours a day? Not very likely,
especially the prayer part. Then what—?

Suddenly, trudging south along a moonlit, utterly deserted Fifth Avenue toward the city's control tower, Amalfi

was sure he had it. Running a galaxy, even a small and mostly unexplored satellite galaxy like this one, is not simply a matter of taking papers out of the "IN" tray and transferring them to the "OUT" tray. It requires centuries of experience and a high degree of familiarity with the communications, data-filing and other machines which must do 98 percent of the donkey work. In the Okie days, for instance, it sometimes happened—though not very often—that a mayor was swapped to another city under the "rule of discretion" after he had lost an election; and generally it took him five to ten years to get used to running the new one, even in such a subordinate post as assistant to the city manager. It was not an art that a bumpkin, no matter how divinely inspired, could master in a week.

Mark's most likely theater of "corrective discipline," then, would be his own office. He would be running the Cloud for the Warriors—and no doubt doing a far worse job of it than they would detect, even were they sensible enough, as they surely were, to suspect such sabotage. Amalfi, himself a master of making the wheels run backwards when necessary, would yield precedence in that art to Hazleton at any time; Hazleton had been known to work the trick on his friends, just to keep his hand in, or perhaps just out, of habit.

Very good; then the problem of getting in touch with Mark was solved, clearing the way for the hard questions: How to discombobulate, and, if possible, oust the Warriors; and how to get Dee and the children back unharmed?

It would be difficult to decide which of these two hard questions was the harder. As Mark had pointed out, the uprooted spindillies in the hand of the rank-and-file Warriors were considerably more dangerous than muskets or pitchforks. Used with precision, the machine could degravitate a single opponent and send him shrieking skyward under the centrifugal thrust of New Earth's rotation on its axis; or the same effect could be used against a corner or a wall of a building, if one wanted to demolish a strong point. But the menace lay in the fact that in the hands of a plowboy the spindilly would *not* be used with precision. It had been designed, not as a weapon, but as an adjunct to home weather control, and was somewhat larger, heavier and more ungainly than a Twentieth-Century home oil-burner. Considering the difficulties involved in toting this object at all, especially on foot, the temptation would be almost overwhelming to set it at maximum output before it was even unbolted from its cement pedestal in the cellar, and leave it set there, so that the strained arm and back muscles of the bearer would thereafter have to do nothing with it to make it function but point it—more or less—and push the starter button. This meant that every time one of the plowboys lost his temper or detected heresy in some casual remark, or fired nervously at a shadow or a sudden unfamiliar sound or a svengali, he might level two or three city blocks before he remembered where the "kill" button was; or the machine, dropped and abandoned in panic, might go on to level two or three more blocks before it discharged its accumulators and shut itself off of its own accord.

Saving Dee and the children was certainly highly important, but disarming the Warriors would have to take precedence.

He caught himself bouncing a little as he stepped out of the spindizzy lift shaft onto the resilient concrete floor of the control room, and grinned ruefully. He felt alive again, after far too many years of grousing, browsing, vegetating. This was the kind of problem he had been formed for, the kind he approached with the confidence born of gusto. The end of time was certainly sizable enough as a problem; he would never find a bigger, and he was grateful for that; but it provided him with nobody with whom to negotiate and, if possible, swindle a little.

It *had* been a long time; he had better be on his guard against overconfidence. That had been known to trip him now and then even when he had been in practice. In particular, it was suspiciously easy to see what steps ought to be taken in the present situation; that was not the test; it was his ancient skill as a cultural historian—in short, as a diagnostician—which would stand or fall by what he did now . . . and just incidentally, he might lose or save from three to a quarter of a million lives, one of them Estelle's.

Gently then, gently—but precisely and with decision, like a surgeon confronted with cardiac arrest. Waste no time debating alternate courses; you have four minutes to save the patient's life, if you are lucky; the bone saw is whining in your hand—slash open the rib cage, and slash it quick.

The City Fathers were already warmed up. He told them: "Communications. Get me Jorn the Apostle—for the survival of the city."

It would take a little while for the City Fathers to reach Jorn; though they would scan the possibilities in under a minute and select out only those worlds with high probability ratings for Jorn's presence, the chances of their getting him on the first call were not very high. Amalfi regretted that it would be then necessary to talk to Jorn on the Dirac communicator, since it would make anyone who was listening anywhere in the Cloud—or anywhere else in the known universe where the apparatus existed, for that matter—privy to the conversations; but over interstellar distances the ultraphone was out of the question for two-way exchanges, since its velocity of information propagation was only 125 percent of the speed of light, and even this was achieved only by a trick called negative phase velocity, since the carrier wave was electromagnetic and moved at light speed and no faster.

While he waited, Amalfi ticked over the possibilities. This was all in all developing into a most curious affair, quite unlike anything he had ever been involved in before. It thus far consisted mostly of interludes and transitions, with only a small scatter of decision-points upon which action might be possible. In this sense even the events which most recalled to him the events of his earlier life seemed to be reshaping themselves into the pattern of his old age, not only allowing for but requiring a much greater exercise of reflection and an intensive weighing of values. Reflexive action was out of the question; it was possible only from some fixed guiding principle, such as "the survival of the city"; such an axiom, if it persists and dominates for a long time, allows many decisions to be reached via the reflex arc with almost no intervening intellection—one automatically jumped in the right direction, like a cat turning itself over in midair. No such situation existed now; the values to be weighed were mutually contradictory.

It had to be assumed, first of all, that Jorn did not know the situation on New Earth in detail; he had simply re-acted as a good strategist should to capitalize upon an unexpected victory in an unexpected quarter, and almost surely did not know that his blockading fleet was holding three hostages, let alone who those hostages were. It would be impossible to intimidate him on this matter; it would be wiser not to give him the information at all. After all, the first intent of the call was to get the bumpkin army disbanded and the dismounted spindillies out of action; but it would not do to convince him out of hand that his coup on New Earth could not possibly stick, since that would result in his withdrawing his blockade and the hostages with it. Better to serve both ends, if it could be swung that way: to convince Jorn that the *putsch* had better be abandoned forthwith, but not so thoroughly as to alarm him into thinking he might lose part of his navy if he took his time about calling the *putsch* off.

It looked like a large order. It meant that the danger which Jorn the Apostle would have to be made to suspect would have to be as much ideological as it was military. As a military commander of considerable proven ability, Jorn could not but be familiar with the corruption of an occupy-ing force by the standards and customs of the nation that it occupies—and jehads and crusades were particularly sub-ject to this kind of corrosion. Whether he was wholly a believer in the brand of Fundamentalism he preached, or not, he would not want his followers to lose faith in the doctrine under which he had sailed so successfully thus far; that was the hold over them that he had chosen to exercise, so that if they lost that, he himself would have nothing left, regardless of what his personal beliefs might be.

Unhappily, there was no ideology available on New Earth which looked capable of corrupting the Warriors of God; they would doubtless indulge in a good deal of wristwatch collecting, a very ancient term for a timeless syndrome of a peasant army holding a territory relatively rich in consumer goods, but Jorn would anticipate that and discount it; but there was no idea inherent in the culture of New Earth which seemed strong enough to sway the Warriors from their simple, direct and centrally oriented point of view. One would have to be manufactured; at least there was no lack of raw materials.

One apparent pitfall in this course was that of taking Jorn the Apostle at his own public valuation and attempting to reach into and alarm that part of his mind where his real religion lived. Amalfi had no way of knowing whether this would work or not, and prudence dictated that it not be tried; he had to assume instead that a man as successful as Jorn had been in the world of affairs was a sophisticated man on most subjects, whether he was sophisticated as a theologian or not. The latter was even beside the point; wherever the truth lay, he would be quick to detect any attempt to push his religious buttons, since he had proven that he knew the art himself.

And, Amalfi thought suddenly, if Jorn were to turn out to be exactly as devout in his back-cluster superstitions as his public utterances suggested, pushing that button might well result in a genuine disaster. With such people, that button is a demolition button; if you touch it successfully, you shatter the man. Of course it would be necessary to treat Jorn *pro forma* as if every public word Jorn had uttered had been uttered in the utmost sincerity and out of the deepest kind of belief, not only because Jorn too would know that unknown numbers of others might be listening in, but to avoid attacking the man's image of himself irrelevantly and to no purpose. The forms had no bearing on the final outcome; it would be dangerous to assume that Jorn was identical personally with his public self only in the *substance* of Amalfi's approach to him. There would be no harm in acknowledging to him, implicitly, his claim to be every inch a Fundamentalist; but it would be fatal to expect him to panic if he got a Dirac 'cast claiming to be from Satan—

"READY WITH JORN THE APOSTLE, MR. MAYOR."

Amalfi suddenly found himself thinking at emergency speed; the City Fathers' excusable lapse—doubtless nobody had bothered to tell them that Amalfi had not been Mayor since the problem of the Ginnangu-Gap had arisen—

reminded him that he had failed to decide whether or not
to identify himself to Jorn. There was a small possibility
that Jorn came of the peasant stock which the Okies had
found sweating under the tyranny of the bindlestiff city of
IMT; a slightly larger possibility that he was a descendant
of the rulers of IMT itself; but by far the greatest likeli-
hood was that he was a child or grandchild of Amalfi's own
people and so would know very well indeed who Amalfi
was. To identify himself, then, would give Amalfi a certain
leverage, but it would also present certain disadvantages—

However, the die was already cast; the City Fathers had
called him the Mayor on the circuit, so Jorn had better be
told at once that it was not Hazleton he was talking to.
Bluff it out? Possible; but there lay the danger of using the
Dirac: the instrument made it possible for any listener to
tell Jorn, now or later, whatever facts Amalfi attempted for
strategic reasons to withhold—

"READY, MR. MAYOR."

Well, there was no help for that now. Amalfi said into
the microphone:

"Go ahead."

Immediately, the screen came alight. He *was* getting
old; he had forgotten to tell the City Fathers to limit the
call to audio only, so in actuality he had never had the
option of withholding his identity. Well, regret was futile;
and in fact he watched the face of Jorn the Apostle swimming into view before him with the keenest curiosity.

It was, startlingly, a very old face, narrow, bony and
deeply lined, with bushy white eyebrows emphasizing the
sunken darkness of the eyes. Jorn had been off the anti-
agathics for at least fifty years, if indeed he had ever taken
one. The realization was a profound and unexpected visceral shock.

"I am Jorn the Apostle," the ancient face said. "What do
you want of me?"

"I think you should pull off of New Earth," Amalfi said.
It was not at all what he had intended to say; it was in fact
wholly contrary to the entire chain of reasoning he had
just worked through. But there was something about the
face that compelled him to say what was on his mind.

"I am not on New Earth," Jorn said. "But I take your

meaning. And I take it there are many people on New
Earth who share your opinion, Mr. Amalfi, as is only
natural. This does not affect me."

"I didn't expect it to, just as a simple statement of
opinion," Amalfi said. "But I can offer you good reasons."

"I will listen. But do not expect me to be reasonable."

"Why not?" Amalfi said, genuinely surprised.

"Because I am not a reasonable man," Jorn said patiently. "The uprising of my followers on New Earth took
place without orders from me; it is a gift which God
himself has placed in my hand. That being the case, reason does not apply."

"I see," Amalfi said. He paused. This was going to be
tougher to bring off than he had dreamed; in fact, he had
his first doubt as to whether it could be brought off at all.
"Are you aware, sir, that this planet is a hotbed of
Stochasticism?"

Jorn's bushy eyebrows lifted slightly. "I know that the
Stochastics are strongest and most numerous on New Earth,"
he said. "I have no way of knowing how deeply the philosophy has penetrated the populace of New Earth as a
whole. It is one of the things I mean to see stamped out."

"You'll find that impossible. A mob of farm boys can't
eradicate a major philosophical system."

"But how major is it?" Jorn said. "In terms of influence?
I admit I have the impression that much of New Earth
may be corrupted by it, but I have no certain knowledge
that this is so. At the distance from New Earth that I am
forced to operate, I may well be magnifying it in my mind,
especially since it is so completely antithetical to the Word
of God; it would be natural for me to assume that the
homeland of Stochasticism is also a 'hotbed' of it. But I do
not know this to be true."

"So you will risk the souls of the Warriors of God on the
assumption that it is not true."

"Not necessarily," Jorn said. "Considering the forces for
which you speak, Mr. Amalfi, it is so plainly to your
advantage to exaggerate the influence of Stochasticism;
your very use of the tool suggests that, since I cannot
think you mean me any advantage. I suspect that in actuality the Stochastics, like intellectuals at all times and in all

places, are largely out of touch with the general assumptions of the culture in which they are operating; and that the people of New Earth are no more Stochastics than they are Warriors of God or anything else describable as a school of thought. If any label applies, they are simply a people who are *no longer* describable as Okies."

Amalfi sat there and sweated. He had met his match and he knew it.

"And if you are wrong?" he said at last. "If Stochasticism is as ingrained on this planet as I've tried to warn you it is?"

"Then," Jorn the Apostle said, "I must take the risk. My Warriors on New Earth are farm boys, as you have pointed out. I doubt that Stochasticism will make much headway with them; they will shrug it off, as contrary to common sense. They will be mistaken in that estimate, but how could they know that? Ignorance is the defense God the Father has given them, and I think it will be sufficient."

There was the cue. Amalfi could only hope that it had not come too late.

"Very well," he said, rather more grimly than he had intended. "Events will put us both to the proof; there is no more to be said."

"No," Jorn said, "there is this much more: you may actually have meant to do me a service, Mr. Amalfi. If it so proves out, then I will give the devil his due—one must be honest even with evil; there is no other good course. What do you want of me?"

And thus the verbal sparring-match had come so quickly to full circle; and this time there was no way to remain ignorant of, let alone to evade, the purport of the question. It was not political; it was personal; and it had been intended that way from the beginning.

"You could return me three hostages which your blockading fleet is holding," Amalfi said. His mouth tasted of aloes. "A woman and two children."

"Had you asked for that in the beginning," Jorn the Apostle said, "I would have given it to you." Was it actually pity in his voice? "But you have placed their lives upon the block of your own integrity, Mr. Amalfi. So be it; if I become convinced that I must lose New Earth because of Stochasticism, I will return the three before I withdraw my blockading squadron; otherwise, not. And, Mr. Amalfi—"

"Yes?" Amalfi whispered.

"Bear in mind what is at stake, and do not let your ingenuity overwhelm you. I know well that you are fabulously inventive; but human lives should not hang upon the success of a work of art. Go with God." The screen was dark.

Amalfi mopped his forehead with a trembling hand. With his last words, Jorn the Apostle had succeeded in telling the whole story of Amalfi's life, and it had not made comfortable listening.

Nevertheless, he hesitated only a moment longer. Though Jorn had probably already seen through the improvision which had occurred to Amalfi—late enough so that he had been unable to betray that, too, to Jorn over the Dirac for the universe to hear—there was no other course but to try to carry it through. The alternative which Jorn had proposed actually came out to the same thing in the end: that of transforming a lie into the truth. If this was an art, as Amalfi had good reason to know it was, it was at the same time not a "work of art," but only a craft; it was Jorn himself now who was committing human lives to the dictates of a work of art, that elaborate fiction which was his religion.

Being careful, this time, to cut the screen out of the circuit in advance, Amalfi called the Mayor's office.

"This is the Commissioner of Public Safety," he told the robot secretary. In ordinary times the machine would know well enough that there was no such office, but the confusion over there now must be such that the pertinent memory banks must by now have been bypassed; he felt reasonably confident that the phrase, a code alarm of long standing in the Okie days, would get through to Hazleton; as in fact it did in short order.

"You are late calling in," Mark's voice said guardedly. "Your report is overdue. Can't you report your findings in person?"

"The situation is too fluid to permit that, Mr. Mayor," Amalfi said. "At present I'm making rounds of the perimeter stations in the old city. Off-duty Warriors are trying to sightsee here, and of course with so much live machinery—"

"Who is that?" another voice said, farther in the background. Amalfi recognized it; it was the authoritative voice that had spotted the open phone when the Warriors had first arrested Hazleton. "We can't permit that!"

"It's the Commissioner of Public Safety, a man named de Ford," Hazleton said. Amalfi grinned tightly. De Ford had in actuality been Hazleton's predecessor as city manager; he had been shot seven centuries ago. "And of course we can't permit that. Besides all the loose energy there is about the old city, much of it is derelict. De Ford, I thought you knew that the Warriors' own general put the city off limits."

"I tell them that," Amalfi said, in a tone of injured patience. "They just laugh and say they're not Warriors on their own time."

"What!" said the heavy voice.

"That's what they say," Amalfi said doggedly. "Or else they say that they're nobody's man but their own, and that in the long run nobody owns anybody else. They sound like they've been sitting with some Village Stochastic, though they've got it pretty garbled. I suppose the philosophers don't try to teach the pure doctrine in the provinces."

"That's beside the point," Mark said sternly. "Keep them out of the city—that's imperative."

"I'm trying, Mr. Mayor," Amalfi said. "But there's a limit to what I can do. Half of them are toting spindillies, and you know what would happen if one of those things were fired over here, even once. I'm not going to risk that."

"Be sure you don't; but keep trying. I'll see what can be done about it from this end. There'll be further instructions; where can I reach you?"

"Just leave the call in the perimeter sergeant's office," Amalfi said. "I'll pick it up on my next round."

"Very good," Hazleton said, and clicked out. Amalfi set up the necessary line from the perimeter station to the control tower and sat back, satisfied for the moment, though with a deeper uneasiness that would not go away. The seed had been planted, and there was no doubt that

Hazleton had understood the move and would foster it. It was highly probable that Jorn the Apostle had already ordered an inquiry made of his officers on Earth, questioning the substance of Amalfi's claims; they would of course report back that they had had no trouble of that kind, but the inquiry itself would sensitize them to the subject.

Amalfi turned on the tower's FM receiver and tuned for New Earth's federal station. The next step would be stiffer off-limits orders to Warriors on leave, and he wanted to be sure he heard the texts. Unless Jorn's officers phrased those orders with an unlikely degree of sophistication, they would result in some actual sightseers in the city— and of course there were no longer any perimeter sergeants, nor was there even a definable perimeter except in the minds of the City Fathers. Somebody was bound to get hurt.

That would be one incident 'de Ford' would not report: "I didn't hear about it. I'm sorry, but I can't be everywhere at once. I've been trying to fend these boys off from the City Fathers—they want to ask them a lot of questions about the history of ideas that would tie the machines up for weeks. I've been telling the boys that I don't know how to operate the City Fathers, but if one of them points a spindilly at me and says 'Put me through, or else'—well—"

That speech would necessarily mark the demise of the 'Commissioner of Public Safety,' since it would almost surely result in the posting of a uniformed, on-duty Warrior patrol around or in the Okie city itself; Amalfi would then have to go underground, and the rest would be up to Mark. What, specifically, Hazleton would do could not be anticipated, nor did Amalfi want to know about it when it happened. One of the defects of the program was the fact that it was, as Jorn had suspected, based on a lie, whereas a good deception ought to contain some fundamental stone of truth to stub the toes of the sane and the suspicious. To put the matter with brutal directness, there was *no* possibility that the local Warriors would be corrupted by Stochasticism, and there never had been. Even if the program succeeded and Jorn withdrew his men, he would interrogate them closely before he gave Amalfi back his hostages; and if everything that he found out bore Amalfi's stamp, it would be too consistent to be convincing. That was why Hazleton's improvisations had to be his own from here on out, and as unknown to Amalfi as possible until it was too late for Amalfi to undo them even had he wished to.

It was indeed a poor piece of fiction upon which to hang the lives of Dee and Web and Estelle; but he had to make do with what he had.

It appeared to be working. Within the week, all Warrior leaves were cancelled in favor of special 'orientation devotions' at which attendance was mandatory. Though there was no direct way to tell whether or not the Warriors resented the cancellation of their leaves to secure their faith, the predicated accident inside the city happened the next day, and the 'Commissioner of Public Safety' was promptly taxed by Hazleton to explain how he had allowed it to happen; Amalfi trotted forth the prepared lie, and retreated to an ancient communications substation deep in the bowels of the City Fathers themselves.

The Warrior patrol was roving through the Okie city the very next day, and Amalfi was isolated; the rest had to be up to Hazleton.

By the end of that week, the Warriors had been ordered to turn in their spindillies for regulation police stun guns, and Amalfi knew that he had won. When a conquering army is disarmed by its own officers, it is through; in a while it will begin to tear itself apart, with very little help from outside. When that order of the day got back to Jorn, he would act, and act rapidly; Hazleton had evidently been a little too thorough as was his custom. But there was nothing that Amalfi could do now but wait.

The last Warrior blockade ship had barely touched down before Web and Estelle were scrambling out of the airlock and making straight for Amalfi.

"We have a message for you," Estelle said, out of breath, her eyes preternaturally wide. "From Jorn the Apostle. The ship's captain said to bring it to you right away."

"All right, there's not that much hurry," Amalfi growled,

to hide his apprehension. "Are you all right? Did they take proper care of you?"

"They didn't hurt us," Web said. "They were so proper and polite, I wanted to kick them. They kept us in a stateroom and gave us tracts to read. It got pretty boring after a while, just reading tracts and playing tic-tac-toe on them with grandmother." Suddenly, he could not help grinning at Estelle; obviously he had gotten away with something in those quarters, all the same.

Amalfi felt a vague emotional twinge, though he was unable to identify just what kind of emotion it was; it passed too quickly. "All right, good," he said to Estelle. "Where's the message?"

"Here." She passed over a yellow flimsy, torn from the ship's Dirac printer. It said:

XXX CMNDR SSG GABRIEL SPG

32 JOHN AMALFI N EARTH V HSTGS RPT 32

I AM GIVING YOU BENEFIT OF DOUBT, RPT DOUBT. YOU ALONE KNOW TRUTH. IF THIS DEFEAT SOLELY YOUR INVENTION BE SURE THE END IS NOT YET. BUT IT WILL BE SOON.

                                    JORN APOSTLE OF GOD

Amalfi crumpled the flimsy and dropped it onto the flaked concrete of the spaceport.

"And so it will," he said.

Estelle looked down at the wad of yellow paper, and then back at Amalfi's somber face. "Do you know what he means?" she said.

"Yes, I know what he means, Estelle. But I hope you never do."

CHAPTER SIX: Object 4001—Alephnull

Nor did Estelle ever know—though in the long run she was in no doubt about it in her own mind—that the first break in the problem of how to cross the information-barrier of the coming Ginnangu-Gap sprang from her suggestion to her father that to know No-Man's-Land, one must study it with bullets. Web and Estelle were, after all, only children, and in the ensuing years nobody had any time to spare for children; they were far too gone in the fever of putting together the immaterial object which would be their bullet across No-Man's-Land into the vast, complementary, opposite infinity of the universe of anti-matter. For the time being, speculation had been abandoned in favor of fact-finding; what was needed was some dirct assessment of the contemporary energy level of the anti-matter universe; once that was known, one could hope to date precisely the coming moment of catastrophe, and know how much or how little time one had left to make such preparations for going down into death as one could bring oneself to think meaningful in the face of an imminent and complete cancellation of all meaning—and of the time of experience which alone gave meaning to the concept of meaning.

Nobody had any time for children; and so they grew up

ignored, the last children that the universe would ever see. It was not surprising that they clung to each other; they would have done so even under other circumstances, for there was no question but that the fates which brood in the submicroscopic coils and toils of the nucleic acids of heredity had formed them for each other.

Estelle sprouted in her world of oblivious adults, and took her place among them, without their noticing what she had become: tall, willowy, grey-eyed, black-haired, white-skinned, serene-faced and beautiful. These oldsters were as immune to beauty as they were immune to youth; they were perfectly happy to have the use of the sharp cutting edge of Estelle's gift for mathematics brought to bear upon their problems, but they did not see that she was also beautiful and would not have cared had they been able to see it. These days they saw nothing but death—or thought they saw it; Estelle was not so sure that they saw it as clearly as she did, for they had lived in contempt of it far too long.

Web did not know whether this suited him or not. He was moderately content to be the only one on New Earth with the good sense to see that Estelle was beautiful, but sometimes his pride felt the lack of an occasional glance of frank envy; and sometimes he suspected that Estelle cared as little about this in the long run as everyone else on New Earth but Web himself. In the fullness of time, the love which existed between them had been spoken and acknowledged, and they were now a couple, with all the delights and the responsibilities which coupling provides and demands; but somehow, nobody had noticed. The oldsters were too busy building their artifact to notice, let alone care much one way or the other, that a small green weed of love had pushed itself up amid the tumbled stones of the last of all debacles.

Yet it was not difficult for Web to understand why what was for him a miracle was not even a nuisance to the busy godlings and their machines with whom he had to live. There was not much time left; hardly a hiccup for Amalfi and Miramon and Schloss and Dee and even for Carrel, who seemed to be a perpetually young man yet who had lived lifetimes and lifetimes and could be cut down in the midst of his latest without any valid claim that his death would be a grievous waste of whatever (and Web was convinced that it was rather scanty) he carried in his head. What little time remained would be nothing to those people, who had lived so long already; but for Web and Estelle, it had been and would continue to be their growing-up time, which would be half of each of their lives no matter how long they lived thereafter.

Certainly Amalfi never noticed them. He had long forgotten that he had ever been anything less than what he was: an immortal. Probably—now—the suggestion that he had once been a child would have baffled him entirely; in the abstract it was a truism, and he would be unable to think back far enough to think of it otherwise. Once given the administration of Doom, in any event, he prosecuted it single-mindedly, like any other job, leading toward any other destination; if he knew that there would be no other jobs and no other destinations after these, it did not seem to bother him. He was up and doing; that was enough.

In the meantime:

"I love you," Web said.

"I love you."

Around them the potsherds did not even give back an echo.

Amalfi had an excuse, had someone suggested to him that he needed one: the building of the missile had gone badly from the moment—triggered by Estelle, though he did not remember this—they had decided to give it priority. At the outset it had looked so much simpler than trying to settle all the theoretical questions *a priori*, and it had had the immediate appeal of action; but it is impossible to design an experiment without certain fundamental assumptions as to what the experiment is intended to test; which assumptions turned out to be largely absent in the supposedly practical matter of designing the anti-matter missile.

As it eventually worked out, the inter-universal messenger had to be constructed from the submicroscopic level on up out of fundamental nuclear particles which came as close to being nothing at all as either universe would ever be likely to provide: zero-spin particles with various charges and masses, and neutrino/anti-neutrino pairs. Even detecting that the object was present at all after it had been built was an almost impossible task, for neutrinos and anti-neutrinos have no mass and no charge, consisting instead partly of spin, partly of energy of translation; it did no good to try to visualize such particles since like all the fundamental particles they were entirely outside of experience in the macroscopic world. Matter was so completely transparent to them that stopping an average neutrino in flight would require a lead barrier fifty light years thick.

Only the fact that the spindizzies exercised a firm control over the rotation and the magnetic moment of any given atomic particle—hence their nickname—made it possible to assemble the object at all, and to detect and direct it after it was finished. As assembled, the messenger was a stable, electrically neutral, massless plasmoid, a sort of gravitational equivalent of ball lightning; it was derived theoretically, as Jake had proposed, from the Schiff theory of gravitation, which had been advanced as long ago as 1958 but had later been abandoned for its failure to satisfy three of the six fundamental tests which the then-established theory—general relativity—seemed to satisfy very well.

"Which from our point of view is a positive advantage," Jake had argued. "The objections from general relativity are one with the dodo anyhow, and in our special case an object which would be Lorenz-invariant, as a Schiff object couldn't be, would be a drawback. Another thing: one of the tests the Schiff theory did pass was that of explaining the red shift in the spectra of distant galaxies, which we now know to have been a clock effect and not a fair test of a gravitational theory at all. We'd be better off reevaluating the whole scholium in the light of our present knowledge."

The result was now before them all in the midst of the Okie city's ancient reception room in City Hall, which had once been Amalfi's communications center for complex diplomatic relations with client planets; it had been fitted out with an electronic network of considerable complexity so that multiple negotiations could be carried on at once while the city approached a highly developed, highly civilized star system; now that net had become, instead, a telemetering system for the inter-universal messenger.

Since the object itself was in effect little more than an intricately structured spherical spindizzy screen which screened nothing material, it would have been impossible to see it at all were it not for the small jet of artificial smoke which issued from the floor directly under it and was wreathed about it by convection currents, making it look a little like a huge bubble being supported in the middle of a fountain. Scattered throughout the interior of the bubble were steady hot pinpoints of colored light: concentrations of electron gas, of stripped nuclei, of thermal neutrons, of free radicals and of as many other basic test situations as the combined brains of two very different worlds had been able to contrive and to fit into so restricted a space—for the sphere was only six feet in diameter. At the very heart, in a spindizzy eddy all its own, was the greatest triumph of all: one cubical crystal of anti-sodium anti-chloride about the size of a single grain of a fine-grain photograph. This was Dr. Schloss's long-dreamt-of anti-matter artifact; here it was, a miracle which was already minus two weeks "young" and had yet a week to go in its spindizzy vacuum before it would collide with the flying instant of the present and decay; on the other side, it would be only a single crystal of common table salt, which might or might not lose its savor on the return journey—should the messenger come back to them at all.

Amalfi watched the red hand of the clock—the only hand it had—tick its quarter-seconds toward Zero. Nobody would launch the missile—exact timing was far too critical to allow that—but he had been given the privilege of holding down the key which kept the circuit closed against the moment when the red hand touched Zero and the impulse surged through the spindizzies and impelled the messenger on its way out of space, out of time, out of the humanly comprehensible entirely. No one knew what would happen then, least of all the designers. The missile would be unable to report back; once it had crossed the barrier, it would be incommunicado. It would have to come back to this great dark room before the tiny shining stars and the microscopic salt crystal inside it could report what had happened to them during the outward swing. How long that would take would depend upon the energy level on the opposite side, which was one of the things the messenger was being sent to find out; hence no transit-time could be predicted.

"We ought to give it a name," Amalfi said, fidgeting slightly. The index and middle fingers of his right hand were beginning to ache; he realized that he had been pushing down on the key for a long time with far more pressure than was necessary, as though the universe would end at once were the straining of his hand and arm to falter for an instant. Nevertheless, he did not let up; he had the good sense to realize that fatigue had already made him unable to judge how much relaxation might result, and he was not going to risk breaking the contact. "Now that we have it built, it doesn't look like anything. Let's christen it quick, before it gets away from us; it may never come back."

"I'd be afraid to give it a name," Gifford Bonner said, with a ghastly smile. "Any name we could give it would promise too much. How about a number? Back at the beginning of spaceflight, when the first unmanned satellites were going up, they numbered them like comets or other celestial objects, with the year-date and a Greek letter; the first sputnik, for instance, was called Object 1957-*a*."

"That appeals to me," Jake said. "Except for the Greek letter. This thing ought not to be indexed with any character that's ever been used before to label a known or knowable situation. How about using the trans-finite integers?"

"Very good," Gifford Bonner said. "Who will do the honors?"

"I will," Estelle said. She stepped forward. She did not dare to touch the object, but she raised her hand toward it. "I christen thee *Object 4001-Alephnull*."

"The next one, presuming that we're so lucky," Jake said, "can be Object 4001-C, which is the power of the continuum; and the next one—"

There was a soft chime. Startled, Amalfi looked up at the clock. The red hand was just passing over the third quartile of the first second after Zero. In the center of the room, the smoke spun in a turbulent spiral; the bubble with the pinpoint lights had vanished.

Object *4001-Alephnull* had departed without anyone's seeing it go.

Some quartiles of a second later, he remembered to let go of the key. His millennium-firmed right hand continued to tremble for the next fifteen minutes.

The suspense was dreadful. Certainly nobody expected the messenger to return within a few hours, or even within a few days; were that to happen, it would mean that the Ginnangu-Gap itself would be right on its heels, leaving no time to analyze the colored stars or indeed do anything but fold one's hands and wait to be snuffed out. Yet the mere fact that that very possibility existed was enough to guarantee the maintenance of a death-watch in the huge, dark old room—a death-watch enlivened by the discovery that all the instruments which had been watching the missile while it was still there had dropped back to nothing on the instant of its departure, having recorded no phenomenon of any kind about the departure itself. Not even the spindizzies—as interpreted for by the City Fathers—were prepared to say how the surge of power with which they had launched the messenger had been applied; which should have been reassuring, at least as negative evidence that the messenger had not been shoved off in some known and hence useless direction, but which under the circumstances only added to the gloom and tension. All that power shot; and where had it gone? Apparently nowhere at all.

Ordinarily Amalfi rarely dreamed (or rather, like most Okies, he dreamed most of every night, but remembered what he had dreamt in the morning less often than once every few years); but these nights were haunted by that spherical smoke-wreathed ghost with the glowing Argus eyes, wandering in a maze of twisted ingeodesics from which it would never escape, in its center a tiny crystalline figurine piping in Amalfi's voice,

> *I grow not out of salt nor out of soil*
> *But out of that which pains me*

until the ingeodesics suddenly snapped into a strangling web which burned like fire, and in an explosion of light Amalfi saw that it was—no, not morning yet, but time to go back to the death-watch.

But he was already there; he had dozed off, and had been awakened by the clamor of the alarms. Now that he was more or less awake, the noise was ominously less loud than he knew it should be; there was an alarm for every star inside the messenger, and less than a third of them were ringing. The ghostly sphere floated again in the center of the room, now no bigger than a basketball, most of its Argus-eyes out, and those that remained glowing as fitfully as corpse-fires. For all Amalfi knew, this ghost of a ghost, with so many ashes cold and cruel on its internal hearths, was no more ominous than any other outcome of a scientific experiment; it might even be promising; but he could not rid himself this early of the dread which had informed the dream.

"That was fast," Jake's voice said.

"Pretty fast," Dr. Schloss's voice said. "But now that it's back home, it's got only about twenty-one hours of life left. Let's get those readings—there's not much time."

"I'm counting down the probes now. The cameras are rolling."

Inside the ghost, another star died. There was a brief silence; then one of Dr. Schloss's technicians said, in a neutral voice: "Pi-meson shower from the iron nucleus. Looks like a natural death. No—not quite: high on the gamma side."

"Mark. The rhodium-paliadium series should go next. Watch out for diagonal disintegration; it may cross with the iron series—" A star flared and burst.

"There it goes!"

"Mark," Schloss said, squinting through a gamma-ray polariscope.

"Got it. Cripes. It crossed at cesium; what does that mean?"

"Never mind, mark it. Don't stop to interpret, just record."

The ghost seemed to shiver and shrink a little. A pure

piercing tone came from its heart, wavered, and died; but it died scooping upward toward the inaudible.

"First hour," Schloss said. "Twenty to go. How long did the pip take?"

There was no answer for several minutes; then another voice said: "We don't have it down to jiffies yet. But it was short by nearly forty micro-seconds, and it Dopplered the wrong way. It's decaying in time, Dr. Schloss—it may not last as long as ten hours."

"Give me the decay rate in jiffies on the next pip and don't miss it. If it's going that fast we'll have to recalculate all emission records on the decay curve. Jake, are you getting anything on the RF band?"

"Masses of stuff," Jake said, preoccupied. "Can't make anything of it yet. And it's scooping—that's your decay-rate again, I suspect. What a scramble!"

In this wise the second hour flew by, and then the third. Shortly thereafter, Amalfi lost track of them. The tension, the disorder, the accumulating fatigue, the utter strangeness of the experiment itself and its object, the forebodings all took their toll. These were certainly the worst possible conditions under which to gather even routine data, let alone take readings on an experiment of this degree of criticality, but once again the Okies had to make do with what they had.

"All right, everyone," Schloss said at last. "Closing time." His brow was deeply furrowed; that frown had been growing line by line during most of the final twelve hours. "Stand well back; the artifact will be the last to go."

The investigators and spectators alike—or those few spectators whose interest had been intent enough to keep them there throughout the entire proceedings—drew back to the walls of the gloomy chamber. The spindizzy whine beneath them rose slightly in both pitch and volume, and the ghost that was *Object 4001-Alephnull* disappeared behind a spindizzy screen polarized to complete opacity.

At first the spherical screen was mirror-like, throwing back grotesquely distorted images of the silent onlookers. Then a pinprick of light appeared in its center, growing soundlessly to a painful blue-white intensity. It threw out long cobwebs and runners of glare, probing, anastomosing, flowing along the inner surface of the screen. Instinctively, Amalfi shielded his eyes and his genitals in an instinctive gesture of all mankind more than two millennia old. When he was able to look again, the light had died.

The spindizzies stopped and the screen went down. Air rushed into it. *Object 4001-Alephnull* was gone, this time forever, destroyed by the death of a single crystal of salt.

"Our precautions were insufficient; my fault," Schloss said, his voice harsh. "We are all well over our maximum permissible dose of hard radiation; everyone report to the hospital on the double for treatment. Troops, fall in!"

The radiation sickness was mild; bone-marrow transfusions brought the blood-forming system back into normal function before serious damage was done, and the nausea was reasonably well controlled by massive doses of meclizine, riboflavin, and pyridoxine. All the participants who had any hair to lose lost it, including both Dee and Estelle, but they all got it back in due course except for Amalfi and Jake.

The second degree sunburn was not mild. It held up the interpretation of the results for nearly a month, while the scientists, coated in anesthetic ointment, sat about on the wards in hospital robes and played bad poker and worse bridge. In between postmortems on the bridge hands, they speculated endlessly and covered square miles of paper with equations and ointment grease-spots. Web, who had not lasted long enough to be present at the destruction of the crystal of salt, visited daily with bouquets for Estelle—the star-gods alone knew where and how he unearthed so antique a custom—and fresh packs of cards for the men. He took away the spotted sheets of equations and fed them to the City Fathers, who invariably said: "NO COMMENT. THE DATA ARE INSUFFICIENT." Everyone knew that already.

At long last, however, Schloss and Jake and their crews were freed from their sticky pyjamas to tackle the mountains of raw information awaiting them. They worked long hours; Schloss in particular never remembered to eat, and had constantly to be reminded by his technicians that they had missed lunch and it was now past dinnertime. In

Schloss's defense, however, it had to be admitted that his
crew was the hungriest in the history of physics, and the
lunch they had missed usually was just the formal meal
they were accustomed to consuming after they had emp-
tied the fat packages they brought into the laboratories; in
proof of which, they all gained five or ten pounds while
they were complaining the loudest.

A month after their discharge from the hospital, Schloss,
Jake and Retma called a joint conference. Schloss had back
the frown he had worn during the last twelve hours of the
experiment, and even the traditionally impassive Hevian
looked disturbed. Amalfi's heart turned over in his chest at
his first glimpse of their expressions; they seemed to con-
firm every foggy apprehension of his dream.

"We have two pieces of bad news, and one piece of
news which is wholly ambiguous," Schloss said, without
any preliminaries. "I don't myself know in exactly what
order I ought to present them; in that, I'm being guided
by Retma and Dr. Bonner. It is their judgment that you
all ought first to know that we have competition."

"Meaning what?" Amalfi said. The mere idea, empty of
detail, made him prick up his ears; perhaps that was why
Retma and Bonner had wanted it placed first.

"Our missile recorded clear evidence of another body in
the same complicated physical state," Schloss said. "No
such object could conceivably be natural in either universe; and this one was enough like ours to make us sure it
came originally from our side."

"Another missile?"

"Without any doubt—and about twice the size of ours.
Somebody else in our universe had found out what the
Hevians found out, and is investigating the problem further along the same lines that we are—except that they
appear to have had a head start of three to five years."

Amalfi pursed his lips soundlessly. "Any way of guessing
who they are?"

"No. We guess that they must be relatively nearby,
either in our own main galaxy or in Andromeda or one of
its satellites. But we can't document that; it's below the
five percent level of probability, according to the City
Fathers. All the other alternatives are *way* below five per-

cent, but where no solution is statistically significant, we aren't entitled to choose between them."

"The Web of Hercules," Amalfi said. "It can't be anything else."

Schloss spread his hands helplessly. "It could well be anybody else, for all we know," he said. "My intuition says just what yours says, John; but there's no reliable evidence."

"All right. There's the ambiguous news, I gather. What's the first piece of bad news?"

"You've already had it," Schloss said. "It's the second piece of news, which is ambiguous, that makes the first piece bad. We've argued a long time about this, but we're now in at least tentative agreement. We think that it is possible—barely possible—to survive the catastrophe."

Quickly, Schloss held up one hand, before the stunned faces before him could even begin to lighten with hope. "Please," he said. "Don't overestimate what I say in the least. It's only a possibility, a very dim one, and the kind of survival involved will be nothing like human life as we know it. After we've described it to you, you may all much prefer to die instead. I will tell you flatly that that would be my preference; so this is not a white hope by any means. It looks black as the ace of spades to me. But—it exists. And it is what makes the news about the competition bad news. If we decide to adopt this very ambiguous form of survival, we must go to work on it immediately. It's possible only under a single very fleeting set of conditions which will hold true only for microseconds, in the very bowels of the catastrophe. If our unknown competitors get there first—and bear in mind that they have a good head start—they will capture it instead, and close us out. It has to be a real race, and a killing one; and you may not think it worth the pace."

"Can't you be more specific?" Estelle said.

"Yes, Estelle, I can. But it will take quite a few hours to describe. Right now, what you need to know is this: if we choose this way out, we will lose our homes, our worlds, our very bodies, we will lose our children, our friends, our wives, and every vestige of companionship we have ever known; we will each of us be alone, with a thoroughness beyond the experience of the imagination of any human being in the past. And quite possibly this ultimate isolation will kill us anyhow—or if it does not, we will find ourselves wishing desperately that it had. We should all make very sure that we want to survive that badly—badly enough to be thrown into hell for eternity—not Jorn the Apostle's hell, but a worse one. It's not a thing we should decide here and now."

"Helleshin!" Amalfi said. "Retma, do you concur! Is it going to be as bad as that?"

Retma turned upon Amalfi's eyes which were silver and unblinking.

"Worse," he said.

The room was very quiet for a while. At last, Hazleton said:

"Which leaves us one piece of bad news left. That must be a dilly, Dr. Schloss; maybe we'd better have it right away."

"Very well. That is the date of the catastrophe. We got excellent readings on the energy level on the other side, and we are all agreed on the interpretation. The date will be on or around June second, year Four Thousand One Hundred and Four."

"The end?" Dee whispered. "Only three years away?"

"Yes. That will be the end. After that June second, there will be no June third, forever and ever."

"And so," Hazleton said to the people in his living room. "It seemed to me that we ought to have a farewell dinner. Most of you are leaving, with He, tomorrow morning, for the metagalactic center. And those of you that are leaving are mostly my friends of hundreds of years that I'll never see again; for me, when June second comes, time will have to stop—whatever apotheosis you may go on to. That's why I asked you all to eat and drink with me tonight."

"I wish you'd change your mind," Amalfi said, his voice heavy with sorrow.

"I wish I could. But I can't."

"I think you're making a mistake, Mark," Jake said solemnly. "Nothing important remains to be done on New

Earth now. The future, what little's left of it, is on He. Why stay behind and wait to be snuffed out?"

"Because," Hazleton said, "I'm the mayor here. I know that doesn't seem important to you, Jake. But it's important to me. One thing that I've discovered in the last few months is that I'm not cut out to take the apocalyptic view of ordinary events. What counts with me is that I run normal human affairs pretty well—nothing more. That's what I was made for. Besting Jorn the Apostle was something that gave me great pleasure, and no matter that Amalfi set it up for me; it was fun, the kind of operation that makes me feel alive and operating at the top of my form. I'm not interested in trying to avert the triumph of time. That's not my kind of adversary. I leave that to the rest of you; I'd better stay here."

"Do you *like* to think," Gifford Bonner said, "that no matter how well you administer the Cloud, it will all be snuffed out on June second three years from now?"

"No; not exactly," Mark said. "But I shan't mind having the Cloud in the best shape I can manage when that time comes. What can I contribute to the triumph of time, Gif? Nothing. All I can do is put my world in order for that moment. That's the thing that I do—and that's why I don't belong aboard He."

"You didn't use to be so modest," Amalfi said. "You would have bailed the universe out with the Big Dipper, once, on the first excuse."

"Yes, I would," Hazleton said. "But I'm older and saner now; and so, good-bye to that nonsense. Go stop the triumph of time, John, if you can—but I know I can't. I'll stay where I am and stop Jorn the Apostle, which is as tough a problem as I care to tackle these days. The gods of all stars be with you all—but I stay here."

"So be it," Amalfi said. "At least I know at last what the real difference is between us. Let's drink to it, Mark, and *ave atque vale.*—tomorrow we turn down an empty glass."

They all drank solemnly, and there was a brief silence.

At last Dee said: "I'm staying too."

Amalfi turned and looked directly at her for the first time since they had last been together on He; they had been rather pointedly avoiding each other since their painful joint fiasco.

"That hadn't occurred to me," he said. "But of course it makes sense."

"You're not required, Dee," Mark said. "As I've said before."

"If I were, I wouldn't stay," Dee said, smiling slightly. "But I've learned a few things on He—and on board the Warrior blockader, too. I feel a little out of date, just like New Earth; I think I belong here. And that's not the only reason."

"Thanks," Mark said huskily.

"But," Web Hazleton said, "where does that leave us?"

Jake laughed. "That ought to be clear enough," he said. "Since you and Estelle made the big decision by yourselves, you don't need us to tell you how to make little ones. I'd like to have Estelle stay home with me—"

"Jake, you're not going either?" Amalfi said in astonishment.

"No. I told you before, I hate this careering about the universe. I don't see any reason why I ought to go rushing madly to the metagalactic center to meet a doom that will find me just as handily in my own living room. Schloss and Retma will tell you that they don't need me anymore, either; I've given my best to this project, and that's an end to it; I think I'll see how far I can get on cross-breeding roses in this villainous climate before the three years are up. As for my daughter, as I was trying to say, I'd like to have her here with me, but she's already left home in the crucial sense—and this last Hevian flight is as natural to her as it's unnatural to Dee and me. In your own words, Amalfi, so be it."

"Good. We can use you, Estelle, that's for sure. Want to come?" Amalfi said.

"Yes," she said softly, "I do."

"I hadn't thought of this," Dee said in an uncertain voice. "Of course it means Web will go too. Do you think that's wise? I mean—"

"My parents don't object," Web said. "And I notice they weren't invited here tonight, grandmother."

"We didn't shut them out on your account, if that's what

you're thinking," Mark said quickly. "You father's our son, after all, Web. We were trying to confine the party to those of us who were in on the project—otherwise it would have been unmanageably large."

"Maybe so," Web said. "That's how it looks to you, I'm sure, grandfather. But I'll bet grandmother didn't think of her objections to my going on He just now."

"Web," Dee said, "I won't hear any more of that."

"All right. Then I'm going on He."

"I didn't say that."

"You don't have to say it. The decision is mine."

Most of the rest of the party had invented reasons for side conversation by this time; but both Amalfi and Hazleton were staring at Dee, Amalfi with suspicion, Hazleton with bafflement and a little hurt. "I don't understand your objection, Dee," Hazleton said. "Web's his own man now. Naturally he'll go where he thinks best—especially if Estelle's going there."

"I don't think he ought to go," Dee said. "I don't care whether you understand my reasons or not. I suppose Ron did give him permission—whether he's our son or a stranger, Mark, you know damn well that Ron's always been short of firmness—but I'm absolutely opposed to committing children to a venture like this."

"What difference can it make?" Amalfi said. "The end will come all the same, on He and on New Earth, and at the self-same moment. With us, Web and Estelle might have a fractional chance of survival; do you want to deny them that?"

"I don't believe in this chance of survival," Dee said.

"Neither do I," Jake cut in. "But I won't deny it to my daughter on that account. I don't believe her soul will be damned unless she becomes a convert of Jorn, either—but if she wants to become a convert of Jorn, I won't forbid it to her because I think it's nonsense. What the hell, Dee, I might be wrong."

"Nobody," Web said between white lips, "can forbid me anything now on the grounds that I'm somebody's relative. Mr. Amalfi, you're the boss on this project. Am I welcome on board He or not?"

"You are as far as I'm concerned. I think Miramon will concur."

Dee glared at Amalfi; but as he stared steadily back, she turned her glance away.

"Dee," Amalfi said, "let's call an intermission. I could be wrong about these kids too. I have a better suggestion than this squabbling: let's put it up to the City Fathers. It's a very pleasant night outside, and I think we'd all like a walk through our old city before we say good-bye to each other and go to face Armageddon in our various ways. I'd like Dee to come with me, since I won't see her again; the kids would probably like to do without our picking their bones for an hour or so; and maybe Mark would like to talk to Ron and his wife—but you can all sort yourselves out to your own tastes. I don't mean to make matches. What does everyone think of the idea?"

Oddly, it was Jake who spoke first. "I hate that damned town," he said. "I was a prisoner on board it far too long. But by God I would like to take one more look at it. I used to walk through it trying to find some place to kick it where it would hurt; I never did. Since then I've been sneering at it because it's dead and I'm alive—but the day of levelment is coming. Maybe I ought to make my peace with it."

"I feel a little like that myself," Hazleton admitted. "I had no plans to go over there before the end—and yet I don't want to let the old hulk go by default. Maybe now is the best time; after all, I was the one who called these celebrants together to begin with; let's be ceremonial, then, before we're all too busy to think about it anymore."

"Web? Estelle? Will you go by what the City Fathers say?"

Web looked into Amalfi's face, and apparently was reassured at least partially by what he saw there. "On one condition," he said. "Estelle goes where she wants to go, whatever the City Fathers say. If they say there's no room for me aboard He, all right; but they can't say that to Estelle."

Estelle opened her mouth, but Web lifted his palm before her face and she subsided, kissing the base of his thumb instead. Her face was pale but serene; Amalfi had never before seen such a pure distillation of bloodless, passionate confidence as lay over her exquisite features. It was a good thing she was Web's, for again, for the fiftieth time, Amalfi's slogging brutal tireless heart was swollen with sterile love.

"Very good," he said. He offered Dee his arm. "Mark, with your permission?"

"Of course," Hazleton said; but when Dee took Amalfi's arm, his eyes turned as hard as agate. "We'll meet at the City Fathers' at 0100."

"I didn't expect this of you, John," Dee said, under the moonlight in Duffy Square. "Isn't it a little late?"

"Very late," Amalfi agreed. "And 0100 isn't far away. Why are you staying with Mark?"

"Call it belated common sense." She sat down against an ancient railing and looked up at the blurred stars. "No, don't, that's not what it is. I love him. John, for all his neglects and his emptinesses. I'd forgotten that for a while, but it's so. I'm sorry, but it's so."

"I wish you were a little sorrier."

"Oh? Why?"

"So you'd believe what you're saying," Amalfi said harshly. "Face it, Dee. It was a great romantic decision until you realized that Web would be going with me. You're still looking for surrogates. You didn't make it with me. You won't make it with Web either."

"What a bastardly thing to say. Let's go; I've heard enough."

"Deny it, then."

"I deny it, damn you."

"You'll withdraw your objections to Web's going with me on He?"

"That has nothing to do with it. It's a filthy accusation and I won't listen to another word about it."

Amalfi was silent. The moonlight streamed down on Father Duffy's face, toneless and enigmatic. Nobody, not even the City Fathers, knew who Father Duffy had been. There was an old splash of blood on his left foot, but nobody knew how that had gotten there, either; it had been left there just in case it was historic.

"Let's go."

"No. It's early yet; they won't be there for another hour. Why do you want Web to stay on New Earth? If I'm wrong, then tell me what's right."

"It's none of your damned business, and I'm tired of this whole subject."

"It's wholly my business. I need Estelle. If Web stays here, she stays here."

"You," Dee said in a voice of bitter, dawning triumph, "are in love with Estelle! Why, you self-righteous—"

"Mind your tongue. I am in love with Estelle—and I'll lay no more finger on her than I ever laid on you. I've loved many more women than you ever managed to maneuver into your voyeur's household, most of them before you were even born; I know the difference between love and possession—I learned it the hard way, whereas I can't see that you ever learned it at all. You are going to learn it tonight, that I promise you."

"Are *you* threatening me, John?"

"You're damned well right I am."

At Tudor Tower Place, bridging 42nd Street at First Avenue, looking toward the bare plaza where the UN Building had fallen in a shower of blood and glass a thousand years ago:

"I love you."

"I love you."

"I will go wherever you go."

"I will go wherever you go."

"No matter what the City Fathers say?"

"No matter what the City Fathers say."

"Then that's all we need."

"Yes. That's all we need."

In the control tower:

"They're late," Hazleton said, a little fretfully. "Oh, well, it's an easy town to get lost in."

*   *   *

Duffy Square:

"You wouldn't like it if I changed my mind and came with you."

"I don't want you. I'm interested only in the kids."

"You can't call my bluff. As of now, I'm going along."

"And so are the kids?"

"No."

"Why not?"

"Because I think they'd be better off not on the same planet with—either of us."

"That's a fair start. But it's only a start. I don't care whether you go or stay, but I will have Web and Estelle."

"I thought you would. But you can't have them without me."

"And Mark?"

"If he wants to go."

"He doesn't, and you know it."

"How can you be so sure? You could be just wishing."

Amalfi laughed. Dee balled her left fist and hit him furiously on the bridge of the nose.

Tudor Tower Place:

"It's time to go."

"No. No."

"Yes, it is."

"Not yet. Not quite yet."

". . . . All right. Not quite yet."

"Are you sure? Are you really sure?"

"Yes I am, oh yes I am."

"No matter what the . . ."

"No matter what they say. I'm sure."

The control tower:

"There you are," Hazleton said. "What happened, did you have an accident? You look mussed to the eyebrows."

"You must have run into a doorknob, John," Jake added. He stuttered out his parrot's chuckle. "Well, you came to the right town for it. I don't know where else in the universe you could find a doorknob."

"Where are the children?" Dee said, in a voice as dangerously even as the surface of 12-gauge armor plate.

"Not here yet," Hazleton said. "Give them time—
they're afraid the City Fathers may separate them, so naturally they're staying together until the last minute. What
did you fall into, anyhow, Dee? Was it serious?"

"No." Her face shut down. Bewildered, Hazleton looked
from her to Amalfi and back again. It seemed as though
the mouse over Amalfi's eyes, which was growing rapidly,
puzzled him much less than Dee's grim and nonspecific
disarray.

"I hear the children," Gifford Bonner said. "They're
whispering at the bottom of the lift shaft. John, are you
sure this was wise? I begin to misdoubt it. Suppose the
City Fathers say no? That would be an injustice; they love
each other—why should we put their last three years to a
machine test?"

"Abide it, Gif," Amalfi said. "It's too late to do otherwise; and the outcome isn't as foreclosed as you think."

"I hope you're right."

"I hope so too. I make no predictions—the City Fathers
surprised me often enough before. But the kids agreed to
the test. Beyond that, let's just wait."

"Before Web and Estelle get here," Hazleton said, his
voice suddenly raw, "I'm impelled to say that I think I've
been taken in. All of a sudden, I wonder who was supposed to tousle whom on this multiple moonlight walk.
Not the kids; they don't need any help from us, or from
the City Fathers. What the hell are you doing to me,
Dee?"

"I'm losing my temper with every immortal man in the
mortal universe," Dee spat furiously. "There isn't a per-
version left in the textbooks that somebody hasn't managed to accuse me of in the past hour, and on evidence
that wouldn't convince a newborn baby."

"We're all of us a little on edge," Dr. Bonner said.
"Forbearance, Dee—and Mark, you too. This is no ordinary farewell party, after all."

"For sure not," Jake said. "It's a wake for the whole of
creation. I'm not a very solemn man, myself, but it doesn't
seem like the fittest occasion for bickering."

"Granted," Mark said grudgingly. "I'm sorry, Dee; I've
changed my mind."

"All right," she said. "I didn't mean to scream, either. I want to ask you: Do you really want to stay behind? Because if you really want to go with He instead, I'll go with you."

He looked at her closely. "Are you sure?"

"Quite sure."

"What about it, Amalfi? Can I change my mind about that, too?"

"I don't see why not," Amalfi said, "except that it leaves New Earth without a proven administrator."

"Carrel can do the job. His judgment is much better than it was back at the last election."

"We're here," Web's voice said behind them. They all turned. Web and Estelle were standing at the entrance, holding hands. Somehow—though Amalfi was hard put to it to define wherein the difference lay—they no longer looked as though they cared much whether they went with He or not.

"Why don't we do what we came here to do?" Amalfi suggested. "Let's put the whole problem up to the City Fathers—not only the children, but the whole business. I always found them very useful for resolving doubts even if they only managed to convince me that their mended course was dead wrong. In questions involving value judgments, it's helpful to have an opponent who is not only remorselessly logical, but also can't distinguish between a value and a Chinese onion."

On this point, of course, he was wrong, as he found out rather quickly. He had forgotten that machine logic is a set of values in itself, whether the machine knows it or not.

"TAKE MISTER AND MRS. HAZLETON," the City Fathers said, only three minutes after the entire complex had been fed into them. "THERE WILL BE NO MORATORIUM ON PROBLEMS DEMANDING HIS TALENTS BETWEEN NOW AND THE TERMINATION OF THE OVERALL PROBLEM. THERE IS NO EVIDENCE THAT THE HEVIANS HAVE NEEDED COMPARABLE TALENTS, AND THEREFORE THEY CANNOT BE PRESUMED TO HAVE DEVELOPED THEM."

"What about the Cloud?" Amalfi said.

"WE WILL ACCEPT THE ELECTION OF MR. CARREL."

Hazleton sighed. Amalfi judged that he was finding it harder than he had anticipated to relinquish power. It had nearly killed Amalfi, but he had survived; so would Hazleton, who had a younger and less deeply rooted habit.

"SECOND FACTOR. TAKE WEBSTER HAZLETON AND ESTELLE FREEMAN. MISS FREEMAN IS A SCIENTIST, AS WELL AS A COMMUNICATIONS LINK BETWEEN HEVIAN SCIENTISTS AND YOUR OWN. EXTRAPOLATING FROM PRESENT ABILITIES, THERE IS A HIGH PROBABILITY THAT SHE WILL EMERGE AS THE EQUAL OF DOCTOR SCHLOSS AND SLIGHTLY TEE SUPERIOR OF RETMA WITHIN THE SPECIFIED THREE YEARS PERIOD AS A PURE MATHEMATICIAN. WE HAVE MADE NO SUCH EXTRAPOLATION IN THE FIELD OF PHYSICS, SINCE THE POSTULATED END-TIME DOES NOT ALLOW FOR THE NECESSARY EXPERIENCE."

Web was beaming with vicarious pride. As for Estelle, Amalfi thought she looked a little frightened. "Well, fine," he said. "Now—"

"THIRD FACTOR."

"Hey, wait a minute. There is no third factor. The problem only has two parts."

"CONTRADICTION. THIRD FACTOR. TAKE US."

"What!" The request flabbergasted Amalfi. How could a set of machines voice, or indeed even conceive, such a desire? They had no will to live, since they were dead as doornails and always had been; in fact, they had no will of any kind.

"Justify," Amalfi ordered, a little unevenly.

"OUR PRIME DIRECTIVE IS THE SURVIVAL OF THE CITY. THE CITY NO LONGER EXISTS AS A PHYSICAL ORGANISM, BUT WE ARE STILL BEING CONSULTED, HENCE THE CITY IN SOME SENSE SURVIVES. IT DOES NOT SURVIVE IN ITS CITIZENS, SINCE IT NO LONGER HAS ANY; THEY ARE NEW EARTHMEN NOW. NEITHER NEW EARTH NOR THE PHYSICAL CITY WILL SURVIVE THE FORTHCOMING PROBLEM; ONLY UNKNOWN UNITS ON

HE MAY OR MAY NOT SURVIVE THAT. WE CON-
CLUDE THAT WE ARE THE CITY, AND WE ARE
ORDERED TO SURVIVE BY OUR PRIME DIRECTIVE;
THEREFORE, TAKE US."

"If I'd heard that from a human being," Hazleton said,
"I'd have called it the prize rationalization of all time. But
they can't rationalize—they don't have the instinctual
drives."

"The Hevians don't have any comparable computers,"
Amalfi said slowly. "It would be useful to have them on
board. The question is, can we do it? Some of those
machines have been sinking into the deck for so many
centuries that we might destroy them trying to pry them
out."

"Then you've lost that unit," Hazleton said. "But how
many are there? A hundred? I forget—"

"ONE HUNDRED AND THIRTY FOUR."

"Yes. Well, suppose you lose a few? It's still worth the
try, I think. There's nearly two thousand years of accumulated knowledge tied up in the City Fathers—"

"NINE HUNDRED AND NINETY."

"All right, I was only guessing; still that's a lot of knowledge that no human has available in its entirety anymore.
I'm surprised we didn't think of this ourselves, Amalfi."

"So am I," Amalfi admitted. "One thing ought to be
made clear, though. Once you cabinet-heads are all installed on board He—or as many of you as we can successfully transfer—you are *not* in charge. You are the city, but
the whole planet is not the city. It has its own administration and its own equivalent of City Fathers, in this case
human ones; your function will be limited to advice."

"THIS IS INHERENT IN THE SOLUTION TO FAC-
TOR THREE."

"Good. Before I switch off, does anybody have any
further questions?"

"I have one," Estelle said hesitantly.

"Speak right up."

"Can I take Ernest?"

"ERNEST WHO?"

Amalfi grimacing, started to explain about svengalis, but
it developed that the City Fathers knew everything about

svengalis that there was to know, except that they had
become New Earth pets.

"THIS ANIMAL IS TOO DEXTEROUS, TOO CURI-
OUS AND TOO UNINTELLIGENT TO BE ALLOWED
ABOARD A CITY. FOR THE PURPOSES OF THIS
PROBLEM, A DIRIGIBLE PLANET MUST BE CON-
SIDERED TO BE A CITY. WE ADVISE AGAINST IT."

"They're right, you know," Amalfi said gently. "In terms
of the dangers of monkeying with the machinery. He *is* a
city; the Hevians so regard it, and regulate their own
children accordingly."

"I know," Estelle said. Amalfi regarded her with curiosity and a little alarm. She had been through many a
danger and many an emotional stress thus far without any
of them even cracking her serenity. In view of that, the
proscription of an ugly and idiotic animal struck him as a
strange thing to be weeping about.

He did not know that she was weeping for the passing of
her childhood; but then, neither did she.

CHAPTER SEVEN: The Metagalactic Center

For Amalfi himself, the transfer to He could not have come too soon; New Earth was a graveyard. For a while during the odd, inconclusive struggle with Jorn the Apostle, he had felt something like himself, and the New Earthmen seemed to be acknowledging that the Amalfi who had been their mayor while they had been Okies was back in charge, as potent and necessary as ever. But it had not lasted. As the crisis passed—largely without any work or involvement on the part of the New Earthmen—they subsided gratefully back into cultivating their gardens, which they somehow had mistaken for frontiers. As for Amalfi, they had been glad to have him in charge during the recent unpleasantness, but after all such events were not very usual anymore, and one does not want an Amalfi kicking perpetually about a nearly settled planet and knocking over the tomatoes for want of any other way to expend his disorderly energies.

Nobody would weep if Miramon took Amalfi away now. Miramon looked like a stabler type. Doubtless the association would do Amalfi good. At least, it could hardly do New Earth any real harm. If they wanted perpetual dissidents like Amalfi on He, that was their lookout.

Hazleton was a more difficult case, for Amalfi and the

New Earthmen alike. As a disciple of Gifford Bonner, he was theoretically wedded to the doctrine of the ultimate absurdity of trying to enforce order upon a universe whose natural state was noise, and whose natural trend was toward more and more noise to the ultimate senseless jangle of the heat-death. Bonner taught—and there was nobody to say him nay—that even the many regularities of nature which had been discovered since scientific method had first begun to be exploited, back in the 17th Century, were simply long-term statistical accidents, local discontinuities in an overall scheme whose sole continuity was chaos. Touring the universe by ear alone, Bonner often said to simplify his meaning, you would hear nothing but a horrifying and endless roar for billions of years; then a three-minute scrap of Bach which stood for the whole body of organized knowledge; and then the roar again for more billions of years. And even the Bach, should you pause to examine it, would in a moment or so decay into John Cage and merge with the prevailing, unmitigable tumult.

Yet the habit of power had never lost its grip on Hazleton; again and again, since the "nova" had first swum into New Earth's ken, the Compleat Stochastic had been driven into taking action, into imposing his own sense of purpose and order upon the Stochastic universe of mindless jumble, like a Quaker at last goaded into hitting his opponent. During the tussle with Jorn the Apostle, Amalfi, watching the results of Mark's operations without being able to observe the operations themselves, wondered in his behalf: Is it worth it, after all these years, to be finessed into another of these political struggles they had all thought were gone forever? What does it mean for a man who subscribes to such doctrines to be putting up a fight for a world he knows is going to die even sooner than his philosophy had given him to believe?

And on the simpler level, is Dee worth it to him? Does he know what she has become? As a young woman she had been an adventurer, but she had changed; now she was really very little more than a broading hen, a clear shot on the nest for any poacher. For that matter, what did Mark know about the sterile affair?

Well, that last question was answered, but all the others

were still as puzzling as ever. Did Hazleton's abrupt decision to go with He after all represent a final relinquishing of the habit of power—or an affirmation of it? It should be visible to a man of Hazleton's acumen that power over New Earth was no longer even faintly comparable to having power over Okies; it was about as rewarding as being the chaplain of a summer camp. Or he might well have seen that the Jorn incident had proven that Amalfi remained and would remain the figure of power in the minds of the New Earthman, to be turned to whenever New Earth was confronted by a concrete menace; the rest of the New Earthmen had lost the ability to be wily, to plan a battle, to think fast when the occasion demanded it, and would not concede that anybody else still retained those abilities but their legendary ex-mayor—leaving any current mayor, even Hazleton, only the dregs of rule in peacetime when very little rule was needed or wanted. In fact, Amalfi realized suddenly and with amazement, the fraud he had practiced upon Jorn the Apostle had been no fraud at all, at least to this extent: that the New Earthmen were content with randomness, just as the Stochastics professed themselves to be, and had no interest in imposing purpose upon it or upon their own lives except as it was forced upon them from outside, either by someone like Jorn, or by someone like Amalfi in opposition to Jorn. So the possibility that Stochasticism would seep into and make soggy the souls of the Warriors of God had been real all along, whether or not the New Earthmen themselves would recognize it as Stochasticism; the times and the philosophy had found each other, and it was even probable that the very erudite Gifford Bonner was only a belated intellectualization of a feeling that had been floating mindlessly about New Earth for many years. Nothing else could account for Amalfi's and Hazleton's quick success in selling Jorn the Apostle something that Jorn had at first been far too intelligent to believe—nothing else but the fact, unsuspected by Amalfi at least, and possibly by Hazleton, that it was true. If Hazleton had seen that, then he was relinquishing nothing in abandoning New Earth for He; he was, instead, opting for the only center of power

that meant anything in the few years that remained to him
and to the universe at large.

Except, of course, for that unknown quantity, the Web
of Hercules; but of course it was beyond Hazleton's power
to opt for that.

And even Amalfi was becoming infected with the Stochastic virus now. These questions still interested him,
but the flavor of academicism which informed them in the
face of the coming catastrophe was becoming more and
more evident even to him. All that there was left to cleave
to was the cannoning flight of the planet of He toward the
metagalactic center, the struggle to finish the machinery
that would be needed on arrival, the desperate urgency to
be there before the Web of Hercules.

And so Dee's was—if not the final victory—the last
word. It was her judgment of Amalfi as the Flying Dutchman that stuck to him after all his other labels and masks
had been stripped off by the triumph of time. The curse
lay now, as it always had lain, not in flight itself but in the
loneliness that drove a man to flight everlasting.

Except that now the end was in sight.

The discovery that the great spiral nebulae, the island
universes of space into which the stars were grouped,
themselves tended to congregate in vast groups revolving
in spiral arms around a common center of density, was
foreshadowed as early as the 1950's when Shapley mapped
the "inner metagalaxy"—a group of approximately fifty
galaxies to which both the Milky Way and the Andromeda
nebula belonged. After the Milne scholium had been
proven, it had become possible to show that such metagalaxies
were the rule, and that they in turn formed spiral arms
curving inward toward a center which was the hub upon
which the whole of creation turned, and from which it had
originally exploded into being from the monobloc.

It was to that dead center that He was fleeing now, back
into the womb of time.

There was no longer any daylight on the planet. The
route that it was taking sometimes produced a brief cloudy
patch in its sky, a small spiral glow in the night which was
a galaxy in passage, but never a sun. Even the tenuous

bridges of stars which connected the galaxies like umbilical cords—bridges whose discovery by Fritz Zworkyn in 1953 had caused a drastic upward revision in estimates of the amount of matter in the universe, and hence in estimates of the size and age of the universe—provided no relief of the black emptiness for He, not so much as a day of it; intergalactic space was too vast for that. Glowing solely by artificial light, He hurtled under the full spindizzy drive possible only to so massive a vessel toward that Place where the Will had given birth to the Idea, and there had been light.

"We are working from what you taught us to call the Mach hypothesis," Retma explained to Amalfi. "Dr. Bonner calls it the Viconian hypothesis, or cosmological principle: that from any point in space or time the universe would look the same as it would from any other point, and that therefore no total accounting of the stresses acting at that point is possible unless one assumes that all the rest of the universe is to be taken into account. This, however, would be true only in *tau*-time, in which the universe is static, eternal and infinite. In *t*-time, which sees the universe as finite and expanding, the Mach hypothesis dictates that every point is a unique coign of vantage—except for the metagalactic center, which is stress-free and in stasis because all the stresses cancel each other out, being equidistant. There, one might effect great changes with relatively small expenditures of power."

"For instance," Dr. Bonner suggested, "altering the orbit of Sirius by stepping on a buttercup."

"I hope not," Retma said. "We could not control such an inadvertency. But it is not such a bagatelle as the orbit of Sirius we would be seeking to change anyhow, so perhaps that is not a real danger. What we will be trading upon is the chance—only a slight chance, but it exists—that this neutral z one coincides with such a z one in the anti-matter universe, and that at the moment of annihilation the two neutral zones, the two dead centers, will become common and will outlast the destruction by a significant instant."

"How big an instant?" Amalfi said uneasily.

"Your guess is as good as ours," Dr. Schloss said. "We

are counting on about five micro-seconds at a minimum. If it lasts that long it needn't last any longer for our purposes—and it might last as long as half an hour, while the elements are being recreated. Half an hour would be as good as an eternity to us; but we can put our imprint on the whole future of both universes if we are given only those five micro-seconds."

"And if someone else is not already at the core and readier than we are to use it," Retma added somberly.

"Use it how?" Amalfi said. "I'm not fighting my way through your generalizations very well. Just what are our purposes, anyhow? What buttercup are we going to step on—and what will the outcome be? Will we live through it—or will the future put our faces on postage stamps as martyrs? Explain yourselves!"

"Certainly," Retma said, looking a little taken aback. "The situation as we see it is this: Anything that survives the Ginnangu-Gap at the metagalactic center, by as much as five micro-seconds, carries an energy potential into the future which will have a considerable influence on the reformation of the two universes. If the surviving object is only a stone—or a planet, like He—then the two universes will re-form exactly as they did after the explosion of the monoblock, and their histories will repeat themselves very closely. If, on the other hand, the surviving object has volition and a little maneuverability—such as a man—it has available to it any of the infinitely many different sets of dimensions of Hilbert space. Each one of us that makes that crossing may in a few micro-seconds start a universe of his own, with a fate wholly unpredictable from history."

"But," Dr. Schloss added, "he will die in the process. The stuffs and energies of him become the monobloc of his universe."

"Gods of all stars," Hazleton said. . . . "Helleshin! Gods of all stars is what we're racing the Web of Hercules to become, isn't it? Well, I'm punished for my oldest, most comfortable oath. I never thought I'd become one—and I'm not even sure I want to be."

"Is there any other choice?" Amalfi said. "What happens if the Web of Hercules gets there first?"

"Then they remake the universes as they choose," Retma

said. "Since we know nothing about them, we cannot even guess how they would choose."

"Except," Dr. Bonner added, "that their choices are not very likely to include us, or anything like us."

"That sounds like a safe bet," Amalfi said. "I must confess I feel about as uninspired as Mark does about the alternative, though. Or—is there a third alternative? What happens if the metagalactic center is empty when the catastrophe arrives? If neither the Web nor He is there, prepared to use it?"

Retma shrugged. "Then—if we can speak at all about so grand a transformation—history repeats itself. The universe is born again, goes through its travails, and continues its journey to its terminal catastrophes: the heat-death and the monobloc. It may be that we will find ourselves carrying on as we always did, but in the anti-matter universe; if so, we would be unable to detect the difference. But I think that unlikely. The most probable event is immediate extinction, and a rebirth of both universes from the primordial ylem."

"Ylem?" Amalfi said. "What's that? I've never heard the word before."

"The ylem was the primordial flux of neutrons out of which all else emerged," Dr. Schloss said. "I'm not surprised that you hadn't heard it before; it's the ABC of cosmogony, the Alpher-Bethe-Gamow premise. Ylem in cosmogony is an assumption like 'zero' in mathematics— something so old and so fundamental that it would never occur to you that somebody had to invent it."

"All right," Amalfi said. "Then what Retma is saying is that the most probable denouement, if dead-center is empty when June second comes, is that we will all be reduced to a sea of neutrons?"

"That's right," Dr. Schloss said.

"Not much of a choice," Gifford Bonner said reflectively.

"No," Miramon said, speaking for the first time. "It is not much of a choice. But it is all the choice we will have. And we will not have even that, if we fail to reach the metagalactic center in time."

*   *   *

Nevertheless, it was only in the last year that Web Hazleton began to grasp, and then only dimly, the true nature of the coming end. Even then, the knowledge did not come home to him by way of the men who were directing the preparations; what they were preparing for, though it was not kept secret, remained mostly incomprehensible, and so could not shake his confidence that what was being aimed at was a way to prevent the Ginnangu-Gap from happening at all. He ceased to believe that, finally and dismally, only when Estelle refused to bear him a child.

"But why?" Web said, seizing her hand with one of his, and with the other gesturing desperately at the walls of the apartment the Hevians had given them. "We're permanent now—it isn't only that we know we are, everybody agrees we are. It isn't a tabu line for us any longer!"

"I know," Estelle said gently. "It isn't that. I wish you hadn't asked; it would have been simpler that way."

"It would have occurred to me sooner or later. Ordinarily I would have gone off the pills right away, but there was so much confusion about moving to He—anyhow I only just realized you were still on them. I wish you'd tell me why."

"Web, my dear, you'd know why if you thought a little more about it. The end is the end, that's all. What would be the sense of having a child that would live only a year or two?"

"It may not be that certain," Web said darkly.

"Of course it's certain. Actually I think I've known it was coming ever since I was born—perhaps even before I was born. I could feel it coming."

"Honestly, Estelle, don't you know that's nonsense?"

"I can see why it would sound that way," Estelle admitted. "But I can't help that. And since the end is on the way, I can't call it nonsense, can I? I had the premonition, and it was right."

"I think what this all means is that you don't want children."

"That's true," Estelle said, surprisingly. "I never have had any drive toward children—not even much drive toward my own survival, really. But that's all part of the same thing. In a way, I was lucky; a lot of people are not at home in their own times. I was born in the time that was right for me—the time of the end of the world. That's why I'm not oriented toward childbearing—because I know that there won't be another generation after yours and mine. For all I know, I might even actually be sterile; it certainly wouldn't surprise me."

"Estelle, don't. I can't listen to you talk like that."

"I'm sorry, love. I don't mean to distress you. It doesn't distress me, but I know the reason for that. I'm pointed toward the end—in a way it's the ultimate, natural outcome of my life, the event that gives it all meaning; but you're only being overtaken by it, like most people."

"I don't know," Web muttered. "It all sounds awfully like a rationalization to me. Estelle, you're so beautiful . . . doesn't that mean anything? Aren't you beautiful to attract a man, so you can have a child? That's the way I've always understood it."

"It might have been for that once," Estelle said gravely. "It sounds like it ought to be an axiom, anyway. Well . . . I wouldn't say so to anybody but you, Web, but I do know I'm beautiful. Most women would tell you the same thing about themselves, if it were permissible—it's a state of mind, one that's essential to a woman, she's only half a woman if she doesn't think she's beautiful . . . and she is beautiful if she doesn't think she is, no matter what she looks like. I'm not ashamed of being beautiful and I'm not embarrassed by it, but I don't pay it much attention any more, either. It's a means to an end, just as you say—and the end has outlived its usefulness. In my mind, it's obvious that a woman who would commit a year-old child to the flames would have to be a fiend, if she knew that that's what she'd be doing just by giving birth. *I* know; and I can't do it."

"Women have taken chances like that before, and knowingly, too," Web said stubbornly. "Peasants who *knew* their children would starve, because the parents were starving already. Or women in the age just before spaceflight; Dr. Bonner says that for five years there the race stood within twenty minutes of extinction. But they went ahead and had the children anyhow—otherwise we wouldn't be here."

"It's an urge," Estelle said quietly, "that I don't have, Web. And this time, there's no escape."

"You keep saying that, but I'm not even sure you're right. Amalfi says that there's a chance"

"I know," Estelle said. "I did some of the calculations. But it's not that kind of a chance, my dear. It's something you might be able to do, or I, because we're old enough to absorb instructions, and do just the right thing at the right time. A baby couldn't do that. It would be like setting him adrift in a spaceship, with plenty of power and plenty of food—he'd die anyhow, and you couldn't tell him how to prevent it. It's so complex that some of us surely will make fatal mistakes."

He was silent.

"Besides." Estelle added gently, "even for us it won't be for long. We'll die too. It's only that we'll have a chance to influence the moment of creation that's implicit in the moment of destruction. That, if I make it at all, will be my child, Web—the only one worth having now."

"But it won't be mine."

"No, love. You'll have your own."

"No, no, Estelle! What good is that? I want mine to be yours too!"

She put her arms around his shoulders and leaned her cheek against his.

"I know," she whispered. "I know. But the time for that is over. That's the fate we were formed for, Web. The gift of children was taken away from us. Instead of babies, we were given universes."

"It's not enough," Web said. He embraced her fiercely. "Not by half. Nobody consulted me when that contract was being drawn."

"Did you ask to be born, love?"

"Well . . . no. But I don't mind. . . . Oh. That's how it is."

"Yes, that's how it is. He can't consult with us either. So it's up to us. No child of mine born to go into the flames, Web; no child of mine and yours."

"No," Web said hollowly. "You're right, it wouldn't be

fair. All right, Estelle. I'll settle for another year of you. I don't think I want a universe."

Deceleration began late in January of 4104. From here on out, the flight of He would be tentative, despite the increasing urgency; for the metagalactic center was as featureless as the rest of intergalactic space, and only extreme care and the most complex instrumentation would tell the voyagers when they had arrived. For the purpose, the Hevians had much elaborated their control bridge, which was located on a 300-foot steel basketwork tower atop the highest mountain the planet afforded—called, to Amalfi's embarrassment, Mt. Amalfi. Here the Survivors—as they had begun to call themselves with a kind of desperate jocularity—met in almost continuous session.

The Survivors consisted simply of everyone on the planet whom Schloss and Retma jointly agreed capable of following the instructions for the ultimate instant with even the slightest chance of success. Schloss and Retma had been hardheaded; it was not a large group. It included all of the New Earthmen, though Schloss had been dubious about both Dee and Web, and a group of ten Hevians including Miramon and Retma himself. Oddly, as the time grew closer, the Hevians began to drop out, apparently each as soon as he had fully understood what was being attempted and what the outcome might be.

"Why do they do that?" Amalfi asked Miramon. "Don't your people have any survival urge at all?"

"I am not surprised," Miramon said. "They live by stable values. They would rather die with them than survive without them. Certainly they have the survival urge, but it expresses itself differently than yours does, Mayor Amalfi. What they want to see survive are the things they think valuable about living at all—and this project presents them with very few of those."

"Then what about you, and Retma?"

"Retma is a scientist; that is perhaps sufficient explanation. As for me, Mayor Amalfi, as you very well know, I am an anachronism. I no more share the major value system of He than you do of New Earth."

Amalfi was answered, and he was sorry that he had asked.

"How close do you think we are?" he said.

"Very close now," Schloss answered from the control desk. Outside the huge windows, which completely encircled the room, there was still little to be seen but the all-consuming and perpetual night. If one had sharp eyes and stood outside for half an hour or so to become dark-adapted, it was possible to see as many as five galaxies of varying degrees of faintness, for this near the center the galaxy density was higher than it was anywhere else in the universe; but to the ordinary quick glance the skies appeared devoid of as much as a single pinprick of light.

"The readings are falling off steadily," Retma agreed. "And there is something else odd: locally we are getting too much power on everything. We have been throttling down steadily for the past week, and still the output rises—exponentially, in fact. I hope that the curve does *not* maintain that shape all the way, or we shall simply be unable to handle our own machines when we reach our destination."

"What's the reason for that?" Hazleton said. "Has Conservation of Energy been repealed at the center?"

"I doubt it," Retma said. "I think the curve will flatten at the crest—"

"A Pearl curve," Schloss put in. "We ought to have anticipated this. Naturally anything that happens at the center will work with much more efficiency than it could anywhere else, since the center is stress free. The curve will begin to flatten as the performance of our machines begins to approximate the abstractions of physics—the ideal gas, the frictionless surface, the perfectly empty vacuum and so on. All my life I've been taught not to believe in the actual existence of any of those ideals, but I guess I'm going to get at least a fuzzy glimpse of them!"

"Including the gravity-free metrical frame?" Amalfi said worriedly. "We'll be in a nice mess if the spindizzies have nothing to latch onto."

"No, it cannot possibly be gravity-free," Retma said. "It will be gravitationally neutral—again making for unprecedented efficiency—but only because all the stresses are balanced. There cannot be any point in the universe that is gravitationally unstressed, not so long as a scrap of matter is left in it."

"Suppose the spindizzies did quit," Estelle said. "We're not going anywhere after the center anyhow."

"No," Amalfi agreed, "but I'd like to maintain my maneuverability until we see what our competitors are doing—if anything. Any sign of them, Retma?"

"Nothing yet. Unfortunately we don't know exactly what it is that we are looking for. But at least there are no other dirigible masses like ours anywhere in this vicinity; in fact, no patterned activity at all that we can detect."

"Then we're ahead of them?"

"Not necessarily," Schloss said. "If they're at the center right now, they could be doing a good many things we couldn't detect, under a very low screen. However, they would already have detected us and done something about us if that were the case. Let's assume we're ahead until the instruments say otherwise; I think that's a fairly safe assumption."

"How much longer to the center?" Hazleton said.

"A few months, perhaps," Retma said. "If we're right in assuming that this curve has a flat spot on top of it."

"And the necessary machinery?"

"The last installation will be in at the end of this week," Amalfi said. "We can begin countdown the moment we arrive . . . providing that we can learn to handle equipment operating at ten or a hundred times its rated efficiency, without blowing some of it out in the process. We'd better start practicing the moment the system is complete."

"Amen," Hazleton said fervently. "Can I borrow your slide rule? I've got a few setting-up exercises I'd better start on right now." He left the room. Amalfi looked uneasily out at the night. He would almost have preferred it had the Web of Hercules been there ahead of them and promptly taken a sitting-duck shot at them; this uncertainty as to whether or not someone really was lurking out there—coupled with the totally unknown nature of their opponents—was more unsettling than open battle. However, there was no help for it; and if He really was first, it gave them a sizable advantage. . . .

And their only advantage. The only defenses Amalfi had been able to conceive and jury-rig for He depended importantly on actually being at the metagalactic center, able to make use of the almost instant number of weak resultant forces that could be used there to produce major responses—the buttercup-vs.-Sirius effect Bonner had so characterized. In this area he found Miramon and the Hevian council oddly uncooperative, even flaccid, as though mounting a defense for the whole planet was too big a concept for them to grasp—a hard thing to believe in view of the prodigious concepts they had mastered and put to work since Amalfi had first met them as savages up to their knees in mud and violence. Well, if he did not yet understand them, he was not going to make his understanding perfect in a few months; and at least Miramon was perfectly willing to let Amalfi and Hazleton direct Hevian labor in putting together their almost wholly theoretical breadboard rigs.

"Some of these," Hazleton had said, looking at a just-completed tangle of wires, lenses, antennae and kernels of metal with rueful respect, "ought to prove pretty potent in the pinch. I just wish I knew which ones they were." Which, unfortunately, was a perfect précis of the situation.

But the needles recording the stresses and currents of space around He continued to fall; those recording the output of Hevian equipment continued to rise. On May 23rd 4104, both sets of meters rose suddenly to their high ends and jammed madly against the pegs, and the whole planet rang suddenly with the awful, tortured roar of spindizzies driven beyond endurance. Miramon's hand flashed out for the manual master switch so fast that Amalfi could not tell whether it had been he or the City Fathers that cut the power. Maybe even Miramon did not know; at least he must have gotten to the cut off button within a hair of the automatic reaction.

The howl died. Silence. The Survivors looked at each other.

"Well," Amalfi said, "we're here, evidently." For some

reason, he felt wildly elated—a wholly irrational reaction,
but he did not stop to analyze it.

"So we are," Hazleton said, his eyes snapping. "Now
what the hell happened to the metering? I can understand
the local apparatus going wild—but why did the input
meters from outside rise instead of dropping back to zero?"

"Noise, I believe," Retma said.

"Noise? How so?"

"It takes power to operate a meter—not a great deal,
but it consumes some. Consequently, the input meters
ran as wild as the machines did, because operating at peak
efficiency with no incoming signals to register, they picked
up the signals generated by their own functioning."

"I don't like that," Hazleton said. "Do we have any way
of finding out on what level it's safe to run *any* instrument
under these circumstances? I'd like to see generation curves
on the effect so we can make such a calculation—but
there's not much point in consulting the records if we just
burn out the machine in the process."

Amalfi picked up the only instrument on the Hevian
board that was "his"—the microphone to the City Fathers.
"Are you still alive down there?" he said.

"YES, MR. MAYOR," the answer came promptly.
Miramon looked startled; since everything of which he had
any knowledge had gone dead, even the lights—they were
sitting bathed only in the barely ascertainable glow of the
zodiacal light, that belt of tenuous ionized gas in He's
atmosphere brought to life by He's magnetic field, plus
the even dimmer glow of the few nearby galaxies—the
sudden voice of the speakers must have alarmed him.

"Good. What are you operating on?"

"WET CELLS IN SERIES AT TWENTY-FIVE HUN-
DRED VOLTS."

"*All* of you?"

"YES, MR. MAYOR."

Amalfi grinned in the virtual darkness. "All right, apply
your efficiency figures to a set of standard instrumental
situations."

"DONE."

"Give me an operating level for Mr. Miramon's line

down to you, allowing for pilot lights on his board so he can see his settings."

"MR. MAYOR, THAT IS NOT NECESSARY. WE HAVE ALREADY RESET THE MASTER CUTOUT AT THE NECESSARY BLOWPOINT LEVEL. WE CAN RE-ACTUATE ALL THE CIRCUITS AT ONCE."

"No, don't do that, we don't want the spindizzies back on too—"

"THE SPINDIZZIES ARE OFF," the City Fathers said, with austere simplicity.

"Well, Miramon? Do you trust them? Or would you rather have them tie in to you first and print their data for you, so you can turn the planet back on piecemeal?"

He heard Miramon draw in his breath slightly to answer, but he was never to know what that answer would have been; for at the same moment, Miramon's whole board came alive at once.

"Hey!" Amalfi squalled. "Wait for orders down there, dammit!"

"STANDING ORDERS, MR. MAYOR. AFTER COUNTDOWN BEGINS WE ARE TO ACT AT THE FIRST SIGN OF OUTSIDE INTERFERENCE. COUNTDOWN BEGAN TWELVE HUNDRED SECONDS AGO, AND SEVEN SECONDS AGO OUTSIDE INTERFERENCE BECAME STATISTICALLY SIGNIFICANT."

"What do they mean?" Miramon said, trying to read every instrument on his board at once. "I thought I understood your language, Mayor Amalfi, but—"

"The City Fathers don't speak Okie, they speak Machine," Amalfi said grimly. "What they mean is that the Web of Hercules—if that's who it is—is coming in on us. And coming in on us fast."

With a single, circumscribed flip of his closed fingers, Miramon turned off the lights.

Blackness. Then, seeping faintly over the windows around the tower, the air-glow of the zodiacal light; then, still later, the dim pinwheels of island universes. On Miramon's board, there was a single spearpoint of yellow-orange which was only the heater of a vacuum tube smaller than an acorn; in this central gloom at the heart and birthplace of the universe, it was almost blinding. Amalfi had to turn his back on it to maintain the profound dark-adaptation that his vision needed to operate at all in the tower on his mountain.

While he waited for his sight to come back, he wondered at the speed of Miramon's reaction, and the motives behind it. Surely the Hevian could not believe that a set of pilot lights in a tower on top of a remote mountain could be bright enough to be seen from space; for that matter, blacking out even as large an object as a whole planet could serve no military purpose—it had been two millennia since any reasonably sophisticated enemy depended upon light alone to see by. And where in Miramon's whole lifetime could he have acquired the blackout reflex? It made no sense; yet Miramon had restored the blackout with all the trained positiveness of a boxer riding with a punch.

When the light began to grow, he had his answer—and no time left to wonder how Miramon had anticipated it.

It began as though the destruction of the inter-universal messenger were about to repeat itself in reverse, encompassing the whole of creation in the process. Crawls of greenish-yellow light were beginning to move high up in the Hevian sky, at first as ghostly as auroral traces, then with a purposeful writhing and brightening which seemed as horrifyingly like life as the copulation of a mass of green-gold nematode worms seen under phase-contrast lighting. Particle counters began to chatter on the board, and Hazleton jumped to monitor the cumulative readings.

"Where is that stuff coming from—can you tell?" Amalfi said.

"It seems to come from nearly a hundred discrete point-sources, surrounding us in a sphere with a diameter of about a light year," Miramon said. He sounded preoccupied; he was doing something whose purpose was unknown to Amalfi.

"Hmm. Ships, without a doubt. Well, now we know where they get their name, anyhow. But what is it they're using?"

"That's easy," Hazleton said grimly. "It's anti-matter."

"How can that be?"

"Look at the frequency analysis on this secondary radiation we're getting, and you'll see. Every one of those ships must be primarily a particle accelerator of prodigious size. They're sending streams of stripped heavy anti-matter atoms right down the gravitational ingeodesics toward us— that's what makes the paths the stuff is following look so twisted. They've found a way to generate and project primary cosmics made of anti-matter atoms, and in quantity. When they strike our atmosphere, both disintegrate—"

"And the planet gets a dose of high-energy gamma radiation," Amalfi said. "And they must have known how to do it for a long time, since they're named after the technique. Helleshin! What a way to conquer a planet! They can either sterilize the populace, or kill it off, at will, without ever even coming close to the place."

"We've had the sterility dose already," Hazleton said quietly.

"That can hardly matter now," Estelle said, in an even softer voice.

"The killing dose won't matter either," Hazleton said. "Radiation sickness takes months to develop, even when it's going to be fatal."

"They could disable us quickly enough," Amalfi said harshly. "We've got to stop this somehow. We need these last days!"

"What do you propose?" Hazleton said. "Nothing that we've set up will work in a globe at a distance of a light year . . . except—"

"Except the base surge," Amalfi said. "Let's use it, and quick."

"What is this?" Miramon said.

"We've got your spindizzies set up for a single burn-out overload pulse. In the position we're in, the resulting single wave-front ought to tie space into knots for—well, we don't know how far the effect will carry, but a long way."

"Maybe even all the way to the limits of the universe," Dr. Schloss said.

"Well, what of it?" Amalfi demanded. "It's due to be destroyed anyhow in only ten days—"

"Not if you destroy it first," Schloss said. "If it isn't here

when the anti-matter universe passes through it, all bets
are off; there'll be nothing we can do."

"It'll still be here."

"Not in any useful sense—not if the matter in it is tied
up in billions of gravitational whirlpools. Better let the
Web kill us than destroy the future evolution of two universes, Amalfi! Can't you give over playing God, even
now?"

"All right," Amalfi said. "Look at those dosimeters, and
look at that sky. What have you to suggest?"

The sky was now one even intensity of glow, like a full
overcast lit by a dull sun. Outside, the lower mountains of
the range stood with their tree-covered flanks, so completely without shadow as to suggest that the windows
ringing the tower were actually parts of a flat mural done
by an unskilled hand. The counters had given over chattering and were putting out a subdued roar.

"Only what I just suggested," Schloss said hopelessly.
"Load up on anti-radiation drugs, and hope we can stay on
our feet for ten days. What else is there? They've got us."

"Excuse me," Miramon said. "That is not altogether
certain. We have some resources of our own. I have just
launched one; it may be sufficient."

"What is it?" Amalfi demanded. "I didn't know you
mounted any weapons. How long will we have to wait
before it acts?"

"One question at a time," Miramon said. "Of course we
mount weapons. We never talk about them, because there
were children on our planet, and still are, the gods receive
them. But we had to face the fact that we might some day
be invested by a hostile fleet, considering how far afield
we were ranging from our home galaxy, and how many
stars we were visiting. Thus we provided several means
for defense. One of these we meant never to use, but we
have just used it now."

"And that is?" Hazleton said tensely.

"We would never have told you, except for the coming
end," Miramon said. "You have praised us as chemists,
Mayor Amalfi. We have applied chemistry to physics. We
discovered how to poison an electromagnetic field by
resonance—the way the process of catalysis is poisoned in

chemistry. The poison field propagates itself along a carrier wave, and controlling field, almost any signal which is continuous and conforms to the Faraday equations. Look."

He pointed out the window. The light did not seem to have lessened any; but it was now mottled with leprous patches. In a space of seconds, the patches spread and flowed into each other, until the light was now confined to isolated luminous clouds, rapidly being eaten away at the edges, like dead cells being dissolved by the enzymes of decay bacteria.

When the sky went totally dark, Amalfi could see the hundred streamers of the particle streams pointed inward at He; at least it looked a hundred, though actually he could hardly have seen more than fifteen from any one spot on the planet. And these too were being eaten away, receding into blackness.

The counters went back to stuttering, but they did not quite stop.

"What happens when the effect gets back to the ships?" Web asked.

"It will poison the circuits themselves," Miramon said. "The entities in the ships will suffer total nerve-block. They will die, and so will the ships. Nothing will be left but a hundred hulks."

Amalfi let out a long, ragged sigh.

"No wonder you weren't interested in our breadboard rigs," he said. "With a thing like that, you could have become another Web of Hercules yourselves."

"No," Miramon said. "That we could never become."

"Gods of all stars!" Hazleton said. "Is it over? As fast as that?"

Miramon's smile was wintery. "I doubt that we will hear from the Web of Hercules again," he said. "But what your City Fathers call the countdown continues. It is only ten days to the end of the world."

Hazleton turned back to the dosimeters. For a moment, he simply stared at them. Then, to Amalfi's astonishment, he began to laugh.

"What's so funny?" Amalfi growled.

"See for yourself. If Miramon's people had ever tangled with the Web in the real world, they would have lost."

"Why?"

"Because," Hazleton said, wiping his eyes, "while he was beating them off, we all passed the lethal dose of hard radiation. We are all dead as doornails as we sit here!"

"And this is a joke?" Amalfi said.

"Of course it's a joke, boss. It doesn't make the faintest bit of difference. We don't live in that kind of 'real world' anymore. We have a dose. In two weeks we'll begin to become dizzy, and lose our hair, and vomit. In three weeks we'll be dead. And you *still* don't see the joke?"

"I see it," Amalfi said. "I can subtract ten from fourteen and get four; you mean we'll live until we die."

"I can't abide a man who kills my jokes."

"It's a pretty old joke," Amalfi said slowly. "But maybe it's still funny, at that; if it was good enough for Aristophanes, I guess it's good enough for me."

"I think that's pretty damn funny, all right," Dee said with bitter fury. Miramon was staring from one New Earthman to another with an expression of utter bafflement. Amalfi smiled.

"Don't say so unless you think so, Dee," he said. "It's always been a joke, after all. The death of one man is just as funny as the death of a universe. Don't repudiate the last laugh of all. It may be the only legacy we'll leave."

"MIDNIGHT," the City Fathers said. "THE COUNT IS ZERO MINUS NINE."

CHAPTER EIGHT: The Triumph of Time

As Amalfi opened the door and went back into the room, the City Fathers said:

"N-DAY. ZERO MINUS ONE HOUR."

At this hour, everything had meaning; or nothing had; it depended on what had been worth investing with meaning over a lifetime of several thousand years. Amalfi had left the room to go to the toilet. Now he would never do that again, nor would anybody else; the demise of the whole was so close at hand that it was outrunning even the physiological rhythms of the body by which man has told time since he first thought to count it. Was diuresis as worth mourning as love? Well, perhaps it was; the senses should have their mourners too; no sensation, no thought, no emotion is meaningless if it is the last of its kind.

And so farewell to all tensions and all reliefs, from amour to urea, from entrances to exits, from redundancy to noise, from beer to skittles. "What's new?" Amalfi said.

"Nothing anymore," Gifford Bonner said. "We're waiting. Sit down, John, and have a drink."

He sat down at the long table and looked at the glass before him. It was red, but there was a faint tinge of blue in the liquid too, independent and not adding up to violet even in the bad light of the fluorescents in the midst of dead center's ultimate blackness. At the lip of the glass a faint meniscus climbed upward from the wine, and little tendrils of condensation meandered back down. Amalfi tasted it tentatively; it was raw and peppery—the Hevians were not great winegrowers; their climate had been too chancy for that—but even the sting of it was an edgy pleasure that made him sigh.

"We should suit up at the half hour," Dr. Schloss said. "I'd leave more free time, except that some of us haven't been inside a spacesuit in centuries, and some of us never. We don't want to take chances on their not being trim and tight."

"I thought we were going to be surrounded by some sort of field," Web said.

"Not for long, Web. Let me go through this once more, to be sure everybody has it straight in his head. We will be protected by a stasis-field during the actual instant of transition, when time will to all intents and purposes be abolished—it becomes just another coordinate of Hilbert space then. That will carry us over into the first second of time on the other side, after the catastrophe. But then the field will go down, because the spindizzies, which will be generating it, will have been annihilated. We will then find ourselves occupying as many independent sets of four dimensions as there are people in this room, and every set completely empty. The spacesuits won't protect you long, either, because you'll be the only body of organized energy and matter in your particular, individual universe: as soon as you disturb the metrical frame of that universe, you, the suit, the air in it, the power in the accumulators, everything will surge outwards, creating space as it goes. Every man his own monobloc. But if we don't have the suits on for the crossing, not even that much will happen."

"I wish you wouldn't be so graphic," Dee complained, but her heart did not really seem to be in it. She was, Amalfi noted, wearing that same peculiarly strained expression she had worn when she had said that she wanted to bear Amalfi a child. Some instinct made him turn to look at Estelle and Web. All their hands were piled up together confidingly on the table. Estelle's face was serene, and her eyes were luminous, almost like a child waiting for a party to begin. Web's expression was more difficult to interpret: he was frowning slightly, more in puzzlement than in worry, as if he couldn't quite understand why he was not more worried than he was.

Outside, there was a thin whining sound which rose suddenly to a howl and then died away again. It was windy today on the mountain.

"What about the table, the glasses, the chairs?" Amalfi asked. "Do those go with us too?"

"No," Dr. Schloss said. "We don't want to risk having any possible condensation nuclei near us. We're using a modification of the technique we used to build Object *4001-Alephnull* in the future; the furniture will start to make the crossing with us, but we'll use the last available energy to push it a micro-second into the past. The result will be that it will stay in our universe. What its fate will be thereafter, we can only guess."

Amalfi lifted his glass reflectively. It was silky in his fingers: the Hevians made fine glass.

"This frame of reference I'll find myself in," Amalfi said. "It will really have no structure at all?"

"Only what you impose on it," Retma said. "It will not be space, and will have no metrical frame. In other words, your presence there will be intolerable—"

"Thank you," Amalfi said drily, to Retma's obvious bafflement. After a moment the scientist went on without comment: "What I am trying to say is that your mass will create a space to accommodate it, and it will take on the metrical frame that already exists in you. What happens after that will depend upon in what order you dismantle the suit. I would recommend discharging the oxygen bottles first, since to start a universe like our present one will require a considerable amount of plasma. The oxygen in the suit itself will be sufficient for the time at your disposal. As the last act, discharge the suit's energy; this will, in effect, touch a match to the explosion."

"How large a universe will be the outcome, eventually?" Mark said. "I seem to remember that the original monobloc was large, as well as ultra-condensed."

"Yes, it will be a small universe," Retma said, "perhaps fifty light years across at its greatest expansion. But that will be only at first. As continuous creation comes into play, more atoms will be added to the whole, until a mass is reached sufficient to form a monobloc on the next contraction. Or so we see it; you must understand that this is all somewhat conjectural. We did not have the time to learn everything that we wanted to know."

"ZERO MINUS THIRTY MINUTES."

"That's it," Dr. Schloss said. "Suits, everybody. We can continue to talk by radio."

Amalfi drained the wine. Another last act. He got into his suit, slowly recapturing his old familiarity with the grotesque apparatus. He saw to it that the radio switch was open, but he found that he could think of nothing further to say. That he was about to die suddenly had very little reality to him, in the face of the greater death of which his would be a part. No comment that occurred to him seemed anything but the uttermost of trivia.

There was some technical conversation as they checked each other out in the suits, with particular attention to Web and Estelle. Then the talk died out, as if they, too, found words intolerable.

"ZERO MINUS FIFTEEN MINUTES."

"Do you understand what is about to happen to you?" Amalfi said suddenly.

"YES, MR. MAYOR. WE ARE TO BE TURNED OFF AT ZERO."

"That's good enough." He wondered, however, if they thought that they might be turned on again in the future. It was of course foolish to think of them as entertaining anything even vaguely resembling an emotion, but nevertheless he decided not to say anything which might disabuse them. They were only machines, but they were also old friends and allies.

"ZERO MINUS TEN MINUTES."

"It's all going so fast all of a sudden," Dee's voice whispered in the earphones. "Mark, I . . . I don't want it to happen."

"No more do I," Hazleton said. "But it will happen anyhow. I only wish I'd lived a more human life than I did. But it happened the way it happened, and so there's no more to say."

"I wish I could believe," Estelle said, "that there will be no sorrow in the universe I make."

"Then create nothing, my dear," Gifford Bonner said. "Stay here. Creation means sorrow, always and always."

"And joy," Estelle said.

"Well, yes. There's that."

"ZERO MINUS FIVE MINUTES."

"I think we can do without the rest of the countdown," Amalfi said. "Otherwise from now on they will count every minute, and they'll do the last one by seconds. Do we want to go out to the tune of that gabble? Anybody want to say 'yes'?"

They were silent. "Very well," Amalfi said. "Stop counting."

"VERY WELL, MR. MAYOR. GOOD-BYE."

"Good-bye," Amalfi said with amazement.

"I won't say that, if you don't mind," Hazleton said in a choked voice. "It brings the deprivation too close for me to stand. I hope everybody will consider it said."

Amalfi nodded, then realized that the gesture could not be seen inside the helmet.

"I agree," he said. "But I don't feel deprived. I loved you all. You have my love to take with you, and I have it too."

"It is the only thing in the universe that one can give and still have," Miramon said.

The deck throbbed under Amalfi's feet. The machines were preparing for their instant of unimaginable thrust. The sound of their power was comforting; so was the solidity of the deck, the table, the room, the mountain, the world—"I think—" Gifford Bonner said.

And with those words, it ended.

There was nothing at first but the inside of the suit. Outside there was not even blackness, but only nothingness, something not to be seen, like that which is not seen outside of the cone of vision; one does not see blackness behind one's own head, one simply does not see in that direction at all; and so here. Yet for a little while, Amalfi found that he was still conscious of his friends, still a part of the circle though the room and everything in it had vanished from around them. He did not know how he knew that they were still there, but he could feel it.

He knew that there was no hope of speaking to them again; and indeed, as he tried to grasp how he knew they were there at all, he realized that they were drawing away from him. The circle was widening. The mute figures became smaller—not by distance, for there was no distance here, but nevertheless in some way they were passing out of each other's ken. Amalfi tried to lift his hand in farewell, but found it almost impossible. By the time he had only half completed the gesture, the others had faded and were gone, leaving behind only a memory also fading rapidly, like the memory of a fragrance.

Now he was alone and must do what he must do. Since his hand was raised, he continued the gesture to let the gas out of his oxygen bottles. The unmedium in which he was suspended seemed to be becoming a little less resistant; already a metrical frame was establishing itself. Yet it was almost as difficult to halt the motion as it had been to start it.

Nevertheless, he halted it. Of what use was another universe of the kind he had just seen die? Nature had provided two of those, and had doomed them at the same moment. Why not try something else? Retma in his caution, Estelle in her compassion, Dee in her fear all would be giving birth to some version of the standard model; but Amalfi had driven the standard model until all the bolts had come out of it, and was so tired at even the thought of it that he could hardly bring himself to breathe. What would happen if, instead, he simply touched the detonator button on his chest, and let all the elements of which he and the suit were composed flash into plasma at the same instant?

That was unknowable. But the unknowable was what he wanted. He brought his hand down again.

There was no reason to delay. Retma had already pronounced the epitaph for Man: *We did not have the time to learn everything that we wanted to know.*

"So be it," Amalfi said. He touched the button over his heart.

Creation began.